Y0-CBI-155

Storming

the

Reality

Studio

RE
W
Moc
readin

mcaffer@inreach.com
. m word 6. 0
RTF

STORMING

THE

REALITY

STUDIO

Edited by Larry McCaffery

■ A

Casebook

of

Cyberpunk

and

Postmodern

Science

Fiction

Duke University Press   Durham & London 1991

Sixth printing in paperback, 1994
© 1991 Duke University Press
All rights reserved
Printed in the United States of America
on acid-free paper ∞

Library of Congress Cataloging-in-Publication Data
Storming the reality studio : a casebook of cyberpunk and
postmodern science fiction / edited by Larry McCaffery.
Includes bibliographical references and index.
ISBN 0-8223-1158-5 (cloth).—ISBN 0-8223-1168-2 (paper)
1. Science fiction, American—History and criticism.
2. Postmodernism (Literature)—United States. 3. Literature and
technology—United States. 4. Science fiction, American.
5. Technology—Fiction. I. McCaffery, Larry, 1946–
PS374.S35S76 1991
813'.0876209—dc20 91–14316 CIP

For Raymond Federman
(for all his vain repetitions)
and for Sinda (of course)

Contents

Acknowledgments   xi

Introduction: The Desert of the Real, Larry McCaffery   1

Cyberpunk 101: A Schematic Guide to *Storming the Reality Studio*, Richard Kadrey and Larry McCaffery   17

Fiction and Poetry

Beyond the Extinction of Human Life (*from* Empire of the Senseless), Kathy Acker   33

From Crash, J. G. Ballard   41

Mother and I Would Like to Know (*from* The Wild Boys), William S. Burroughs   44

Rock On, Pat Cadigan   48

Among the Blobs, Samuel R. Delany   56

From White Noise, Don DeLillo   63

From Neuromancer, William Gibson   65

Fistic Hermaphrodites, Rob Hardin   75

Microbes, Rob Hardin   76

Penetrabit: Slime Temples, Rob Hardin   77

nerve terminals, Rob Hardin   79

Max Headroom, Harold Jaffe   80

From Straight Fiction, Thom Jurek   85

The Toilet Was Full of Nietzsche (*from* Metrophage),
Richard Kadrey   87

Office of the Future (*from* Dad's Nuke), Marc Laidlaw   98

I Was an Infinitely Hot and Dense Dot (*from* My Cousin,
My Gastroenterologist), Mark Leyner   102

From Plus, Joseph McElroy   109

Wire Movement #9, Misha   112

Wire for Two Tims, Misha   114

From Easy Travel to Other Planets, Ted Mooney   116

Frame 137, Jim O'Barr   118

From The Crying of Lot 49, Thomas Pynchon   122

From Software, Rudy Rucker   125

From Life During Wartime, Lucius Shepard   132

Stoked, Lewis Shiner   134

Wolves of the Plateau, John Shirley   139

Twenty Evocations, Bruce Sterling   154

The Mare Tranquillitatis People's Circumlunar Zaibatsu:
2-1-'16 (*from* Schismatrix), Bruce Sterling   162

The Indigo Engineers (*from* The Rainbow Stories),
William T. Vollmann   168

Non-Fiction

Before the Lights Came On: Observations of a Synergy,
Steve Brown   173

The Automation of the Robot (*from* Simulations),
Jean Baudrillard   178

Cyberpunk and Neuromanticism, Istvan Csicsery-Ronay, Jr.   182

From Of Grammatology, Jacques Derrida   194

Yin and Yang Duke It Out, Joan Gordon   196

Cybernetic Deconstructions: Cyberpunk and Postmodernism,
Veronica Hollinger   203

From Postmodernism, or The Cultural Logic of Late Capitalism,
Fredric Jameson   219

Television and the Triumph of Culture (*from* The Postmodern Scene),
Arthur Kroker and David Cook   229

Bet On It: Cyber/video/punk/performance, Brooks Landon   239

The Cyberpunk: The Individual as Reality Pilot,
Timothy Leary   245

The Postmodern (*from* The Postmodern Condition),
Jean-François Lyotard   259

An Interview with William Gibson, Larry McCaffery   263

Cutting Up: Cyberpunk, Punk Music, and Urban
Decontextualizations, Larry McCaffery   286

POSTcyberMODERNpunkISM, Brian McHale   308

The Wars of the Coin's Two Halves: Bruce Sterling's
Mechanist/Shaper Narratives, Tom Maddox   324

Frothing the Synaptic Bath, David Porush   331

Literary MTV, George Slusser   334

Preface from Mirrorshades, Bruce Sterling   343

On Gibson and Cyberpunk SF, Darko Suvin   349

The Japanese Reflection of Mirrorshades, Takayuki Tatsumi   366

Bibliography   375

Contributors   385

Acknowledgments

This volume could never have been assembled without the generous help, support, and suggestions of many different people. Let me trace through some of the main points along the winding path that has led to this book's publication: My thanks, first of all, to Samuel R. Delany, who suggested over lunch one day in 1986 that I take a look at William Gibson's *Neuromancer*. Thanks, too, goes to Gibson, who agreed to do an interview with me. Frederick Barthelme, the editor of *The Mississippi Review*, accepted my Gibson interview for his journal, and then asked me if I could assemble an entire issue devoted to cyberpunk. Mega-thanks, next, to all the cyberpunk authors and critics who generously allowed me to publish their work in the *Mississippi Review* issue that resulted from Barthelme's invitation. In gathering the materials for that *MR* issue—which was the starting point for this current *Storming the Reality Studio* casebook—I was given advice at every step of the way by nearly all the members of the cyberpunk movement (who turned out to be much warmer, funnier, and friendlier than their black leather-jacketed press clippings might lead one to believe). This was especially true of Bruce Sterling and John Shirley, both of whom provided invaluable assistance in suggesting names, works, addresses, and phone numbers for that volume.

Once I decided to expand the boundaries of the *MR* issue into something resembling the current volume, Joanne Ferguson of Duke University Press provided invaluable editorial insights, suggestions, and encouragement at every stage of the process of this book's formulation. Once again, the cyberpunk authors themselves—as well as the noncyberpunk authors and critics included in *Storming the Reality*

Studio—were generous with their suggestions and with their willingness to allow me to reprint their work. Neil Barron, science fiction's bibliographer *extraordinaire*, was always available to help me track down references, titles, and addresses at a moment's notice. Jim McMenamin helped hold things together during the year I spent in Beijing by handling most of my correspondence, and generally keeping things cool until I returned.

My thanks to my son, Mark Urton, whose encouragement and advice I relied upon at various stages of this volume's evolution. Finally, my deepest debt ("of course") goes to my wife and collaborator, Sinda J. Gregory, who has been with me every step of the way for twenty years on our journeys across these wounded galaxies—and who has, in fact, been the point-person on our own personal efforts to storm the reality studio of postmodern culture. Thanks for being willing to take the white light and white heat when the going got tough, Sinda—and for being there when the reality studio emptied out and it was just us.

My thanks, too, to all the authors and their publishers for granting permission to reprint the following materials:

"Beyond the Extinction of Human Life," from *Empire of the Senseless* (31–39), by Kathy Acker. Copyright 1988 by Kathy Acker. Reprinted by permission of the author.

Excerpt from *Crash* (15–17), by J. G. Ballard. Copyright 1973 by J. G. Ballard. Reprinted by permission of the author.

"The Automation of the Robot," from *Simulations* (92–96), by Jean Baudrillard. Copyright 1983 by *Semiotext(e)* and Jean Baudrillard. Reprinted by permission of *Semiotext(e)*.

"Mother and I Would Like to Know," from *The Wild Boys* (502–5), by William S. Burroughs. Copyright 1969, 1970, 1971 by William S. Burroughs. Reprinted by permission of Grove Press, Inc.

"Rock On," by Pat Cadigan, originally appeared in *Light Years and Dark* (Berkeley, 1984 [32–42]). Copyright 1984 by Pat Cadigan. Reprinted by permission of the author.

"Cyberpunk and Neuromanticism," by Istvan Csicsery-Ronay, Jr., originally appeared in *Mississippi Review* 47/48 (1988): 266–78. Reprinted by permission of the author.

"Among the Blobs," by Samuel R. Delany, originally appeared in *Mississippi Review* 47/48 (1988): 86–92. Reprinted by permission of the author.

Excerpt from *White Noise* (12–13), by Don DeLillo. Copyright 1984, 1985 by Don DeLillo. Reprinted by permission of Viking Penguin, Inc.

Excerpt from *Of Grammatology* (9), by Jacques Derrida. English translation Copyright 1976 by Jacques Derrida and Johns Hopkins University Press. Reprinted by permission of Johns Hopkins University Press.

Excerpt from *Neuromancer* (3–8, 76–79, 238–40), by William Gibson. Copyright 1984 by William Gibson. Reprinted by permission of the author.

"Yin and Yang Duke It Out," by Joan Gordon, originally appeared in *Science Fiction Eye* 2, no. 1 (February 1990): 37–40. Reprinted by permission of the author.

"Cybernetic Deconstructions: Cyberpunk and Postmodernism," by Veronica Hollinger, originally appeared in *Mosaic* 23, no. 2 (Spring 1990): 29–44. Reprinted by permission of the author.

"Fistic Hermaphrodites," "Microbes," and "nerve terminals," by Rob Hardin, originally appeared in *Mississippi Review* 47/48 (1988): 156–58. Reprinted by permission of the author.

"Max Headroom," by Harold Jaffe, originally appeared in *Mississippi Review* 47/48 (1988): 130–35. Copyright 1988 by Harold Jaffe. Reprinted by permission of the author.

Excerpts from "Postmodernism, or the Cultural Logic of Late Capitalism" (53–54, 64, 65–66, 67, 72–73, 75–76, 78–80, 89–90, 92), by Fredric Jameson, originally appeared in *New Left Review* 146 (July–August 1984): 53–92. Reprinted by permission of the author.

"The Toilet Was Full of Nietzsche," by Richard Kadrey, originally appeared in *Mississippi Review* 47/48 (1988): 159–69. Reprinted by permission of the author.

"Television and the Triumph of Culture," from *The Postmodern Scene: Excremental Culture and Hyper-Aesthetics* (St. Martin's Press, 1986 [270–79]), by Arthur Kroker and David Cook. Reprinted by permission of St. Martin's Press, Inc.

"Office of the Future," from *Dad's Nuke* (194–97), by Marc Laidlaw. Copyright 1984 by Marc Laidlaw. Reprinted by permission of the author.

"Bet On It: Cyber/video/punk/performance," by Brooks Landon, originally appeared in *Mississippi Review* 47/48 (1988): 245–51. Reprinted by permission of the author.

"Cyberpunk: The Individual as Reality Pilot," by Timothy Leary, originally appeared in *Mississippi Review* 47/48 (1988): 252–65. Reprinted by permission of the author.

"I Was an Infinitely Hot and Dense Dot," from *My Cousin, My Gastroenterologist* (3–8), by Mark Leyner. Copyright 1990 by Mark Leyner. Reprinted by permission of Harmony Books, a division of Crown Publishers, Inc.

"The Postmodern," from *The Postmodern Condition* (79–82), by Jean-François Lyotard. English translation Copyright 1984 by the University of Minnesota Press. Reprinted by permission of the University of Minnesota Press.

"The Wars of the Coin's Two Halves: Bruce Sterling's Mechanist/ Shaper Narratives," by Tom Maddox, originally appeared in *Mississippi Review* 47/48 (1988): 237–44. Reprinted by permission of the author.

Excerpt from *Plus* (9–12), by Joseph McElroy. Copyright 1976 by Joseph McElroy. Reprinted by permission of Alfred A. Knopf, Inc.

"Wire Movement #9" and "Wire for Two Tims," from *Prayers of Steel* (29–32), by Misha. Copyright 1983 by Misha. Reprinted by permission of the author.

Excerpts from *Easy Travel to Other Planets* (18, 24), by Ted Mooney. Copyright 1981 by Ted Mooney. Reprinted by permission of Farrar, Strauss & Giroux.

Excerpt from *The Crying of Lot 49* (24–25), by Thomas Pynchon. Copyright 1965, 1966 by Thomas Pynchon. Reprinted by permission of Harper & Row, Publishers, Inc.

Excerpts from *Software* (15–19, 30–34), by Rudy Rucker. Copyright 1982 by Rudy Rucker. Reprinted by permission of the author.

Excerpt from *Life During Wartime* (131–32), by Lucius Shepard. Copyright 1987 by Lucius Shepard. Reprinted by permission of Bantam Books.

"Wolves of the Plateau," by John Shirley, originally appeared in *Mississippi Review* 47/48 (1988): 136–50. Reprinted by permission of the author.

"Stoked," by Lewis Shiner, originally appeared in *Re: Artes Liberales* (Spring/Fall 1988): 198–202. Reprinted by permission of the author.

"Literary MTV," by George Slusser, originally appeared in *Mississippi Review* 47/48 (1988): 279–88. Reprinted by permission of the author.

Excerpt from *Schismatrix* (39–44), by Bruce Sterling. Copyright 1985 by Bruce Sterling. "Preface," in *Mirrorshades: The Cyberpunk Anthology.* Copyright by Bruce Sterling. "20 evocations," by Bruce Sterling, originally appeared in *Interzone* and in *Mississippi Review* 47/48 (1988): 122–29. All reprinted by permission of the author.

"On Gibson and Cyberpunk," by Darko Suvin, originally appeared in *Foundation* 46 (Autumn 1989): 40–51. Reprinted by permission of the author.

Excerpts from "The Indigo Engineers," (443–44, 457–59), in *The Rainbow Stories*, by William T. Vollmann. Copyright 1979 by William T. Vollmann. Reprinted by permission of Atheneum Publishers, an imprint of Macmillan Publishing Company.

Storm The Reality Studio.

And retake the universe.

—William S. Burroughs, *Nova Express*

Larry McCaffery

Introduction:
The Desert
of the
Real

But how could we know when I was young
All the changes that were to come?
All the photos in the wallets on the battlefield
And now the terror of the scientific sun?
—The Clash, "Something About England"

It is the real, and not the map, whose vestiges
subsist here and there, in the deserts which
are no longer those of the Empire, but our
own. The desert of the real itself.
—Jean Baudrillard, "The Precession of the
Simulacra"

i haven't fucked much w/ the past but i've
fucked plenty w/ the future.
—Patti Smith, "babelogue"

In gathering together the materials contained in *Storming the Reality
Studio*, I hope to create a context that will illuminate and broaden our
understanding of two enormously exciting topics that have broad significance for postmodern culture generally. The first of these has to do
with the recent evolution of what I will call "postmodern science
fiction." This evolution was spurred on within genre SF by the "cyberpunk controversy" during the 1980s. Sparked initially by the publication of William Gibson's *Neuromancer* in 1984, this controversy
spawned numerous critical debates in SF fanzines and at SF conferences and ultimately had the effect of opening up a dialogue within
the field that encouraged even cyberpunk's most hardened opponents
to examine the nature and roles of the genre, especially as these have
been changing in response to postmodern culture. Equally significant

in SF's recent transformations has been the development of experimental, quasi-SF works created by a number of major "mainstream" literary innovators (Pynchon, Burroughs, Ballard, Mooney, DeLillo and many others) that featured themes, motifs, and other elements that would previously have been associated with SF.

The nature and background of these parallel developments are discussed by a number of the critical essays included here as well as being schematically introduced in the Kadrey/McCaffery "Cyberpunk 101" text that follows this introduction. I have also aimed at presenting a range of stories, novel excerpts, poems, and other materials that can suggest something of the richness of theme and variety of stylistic innovation that characterizes contemporary SF and its many hybrid forms. A number of recurrent issues that emerge from the interaction of primary and secondary sources here—particularly those having to do with the meaning of artistic "realism" in our postfuturist age, the concepts of literary "authenticity" and "originality," and the paradoxes involved in artistic rebellion when "rebellion" is now a commodifiable *image* that is regularly employed as a "counterculture" marketing strategy—can all be shown to reflect and relate to similar issues being debated by nearly all artists and critics associated with postmodernism.

Indeed, the central topic addressed by this casebook is the way in which cyberpunk and other innovative forms of SF are functioning within the realm of postmodern culture generally: that is, the broader significance of SF's relationship to the complex set of radical ruptures—both within a dominant culture and aesthetic and also within the new social and economic media system (or "postindustrial society") in which we live. These are the ruptures and dislocations associated with postmodernism, as that term is used in this volume by critics such as Jean-François Lyotard, Fredric Jameson, Brian McHale, Dave Porush, Arthur Kroker and David Cook, and Jean Baudrillard, as well as by other critics not included here, such as David Bell, Gilles Deleuze, O. B. Hardison, and Kate Hayles.

The Desert of the Real: A Brief History of the Postmodern Universe

To one degree or another, all the critics cited above closely tie the evolution of postmodern culture to technological developments. *Storm-*

ing the Reality Studio specifically explores this connection, for it is my conviction that the myriad features and tendencies associated with the slippery term "postmodernism" can be understood best by examining what is unique about our contemporary condition. And it seems undeniable that this condition derives its unique status above all from technological change. Almost inevitably, those artists who have been most in touch with these changes, intuitively as well as intellectually, have relied on themes and aesthetic modes previously associated with SF. Some of these artists have naturally been genre SF writers working within the relatively insular SF publishing scene. Others have arrived at SF modes from without—from "mainstream" postmodernist experimentalism, including fictional forms, but also poetry, drama, rock music, television and video art, performance art, and many other modes. In a basic sense, then, this book is dedicated to the proposition that the interaction between genre SF and the literary avant-garde— two groups historically segregated (at least in the United States) and, hence, not influencing one another directly—needs to be noted, discussed, and encouraged.

It is to be expected that critics seeking to account for the central features of postmodern culture exhibit considerable differences in the nature and scope of their inquiries, as well as their particular emphases. But underlying most of their investigations—which are grounded less in literary criticism than in economics, philosophy, political science, semiology, and cultural anthropology—is a view that the past several decades have seen the evolution of a new network of political and economic systems, a global movement away from local, nationalistic sources of economic and political control (and other forms of power wielding) toward multinational ones. This shift is intimately connected with the arrival of what Ernest Mandel (in his influential study, *Late Capitalism*) has termed the "Third Stage" in capitalist expansion—that of "postindustrial capitalism," which has followed the earlier stages of market capitalism and the monopoly (or imperialist) stage. This new stage, emerging roughly in the years immediately following WWII, has produced our own postmodern world by expanding capitalism's operations, by eliminating those areas of precapitalist organizations previously tolerated and exploited, and, as Fredric Jameson summarizes, by creating "a new and historically original penetration and colonization of Nature and the Unconscious" (1984a:78). This unprecedented expansion, made possible specifically by the exponential growth of technology, has profoundly altered not only the daily textures of the world(s) we inhabit but the way we think about the world and ourselves in it. The new economic and political systems responsible for multinational capitalism are highly dependent upon rapid technological advancements that will allow them to compete successfully for global resources and further expansion. Because competition among the multinationals is so intense and because success within this competition depends so much upon gathering highly specialized marketing information (including political and social information for insurance and investment purposes, etc.), the development of highly sophisticated methods of information gathering and data storage has been a key priority in technological research and production—so much so that one can say now that the key "global resource" is the *information itself* rather than the oil, farm goods, or other resources usually associated with capitalist market systems.

These technological advancements have introduced a broad range of new "high-tech" products into postmodern society, such as sophisticated offensive and defensive military weaponry and surveillance to protect the resources and markets of the multinationals; increasingly complex (and expensive) medical equipment and supplies, including a new array of prosthetic devices; and a whole host of consumer products, from automobiles to chain saws, cellular phones, trash compactors, microwave ovens, and so forth.

But even more significant than these "tangible products" has been the rapid proliferation of technologically mass-produced "products" that are essentially *reproductions* or *abstractions*—images, advertising, information, memories, styles, simulated experiences, and copies of original experiences. Particularly notable in this regard has been the prodigious expansion in the past several decades of three industries: advertising, information, and what is referred to as "the media (or culture) industry." As Greil Marcus has noted, in different ways all three industries have "turned upon individual men and women, seized their subjective emotions and experiences, changed those once evanescent phenomena into objective, replicatable commodities, placed them on the market, set their prices, and sold them back to those who had, once, brought emotions and experiences out of themselves—to people who, as prisoners of the spectacle, could now find such things only on the market" (1989:101). Created for consumers by other products (TVs and film projectors, VCRs, CDs, computers, instacams, cameras, xerox and fax machines), these commodities can be reproduced (and then consumed) more easily than previous, unwieldy consumer products (cars, shoes, tanks); increasingly, they have thoroughly interpenetrated our daily lives with their "virtual realities," and begun to inhabit and colonize our imaginations and desires, even our unconscious, in a manner whose full implications are only now beginning to be recognized.

Overall, of course, such developments have enormously benefited the multinational system, for they have created a huge expansion of the *realm* in which the "dance of biz" (Gibson) can now whirl and infiltrate the desires of the soul. Together with the collective failure of communism to provide a viable alternative, the expansion of capitalism into its third stage has consolidated multinationalism's position so that virtually every corner of the globe is being successfully colonized by, for example, American popular culture. Thus, even in China, where these developments have met with massive political and cultural resistance, rock music is flourishing, Mickey Mouse and Donald Duck are national icons, and Rambo and Marlboro Men stalk the imaginations of the public. Even before the startling political events in China and Eastern Europe in 1989 (surely a pivotal year in this century's history), it seemed only a matter of time before the entire world would become united as one huge consumer market for the "free enterprise system." But as Greil Marcus notes, the success of this particular system of "freedom" has paradoxically created new forms of social control: "This was the modern world; to the degree that the real field of freedom had expanded, so had the epistemology, the aesthetics, the politics and the social life of control" (1989:101).

Although the general results of these developments are evident globally, the specific effects have inevitably been most far-reaching in those countries where technological advancement, together with social and economic pressures, are most intense—particularly the United States and Japan, but also Western Europe. The routine introduction of high-tech artifacts into these countries provides their citizens with a host of stimulating possibilities—but an equal number of troubling psychological, moral, and epistemological quandaries, as well. Many of these quandaries can be framed within age-old, venerable terminologies that go back as far as Plato and Eastern mysticism: What is real and what is illusion? What does it mean to be "alive" or "dead"? to be "conscious"? to be "immortal"? But in many cases, terms that were previously purely speculative abstractions ("immortality," "illusion") whose "existence" was tied to matters of semiotics and definition have now suddenly become literalized. Throughout history, for example, people have debated the nature of "life" and "death," and have argued about how one might go about achieving "immortality." Despite their vast emotional and psychological resonances, however, such discussions had little practical relevance until we began to develop technologies that allowed us to keep brain-damaged (or otherwise physically impaired people) "alive" indefinitely, or to replace our body parts with organ transplants, or to create computer and robotic systems that can "talk" and otherwise simulate the features of a "conscious" human being.

Such technological systems and artifacts that people can interface with (physically and imaginatively) or that can recreate experiences and "realize" desires, illusions, and memories have created vast new "areas" of sensory experience with their own spatial and temporal coordinates, their own personal and metaphysical dimensions. These new realms of experience—theorized by Guy Debord's "Society of the Spectacle," Baudrillard's "precession of simulacra," and Cook and Kroker's "hyperreality," and metaphorized perhaps most vividly by Gibson's "cyberspace"—have become integrated so successfully into the daily textures of our lives that they often seem more "real" to us than the presumably more "substantial," "natural" aspects. Indeed, these reproduced and simulated realities, whose objective forms serve as a disguise for their subjective content, have begun subtly to actually *displace* the "real," rendering it superfluous. Even as early as the 1950s, Guy Debord theorized this obsolescence of the real by describing contemporary life as now belonging to the "Society of the Spectacle" where "everything that was directly lived has moved away into a representation" (1977:1). Similarly, Jean Baudrillard, borrowing an image from Borges, has summarized this process as the replacement of the territory by the map so that the postmodern realm is now "the desert of the real." This is the postmodern desert inhabited by people who are, in effect, consuming *themselves* in the form of images and abstractions through which their desires, sense of identity, and memories are replicated and then sold back to them as products.

The psychological and metaphysical implications of such developments are explored by most of the fiction writers included in this volume, many of whom take already extant technological realities and push them (often only slightly) into more extreme possibilities. Similar extrapolative approaches can be found in many recent popular films (*Robocop* [1987], *The Terminal Man* [1974], *Videodrome* [1983], *Total Recall* [1990]), music (Sonic Youth's *Daydream Nation* [1988] or the performance art and albums by Laurie Anderson), and in the "mechanized, industrial sculptures" created by Mark Pauline and the Survival Research Lab. But even much more ordinary, familiar examples demonstrate the striking ways in which technology is transforming our perceptions of our relationship to time, memory, self-identity, and "reality." Consider the relatively mundane example of the effect that photography has had on our relationship to memory, a theme richly explored by Philip K. Dick in *Do Androids Dream of Electric Sheep?* (1968) and in Ridley Scott's adaptation of Dick's novel in the film *Blade Runner* (1982), and by Don DeLillo's *White Noise* (1985). Basically, our memories of many of the key events of our past are now recollections not of "actual" past events, but of the photographs or videos we have taken of them. In a sense, people now often use the "real experience"—a trip to the Grand Canyon, our daughter's wedding—primarily as a "pretext" for the more "substantial" later experience of "reliving" these experiences through reproduced sounds and images that magically conjure up for us our past, a conjuration that seems more "substantial" precisely because it can be endlessly reproduced.

Clearly these developments in technology and critical theory require some radical rethinking of several of the basic paradigms and metaphors through which West Europeans have viewed themselves since the time of the ancient Greeks. As noted earlier, these concepts are as fundamental as the nature of "consciousness" and "desire," or the familiar set of categorical oppositions that we rely upon to understand ourselves and our relationship to the universe: male/female, organic/inorganic, artifice/nature, reality/illusion, originality/duplication, life/death, human/inhuman. The breakdown of these concepts and distinctions, as well as the rise of new metaphors and categories of perception, is obsessively explored (often with startling and provocative results) by nearly all the critics and fiction writers included in this volume. In a basic sense, then, the works contained in this volume continually return to the same questions: What does it mean to be *human* in today's world? What has stayed the same and what has changed? How has technology specifically changed the answers we supply to such questions? And what does all this suggest about the future we will inhabit?

These are obviously important questions that not only have no simple answers, but that also are difficult (maybe impossible) to formulate within the conventions of so-called "traditional realism." The nature and sources of this difficulty are varied and complex. For one thing, the scientific, economic, and metaphysical principles producing these massive transformations often require specialized knowledge and intellectual skills not readily accessible to most artists. While railroads, steel mills, and assembly lines were fundamentally altering America's landscapes and mind-sets during the nineteenth century, it was still possible for the average American to grasp the mechanisms and principles responsible for such changes. Today, an analogous understanding of what is taking place in computer technology, astronomy, biology, and chemistry is simply too difficult. Consider the following list of some of the recurrent political, philosophical, moral, and cultural issues that postmodern SF and cyberpunk have been exploring: the far-reaching implications of the recent breakthroughs in cybernetic and genetic engineering, organ transplants, virtual reality, and artificial intelligence research; the equally significant developments involving information storage, and, in particular, the ways in which computerized data, microstorage, and data bank development are controlled and owned by multinationals (in short, the increasing monopolization of information by private business for the purposes of wielding power and control over nation-states and individuals); the social, psychic, political, and behavioral impact resulting from the shift away from the older industrial technologies to the newer information and cybernetic ones; the massive expansion of the "culture industry," an industry indiscriminately seeking profits from the sale of everything from "lite" beer to presidential images, detox centers, napalm, famine relief, invasion, and salvation; the assistance given to this expansion by technology's greater facility to introduce media images, print, and other informational sources directly into our homes, cars, and offices—and consequently, into the most intimate reaches of our imaginations, our self-definitions, our desires; the resulting "new and historically original penetration and colonization of Nature and the Unconscious" (Jameson 1984a:76).

Issues such as these, which are so massive, troubling, and profoundly disruptive, are rarely dealt with by mainstream "realistic" writers, not only because of the specialized knowledge required, but also because they challenge the normative bedrocks upon which the fantasies of "realism" are grounded. Thus, with only a handful of exceptions, most contemporary American authors continue to write novels as if these key issues (and the forces that produced them) did not exist. With the gap between the future and the present narrowing every day—and, paradoxically, with the growing recognition that if we move even "twenty minutes into the future" (à la *Max Headroom* [1985]), we will encounter a world as unimaginably transformed as what we find in Bruce Sterling's *Schismatrix* (1985)—the potential importance of informed, aesthetically innovative SF becomes obvious; here we have a form whose maximal level of artifice and focus on the future permit it to jettison the familiar, "correct" images, narratives, and implications that combine to produce the realistic illusions projected in most art. Freed from the requirements of "realism," and sensitive to the ways in which the "real" and the "true" are being systematically replaced (even *excluded*) by the "hyperreal" of images, statistics, and other abstractions whose role is to "stand in" for reality, postmodern SF has recently produced the only art systematically exploring this "desert of the real(s)."

SF and the Literary Avant-Garde

As I have just summarized, the challenge of finding a suitable means to examine the "postmodern condition" has produced a vigorous and highly energized response from a new breed of SF authors who combine scientific know-how with aesthetic innovation. But because much of this writing *is* so radical and formally experimental, and because writing which bears the imprint of "SF" has been so commonly relegated to pop-culture ghettos, it has remained until recently largely ignored, except within its own self-contained world. Examples of important, aesthetically radical SF exhibiting many of the features associated with postmodernism are evident as early as the mid-1950s and early 1960s, when literary mavericks like Alfred Bester, William

S. Burroughs, J. G. Ballard, Philip K. Dick, and Thomas Pynchon began publishing books that self-consciously operated on the fringes of SF and the literary avant-garde.

During the 1970s and 1980s, a few other authors working at the boundaries of SF and postmodern experimentalism continued to borrow the use of motifs, language, images—as well as the "subject matter"—of SF. Important examples would include Don DeLillo's *Ratner's Star* (1976) and *White Noise*, Ted Mooney's *Easy Travel to Other Planets* (1981), Joseph McElroy's *Plus* (1976) and *Women and Men* (1986), Denis Johnson's *Fiskadoro* (1985), Margaret Atwood's *The Handmaid's Tale* (1985), William T. Vollmann's *You Bright and Risen Angels* (1987), Kathy Acker's *Empire of the Senseless* (1988), and Mark Leyner's *My Cousin, My Gastroenterologist* (1990). While writing outside the commercial SF publishing scene, these writers produced works that perfectly fulfill the generic task of SF, described by Vivian Sobchack as "the cognitive mapping and poetic figuration of social relations as these are constituted by new technological modes of 'being-in-the-world'" (1987:225). As is true of the cyberpunk novels that began appearing in the early 1980s, these mainstream works (recently dubbed "slipstream" novels by cyberpunk theoretician Bruce Sterling) typically portrayed individuals awash in a sea of technological change, information overload, and random—but extraordinarily *vivid*—sensory stimulation. Personal confusion, sadness, dread, and philosophical skepticism often appeared mixed with equal measures of euphoria and nostalgia for a past when centers could still hold. The characters and events in these works typically exist within narrative frameworks that unfold as a barrage of words, data, and visual images drawn from a dissolving welter of reference to science and pop culture, the fabulous and the mundane, a tendency that reaches its most extreme expression in William Burroughs's hallucinatory mid-1960s novels.

A few of these "mainstream" postmodern writers have drawn very self-consciously from genre SF for specific tropes and narrative devices. This is very obvious in, for example, Burroughs's use of the motifs of the 1930s space opera works he read as a youth, in DeLillo's borrowing of dystopian elements in *White Noise*, in Vollman's improvisational treatment of a much wider range of SF modes in *You Bright and Risen Angels*, or Kathy Acker's borrowing of specific passages from *Neuromancer* in *Empire of the Senseless*. But typically one gets less a sense of these authors consciously borrowing from genre SF norms than of their introducing these elements simply because the world around them demands that they be present.

What Becomes a Mirrorshade Most?
Enter Cyberpunk

Not surprisingly, however, it has been within the realm of genre SF that technology's role in the evolution of postmodern life has been most frequently scrutinized and transformed into narratives and metaphors. One way to view the mid-1980s cyberpunk phenomenon is to suggest that it represented a synthesis of SF with postmodern aesthetic tendencies and thematic impulses. This synthesis could be loosely paralleled with the much-documented integration of "modernism" and SF during the 1960s, when SF experienced its last series of major formal disruptions during its "New Wave" period. Such a summary is misleading in several respects. For instance, while SF's New Wave self-consciously adopted specific modernist devices—Brian Aldiss's borrowing of Joyce (*Barefoot in the Head* [1969]), John Brunner's use of Dos Passos (*Stand on Zanzibar* [1968]), or Gene Wolfe's and Gregory Benford's employment of Faulkner (*The Fifth Head of Cerberus* [1972] and *Against Infinity* [1983])—it also produced a number of works as fully grounded in "postmodernist" impulses as those appearing in the 1980s (cyberpunk or otherwise). These would include several of the major works by SF innovators such as Samuel R. Delany, Joanna Russ, Thomas Disch, Ursula K. Le Guin, and Philip K. Dick. Nor does this cyberpunk-as-postmodernism equation provide much information about cyberpunk's *particular* aesthetic and thematic orientations. Books such as Le Guin's *Always Coming Home* (1985), Russ's *Extra(Ordinary) People* (1985), and Delany's *Triton* (1976) or his Nevèrÿon series are every bit as "postmodern" in their formal innovations and thematic concerns as anything written by the cyberpunks. Nevertheless, the premise that cyberpunk represents one particularly intriguing example of the "postmodernization" of SF generally suggests one of the theses governing this casebook.

The cyberpunk SF "movement" first came into prominence in 1984, when William Gibson's *Neuromancer* was published to considerable popular and critical success (it was the first SF novel to garner all three of SF's major awards, winning the Hugo, Nebula, and Philip K. Dick awards). But the seeds of its development were actually planted several years earlier, when Gibson and other writers later associated with cyberpunk began publishing stories and novels that had a different edge from other SF works dealing with similar issues. Cyberpunk was written by a generation of authors once-removed from the 1960s New Wave innovators, and this ten- or fifteen-year age difference was evident in their work in several ways. (The same point can be made about the differences between the "mainstream" innovators of the 1960s [Coover, Barth, and Gass] and their 1980s counterparts [Leyner, Vollmann, and Ann Beattie].) For one thing, the cyberpunks were the first generation of artists for whom the technologies of satellite dishes, video and audio players and recorders, computers and video games (both of particular importance), digital watches, and MTV were not exoticisms, but part of a daily "reality matrix." They were also the first generation of writers who were reading Thomas Pynchon, Ballard, and Burroughs as teenagers, who had grown up immersed in technology but also in pop culture, in the values and aesthetics of the counterculture associated with the drug culture, punk rock, video games, *Heavy Metal* comic books, and the gore-and-spatter SF/horror films of George Romero, David Cronenberg, and Ridley Scott.

In their works and in numerous, highly contentious public debates that took place at SF conferences and conventions, the cyberpunks presented themselves as "techno-urban-guerilla" artists announcing that both the technological dreams and nightmares envisioned by previous generations of SF artists were already in place, and that writers as well as the general public needed to create ways of using this technology for our own purposes before we all became mere software, easily deletable from the hard drives of multinationalism's vast mainframe. Cyberpunk, then, became a significant movement within postmodernism because of its ability to present an intense, vital, and often darkly humorous vision of the world space of multinational capitalism—and to render this vision both formally (through a style appropriate to its age) and concretely (through the dominant cultural imagery). Like their avatars Pynchon, Ballard, Dick, and Burroughs, cyberpunk authors constructed works that moved seamlessly through the realms of hard science and pop culture, realms that included chaos theory and Madonna, dada and punk rock, MTV and *film noire*, Arthur Rimbaud and Lou Reed, Arnold Schwarzenegger and Oliver North, instant reruns and AI. Decked out in mirrorshades and leather jackets, the cyberpunks projected an image of confrontational "reality hacker" artists who were armed, dangerous, and jacked into (but not under the thumb of) the Now and the New.

The overall effect of cyberpunk within SF is analogous to what occurred within rock music in the mid-1970s when punk music rudely and crudely deconstructed nearly everyone's relationship to popular music. When the slam dancers cleared out, and the pieces of amps, guitars, and vocal sounds were once again rejoined into something that seemed vaguely recognizable, there was a certain sense of sane clarity (or clear insanity) in the air. In the case of both punk and cyberpunk, however, this sense did not produce a constricting attitude of conformity among ambitious writers and musicians. While inevitably there were artists in both fields who were merely blindly mimicking the successful patterns of more creative counterparts, truly imaginative artists hardly felt that they were now required to narrowly imitate, say, punk and cyberpunk's emphasis on sensationalized, S&M surface textures, its Benzedrine-rush pacings, or its parodically nonconformist stance. Rather, there was a feeling in both the rock and SF communities that *whatever direction* these forms were now taking, they could be reconstructed afresh so that priorities could once again be recognized. With music there was an immediate series of healthy mutations, as with the Clash's incorporation of reggae and jazz, the cool, funky minimalism of Talking Heads (who later ventured into more complex arrangements influenced by African rhythms and Brian Eno), the cowpunk sounds of the Meat Puppets (whose name Gibson uses as a central motif in *Neuromancer*), and the speed-metal transformations of punk and blues elements.

Similarly, cyberpunk writers soon began producing works that defy easy categorization. It is precisely at this point of transformation and mutation that cyberpunk's evolution within genre SF begins to interact with the world outside—with the literary world of Don De-Lillo, for instance, or of William S. Burroughs, Ted Mooney, Kathy Acker, William T. Vollmann, J. G. Ballard, Harold Jaffe, and Mark Leyner. At this point, it also becomes clear that the cyberpunk phenomenon is important for reasons that lie far outside its impact on the recent direction of SF. These reasons, as I have already suggested, are related to a series of broad issues pertaining to postmodernist art in general: the breakdown of genre distinctions, for example, and the increasingly arbitrary separation of pop art from "serious art" (or art from advertising, image from referent, the natural from the conventionalized, originality from imitation, fiction from criticism, man-made from machine-made, live from Memorexed) and to the vital artistic interactions resulting from these interminglings. But most centrally these reasons involve the shared perception among a significant number of postmodern artists that art which fails to come to grips, formally or thematically, with these changes is irrelevant or (less harshly) out of sync with the times.

Thus, this casebook presents cyberpunk and related "mainstream" forays into quasi-SF forms as the inevitable result of art responding to the technological milieu that is producing postmodern culture at large. The critical debate spawned by postmodernism which has emphasized the semiological, *conventional* bases of all fictional forms (including the "natural" forms of realism) makes it easier to recognize the common aesthetic grounds shared by cyberpunk (and all SF) and other highly stylized forms. In this respect, SF's aesthetics can be seen as extending the implications of the surfictionist, metafictionist, and fabulist experiments of the 1960s in using its highly stylized codes and conventions to produce textual "meaning" in a manner as fully distinctive as the linguistic systems that give rise to meaning in a Shakespearean sonnet, a medieval morality fable, or a postmodernist story by Coover or Barth. Once the complex nuances of these codes and conventions are recognized, however, cyberpunk's narrative strategies can be shown to unfold in a typically postmodernist way: mixing together genres, borrowing devices from the cinema, computer systems, and MTV, infusing the rhythms of its prose with those of rock music and TV advertising, pastiching prior literary forms and otherwise playing with literary elements, and, above all, adopting the familiar postmodernist device of developing familiar "mythic" structures and materials which can then be undercut and exploited for different purposes.

It is this latter device that has been perhaps the most misunderstood and misrepresented by cyberpunk's critics, who have constantly pointed toward cyberpunk's appropriation of devices and materials associated with other genres—the use of hard-boiled detective formulas in *Blade Runner* and in Gibson's *Neuromancer*, the analogous use of gothic horror in *Alien* (1979) and of cop formulas in *Robocop* and *The Terminal Man*—as exhibiting its superficiality and collective failure of imagination. What such criticism ignores, however, is cyberpunk's postmodernist spirit of free play (*jouissance*) and collaboration, its delight in creating cut-ups and collages (à la Burroughs) in which familiar objects and motifs are placed in startling, unfamiliar contexts. To take an obvious example, when Gibson relocates hundreds of semiological fragments within the dissolving, surreal electronic nightworld he invents for his cyberspace trilogy, a new discourse is established, different messages conveyed. Yes, *Neuromancer*'s hero, Case, is a computer "cowboy" and "detective," and his mission is the familiar "Big Heist" with all the plot trappings, Molly is a "moll" out of a 1940s *film noire*, and Case's psychological motives center on his desire to seek revenge against the forces who fucked him over. True, the "messages" occasionally bear similarities to what we find in Chandler and Hammett: the hero lost in a society of criminal and impersonal forces, a nostalgic longing for a more authentic, uncorrupted past. But Gibson is also using the framework of *Neuromancer* to introduce his own agenda, which is a veritable casebook of postmodern SF concerns: the contrast between the human "meat" and metal, the relationship betwen human memory and computer memory; the denaturing of the body and the transformation of time and space in the postindustrial world; the increasingly abstract interaction of data and images in this world; the primacy of information in the "dance of data" that comprises so much of life today (a "dance" which Gibson employs as a metaphor for everything from the interaction of subatomic particles to the interactions of multinational corporations); the ongoing angst and paranoia (evident, as well, in the works of Burroughs, Dick, Pynchon, and DeLillo) that some overarching demiurge is manipulating individuals and international politics; the mystical sense that our creation and re-creation of data and images produces systems capable of merging with one another into new intelligences; and the spectre haunting nearly all postmodern SF—the uneasy recognition that our primal urge to replicate our consciousness and physical beings (into images, words, machine replicants, computer symbols) is *not* leading us closer to the dream of immortality, but is creating merely a pathetic parody, a metaexistence or simulacra of our essences that is supplanting us, literally taking over our physical space and our roles with admirable proficiency and without the drawbacks of human error and waste, without the human emotions of love, anger, ambition, and jealousy that jeopardize the efficiency and predictability of the capitalistic exchange—without, in short, the messy, unruly passions which also make the brief movement from conception to death so exhilarating and so frightening. And so human.

Near the end of "Postmodernism, or the Cultural Logic of Late Capitalism," Fredric Jameson announces the need for contemporary artists to invent "radically new forms" capable of responding to the complexities and textures of our historical moment. These new forms, he argues, would contain the possibilities for a new kind of "political art" that does more than either long for the past or merely represent our current "world space of multinational capital." This world space would indeed be represented in such art, Jameson notes, but it would achieve "a breakthrough to some as yet unimaginable new mode of representing this last, in which we may again begin to grasp our position as individual and collective subjects and regain a capacity to act and struggle which is at present neutralized by our spatial as well as our social confusion" (1984a:92).

I hope to establish that Jameson's eloquent and timely call for new art forms capable of assisting us in clarifying the nature and meaning of our lives has in fact already begun to be answered by some of the artists and critics who are represented here. Their work represents the most concerted effort yet by artists to find a suitable means for displaying the powerful and troubling technological logic that underlies the postmodern condition. Mixing equal measures of anger and bitter humor, technological know-how and formal inventiveness, postmodern SF should be seen as the breakthrough "realism" of our time. It is an art form that vividly represents the most salient features of our lives, as these lives are being transformed and redefined by technology. It also seeks to empower us by providing a cognitive mapping that can help situate us in a brave new postmodern world that systematically distorts our sense of who or where we are, of what is "real" at all, of what is most valuable about human life.

Richard Kadrey & Larry McCaffery

Cyberpunk 101:
A Schematic Guide
to *Storming the*
Reality Studio

A quick list of the cultural artifacts that helped to shape
cyberpunk ideology and aesthetics, along with books by the
cyberpunks themselves, in roughly chronological order.

Frankenstein (Mary Shelley, 1989 [1818], Penguin). The recycling of
body parts, the creation of life (or monster making), murder, sex,
revenge, the epic chase, the brilliant scientist working outside the law,
a brooding, romantic atmosphere—this book is a veritable sourcebook
for SF motifs and clichés. It also created the first great myth of the
industrial revolution, and reflects the deeply schizophrenic attitude
toward science so evident in postmodern culture and in the fiction
emerging from this culture.

Red Harvest (Dashiell Hammett, 1929, Vintage). Established the basic
template for the hard-boiled detective format. The tough guy–loner
confronting a vast system of corruption with his own private code of
ethics, the vividly drawn underworld populated by sleazy criminal
types, the richly idiosyncratic lingoes, the violence and surrealism of
urban life—these motifs proved readily transferable to cyberpunk's
portrayal of survival in a multinational version of street life.

Last and First Men (Olaf Stapledon, 1937, Dover). Hardly a novel at
all. More like a long, brilliant encyclopedic essay on the next million-
or-so years of human evolution.

The Big Sleep (Raymond Chandler, 1939, Random House). Chandler's
smooth, polychromatic prose style and vision of the detective as knight-
errant has influenced more than one cyberpunk.

"Coming Attraction" (Fritz Leiber, 1950, in *The Best of Fritz Leiber*, 1974, Ballantine). Virtually without precedent in 1950s SF, this grim short story of the future was told in sharp, surreal images, highlighted by an unflinching *noir* viciousness and terse prose. Its opening sentence is a paradigm for much of cyberpunk: "The coupe with the fishhooks welded to the fender shouldered up over the curb like the nose of a nightmare."

Limbo (Bernard Wolfe, 1988 [1952], Carroll & Graf). Wolfe, ex-Trotsky bodyguard, wrote this great American dystopia (and proto-cyberpunk) novel. Self-mutilation, lobotomy, and prosthetics are seen in a postnuke North America as the cure for war. *Limbo* is a brilliant black comedy, which is probably why it has been so neglected. Average SF readers don't score high on *irony* tests.

The Stars My Destination (Alfred Bester, 1956 [1955], Sidgwick & Jackson). Body modification, corporate intrigue, baroque settings and characters, and a walk down the gray line that separates criminals from the straight world. But it's the protagonist's purely anarchic belief in humanity that makes this book remarkable. This remains one of the few truly subversive novels ever to come out of science fiction.

Naked Lunch (William S. Burroughs, 1962 [1959], Grove). A blast of maniacal laughter from Hell. A combination of comedy as black as clotted blood. Dr. Benway's twisted medical speculations, tales of the criminal underground, and sexual fantasies that tear at your inseams like a rabid brontosaurus, all told in a fragmented prose style that still reads like the raw, beautiful poetry it is. The influence of this book is enormous. Without *Naked Lunch* there would probably be no cyberpunk.

The Gutenberg Galaxy, Understanding Media, and *The Medium Is the Massage* (Marshall McLuhan, 1962, University of Toronto Press; 1964, NAL; 1967, Random House). McLuhan was to the 1960s what Baudrillard, Kroker and Cook, and Deleuze and Guattari are to the postcyberpunk era: grasping the profound implications of how technological change (in the form of the printing press, television, movies, the telephone, and so on) was reshaping human interactions, perceptions, and self-concepts, McLuhan presented his message in a medium that was "postmodern" before its time—that is, via a jagged mosaic of audacious speculations, samplings of quotes, photographs, footnotes, digressions. Another candidate for the "Godfather of Cyberpunk."

A Clockwork Orange (Anthony Burgess, 1962, Norton). Alex is the subject of a mind control experiment in a bleak near-future world overrun by youth gangs obsessed with violence and trendy fashion. Told in a well thought-out patois collaging bits of Cockney rhyming slang and various Eastern languages.

The Soft Machine, The Ticket That Exploded, Nova Express, The Wild Boys (William S. Burroughs, 1966 [1961], 1967 [1962], 1964, 1971). In this sequence of novels (or prose poems), Burroughs draws more heavily on the SF pulp motifs of his childhood than in *Naked Lunch*. Space odysseys, Uranium Willy and the Heavy Metal Kid, image banks and silence viruses, protopunk "wild boys" engaged in apocalyptic guerilla warfare, body and mind invasion, the Nova Mob matching wits with the Nova police (hampered by the corrupt Biologic Courts) for control of the Reality Studio—these hallucinatory SF elements interact with shards of poetry by Rimbaud, Shakespeare, and Eliot (and much, much more) to fuel Burroughs's atomic-powered strap-on, which probes the asshole of society with more glee and wicked humor than anyone since Swift.

The Crying of Lot 49 (Thomas Pynchon, 1966, Perennial). Like Pynchon's first novel, *V.* (1963), this book serves up bits of history, science, philosophy, and pop psychology in a sauce wonderfully spiced with rock lyrics, sophomoric jokes, and truly *twisted* character names and types; when these elements are heated by paranoia and alienation, severe turbulence occurs. Less dense and less grounded in technology than his massive next novel, *Gravity's Rainbow*, *Lot 49* nonetheless anticipates cyberpunk in its wondrous use of scientific metaphors, its slam-dance pacings, its depiction of an exotic underworld of alienated weirdos, and its rapid modulations between the realms of "high culture" and the pop underground of drugs and the media culture.

Andy Warhol Presents the Velvet Underground and Nico (Velvet Underground, 1967, Polygram). Lou Reed and John Cale took pop audiences for harrowing rides into the darkness existing not on the edge of town but right in its center. Combining avant-garde, industrial-strength noise and back-to-basics impulses, VU's brutally honest depiction of drugs, s&m, and desperation was a breakthrough for a pop culture then entranced by the Summer of Love. The epitome of cool, bored-but-hyper hipness and street smarts, Reed—resplendent in black leather jacket and mirrorshades—created adult songs about characters whose arrogance and paranoia clashed headlong with their human frailties. As musicians and as cultural icons, the VU were seminal influences on the 1970s punk and the 1980s cyberpunk scenes.

Do Androids Dream of Electric Sheep? (Philip K. Dick, 1968, Ballantine). Renegade androids escape to earth from off-planet, and robot killer Deckard must track them down. Identity is the big question here: who is more human, the androids who want to live or the cop who wants to kill them? Basis for the film *Blade Runner* (1982).

Nova (Samuel Delany, 1968, Bantam). Stylistically, the bridge between the baroque 1950s SF of *The Stars My Destination* and the harder edge worldview of *Neuromancer*. A space opera full of feuding families and oddball characters, but with a respect for the science that makes it all run.

La Société du Spectacle (Guy Debord, 1967, Buchet-Chastel; trans. *Society of the Spectacle*, Black & Red, 1977). The first comprehensive examination of the far-reaching effects of postindustrial capitalism on individuals. The book opens with the following startling statement: "In societies where modern conditions of production prevail, all of life presents itself as an immense accumulation of *spectacles*. Everything that was directly lived has moved away into a representation." From there, we are only a hop, skip, and a jaunt from Baudrillard's "simulacra," Rucker's software, and Gibson's cyberspace.

The Cornelius Chronicles, volumes 1–3 (Michael Moorcock, 1969, Avon). The semicomplete story of the life/lives of Jerry Cornelius, Nobel Prize–winning scientist and rock and roll musician. The existential plotting, ambiguous sexuality of the main characters, and general low life/high brow feel make these very important works in the canon.

The Atrocity Exhibition (J. G. Ballard, 1990 [1969], Re/Search Publications). Ballard studied medicine while in college and it shows here. Through a series of fragmented "compressed novels," Ballard traces the breakdown of a doctor at a mental hospital.

Future Shock (Alvin Toffler, 1970, Random House). Information increased and comprehension decreased. Sound familiar? Get ready. The future is only going to get weirder.

Dub Music (1970-present). Reggae, all dreads and drive, collides with modern tech toys like digital delays and rhythm machines. That bastard offspring is called Dub, a hypnotic dance music from Jamaica, a brain graft of primitive glee and cool digital grace. Sly & Robbie, Prince Far I, the Mad Professor, as well as British honky Adrian Sherwood, are all masters of the style. This melding of tech and street music was extended even further by adding sampling machines (digital shoplifting of sound) by Rap musicians.

Dog Soldiers (Robert Stone, 1973, Houghton Mifflin). Stone's post-Beat prose style and vision of America as a morally bankrupt party town tearing itself apart is as harrowing as Conrad's "Heart of Darkness." The difference is that like most cyberpunk, the action in *Dog Soldiers* could be happening right next door.

"The Girl Who Was Plugged In" (James Tiptree, Jr., 1973, in *Warm Worlds and Otherwise*, 1975, Ballantine). A near-future Pygmalion story in which a hideous street girl is fitted with a sleek new "perfect" body and groomed for media stardom as a sort of living-breathing ad for all things marketable.

Crash (J. G. Ballard, 1973, Farrar, Straus & Giroux). The erotic thrill of violence, the secret satisfaction of watching machines fuck up and go haywire, and the numbing power of mass-produced imagery have never been presented more convincingly. If you've ever wondered what it would have been like to be approaching orgasm with Jayne Mansfield just before the Fatal Impact, this book is for you.

Gravity's Rainbow (Thomas Pynchon, 1973, Viking). The best cyberpunk ever written by a guy who didn't even know he was writing it. Pynchon's most difficult (and rewarding) book puts you into the bad brains of soldiers, scientists, hookers, losers, and more during World War II, when science was about to Change Everything.

Soon Over Babaluma (Can, 1974, Restless). Trance music from the band that practically invented what we now call "modern rock." Bassist Holger Czukay studied with Stockhausen for several years before jumping into a rock band. Their sound influenced everyone from Soft Machine to Public Image Limited to the Talking Heads.

Horses (Patti Smith, 1975, Arista). Patti Smith's androgynous, defiant, radiantly obscene stage personality showed a generation of would-be women rockers (and a number of cyberpunk authors) that females could be every bit as tough, raunchy, and daring as their male counterparts. Drawing equally from the realms of the artistic avant-garde (Rimbaud, Genet, and Burroughs) and of pop culture, Smith dipped down into the sea of possibilities and conjured up a jagged, delirious vision that drew its intensity from the same sense of desperation and exhilaration that characterized cyberpunk.

Shockwave Rider (John Brunner, 1975, Harper & Row). When people are little more than bytes in the government data stream, can anyone remain human? Fugitive Nickie Heflinger wants to find out, and change a few things.

Galaxies (Barry Malzberg, 1975, Pocket Books). Pure postmodernism in SF drag. A novel about a trip to a "black" galaxy, as well as a novel about writing a novel. Self-referential and reflexive in the extreme. Like reading Wittgenstein in a hall of mirrors.

Plus (Joseph McElroy, 1976, Knopf). A dying engineer who has his brain removed awakens to find he has become, literally, a mere communication device, attached to a computer inside a satellite orbiting the earth. As "he" (Imp Plus) gradually recovers his memories and reinvents language, he transforms himself into a fully conscious biological and chemical laboratory. Eventually he discovers a means of rebellion against the people and world that put him where he is. Told in a dense, poetic blend of Beckett and computerese.

Never Mind the Bollocks (The Sex Pistols, 1976, Warner). The band that shook the world and said "No" in power chords so loud and elegant that they were heard by a whole generation of artists wishing to escape the emptiness and safety of the corporate consumer mentality. The dadaists performing nightly in Zürich's Cabaret Voltaire in 1916 performed an experiment in which the language used to justify the great war raging outside was destroyed. If they had had access to electric guitars and amplifiers, those dadaists would have sounded like this.

Enter cyberpunk, which appropriated punk's confrontational style, its anarchist energies, its crystal-meth pacings, and its central motif of the alienated victim defiantly using technology to blow everyone's fuses.

Second Annual Report (Throbbing Gristle, 1976, Industrial Records). Throbbing Gristle completely abandoned the pretense of playing anything like conventional music. Their albums and performances were psychological assaults of the most extreme, where creative use of pure noise substituted for songs. The Futurists performed similar experiments in the 1920s. Throbbing Gristle's brilliance, however, came when they approached their noise assaults as rock and roll shows, seducing thousands of listeners who would normally run screaming from anything called "art."

Low (David Bowie, 1977, Ryko). Bowie's first collaboration with Brian Eno resulted in *the* album that mended the rift between the razor heat of rock and the cooler geometry of electronic/progressive/avant-garde sounds. A happy mistake early in the recording process resulted in a fresh drum sound still being copied.

The Ophiuci Hotline (John Varley, 1977, Dial). Cyberpunk ideas presented in their larval form are the highlight of this otherwise vastly disappointing first novel. Though the prose is graceless, Varley has a fine feel for the infinite malleability of flesh through technology, and his multiple clones of a single female character and their wildly different fates is an excellent depiction of the fragmentation of a single personality.

Dawn of the Dead (George Romero, 1978, Media). The mindless zombies who can eagerly (but placidly) rip-and-devour the flesh of gun-toting bikers (when they're not riding the escalators or being drawn to Blue Lite Specials) and prowl the shopping mall scene of this classic, horrifically funny film are, of course, the same folks we've hurried past on our way to the Cineplex 12. The nightmarish, punk extremities of surreal violence, the relentless exposure of capitalism's banalizing effect on individuals, the insistence on visceral, bodily reality that our airbrushed, roboticized exteriors deny—all would find their way, in transmuted form, into cyberpunk's own brand of dark humor, aesthetic extremity, and notions of guerilla-tactics survival.

Blood and Guts in High School (Kathy Acker, 1984 [1978], Grove). Her influence is similar to that of Burroughs and Moorcock, but Acker started out as a poet, so her prose is infused with the poet's lust for words. That and her moral outrage make her very important. If Genet had sung for Black Flag, he might have sounded like this.

Survival Research Laboratories (Mark Pauline, Matt Heckert, Erick Werner, ca. 1979–present). These San Francisco–based industrial sculptors and performance artists have literalized the machinery-run-amok theme by staging spectacular, alarming, and often nauseating catastrophes. As these surreal, grotesque mechanical simulacra (which are often rigged up to dead animals magically brought back to a pathetic parody of "life") attack effigies, images, targets, and eventually turn on each other, our culture's deepest emotional responses toward the technological milieu are played out in ways not soon forgotten by anyone who was there (and survived).

The Postmodern Condition (Jean-François Lyotard, 1984 [1979], University of Minnesota Press). This difficult but provocative "Report on Knowledge" lays a philosophical blueprint for cyberpunk (if anyone can read the map). How to react to the computerization of society? or the dystopian prospect of a global private monopoly of information created by the profitability of the new technological and information revolutions? or the crisis of representation? Lyotard has a quietly optimistic view that science's capacity for change, innovation, and renewal will ultimately be the undoing of the repressive system that supplies it with grant money. Stay tuned.

MTV (1981–present). Mundane music (for the most part) is genetically altered into a pure info monster comprising collage, rapid-fire imagery, and a stream-of-consciousness sense of timelessness and placelessness. All these things make MTV an influential point of reference for the age when information overload is more chic than a pierced nipple.

Easy Travel to Other Planets (Ted Mooney, 1981, Farrar, Straus, Giroux). Blending mainstream's emphasis on psychological depth with an eerie ambience of SF (an impending war in the Antarctic, information sickness), this haunting, lyrical novel perfectly exemplifies the blend of the postmodern mainstream and SF that Bruce Sterling has dubbed "slipstream." If affairs with dolphins, the fear of death, the throb of reggae, and the lure of what the next twist of your joystick might bring pretty much describes the world you live in—one that's rushing away from you at every moment—give this book a whirl.

Big Science (Laurie Anderson, 1982, Warner). Okay, so she does seem occasionally too cute, precious, and "profound" to be mingling with this roughhouse gang. But there's an undercurrent of minimalist dread, alienation, and paranoia that wafts over you so gently, as you sit entering spreadsheet data on your laptop while sipping cocktails in the business class of a 747. Slowly it dawns on you that you're only seconds from impact, that the reassuring voice of the "pilot" was only another recorded message, that the arms of the loved one gripping you in a last embrace are really automatic, electronic arms, that all those amazing chemical reactions going on inside your body right now to protect you aren't going to mean a thing when this lumbering, gas-guzzling pile of metal plows into a Kansas cornfield at 600 MPH with you strapped inside like the meat puppet you are. Stand by.

Blade Runner (Ridley Scott, 1982, Embassy). This film has often (and deservedly) been compared with Gibson's *Neuromancer*, and for good reason. The claustrophobic feel of Scott's mise-en-scène, with its over-abundance of exotic images and information, its mixture of Asian and American, glittery high tech and refuse-strewn lowlife, plus the sheer intensity of its presentation—these are the cinematic equivalents of Gibson's prose. Just as important, the movie shares with *Neuromancer* a focus on the moral and epistemological questions created by technology. No answers in sight.

Simulations (Jean Baudrillard, 1983, Semiotext(e)). French Marxist theorist Baudrillard runs amok in the labyrinth of epistemological quandaries, simulated experiences and desires, and all-too-familiar banalities that comprise postmodern American life. His elaborate, playful theorization of the concept of the "simulacra"—a copy of something which has no original—has been a landmark in the theorization of postmodern culture. Beneath all the neologisms, undecipherable rhetoric, and confusing analogies, readers sense that in his probings of Disneyland, Reagan, and celebrity hijackers he has indeed put his finger upon something real in the wispy abstractions of postmodernism. (Or was that finger in a data glove?)

Videodrome (David Cronenberg, 1983, MCA). Cronenberg explores one of cyberpunk's favorite themes—the denaturing of the body, the displacement of the real by the "hyperreal" of television. A Dickian vision, troubling in its gruesome but perceptive take on how society has become transfixed as it consumes its own desires and fears in the form of media-produced images.

Frontera (Lewis Shiner, 1984, Pocket Books). The first privately funded mission to Mars after the collapse of NASA turns nightmarish when the protagonist, Kane, finds himself programmed to bring something back to Earth, at any cost.

The Terminator (James Cameron, 1984, EMI). Arnold Schwarzenegger is a time-traveling killer robot sent to 1980s L.A. to murder the woman destined to give birth to the leader of the future rebellion against the sentient machines who have taken over the planet. Like much cyberpunk, this film is a conscious throwback to earlier pulp forms, full of genre references; a SF potboiler saved by a bent wit and savage speed-freak energy, it was the model for virtually every action movie for the remainder of the decade (and beyond).

Neuromancer, Count Zero, Mona Lisa Overdrive (William Gibson, 1984, Berkley; 1986, Arbor House; 1988, Bantam). The evolution of the Matrix, a computer-generated reality created by data from all the world's computers, and the lives of those that live in and through it.

"Postmodernism, or The Cultural Logic of Late Capitalism" (Fredric Jameson, 1984a, *New Left Review*). This seminal essay remains the most cogent and compelling description of the central features of postmodernism. What is interesting is the way Jameson's central, oft-quoted premises about postmodernism—its impulse toward collage and pastiche, its eschewal of "depth" and its emphasis on "surface," the deliberate foregrounding of sensory overload and proliferation of signs without reference (with the resulting inability of individuals to locate themselves, physically or psychically), the odd response of "euphoria" when confronted with sensory overload, the lack of affect, the "nostalgia mode"—read almost as a litany of cyberpunk thematic and stylistic tendencies.

White Noise (Don DeLillo, 1985, Viking). DeLillo mixes dystopian premises (a toxic cloud raises havoc in an Everytown, U.S.A.) with utopian ones (the development of a drug that eliminates the anxiety of death) in a novel that portrayed the most essential dilemmas, absurdities, and wonders of postmodern life. Wonderfully comic and yet deeply moving, this was written with more wit and sympathy than any other novel of the 1980s.

The Soft Machine: Cybernetic Fiction (David Porush, 1985, Methuen). The first important investigation of the ways in which recent concepts of cybernetics and AI have begun to provide contemporary writers with key sources of images and literary techniques. While Porush focuses mostly on writers whom Bruce Sterling would later dub "slipstream authors" (he examines Burroughs, Barthelme, Vonnegut, McElroy, Beckett, and Pynchon in detail), his analysis of the struggle taking place between those who accept the mechanical model for human intelligence and communication and those who resist it leads him to propose the recent evolution of a literary synthesis that has striking applications for cyberpunk fiction of the 1980s.

Blood Music (Greg Bear, 1985, Arbor House). A renegade gene hacker injects himself with his own experimental microorganisms and gets up close and personal with Information. Theory and a too, too malleable reality. Visually, this book is worthy of Salvador Dalí.

Eclipse, Eclipse Penumbra, Total Eclipse (John Shirley, 1985, 1987, 1989, Warner Books). A large-scale story on the reemergence of fascism as a major political force, told in a vivid, hallucinatory prose style.

Max Headroom (Peter Wagg, producer; Steve Roberts, original screenplay; 1985, MLV-TV [Lorimar]). Traveling just 20 minutes into the future, we arrive in cyberpunk land—a place where video-generated talking heads call the shots for the anonymous guys with *real* power (the multinational bigwigs), where capitalism's goal of transforming every point in space and time into a potential sale opportunity has never been realized, where the present moment seems to disappear into a turbulent sea of disconnected words and images that all seem vaguely exciting *and* banal. And you forgot your life jacket.

Mirrorshades: The Cyberpunk Anthology (ed. Bruce Sterling, 1986, Arbor House). Could be subtitled "A Young Person's Guide to Cyberpunk." The first and still definitive collection of cyberpunk short fiction.

The Postmodern Scene: Excremental Culture and Hyper-Aesthetics (Arthur Kroker and David Cook, 1986, St. Martin's Press). Kroker and Cook examine "sign crimes," "panic sex," "body invaders," the role of television as a "consumption machine," and other central bummers of the technological age. In its own way, their vision is as extreme and hysterical as that of anything found in cyberpunk (for example, they claim that Saint Augustine was the first postmodernist!).

Mindplayers (Pat Cadigan, 1987, Bantam). Deadpan Allie is a sort of future psychiatrist who works on her patients by entering virtual representations of their psyches.

When Gravity Fails (George Alec Effinger, 1987, Bantam). Petty criminals in a postsuperpower Arab world augment themselves with designer drugs and personality chips in a Chandleresque murder mystery.

You Bright and Risen Angels (William T. Vollmann, 1987, Vintage). In one of the most ambitious and original debuts since Pynchon's *V.*, Vollmann develops a dense, sprawling, novelistic "cartoon" in which bugs and electricity become motifs used to explore the revolutionary impulses that have arisen in response to the evils of industrialism. Moving across vast areas of history and geography filled with arcane information and surrealist literalizations of sexual longings and violence, this book's wild flights of improvisational prose and intensity of vision signal the arrival of a major talent.

Daydream Nation (Sonic Youth, 1988, Enigma). The ultimate cyberpunk musical statement to date, this double album evokes the confusion, pain, and exhilaration of sensory overload, via chaos theory–produced blasts of sound and sonic textures whose dissonance and wildness are matched only by their soaring beauty and wicked sense of humor. What becomes a mirrorshade most?

Islands in the Net (Bruce Sterling, 1988, Morrow). A thoughtful extrapolation of a future in which nuclear weapons have been banned and information is the most valuable commodity. Don't overlook Sterling's other books, *Schismatrix* (1985) and *The Artificial Kid* (1980).

Empire of the Senseless (Kathy Acker, 1988, Grove). Thivia (a pirate) and Abhor (part human and part robot) roam through a Sadean future ("dystopia" is much too mild) on a quest to kill-the-father (and hence demolish the world of patriarchy) on as many different levels as possible. Like the cyberpunks (and she appropriates an extended section of *Neuromancer* here), there is something oddly optimistic about Acker's vision of pirate-renegades stealing what they need from The Man and transgressing every taboo imaginable, while still trying to work out their own myth that lies beyond those devised by the hippies or the punks.

Metrophage (Richard Kadrey, 1988, Ace). Art and crime meet literally, in the streets when a strange virus hits Los Angeles. If Tom Waits were a cyberpunk writer, he'd be writing something like *Metrophage* [L.M.]

Wetware (Rudy Rucker, 1988, Avon). Sentient robots ("boppers") on the moon want to interface with human beings and create the first "meatbop." This book recently netted Rudy his second Philip K. Dick Award.

My Cousin, My Gastroenterologist (Mark Leyner, 1990, Harmony). Imagine some sort of metal cylinder of near-infinite diameter that has been twisted into a circle; inside this cylinder, verbal elements of political and lit-crit jargon, cyberpunk, speed-metal rock lyrics, language poetry, movie dialogue, obscure medical and scientific textbooks, television ads, and all manner of pop-cultural discourses have been accelerated to near-warp velocities, until they collide violently and begin to ooze out onto the page. If Rudy Rucker's claim that the essence of cyberpunk fiction lies in its information density and concern with new thought forms is to be taken seriously, Leyner, like Pynchon before him, wrote an instant cyberpunk masterpiece without even knowing he was doing so.

Fiction

and

Poetry

Kathy Acker

Beyond
the Extinction
of Human Life
(*from* **Empire**
of the Senseless)

I asked Abhor what she wanted with me. Did she also want to destroy my identity?

"I work for this man. I'm collecting for him." As if I understood what she meant, blindly, I followed her out of my room. They say love's also blind, but, for me, love has equalled pain.

Her boss's name was Schreber. "I've never seen you before, have I?" he asked.

"No."

"I'm going to tell you something about yourself." Finally perhaps I'd learn something about myself. "You're masochistic to the point of suicidal and, actually, physically damaged. You believe that, and the neurological and hormonal damage probably is, permanent."

"Yes."

He wasn't going to let me interrupt him. "You were . . . disrupted in your childhood by the usual causes. I'm not the least bit interested in psychological interpretations. They're passé. But there's one thing."

I interrupted him. "I don't give a damn. Not only about psychology. About myself." I continued, "You're fat and ugly, sir, but I'm dead. Psychology and my psychology's a dead issue." There were a lot of dead bodies floating around the world. "All I want to know from you is what you want from me." Otherwise, I wanted to be alone.

Because, for me, desire and pain're the same.

I didn't want her. I couldn't so I didn't want. Frigidity was a way of life. I didn't know if phenomena such as desires which're fleeting even mattered. Psychology isn't here a dead issue. I decided I would keep her because I had to because she said I had to be hers.

Ferret

Is reality always this unknown?

My friends informed me that the boss's real name was Schreber. Dr Schreber. He's honest enough, they said, as bosses are honest, to pay me for my work. So I could pay off my last boss so he wouldn't off me. Of course there's no money. Money's flimsy paper people who don't have power carry on them. What they do with money I don't know. I needed drugs.

"Your neurological and hormonal damage is making you degenerate so fast, faster than if you had AIDS," the fat man informed me in front of the cunt, "that within a couple of months you're going to be a mongoloid, even stupider than a lobotomy case, due to all the hatred which is festering in you, unless I inject a certain enzyme into your bloodstream and then enable you to receive a full blood transfusion. You will get this enzyme, your saviour, flea, only if you do what I want."

"What do you want?"

"For you to do exactly what I want until that time."

The trouble was I had no way of knowing if he meant to keep his part of the deal. I couldn't ask the cunt I thought I loved. Since I was thus dragging my tail through unknowable territory, my memory was useless. My memory was as dead as my desire used to be.

The next day, on a street, a garbage dump in front of the river, my former boss himself cut the throat of the fuck who informed on me in front of me. He slaughtered her because it was a practical way of making room for a fresh employee. Capitalism needs new territory or fresh blood.

I saw: blood sprayed from a jugular.

I needed my drug.

For a long time I had remained apathetic. So sure that my words meant nothing to anyone that I no longer spoke unless circumstances forced me to. So sure that my relations to the world were null that it didn't matter to what I said 'yes.' When I was young frivolity and trivia had been my weapons; now I did whatever I was told because I was no longer me. That is, the I who was acting was theirs, separate from the I who knew and whom I had known. Lots of eyes were watching me.

That is, the I who had SEXUAL DESIRES had nothing to do with the high IQ/understanding. This IQ used to be high but, since now was corrupted blinded covered over, wants seemed more capable and intelligent than I had known. I found myself at that point, that bottom.

I thought all I could know about was human separation; all I couldn't know, naturally, was death. Moreover, since the I who desired and the eye who perceived had nothing to do with each other and at the same time existed in the same body—mine: I was not possible. I, in fact, was more than diseased. But Schreber had given me hope of a possible solution. A hope of eradicating disease. Schreber had the enzyme which could change all my blood.

When all that's known is sick, the unknown has to look better. I, whoever I was, had no choice but to go along with Schreber. I, whoever I was, was going to be a construct.

The sky faded to blood, to the color of blood. After I left the doctor and returned home, what I called home, which was better than I had ever had, Abhor had gotten there before me and was waiting for me, so to speak. Asleep. Naked. I saw her. A transparent cast ran from her knee to a few millimeters below her crotch, the skin mottled by blue purple and green patches which looked like bruises but weren't. Black spots on the nails, finger and toe, shaded into gold. Eight derms, each a different color size and form, ran in a neat line down her right wrist and down the vein of the right upper thigh. A transdermal unit, separated from her body, connected to the input trodes under the cast by means of thin red leads. A construct.

In my imagination we were always fucking: the black whip crawls across her back. A red cock rises.

"I don't know who's backing him." Abhor turned around to face me. She must have woken up. "All I know is we call him 'boss' and he gets his orders. Like you and me."

"Somebody knows something. Whoever he is, the knower, must be the big boss."

"Look." Abhor raised herself up on one arm. She smelled warm, as if from kisses, but to my knowledge no kisses had taken place. "All I know is that we have to reach this construct. And her name's Kathy."

"That's a nice name. Who is she?"

"It doesn't mean anything."

"If it doesn't mean anything, it's dead. The cunt must be dead." My puns were dead.

"Look. All I know is we have to reach this construct. I don't know anything else."

"We have the capacities for understanding and, at the same time, we understand nothing," I replied. I understood we had to find some construct.

She told me again. "All I know is we're looking for a certain construct. Somewhere. Nothing else matters." A pulsing red then black cursor crept through the outline of a doorway. With enough endorphin analogue, Abhor could walk on a pair of bloody stumps. "You don't matter and reality doesn't matter." The road away from the airport, which became a series of roads, had been dead straight, like neat incisions, into the open body of the city. Poverty was writhing in pink. I had watched, here and there, a machine glide by, bound by fog and grey. Later on there were tenements called "council housing," walls of mottled aluminum, prison guards' cocks sticking in order to piss through unarranged holes in the brick, more plyboard and corrugated iron walls. The lucky poor had playgrounds. I remembered Abhor was a construct.

Imagination was both a dead business and the only business left to the dead.

In such a world which was non-reality terrorism made a lot of sense.

The modern Terrorists are a new version, a modern version, so to speak, of the hoboes of the 1930s USA. Just as those haters of all work (work being that situation in which they were being totally controlled; the controllers didn't work), as far as they were able took over their contemporary lines of communication, so these Terrorists, being aware of the huge extent to which the media now divorce the act of terrorism from the original sociopolitical intent, were not so much nihilists as fetishists. I had worked with them before in some way which I couldn't quite remember.

Two days after I had met the doctor, I found myself knocking on the door of a record shop somewhere. Terrorism is always a place to start because one has to start somewhere. A boy, or rather a skull, whose teeth were pointed red, as if skulls eat meat, opened the door which was falling apart so badly it was cracking open. I half crawled through a gap, half walked through the door, into a middle-sized record shop storeroom. Discs lay shattered on the floor. A celluloid nun moved her eyes horizontally as if a hand was moving her eyeballs. Smiley with one hand bone pointed me to a couch on which a freezer was sitting.

"Among the American international corporations the practice of setting up mixed affiliates is most widespread in chemicals and petrochemicals, rubber and the extractive industries. These ICs combine production on an international scale and organize the vertical and/or horizontal integration of their plants and thus, finally, control the whole product cycle . . ."

"I'm not interested."

"Du Pont and Union Carbide, Goodyear and Uniroyal, Exxon and Kaiser, for example, organize the supply of semifinished products from overseas enterprises to others on a wide scale, gain access to sources of raw . . ."

"Shut up," I said. "I need to find a code for a certain construct. I know you're planning to knock over the CIA library and the code is there."

Smiley smiled at me again. I remembered we had once been lovers; I had forgotten. We still are, I thought, in that his nastiness and inability to do anything but bite in the face of fear—any human presence triggered fear—matches my deeper nastiness. I never actually worked with the Moderns, but then I only work with people out of my need. Things are always the same.

The fact was that the Moderns talked too much. Their talk, or rhetoric, was blab: they didn't care who heard them; they would happily explain anything to the tiny parrots who shitted on the record discs as they flew around. The Moderns had the same relation to their work, terrorism: they didn't give a damn. They just wanted to have fun. Like parrots, they became easily bored.

On this operation the Moderns planned with great glee to reach Washington DC, the location of the library, via chickenwire. The chickenwire was sets of satellite and radio connectives. Like kids gone mad the Terrorists zoomed through the green purple yellow flashlights which are Manhattan, that absence of people, by using epoxy as they touched the midnight glass to control their movements. Then, over black ghettoes.

Except for Manhattan, which had been left to the rich, all of the eastern American urban centres had been left to the packs of wild dogs, wild cats, and blacks who lived in and under the streets. There were no more whites there except for gays.

The library was the American Intelligence's central control network, its memory, what constituted its perception and understanding.

(A hypothesis of the political uses of culture.) It was called MAINLINE. The perception based on culture is a drug, a necessity for sociopolitical control.

Being a bit behind their times the Moderns only wanted to destruct. On the other hand my construct (a cunt) and I had to find the code. The Modernists planned to shoot misinformation into MAINLINE's internal video. Due to the misinformation each video screen would strobe for twenty seconds in a frequency that would cause the constructs and other robot viewers to have seizures. Pale green apartments strobed emerald at midnight. Simultaneously the audio portion of MAINLINE's internal video, speeding double, would inform its listeners about the army's use of a certain endomorphin, at this moment being tested, to throw human skeletal growth into one thousand percent overkill. The red lights in the brothel tenements strobed blood eyes of Haiti.

The Terrorists would be happy when two minutes later their infiltrated message ended with the main system's end in white noise.

The Terrorists were happy.

In the white noise the cops arrived so that they could kill everybody. Round revolving cars emitted sonar waves. Certain sonar vibrations blinded those not in the cars; other levels numbing effectively chopped-off limbs; other levels caused blood to spurt out of the mouths nostrils and eyes. The buildings were pink. Preferring mutilation the families who lived in bed-sits ran out into the streets. Outside the black ghettoes, through the waters, sea-cruise missiles with two hundred kt. nuclear warheads swam like dolphins. Carrying at least twelve ALCMs on extended pylons and eight on internal rotary launchers, B-52 bombers rode on cars whose trunks held various nerve gases which seeped out through the city atmosphere at designated intervals. "Homing-and-kill" vehicles, upon sensing the presence of any living thing with their infrared sensors, unfurled two-meter-long metal ribs. Metallic weights studded the metal ribs. The insect life moved on. The cops' faces, as they killed off the poor people, as they were supposed to, were masks of human beings. And the faces of the politicians are death. A young boy who lay in the street had hollowed-out eye sockets, skinless arms, and a smile due to the large amounts of acid rain in the air. Red and black deco staircases from the magenta tops of buildings bridged building to building.

Inside the library's research department, the construct cunt inserted a subprogram into that part of the video network. The sub-program altered certain core custodial commands so that she could retrieve the code.

The code said: GET RID OF MEANING. YOUR MIND IS A NIGHTMARE THAT HAS BEEN EATING YOU: NOW EAT YOUR MIND.

The code would lead me to the human construct who would lead me to, or allow me, my drug.

J. G. Ballard

From

Crash

Long before Vaughan died I had begun to think of my own death. With whom would I die, and in what role—psychopath, neurasthenic, absconding criminal? Vaughan dreamed endlessly of the deaths of the famous, inventing imaginary crashes for them. Around the deaths of James Dean and Albert Camus, Jayne Mansfield and John Kennedy he had woven elaborate fantasies. His imagination was a target gallery of screen actresses, politicians, business tycoons, and television executives. Vaughan followed them everywhere with his camera, zoom lens watching from the observation platform of the Oceanic Terminal at the airport, from hotel mezzanine balconies and studio car-parks. For each of them Vaughan devised an optimum auto-death. Onassis and his wife would die in a re-creation of the Dealey Plaza assassination. He saw Reagan in a complex rear-end collision, dying a stylized death that expressed Vaughan's obsession with Reagan's genital organs, like his obsession with the exquisite transits of the screen actress's pubis across the vinyl seat covers of hired limousines.

After his last attempt to kill my wife Catherine, I knew that Vaughan had retired finally into his own skull. In this overlit realm ruled by violence and technology he was now driving forever at a hundred miles an hour along an empty motorway, past deserted filling stations on the edges of wide fields, waiting for a single oncoming car. In his mind Vaughan saw the whole world dying in a simultaneous automobile disaster, millions of vehicles hurled together in a terminal congress of spurting loins and engine coolant.

I remember my first minor collision in a deserted hotel car-park. Disturbed by a police patrol, we had forced ourselves through a hurried

Ferret © 1991

Ferret

sex-act. Reversing out of the park, I struck an unmarked tree. Catherine vomited over my seat. This pool of vomit with its clots of blood like liquid rubies, as viscous and discreet as everything produced by Catherine, still contains for me the essence of the erotic delirium of the car-crash, more exciting than her own rectal and vaginal mucus, as refined as the excrement of a fairy queen, or the minuscule globes of liquid that formed beside the bubbles of her contact lenses. In this magic pool, lifting from her throat like a rare discharge of fluid from the mouth of a remote and mysterious shrine, I saw my own reflection, a mirror of blood, semen, and vomit, distilled from a mouth whose contours only a few minutes before had drawn steadily against my penis.

William S. Burroughs

"Mother and I
Would Like
to Know"
(from The Wild Boys)

The uneasy spring of 1988. Under the pretext of drug control suppressive police states have been set up throughout the Western world. The precise programming of thought feeling and apparent sensory impressions by the technology outlined in bulletin 2332 enables the police states to maintain a democratic façade from behind which they loudly denounce as criminals, perverts and drug addicts anyone who opposes the control machine. Underground armies operate in the large cities enturbulating the police with false information through anonymous phone calls and letters. Police with drawn guns irrupt at the Senator's dinner party a very special dinner party too that would tie up a sweet thing in surplus planes.

"We been tipped off a nude reefer party is going on here. Take the place apart boys and you folks keep your clothes on or I'll blow your filthy guts out."

We put out false alarms on the police short wave directing police cars to nonexistent crimes and riots which enables us to strike somewhere else. Squads of false police search and beat the citizenry. False construction workers tear up streets, rupture water mains, cut power connections. Infra-sound installations set off every burglar alarm in the city. Our aim is total chaos.

Loft room map of the city on the wall. Fifty boys with portable tape recorders record riots from TV. They are dressed in identical grey flannel suits. They strap on the recorders under gabardine topcoats and dust their clothes lightly with tear gas. They hit the rush hour in a flying wedge riot recordings on full blast police whistles, screams, breaking glass crunch of nightsticks tear gas flapping from their clothes. They

John Bergin

scatter put on press cards and come back to cover the action. Bearded Yippies rush down a street with hammers breaking every window on both sides leave a wake of screaming burglar alarms strip off the beards, reverse collars and they are fifty clean priests throwing petrol bombs under every car WHOOSH a block goes up behind them. Some in fireman uniforms arrive with axes and hoses to finish the good work.

In Mexico, South and Central America guerrilla units are forming an army of liberation to free the United States. In North Africa from Tangier to Timbuctu corresponding units prepare to liberate Western Europe and the United Kingdom. Despite disparate aims and personnel of its constituent members the underground is agreed on basic objectives. We intend to march on the police machine everywhere. We intend to destroy the police machine and all its records. We intend to destroy all dogmatic verbal systems. The family unit and its cancerous expansion into tribes, countries, nations we will eradicate at its vegetable roots. We don't want to hear any more family talk, mother talk, father talk, cop talk, priest talk, country talk, *or* party talk. To put it country simple we have heard enough bullshit.

I am on my way from London to Tangier. In North Africa I will contact the wild-boy packs that range from the outskirts of Tangier to Timbuctu. Rotation and exchange is a keystone of the underground. I am bringing them modern weapons: laser guns, infra-sound installations, Deadly Orgone Radiation. I will learn their specialized skills and transfer wild-boy units to the Western cities. We know that the West will invade Africa and South America in an all-out attempt to crush the guerrilla units. Doktor Kurt Unruh von Steinplatz, in his four-volume treatise on the Authority Sickness, predicts these latter-day crusades. We will be ready to strike in their cities and to resist in the territories we now hold. Meanwhile we watch and train and wait. I have a thousand faces and a thousand names. I am nobody I am everybody. I am me I am you. I am here there forward back in out. I stay everywhere I stay nowhere. I stay present I stay absent.

Disguise is not a false beard dyed hair and plastic surgery. Disguise is clothes and bearing and behavior that leave no questions unanswered . . . American tourist with a wife he calls "Mother" . . . old queen on the make . . . dirty beatnik . . . marginal film producer. . . . Every article of my luggage and clothing is carefully planned to create a certain impression. Behind this impression I can operate without interference for a time. Just so long and long enough. So I walk down Boulevard Pasteur handing out money to guides and shoeshine boys. And that is only one of the civic things I did. I bought one of those souvenir matchlocks clearly destined to hang over a false fireplace in West Palm Beach Florida, and I carried it around wrapped in brown paper with the muzzle sticking out. I made inquiries at the Consulate "Now Mother and I would like to know."

And "MOTHER AND I WOULD LIKE TO KNOW" in American Express and the Minzah pulling wads of money out of my pocket "How much shall I give them?" I asked the vice-consul for a horde of guides had followed me into the Consulate. "I wonder if you've met my congressman Joe Link?"

Nobody gets through my cover I assure you. There is no better cover than a nuisance and a bore. When you see my cover you don't look further. You look the other way fast. For use on any foreign assignment there is nothing like the old reliable American tourist cameras and light meters slung all over him.

"How much shall I give him Mother?"

I can sidle up to any old bag she nods and smiles it's all so familiar "must be that cute man we met on the plane over from Gibraltar Captain Clark welcomes you aboard and he says: 'Now what's this form? I don't read Arabic.' Then he turns to me and says 'Mother I need help.' And I show him how to fill out the form and after that he would come up to me on the street this cute man so helpless bobbing up everywhere."

"What is he saying Mother?"

"I think he wants money."

"They all do." He turns to an army of beggars, guides, shoeshine boys and whores of all sexes and makes an ineffectual gesture.

"Go away! Scram off!"

Pat Cadigan

Rock On

Rain woke me. I thought, shit, here I am, Lady Rain-in-the-Face, because that's where it was hitting, right in the old face. Sat up and saw I was still on Newbury Street. See beautiful downtown Boston. Was Newbury Street downtown? In the middle of the night, did it matter? No, it did not. And not a soul in sight. Like everybody said, let's get Gina drunk and while she's passed out, we'll all move to Vermont. Do I love New England? A great place to live, but you wouldn't want to visit here.

I smeared my hair out of my eyes and wondered if anyone was looking for me now. Hey, anybody shy a forty-year-old rock 'n' roll sinner?

I scuttled into the doorway of one of those quaint old buildings where there was a shop with the entrance below ground level. A little awning kept the rain off but pissed water down in a maddening beat. Wrung the water out of my wrap pants and my hair and just sat being damp. Cold, too, I guess, but didn't feel that so much.

Sat a long time with my chin on my knees: you know, it made me feel like a kid again. When I started nodding my head, I began to pick up on something. Just primal but I tap into that amazing well. Man-O-War, if you could see me now. By the time the blueboys found me, I was rocking pretty good.

And that was the punchline. I'd never tried to get up and leave, but if I had, I'd have found I was locked into place in a sticky field. Made to catch the b&e kids in the act until the blueboys could get around to coming out and getting them. I'd been sitting in a trap and digging it. The story of my life.

They were nice to me. Led me, read me, dried me out. Fined me a hundred, sent me on my way in time for breakfast.

Awful time to see and be seen, righteous awful. For the first three hours after you get up, people can tell whether you've got a broken heart or not. The solution is, either you get up *real* early so your camouflage is in place by the time everybody else is out, or you don't go to bed. Don't go to bed ought to work all the time, but it doesn't. Sometimes when you don't go to bed, people can see whether you've got a broken heart all day long. I schlepped it, searching for an uncrowded breakfast bar and not looking at anyone who was looking at me. But I had this urge to stop random pedestrians and say, Yeah, yeah, it's true, but it was rock 'n' roll broke my poor old heart, not a person, don't cry for me or I'll pop your chocks.

I went around and up and down and all over until I found Tremont Street. It had been the pounder with that group from the Detroit Crater—the name was gone but the malady lingered on—anyway, him; he'd been the one told me Tremont had the best breakfast bars in the world, especially when you were coming off a bottle drunk you couldn't remember.

When the c'muters cleared out some, I found a space at a Greek hole in the wall. We shut down 10:30 A.M. sharp, get the hell out when you're done, counter service only, take it or shake it. I like a place with Attitude. I folded a seat down and asked for coffee and a feta cheese omelet. Came with home fries from the home fries mountain in a corner of the grill (no microwave *garbazhe*, hoo-ray). They shot my retinas before they even brought my coffee, and while I was pouring the cream, they checked my credit. Was that badass? It was badass. Did I care? I did not. No waste, no machines when a human could do it, and real food, none of this edible polyester that slips clear through you so you can stay looking like a famine victim, my deah.

They came in when I was half finished with the omelet. Went all night by the look and sound of them, but I didn't check their faces for broken hearts. Made me nervous but I thought, well, they're tired; who's going to notice this old lady? Nobody.

Wrong again. I became visible to them right after they got their retinas shot. Seventeen-year-old boy with tattooed cheeks and a forked tongue leaned forward and hissed like a snake.

"Sssssssinner."

The other four with him perked right up. "Where?" "Whose?" "In here?"

"Rock 'n' roll sssssssinner."

The lady identified me. She bore much resemblance to nobody at all, and if she had a heart it wasn't even sprained a little. With a sinner, she was probably Madame Magnifica. "Gina," she said, with all confidence.

My left eye tic'd. Oh, please. Feta cheese on my knees. What the hell, I thought, I'll nod, they'll nod, I'll eat, I'll go. And then somebody whispered the word, *reward*.

I dropped my fork and ran.

Safe enough, I figured. Were they all going to chase me before they got their Greek breakfasts? No, they were not. They sent the lady after me.

She was much the younger, and she tackled me in the middle of a crosswalk when the light changed. A car hopped over us, its undercarriage just ruffling the top of her hard copper hair.

"Just come back and finish your omelet. Or we'll buy you another."

"No."

She yanked me up and pulled me out of the street. "Come on." People were staring, but Tremont's full of theaters. You see that here, live theater; you can still get it. She put a bring-along on my wrist and brought me along, back to the breakfast bar, where they'd sold the rest of my omelet at a discount to a bum. The lady and her group made room for me among themselves and brought me another cup of coffee.

"How can you eat and drink with a forked tongue?" I asked Tattooed Cheeks. He showed me. A little appliance underneath, like a *zipper*. The Featherweight to the left of the big boy on the lady's other side leaned over and frowned at me.

"Give us one good reason why we shouldn't turn you in for Man-O-War's reward."

I shook my head. "I'm through. This sinner's been absolved."

"You're legally bound by contract," said the lady. "But we could c'noodle something. Buy Man-O-War out, sue on your behalf for non-fulfillment. We're Misbegotten. Oley." She pointed at herself. "Pidge." That was the silent type next to her. "Percy." The big boy. "Krait." Mr. Tongue. "Gus." Featherweight. "We'll take care of you."

I shook my head again. "If you're going to turn me in, turn me in and collect. The credit ought to buy you the best sinner ever there was."

"We can be good to you."

"I don't have it anymore. It's gone. All my rock 'n' roll sins have been forgiven."

"Untrue," said the big boy. Automatically, I started to picture on him and shut it down hard. "Man-O-War would have thrown you out if it were gone. You wouldn't have to run."

"I didn't want to tell him. Leave me alone. I just want to go and sin no more, see? Play with yourselves, I'm not helping." I grabbed the counter with both hands and held on. So what were they going to do, pop me one and carry me off?

As a matter of fact, they did.

In the beginning, I thought, and the echo effect was stupendous. *In the beginning . . . the beginning . . . the beginning. . . .*

In the beginning, the sinner was not human. I know because I'm old enough to remember.

They were all there, little more than phantoms. Misbegotten. Where do they get those names? I'm old enough to remember. Oingo-Boingo and Bow-Wow-Wow. Forty, did I say? Oooh, just a little past, a little close to a lot. Old rockers never die, they just keep rocking on. I never saw The Who; Moon was dead before I was born. But I remember, barely old enough to stand, rocking in my mother's arms while thousands screamed and clapped and danced in their seats. *Start me up . . . if you start me up, I'll never stop. . . .* 763 Strings did a rendition for elevator and dentist's office, I remember that, too. And that wasn't the worst of it.

They hung on the memories, pulling more from me, turning me inside out. *Are you experienced?* On a record of my father's because he'd died too, before my parents even met, and nobody else ever dared ask that question. *Are you experienced? . . . Well, I am.*

(Well, *I* am.)

Five against one and I couldn't push them away. Only, can you call it rape when you know you're going to like it? Well, if I couldn't get away, then I'd give them the ride of their lives. *Jerkin' Crocus didn't kill me but she sure came near. . . .*

The big boy faded in first, big and wild and too much badass to him. I reached out, held him tight, showing him. The beat from the night in the rain, I gave it to him, fed it to his heart and made him live it. Then came the lady, putting down the bass theme. She jittered, but mostly in the right places.

Now the Krait, and he was slithering around the sound, in and out. Never mind the tattooed cheeks, he wasn't just flash for the fools. He knew; you wouldn't have thought it, but he knew.

Featherweight and the silent type, melody and first harmony. Bad. Featherweight was a disaster, didn't know where to go or what to do when he got there, but he was pitching ahead like the S.S. *Suicide*.

Christ. If they had to rape me, couldn't they have provided someone upright? The other four kept on, refusing to lose it, and I would have to make the best of it for all of us. Derivative, unoriginal— Featherweight did not rock. It was a crime, but all I could do was take them and shake them. Rock gods in the hands of an angry sinner.

They were never better. Small change getting a glimpse of what it was like to be big bucks. Hadn't been for Featherweight, they might have gotten all the way there. More groups now than ever there was, all of them sure that if they just got the right sinner with them, they'd rock the moon down out of the sky.

We maybe vibrated it a little before we were done. Poor old Featherweight.

I gave them better than they deserved, and they knew that too. So when I begged out, they showed me respect at last and went. Their techies were gentle with me, taking the plugs from my head, my poor old throbbing abused brokenhearted sinning head, and covered up the sockets. I had to sleep and they let me. I hear the man say, "That's a take, righteously. We'll rush it into distribution. Where in *hell* did you find that sinner?"

"Synthesizer," I muttered, already asleep. "The actual word, my boy, is synthesizer."

Crazy old dreams. I was back with Man-O-War in the big CA, leaving him again, and it was mostly as it happened, but you know dreams. His living room was half outdoors, half indoors, the walls all busted out. You know dreams; I didn't think it was strange.

Man-O-War was mostly undressed, like he'd forgotten to finish. Oh, that *never* happened. Man-O-War forget a sequin or a bead? He loved to act it out, just like the Krait.

"No more," I was saying, and he was saying, "But you don't know anything else, you shitting?" Nobody in the big CA kids, they all shit; loose juice.

"Your contract goes another two and I get the option, I always get the option. And you love it, Gina, you know that, you're no good without it."

And then it was flashback time and I was in the pod with all my sockets plugged, rocking Man-O-War through the wires, giving him the meat and bone that made him Man-O-War and the machines picking it up, sound and vision, so all the tube babies all around the world could play it on their screens whenever they wanted. Forget the road, forget the shows, too much trouble, and it wasn't like the tapes, not as exciting, even with the biggest FX, lasers, spaceships, explosions, no good. And the tapes weren't as good as the stuff in the head, rock 'n' roll visions straight from the brain. No hours of setup and hours more doctoring in the lab. But you had to get everyone in the group dreaming the same way. You needed a synthesis, and for that you got a synthesizer, not the old kind, the musical instrument, but something—somebody—to channel your group through, to bump up their tube-fed little souls, to rock them and roll them the way they couldn't do themselves. And anyone could be a rock 'n' roll hero then. Anyone!

In the end, they didn't have to play instruments unless they really wanted to, and why bother? Let the synthesizer take their imaginings and boost them up to Mount Olympus.

Synthesizer. Synner. Sinner.

Not just anyone can do that, sin for rock 'n' roll. I can.

But it's not the same as jumping all night to some bar band nobody knows yet. . . . Man-O-War and his blown-out living room came back, and he said, "You rocked the walls right out of my house. I'll never let you go."

And I said, "I'm gone."

Then I was out, going fast at first because I thought he'd be hot behind me. But I must have lost him and then somebody grabbed my ankle.

Featherweight had a tray, he was Mr. Nursie-Angel-of-Mercy. Nudged the foot of the bed with his knee, and it sat me up slow. She rises from the grave, you can't keep a good sinner down.

"Here." He set the tray over my lap, pulled up a chair. Some kind of thick soup in a bowl he'd given me, with veg wafers to break up and put in. "Thought you'd want something soft and easy." He put his left foot up on his right leg and had a good look at it. "I *never* been rocked like that before."

"You don't have it, no matter who rocks you ever in this world. Cut and run, go into management. The *big* Big Money's in management."

He snacked on his thumbnail. "Can you always tell?"

"If the Stones came back tomorrow, you couldn't even tap your toes."

"What if you took my place?"

"I'm a sinner, not a clown. You can't sin and do the dance. It's been tried."

"*You* could do it. If anyone could."

"No."

His stringy cornsilk fell over his face and he tossed it back. "Eat your soup. They want to go again shortly."

"No." I touched my lower lip, thickened to sausage size. "I won't sin for Man-O-War and I won't sin for you. You want to pop me one again, go to. Shake a socket loose, give me aphasia."

So he left and came back with a whole bunch of them, techies and do-kids, and they poured the soup down my throat and gave me a poke and carried me out to the pod so I could make Misbegotten this year's firestorm.

I knew as soon as the first tape got out, Man-O-War would pick up the scent. They were already starting the machine to get me away from him. And they kept me good in the room—where their old sinner had done penance, the lady told me. Their sinner came to see me, too. I thought, poison dripping from his fangs, death threats. But he was just a guy about my age with a lot of hair to hide his sockets (I never bothered, didn't care if they showed). Just came to pay his respects, how'd I ever learn to rock the way I did?

Fool.

They kept me good in the room. Drunks when I wanted them and a poke to get sober again, a poke for vitamins, a poke to lose the bad dreams. Poke, poke, pig in a poke. I had tracks like the old B&O, and they didn't even know what I meant by that. They lost Featherweight, got themselves someone a little more righteous, someone who could go with it and work out, sixteen-year-old snip girl with a face like a praying mantis. But she rocked and they rocked and we all rocked until Man-O-War came to take me home.

Strutted into my room in full plumage with his hair all fanned out (hiding the sockets) and said, "Did you want to press charges, Gina darling?"

Well, they fought it out over my bed. When Misbegotten said I was theirs now, Man-O-War smiled and said, "Yeah, and I bought *you*. You're *all* mine now, you *and* your sinner. My sinner." That was truth. Man-O-War had his conglomerate start to buy Misbegotten right after the first tape came out. Deal all done by the time we'd finished the third one, and they never knew. Conglomerates buy and sell all the time. Everybody was in trouble but Man-O-War. And me, he said. He made them all leave and sat down on my bed to re-lay claim to me.

"Gina." Every see honey poured over the edge of a sawtooth blade? Every hear it? He couldn't sing without hurting someone bad and he couldn't dance, but inside, he rocked. If I rocked him.

"I don't want to be a sinner, not for you or anyone."

"It'll all look different when I get you back to Cee-Ay."

"I want to go to a cheesy bar and boogie my brains till they leak out the sockets."

"No more, darling. That was why you came here, wasn't it? But all the bars are gone and all the bands. Last call was years ago; it's all up here now. All up here." He tapped his temple. "You're an old lady, no matter how much I spend keeping your bod young. And don't I give you everything? And didn't you say I had it?"

"It's not the same. It wasn't meant to be put on a tube for people to *watch*."

"But it's not as though rock 'n' roll is dead, lover."

"You're killing it."

"Not me. You're trying to bury it alive. But I'll keep you going for a long, long time."

"I'll get away again. You'll either rock 'n' roll on your own or give it up, but you won't be taking it out of me any more. This ain't my way, it ain't my time. Like the man said, 'I don't live today.'"

Man-O-War grinned. "And like the other man said, 'Rock 'n' roll never forgets.'"

He called in his do-kids and took me home.

Samuel R. Delany

Among
the Blobs

(1) "I'm terribly sorry, ma'am. I'm sorry." He swayed, one arm raised, torso stalled in the torque of its own turning. His name was Joe. To one side of his back was, not a pain nor even a feeling, but rather a sensational ghost, an unformed blob, where she had lurched against his army jacket, or he had backed into her tweed. "Are you all right?" She probably couldn't hear because of the subway car's roar. "You okay?"

"Yes." (Was she confused a little, a little bewildered?) "That's all right." Swaying by the pole, her fuchsia scarf pulled through something gold, amoeboid, and splattered with ruby glass, she looked like one of the black Miss Subways. He had no idea if she were five years older or five years younger than he. Joe turned, because, after all, all he'd done was bump her a little; or she'd bumped him. But I could have smiled, he thought, reaching for and missing and then getting the next hanger. He knew his smile was good. (2) And Bat D—, in a rocket of luciprene-6 with vytrol fittings, careened at ballistic speeds through interstellar night. Flakes had fallen off the black, letting light: stars. Bat was dubious and alert, with the bellyfeeling that is both anxiety and enthusiasm. His would be the first human encounter with the Blob— which had been reported flûtchüláting (a form of communication? digestion? play?) in sector E-3. Till this report Bat D—, of the blazing death-laser, slayer of twenty-seven seven-foot Uranites, hero of the Kpt rebellion on Formalhaut-G, had poohed the existence of Blobs, but the closer his luciprene hull swooped toward Galactic Council, the more indubitable seemed the Blob's particular order of ontological resolution—what an earlier, less vulgar epoch would have called her "reality." (3) And Joe, on the Broadway Local, headed for Forty-second, wearing a Pendleton that didn't look it because his friend Joe—another Joe—had been in with his truck the day before yesterday, and the two of them had worked on the transmission six hours up at the Dyckman Street garage.

One train door stuck.

Army jacket open, Joe hammered up the concrete steps to the station concourse, loped under pipes and fluorescent fixtures, passed the rack of phone booths, the doughnut emporium. Another twenty-five steps and the florist concession pressed dull plants against glass; then down past the stall of Latin records, across from the hotdog-pasteles, piña-colada-Coca-Cola-cuchifrito counter, and toward the BMT.

He had been moving all this time through the late rush hour crowds, which crowds we have not mentioned till now because he was just about to separate himself from them. Joe thought of these crowds as a Blob, to which he was by and large indifferent.

Neither the Blob nor Joe's indifference, however, were impregnable to analysis. There were the men, of whom he was vaguely resentful, because if he stood too close to one in the crush, or sat too close to one on a subway seat—too much body contact—they might suspect he was not a heterosexual lustful-panting-monster, and the grapevine had it they could get hostile toward the other kind. There were the women, of whom he was vaguely resentful, because, since everyone knew all men were heterosexual lustful-panting-monsters, if he bumped on or brushed one (not to mention stood too near or sat to close), he had to apologize, be appallingly polite, and generally come on far more deferentially than any normal human should be expected to establish that, indeed, he was *not* a heterosexual lustful-panting-monster. At twenty-six, actually, he knew how to deal with the men: stand or sit where you want and fuck 'em. They could move. The women, however, confused him a little, bewildered him. And women were a subject about which the grapevine was distressingly un- (if not ill-) informed. Resentment, however vague, is not pleasant; hence the indifference in which he travelled.

At the blue and white column, Joe swung left toward the john.

The wooden gate—not, this time, "Closed for Cleaning"—was wedged back, askew on its hinges. Some time ago they'd painted the tiled entrance hall blue. Hand-sized paint flakes had fallen away. The antiseptic with which the place was flushed every other day had blistered what paint remained. Sometimes it left fumes so strong you couldn't stay inside long enough to take an honest leak.

In front of five of the ten porcelain urinals—most of the brass flush-treadles lay without tension on the red floor—(4) half the Galactic Council was in attendance. It was a highly formalized gathering. Members came and went according to an arcane protocol Bat D— still did not understand. Each member entered the High and Icy Hall (here and there still crossed with traces of unbreathable fumes) to linger, silently and intently for an arbitrary while, before what looked to Bat D— for all the world like something from a book on Twentieth-Century toilet fixtures.

The members of the Council were laboring to express the Blob.

The Blob was not impregnable to analysis: it was a largely mucusoid emulsion contained in a selectively permeable membrane within which drifted a nucleus, various nucleoli, vacuoles, ribosomes, mitochondria, and chloroplasts, the whole a symbiotic intrusion of eucaryotic and procaryotic cells from a less vulgar moment in the pluroma when all was closer than it is today to organic soup, to inorganic matter.

The Council members, minds on high matters, manipulated their computers.

The Blob was, appropriately, near Betelgeuse.

And Betelgeuse was in E-3. (5) Joe lingered at the next-to-the-end urinal. He had a thing for older guys with big, heavily veined cocks and small hands with overlong nails; and the guy to his left, at the end urinal (Pushing sixty? But that was all right), was probably a librarian. He wore a dumb-silly coat with a fur collar you couldn't button up. Or a designer. The black portfolio leaned on the wall behind them. But that was all right.

A bum lurched through the door (probably not as old as this guy beside him with those long, long nails the color of aluminum in winterlight. In his own too wide, too horny hand, at the memory only a second old—rather than at what was beside him—Joe hardened), moustache full of mucus, missing a lot of hair over one ear, missing shirt buttons; and the breast pocket gone. His pants leg was ripped, knee to cuff, showing a shin like soap. The bum looked around: "Aw, Jesus Christ, nothin' in here but a bunch of . . . I mean ever'body in here is one of them fuckin' . . . Hey you there, I bet you're one of . . ."

To Joe's right, two members of the Galactic Council glanced at each other, smiled. One shook his head. Hands down before white porcelain, busy with calculations, they manipulated and manipulated.

Wilson, the deaf-mute hustler, fists pouched in his frayed windbreaker, came bopping in. Joe knew him because Wilson had once tried to score from Joe, who had brought him a cup of coffee at the hot dog counter across the concourse and explained to him—Joe had two aunts who had been born deaf and with whom he had stayed for a year in Portland when he was ten, which is how he knew the deaf-and-dumb sign language—that at this particular spot there was just too much of it walking around for free to make it worth a working man's time. Wilson came around the bum ("Hey, you ain't interested in these fuckin' faggots, huh . . . ?"), surveyed the Council Members at their stalls, and left.

"Shit . . . !" The bum turned, started out, stumbled into the jamb. An incoming Member—a subway worker Joe had seen here a few times before—steadied him:

"Hey, watch it, old man."

The worker moved the bum out to arm's length and looked down to see a dripping cuff; now the shin was wet. Not having made it to a stall, the bum lurched out, leaving sneaker pissprints on the chalky floor.

Joe turned back to the man beside him: grey hair, Vandyke beard, glasses. They exchanged glances, anxious, enthusiastic, eye to lens, lens to groin. That crank (Joe had grown up in Seattle), those nails: Joe felt the warmth of orgasm heating the backs of his knees. (6) The salmon light of Betelgeuse slanted through the clear wall of Sumpter VII, the Fort named—jokingly—by the first generation of galactic anthropologists, how many years ago now . . . ? And where were they today: reduced to inert jelly during the tragic Kpt. And now, this Blob . . . ? Bat D— walked across reddened tiles of luciprene-57 past the Fort's transparent north facade that looked out across magnetic sands webbed with molten ammonia runulets worming the hyperborean chill, toward the sheer range called Chroma—because of the pink, fuchsia, and vermilion clays streaking its silver slopes. Warily, Bat turned from the window-wall to round a partition studded with ruby vytrol—

She quivered there within the high, luminous geometries of Sumpter VII, contracting her gargantuan bulk inward from those bloated pseudopods into which her viscid soap-collared stuffs had spread. Nucleoli and vacuoles and just plain bubbles puckered her membrane. She could sense him, Bat could tell. Languorously, she heaved herself forward.

Bat D—'s thumb snapped open the cover of his naugahyde holster. He tugged loose his death laser, its handle of black ivory worked into rare scrimshaw by the Little Folk of Antares-10, its symmetrically veined and partitioned barrel molded of clear lucite casting resin by Jonas and Barboli of Fenton, Pennsylvania. Carefully, Bat raised the gun.

The Blob said: "Burble, burble . . . burble." She flattened her amoeboid volume slightly, then heaved again.

Bat fired—and a pseudopod, a little charred, smoking a little, dropped from the ceiling and knocked the death-laser fifteen feet to crack the partition. Ruby vytrol chattered to the floor, glittered on the tiles.

Bat D—, terrified and exuberant, stepped back. The Blob, enraged, hurled herself. Bat D— shrieked and flung up his arms. She smacked him, knee to chin, with a strange and violet warmth that flattened him to the ground. She rolled across him, was in him at every orifice, ears, urethra, anus, mouth, nostrils. She was without him. She was within him. She rolled through him. She flowed around him.

While he lay, gloriously stalled within her circling torque, with her within him within her, the Blob said: "Honey, what's *with* this shit resenting strange niggers on the subway? *That* sort of double-think earns you no popcorn coupons from the Big Movie Theatre in the sky. Try to imagine an older, less vulgar epoch. Just be your sweet self— you *have* a lovely smile. But Lord, this luciprene is getting to me. Tastes like old airplane glue!"

For a moment Bat D— thought he would really die. But the Blob withdrew. Letting a howl that resembled nothing so much as the Twentieth-Century war-whoop of Sheena, Queen of the Jungle, she flung herself at Fort Sumpter VII's north wall.

It shattered.

Eyes still tight, Bat heard fragments thud outward on the sand, clatter inward to the floor.

Moments later when, panting and weak, he pulled himself erect beside the jagged pane—already frosting with ammonia from the hyperborean chill—the Blob, a football field away, was flûtchüláting (a method of transportation? reproduction? art?) across the black sands, making her erratic path between runulets, toward the Chroma's ceramic and silver. (7) Joe leaned his forehead on the tile above the urinal, taking deep breaths.

The man beside him zipped his fly, squeezed Joe's jacketed elbow (with that *fine* hand), and whispered: "You know, fellow, you really get into it, don't you?" (One of the Council's feyer members had actually applauded. Another had gotten scared and run.) "You're too much. . . . Maybe I'll see you in here again sometime . . . ?"

Without lifting his head, Joe grinned; and nodded—because when, on the odd Thursday you found somebody that much what you were into, it took a minute to get it back together. Faint pain pulsed in his spleen—he'd come that hard. He stuffed himself back in his fly, took another breath, looked up—

The man, and his portfolio, were gone.

On the urinal edge, semen trailed the glaze.

Joe shouldered out between two more arriving members (the blue door was marked E-3) and nearly bumped the incoming policeman. Joe grinned at the cop, nodded; automatically, the cop smiled, nodded back—then apparently remembered himself and frowned.

But Joe was already making it down the concrete ramp to the RR—when two high-school girls collided with him from behind. As he turned, "I'm sorry!" started up behind his teeth, but he chewed and chomped it into, "Hello. . . ." And smiled.

One girl giggled over her packages. The other, with more packages, blinked.

After a moment the blinking one said, hesitantly: "Oh . . . excuse me."

"That's okay," Joe said. "What *are* all those?"

The packages were part of an exhibit they were setting up at the Brooklyn Public Library on the History of Puerto Rico. They talked about it through three trains. When they did say goodbye, all three of them were grinning a lot—grinning too much, Joe decided once he was in the car.

Well, old habits die hard. So kill a little harder. Interesting kids, Joe thought. Maybe he should check out the exhibit. Perhaps next

Wednesday, after he'd finished standing around at Unemployment. And he would be at the Fourteenth Street john in ten minutes—unless he stopped in at Twenty-third, which, the grapevine had it, was sort of kicky this month.

Don DeLillo

From

White Noise

Several days later Murray asked me about a tourist attraction known as the most photographed barn in America. We drove twenty-two miles into the country around Farmington. There were meadows and apple orchards. White fences trailed through the rolling fields. Soon the signs started appearing. THE MOST PHOTOGRAPHED BARN IN AMERICA. We counted five signs before we reached the site. There were forty cars and a tour bus in the makeshift lot. We walked along a cowpath to the slightly elevated spot set aside for viewing and photographing. All the people had cameras; some had tripods, telephoto lenses, filter kits. A man in a booth sold postcards and slides—pictures of the barn taken from the elevated spot. We stood near a grove of trees and watched the photographers. Murray maintained a prolonged silence, occasionally scrawling some notes in a little book.

"No one sees the barn," he said finally.

A long silence followed.

"Once you've seen the signs about the barn, it becomes impossible to see the barn."

He fell silent once more. People with cameras left the elevated site, replaced at once by others.

"We're not here to capture an image, we're here to maintain one. Every photograph reinforces the aura. Can you feel it, Jack? An accumulation of nameless energies."

There was an extended silence. The man in the booth sold postcards and slides.

"Being here is a kind of spiritual surrender. We see only what the others see. The thousands who were here in the past, those who will come in the future. We've agreed to be part of a collective perception.

This literally colors our vision. A religious experience in a way, like all tourism."

Another silence ensued.

"They are taking pictures of taking pictures," he said.

He did not speak for a while. We listened to the incessant clicking of shutter release buttons, the rustling crank of levers that advanced the film.

"What was the barn like before it was photographed?" he said. "What did it look like, how was it different from other barns, how was it similar to other barns? We can't answer these questions because we've read the signs, seen the people snapping the pictures. We can't get outside the aura. We're part of the aura. We're here, we're now."

He seemed immensely pleased by this.

William Gibson

From

Neuromancer

The sky above the port was the color of television, tuned to a dead channel.

"It's not like I'm using," Case heard someone say, as he shouldered his way through the crowd around the door of the Chat. "It's like my body's developed this massive drug deficiency." It was a Sprawl voice and a Sprawl joke. The Chatsubo was a bar for professional expatriates; you could drink there for a week and never hear two words in Japanese.

Ratz was tending bar, his prosthetic arm jerking monotonously as he filled a tray of glasses with draft Kirin. He saw Case and smiled, his teeth a webwork of East European steel and brown decay. Case found a place at the bar, between the unlikely tan on one of Lonny Zone's whores and the crisp naval uniform of a tall African whose cheekbones were ridged with precise rows of tribal scars. "Wage was in here early, with two joeboys," Ratz said, shoving a draft across the bar with his good hand. "Maybe some business with you, Case?"

Case shrugged. The girl to his right giggled and nudged him.

The bartender's smile widened. His ugliness was the stuff of legend. In an age of affordable beauty, there was something heraldic about his lack of it. The antique arm whined as he reached for another mug. It was a Russian military prosthesis, a seven-function force-feedback manipulator, cased in grubby pink plastic. "You are too much the artiste, Herr Case." Ratz grunted; the sound served him as laughter. He scratched his overhang of white-shirted belly with the pink claw. "You are the artiste of the slightly funny deal."

"Sure," Case said, and sipped his beer. "Somebody's gotta be funny around here. Sure the fuck isn't you."

The whore's giggle went up an octave.

"Isn't you either, sister. So you vanish, okay? Zone, he's a close personal friend of mine."

She looked Case in the eye and made the softest possible spitting sound, her lips barely moving. But she left.

"Jesus," Case said, "what kinda creepjoint you running here? Man can't have a drink."

"Ha," Ratz said, swabbing the scarred wood with a rag, "Zone shows a percentage. You I let work here for entertainment value."

As Case was picking up his beer, one of those strange instants of silence descended, as though a hundred unrelated conversations had simultaneously arrived at the same pause. Then the whore's giggle rang out, tinged with a certain hysteria.

Ratz grunted. "An angel passed."

"The Chinese," bellowed a drunken Australian, "Chinese bloody invented nerve-splicing. Give me the mainland for a nerve job any day. Fix you right, mate. . . ."

"Now that," Case said to his glass, all his bitterness suddenly rising in him like bile, "that is *so* much bullshit."

The Japanese had already forgotten more neurosurgery than the Chinese had ever known. The black clinics of Chiba were the cutting edge, whole bodies of technique supplanted monthly, and still they couldn't repair the damage he'd suffered in that Memphis hotel.

A year here and he still dreamed of cyberspace, hope fading nightly. All the speed he took, all the turns he'd taken and the corners he'd cut in Night City, and still he'd see the matrix in his sleep, bright lattices of logic unfolding across that colorless void. . . . The Sprawl was a long strange way home over the Pacific now, and he was no console man, no cyberspace cowboy. Just another hustler, trying to make it through. But the dreams came on in the Japanese night like livewire voodoo, and he'd cry for it, cry in his sleep, and wake alone in the dark, curled in his capsule in some coffin hotel, his hands clawed into the bedslab, temperfoam bunched between his fingers, trying to reach the console that wasn't there.

"I saw your girl last night," Ratz said, passing Case his second Kirin.

"I don't have one," he said, and drank.

"Miss Linda Lee."

Case shook his head.

"No girl? Nothing? Only biz, friend artiste? Dedication to commerce?" The bartender's small brown eyes were nested deep in wrinkled flesh. "I think I liked you better, with her. You laughed more. Now, some night, you get maybe too artistic; you wind up in the clinic tanks, spare parts."

"You're breaking my heart, Ratz." He finished his beer, paid and left, high narrow shoulders hunched beneath the rain-stained khaki nylon of his windbreaker. Threading his way through the Ninsei crowds, he could smell his own stale sweat.

Case was twenty-four. At twenty-two, he'd been a cowboy, a rustler, one of the best in the Sprawl. He'd been trained by the best, by McCoy Pauley and Bobby Quine, legends in the biz. He'd operated on an almost permanent adrenaline high, a byproduct of youth and proficiency, jacked into a custom cyberspace deck that projected his disembodied consciousness into the consensual hallucination that was the matrix. A thief, he'd worked for other, wealthier thieves, employers who provided the exotic software required to penetrate the bright walls of corporate systems, opening windows into rich fields of data.

He'd made the classic mistake, the one he'd sworn he'd never make. He stole from his employers. He kept something for himself and tried to move it through a fence in Amsterdam. He still wasn't sure how he'd been discovered, not that it mattered now. He'd expected to die, then, but they only smiled. Of course he was welcome, they told him, welcome to the money. And he was going to need it. Because—still smiling—they were going to make sure he never worked again.

They damaged his nervous system with a wartime Russian mycotoxin.

Strapped to a bed in a Memphis hotel, his talent burning out micron by micron, he hallucinated for thirty hours.

The damage was minute, subtle, and utterly effective.

For Case, who'd lived for the bodiless exultation of cyberspace, it was the Fall. In the bars he'd frequented as a cowboy hotshot, the elite stance involved a certain relaxed contempt for the flesh. The body was meat. Case fell into the prison of his own flesh.

His total assets were quickly converted to New Yen, a fat sheaf of the old paper currency that circulated endlessly through the closed circuit of the world's black markets like the seashells of the Trobriand islanders. It was difficult to transact legitimate business with cash in the Sprawl; in Japan, it was already illegal.

In Japan, he'd known with a clenched and absolute certainty, he'd find his cure. In Chiba. Either in a registered clinic or in the shadowland of black medicine. Synonymous with implants, nerve-splicing, and microbionics, Chiba was a magnet for the Sprawl's techno-criminal subcultures.

In Chiba, he'd watched his New Yen vanish in a two-month round of examinations and consultations. The men in the black clinics, his last hope, had admired the expertise with which he'd been maimed, and then slowly shaken their heads.

Now he slept in the cheapest coffins, the ones nearest the port, beneath the quartz-halogen floods that lit the docks all night like vast stages; where you couldn't see the lights of Tokyo for the glare of the television sky, not even the towering hologram logo of the Fuji Electric Company, and Tokyo Bay was a black expanse where gulls wheeled above drifting shoals of white styrofoam. Behind the port lay the city, factory domes dominated by the vast cubes of corporate arcologies. Port and city were divided by a narrow borderland of older streets, an area with no official name. Night City, with Ninsei its heart. By day, the bars down Ninsei were shuttered and featureless, the neon dead, the holograms inert, waiting, under the poisoned silver sky.

Two blocks west of the Chat, in a teashop called the Jarre de Thé, Case washed down the night's first pill with a double espresso. It was a flat pink octagon, a potent species of Brazilian dex he bought from one of Zone's girls.

The Jarre was walled with mirrors, each panel framed in red neon.

At first, finding himself alone in Chiba, with little money and less hope of finding a cure, he'd gone into a kind of terminal overdrive, hustling fresh capital with a cold intensity that had seemed to belong to someone else. In the first month, he'd killed two men and a woman over sums that a year before would have seemed ludicrous. Ninsei wore him down until the street itself came to seem the externalization of some death wish, some secret poison he hadn't known he carried.

Night City was like a deranged experiment in social Darwinism, designed by a bored researcher who kept one thumb permanently on the fast-forward button. Stop hustling and you sank without a trace, but move a little too swiftly and you'd break the fragile surface tension of the black market; either way, you were gone, with nothing left of you but some vague memory in the mind of a fixture like Ratz, though heart or lungs or kidneys might survive in the service of some stranger with New Yen for the clinic tanks.

Biz here was a constant subliminal hum, and death the accepted punishment for laziness, carelessness, lack of grace, the failure to heed the demands of an intricate protocol.

Alone at a table in the Jarre de Thé, with the octagon coming on, pinheads of sweat starting from his palms, suddenly aware of each tingling hair on his arms and chest, Case knew that at some point he'd started to play a game with himself, a very ancient one that has no name, a final solitaire. He no longer carried a weapon, no longer took the basic precautions. He ran the fastest, loosest deals on the street, and he had a reputation for being able to get whatever you wanted. A part of him knew that the arc of his self-destruction was glaringly obvious to his customers, who grew steadily fewer, but that same part of him basked in the knowledge that it was only a matter of time. And that was the part of him, smug in its expectation of death, that most hated the thought of Linda Lee.

He'd found her, one rainy night, in an arcade.

Under bright ghosts burning through a blue haze of cigarette smoke, holograms of Wizard's Castle, Tank War Europa, the New York skyline. . . . And now he remembered her that way, her face bathed in restless laser light, features reduced to a code: her cheekbones flaring scarlet as Wizard's Castle burned, forehead drenched with azure when Munich fell to the Tank War, mouth touched with hot gold as a gliding cursor struck sparks from the wall of a skyscraper canyon. He was riding high that night, with a brick of Wage's ketamine on its way to Yokohama and the money already in his pocket. He'd come in out of the warm rain that sizzled across the Ninsei pavement and somehow she'd been singled out for him, one face out of the dozens who stood at the consoles, lost in the game she played. The expression on her face, then, had been the one he'd seen, hours later, on her sleeping face in a portside coffin, her upper lip like the line children draw to represent a bird in flight.

Crossing the arcade to stand beside her, high on the deal he'd made, he saw her glance up. Gray eyes rimmed with smudged black paintstick. Eyes of some animal pinned in the headlights of an oncoming vehicle.

Their night together stretching into a morning, into tickets at the hoverport and his first trip across the Bay. The rain kept up, falling along Harajuku, beading on her plastic jacket, the children of Tokyo trooping past the famous boutiques in white loafers and clingwrap capes, until she'd stood with him in the midnight clatter of a pachinko parlor and held his hand like a child.

It took a month for the gestalt of drugs and tension he moved through to turn those perpetually startled eyes into wells of reflexive need. He'd watched her personality fragment, calving like an iceberg, splinters drifting away, and finally he'd seen the raw need, the hungry armature of addiction. He'd watched her track the next hit with a concentration that reminded him of the mantises they sold in stalls along Shiga, beside tanks of blue mutant carp and crickets caged in bamboo.

Case waited for a trans-BAMA local on the crowded platform. Molly had gone back to the loft hours ago, the Flatline's construct in her green bag, and Case had been drinking steadily ever since.

It was disturbing to think of the Flatline as a construct, a hardwired ROM cassette replicating a dead man's skills, obsessions, knee-jerk responses. . . . The local came booming in along the black induction strip, fine grit sifting from cracks in the tunnel's ceiling. Case shuffled into the nearest door and watched the other passengers as he rode. A pair of predatory-looking Christian Scientists were edging toward a trio of young office techs who wore idealized holographic vaginas on their wrists, wet pink glittering under the harsh lighting. The techs licked their perfect lips nervously and eyed the Christian Scientists from beneath lowered metallic lids. The girls looked like tall, exotic grazing animals, swaying gracefully and unconsciously with the movement of the train, their high heels like polished hooves against the gray metal of the car's floor. Before they could stampede, take flight from the missionaries, the train reached Case's station.

He stepped out and caught sight of a white holographic cigar suspended against the wall of the station, FREESIDE pulsing beneath it in contorted capitals that mimicked printed Japanese. He walked through the crowd and stood beneath it, studying the thing. WHY WAIT? pulsed the sign. A blunt white spindle, flanged and studded with grids and radiators, docks, domes. He'd seen the ad, or others like it, thousands of times. It had never appealed to him. With his deck, he could reach the Freeside banks as easily as he could reach Atlanta. Travel was a meat thing. But now he noticed the little sigil, the size of a small coin, woven into the lower left corner of the ad's fabric of light: T-A.

He walked back to the loft, lost in memories of the Flatline. He'd spent most of his nineteenth summer in the Gentleman Loser, nursing expensive beers and watching the cowboys. He'd never touched a deck, then, but he knew what he wanted. There were at least twenty other hopefuls ghosting the Loser, that summer, each one bent on working joeboy for some cowboy. No other way to learn.

They'd all heard of Pauley, the redneck jockey from the 'Lanta fringes, who'd survived braindeath behind black ice. The grapevine—slender, street level, and the only one going—had little to say about Pauley, other than that he'd done the impossible. "It was big," another would-be told Case, for the price of a beer, "but who knows what? I hear maybe a Brazilian payroll net. Anyway, the man was dead, flat down braindeath." Case stared across the crowded bar at a thickset man in shirtsleeves, something leaden about the shade of his skin.

"Boy," the Flatline would tell him, months later in Miami, "I'm like them huge fuckin' lizards, you know? Had themselves two goddam brains, one in the head an' one by the tailbone, kept the hind legs movin'. Hit that black stuff and ol' tailbrain jus' kept right on keepin' on."

The cowboy elite in the Loser shunned Pauley out of some strange group anxiety, almost a superstition. McCoy Pauley, Lazarus of cyberspace. . . .

And his heart had done for him in the end. His surplus Russian heart, implanted in a POW camp during the war. He'd refused to replace the thing, saying he needed its particular beat to maintain his sense of timing. Case fingered the slip of paper Molly had given him and made his way up the stairs.

Molly was snoring on the temperfoam. A transparent cast ran from her knee to a few millimeters below her crotch, the skin beneath the rigid micropore mottled with bruises, the black shading into ugly yellow. Eight derms, each a different size and color, ran in a neat line down her left wrist. An Akai transdermal unit lay beside her, its fine red leads connected to input trodes under the cast.

He turned on the tensor beside the Hosaka. The crisp circle of light fell directly on the Flatline's construct. He slotted some ice, connected the construct, and jacked in.

It was exactly the sensation of someone reading over his shoulder. He coughed. "Dix? McCoy? That you man?" His throat was tight.

"Hey, bro," said a directionless voice.

"It's Case, man. Remember?"

"Miami, joeboy, quick study."

"What's the last thing you remember before I spoke to you, Dix?"

"Nothin'."

"Hang on." He disconnected the construct. The presence was gone. He reconnected it. "Dix? Who am I?"

"You got me hung, Jack. Who the fuck are you?"

"Ca—your buddy. Partner. What's happening, man?"

"Good question."

"Remember being here, a second ago?"

"No."

"Know how a ROM personality matrix works?"

"Sure, bro, it's a firmware construct."

"So I jack it into the bank I'm using, I can give it sequential, real time memory?"

"Guess so," said the construct.

"Okay, Dix. You *are* a ROM construct. Got me?"

"If you say so," said the construct. "Who are you?"

"Case."

"Miami," said the voice, "joeboy, quick study."

"Right. And for starts, Dix, you and me, we're gonna sleaze over to London grid and access a little data. You game for that?"

"You gonna tell me I got a choice, boy?"

"And that's the last thing you remember?" He watched her scrape the last of the freeze-dried hash from the rectangular steel box cover that was their only plate.

She nodded, her eyes huge in the firelight. "I'm sorry, Case, honest to God. It was just the shit, I guess, an' it was . . ." She hunched forward, forearms across her knees, her face twisted for a few seconds with pain or its memory. "I just needed the money. To get home, I guess, or . . . hell," she said, "you wouldn't hardly talk to me."

"There's no cigarettes?"

"God*dam*, Case, you asked me that ten times today! What's wrong with you?" She twisted a strand of hair into her mouth and chewed at it.

"But the food was here? It was already here?"

"I *told* you, man, it was washed up on the damn beach."

"Okay. Sure. It's seamless."

She started to cry again, a dry sobbing. "Well, damn you anyway, Case," she managed, finally, "I was doin' just fine here by myself."

He got up, taking his jacket, and ducked through the doorway, scraping his wrist on rough concrete. There was no moon, no wind, sea sound all around him in the darkness. His jeans were tight and clammy. "Okay," he said to the night, "I buy it. I guess I buy it. But tomorrow some cigarettes better wash up." His own laughter startled him. "A case of beer wouldn't hurt, while you're at it." He turned and re-entered the bunker.

She was stirring the embers with a length of silvered wood. "Who was that, Case, up in your coffin in Cheap Hotel? Flash samurai with those silver shades, black leather. Scared me, and after, I figured maybe she was your new girl, 'cept she looked like more money than you had. . . ." She glanced back at him. "I'm real sorry I stole your RAM."

"Never mind," he said. "Doesn't mean anything. So you just took it over to this guy and had him access it for you?"

"Tony," she said. "I'd been seein' him, kinda. He had a habit an' we . . . anyway, yeah, I remember him running it by on this monitor, and it was this real amazing graphics stuff, and I remember wonderin' how you—"

"There wasn't any graphics in there," he interrupted.

"Sure was. I just couldn't figure how you'd have all those pictures of when I was *little*, Case. How my daddy looked, before he left. Gimme this duck one time, painted wood, and you had a picture of *that*. . . ."

"Tony see it?"

"I don't remember. Next thing, I was on the beach, real early, sunrise, those birds all yellin' so lonely. Scared 'cause I didn't have a shot on me, nothin', an' I knew I'd be gettin' sick. . . . An' I walked an' walked, 'til it was dark, an' found this place, an' next day the food washed in, all tangled in the green sea stuff like leaves of hard jelly." She slid her stick into the embers and left it there. "Never did get sick," she said, as embers crawled. "Missed cigarettes more. How 'bout you, Case? You still wired?" Firelight dancing under her cheek-bones, remembered flash of Wizard's Castle and Tank War Europa.

"No," he said, and then it no longer mattered, what he knew, tasting the salt of her mouth where tears had dried. There was a strength that ran in her, something he'd known in Night City and held there, been held by it, held for a while away from time and death, from the relentless Street that hunted them all. It was a place he'd known before; not everyone could take him there, and somehow he always managed to forget it. Something he'd found and lost so many times. It belonged, he knew—he remembered—as she pulled him down, to the meat, the flesh the cowboys mocked. It was a vast thing, beyond knowing, a sea of information coded in spiral and pheromone, infinite intricacy that only the body, in its strong blind way, could ever read.

The zipper hung, caught, as he opened the French fatigues, the coils of toothed nylon clotted with salt. He broke it, some tiny metal part shooting off against the wall as salt-rotten cloth gave, and then he was in her, effecting the transmission of the old message. Here, even here, in a place he knew for what it was, a coded model of some stranger's memory, the drive held.

She shuddered against him as the stick caught fire, a leaping flare that threw their locked shadows across the bunker wall.

Later, as they lay together, his hand between her thighs, he remembered her on the beach, the white foam pulling at her ankles, and he remembered what she had said.

"He told you I was coming," he said.

But she only rolled against him, buttocks against his thighs, and put her hand over his, and muttered something out of dream.

Rob Hardin

Fistic

Hermaphrodites

The scarab beetle lay on a tiny operating table
until the rain-dotted surfaces of the boulevard appeared,
slow-dancing to idiotic show tunes.
Lines between sidewalk squares deepened to cracks,
and if they won't crack, force them.
They want to know how your gridwork tastes
but *they* will never understand
why our centipede sizzles in the pool
and the stripped lock of bliss falls neatly open.
Her ejaculate coated the walls of the microwave,
thudding against the nerve
of the apartment, leaving the ceiling and floor within inches.
We now come to a clean extreme of motion,
though it is floating sideways and will soon be frustrated
by bits of garden scattered
across a sheet of graph paper. The queen
herself chose this technique; she abides the speculative instinct
with thoughtless precision. *Hold out your hand,* she twitters,
squeeze the heart of it, the guts of the matter.
But the limbs of the male fall from a great height,
wriggle in soot, and are then dislocated from geography.
The newlyweds cough up larvae, smiling apologetically.
Their desires read like a homework assignment
and, at the base of the fifth pair of walking legs,
their genital ducts have not yet evolved.

Rob Hardin

Microbes

—For Tristan Avakian

What you said, on paper.
—an abscess emptied
in slabs its filaments of breath
which discolor these dendritic innards
  and, here, a lattice of antibodies

—I don't want them watching, they say things
too apparent as mist,
as genitals that slide across the visor,
smearing a gray liquid across our field
  of fenestrated tendrils, & shavings of blue dye

all intemperate, flinching, they plummet
into a circle of homicidal deities
incarnated as glass shards, or perhaps
as *nothing*, cold gusts of disembowelled martyrs
  reduced to branches rigidly writhing

until you collect them in fissures
and wave your pin at the strands
of connective tissue, at the gulps & glottal stops,
as the wall sags into tiny figures—once worshipped,
  now vomitted into someone else's hands

a deposit of air, make it stop retching
its bloodless dialect on the last seconds of recollection

Rob Hardin

Penetrabit:
Slime-Temples*

Life is a disease of matter.
—Goethe

I

30 cm. of creeping protoplasm,
absently gibbering spirals, hexahedrons, hillocks, trills,
may indicate an *autocatalytic reaction.*
And the hypnotic figurations of nerve axons—

Receptive, active, quiescent—
turn like scrolls of electrolyzed plasma.
Both substances reveal a talent for spatial organization:
their dead thrashings trace patterns of cerebral complexity.

Similarly, the contractions of human heart muscle
resemble a wave spreading outward.
When the wave is broken, heart fibrillations
exhibit persistent patterns. And, often,

these *autocatalytic spirals* of disease
are attended by failure and death.

II

The surface of the brain
may also erupt in a necropolis of spirals.

*Penetrabit: literally, *I will penetrate*, a medieval inscription adopted by Michelet.

Reverberating cortical depression
brings with it a pattern of self-propagating forms.

Even a disc galaxy follows this rococo pathology:
its tentacles of stars are ragged whorls.
A parahuman architect is endlessly sketching
cochlear temples to its own vacant energies.

If god is dead, he is dressed as a tendrillar Louis XIV,
and his fingers are *twitching*.

Rob Hardin

nerve terminals

Post mortem, stirred tarantulas
trill *HHHHH* through lung-books lined with gauze.
Their cerci writhe outside the frame
 and scythes of come
 spell *No One's Home.*

Reanimated sentences
crawl searchingly through palaces.
. . . .ellipses crumble, swapped for noise. . . .
 our symphonies
 are insect seas.

The number series incubus
drips *oo-spores* in jagged fur.
These | | - | | | | | | merge—interfuse—
 to disinter
 his tactile stare.

Each love-bit scars to antipode.
Catoptromantic unisons
fortell the double's overload:
 undead, Lust puns
 necrotic suns.

Harold Jaffe

Max
Headroom

"One day in Silicon Valley I came upon two
blind men, well-dressed, sitting side by side,
each masturbating the other."

Zero Option

A forty-four-year-old woman, described by her daughter as "emotionally distraught," walked into an elementary school classroom on
Tuesday morning and fatally shot herself in front of twenty-three fifth-
graders.

The twenty-three pupils in Dry Ice Fog Elementary School of
Sector 3 and Ms. Bernice (called "Bunny") Bornagin, their red-haired
teacher, tried to dissuade the woman, who was armed with two Smith
and Wesson .32 caliber revolvers. "I'm sorry I have to do it this way,"
the woman said before firing a bullet into her head.

When it was clear that the woman would not listen to reason, Ms.
Bornagin instructed her students to stare at the side-by-side TV monitors above the blackboard at the front of the room, school officials said.
The first time the woman, identified as Missy Rodriguez, pulled the
trigger of the gun in her right hand, it misfired, so she aimed the gun in
her left hand at the wall, fired a shot, then pointed the gun in her left
hand at her left temple and fired the fatal shot.

Psychologists from the Jesu-Manville Sector were transmitted to
Dry Ice Fog Elementary at once to begin counseling the pupils. The
psychologists were dressed in camouflage fatigues. The pupils received them at their consoles while eating their lunch, with the princi-

pal's permission, since it was a special occasion: TV News was running a 30-second segment on the classroom suicide.

"Very few [pupils] actually saw anything," said Harvey Joy, a high-school principal in the Sector, a former principal of Dry Ice Fog Elementary, and a psychologist in his own right. "Most of the pupils talked about it as though it was something they'd seen on TV," Dr. Joy said. "Each pupil will handle it differently. I was very impressed with the calmness of the pupils."

The woman was declared dead at Sector 3 Hospital at 11:17 A.M., about an hour after the shooting. School officials said there was absolutely no evidence that Rodriguez, the suicide, had any connection with Dry Ice Fog Elementary. Rodriguez was not a parent of any of the school's four hundred twelve students. "She was a shy sort of person," Rodriguez' twenty-seven-year-old daughter, Hortensia, said.

The parents of the twenty-three fifth graders in Sector 3 have met with their attorneys to discuss filing a dual lawsuit (the figure reportedly was nineteen million dollars) against Dry Ice Fog Elementary for inadequate surveillance, and against Hortensia Rodriguez Cora, the sole living relative of the suicide.

"Very few of the pupils, if any, saw anything," Dr. Joy emphasized. "Ms. Bornagin instructed them to stare at the TV monitors above the blackboards, and our indications are that the pupils followed instructions and watched a videotape of themselves at their consoles accessing the geography of Mexico. Nonetheless, the suicide was demonstrably traumatic, and the parents of the twenty-three fifth-graders in Sector 3 are constitutionally entitled to sue."

20 Minutes Into the Future

"There's a real feeling that some of our foreign competitors have eaten our lunch," said Rep. Don Ritter (R-Pa.), who chairs a Task Force on High Technology & Competitiveness. "We can't let that happen in superconductors."

Die- Die- Die- Die- DIET PEPSI!

"The shopping mall is the natural venue for lip sync and air band competitions. Though malls tend to look alike, different malls in different neighborhoods attract contestants with different tastes. 'Like in

Brooklyn you get a lot of break dancing and rapping,' said Dickie. 'But you go to Levittown and you get punk—there's a big punk club there called Spit. And in Staten Island there's more, like, commercial New Wave.'"

The crowning irony, according to NEWSWEEK, is that, "for all his scoffing at the system, Max is, in actuality, the quintessential product of his times—a pop icon designed and manufactured for the video generation with an almost mathematical precision."

Where you from?
Pakistan.
You mean Pakestine?
No.
I think you do, listen up: Pakestine craves Diet Pepsi, that freakin' heat plus your bean-eaters' propensity to put on a pound or two.

Brad likes Lite Beer, scented candles, and environmental music, and plenty of it. Anton lurches towards the synthesizer: Bach's Toccata in B. Above: monitoring satellites and waste disposal modules. And that's how the lifestyle of the Beverly Hills male influences your Japanese designer.

Bind their long hair one to the other, strip them, blind them, grant them long knives, call the survivor TERRORIST. Not long knives but canes, sword-canes, actually sugar cane, they're "undocumented," with bound-to-the-other black coarse hair, each made-blind farmhand a TERROR-IST, the survivor alone called Cain.

"Increasingly the trend is towards large automated systems—so called 'Flexible Manufacturing Systems'—controlled by software written in specialized programming language. This naturally enables robots to perform complex and coordinated actions, and to mimic more closely the flexibility and responsiveness of the non-robotic worker."

How much do you and your lover trust each other, really? These soft ribbons add extra spice to "trust me" fantasy games with that special someone. Unlike other restraints that may chafe and irritate, we selected our tethers of trust especially for their comfort, softness and sensuality. Each set contains two wrist and two ankle tethers, the clasps are velcro, the ribbons are nylon parachute webbing 48-inches long for ultimate versatility, scented.

Diet Pepsi technicians have now successfully demythicized the romantic mumbo-jumbo of the human brain, which fundamentally is no more than a binary system of off-on switches, and employing immaculate logic, the Pepsi team has isolated the consumer principle in a "computer generated" image, which replicates tone without temperament, which is at once the consummate image and the consummate reproduction of images, and which, despite its "marginal humanness" is sexy.

Wargasm

A forty-four-year-old *Hispanic* woman, described by her daughter as "emotionally distraught," walked into an elementary school classroom on Tuesday morning and fatally shot herself in front of twenty-three fifth-graders.

The twenty-three pupils in Dry Ice Fog Elementary School of Sector 3, and Ms. Bernice (called "Bunny") Bornagin, their red-haired *diet-Pepsi-thin* teacher, tried to dissuade the woman, who was armed with two *evidently stolen* Smith & Wesson .32 caliber revolvers. "I'm sorry I have to do it this way," the woman said *in heavily accented English* before firing a bullet into her head.

When it was clear that the woman would not listen to reason, Ms. Bornagin instructed her students to stare at the side-by-side TV monitors above the blackboard at the front of the room, school officials said. The first time the woman, identified as Missy Rodriguez, *and overweight,* pulled the trigger of the gun in her right hand, it misfired, so she aimed the gun in her left hand at the wall, fired a shot, then pointed the gun in her left hand at her left temple and fired the fatal shot.

Psychologists from the Jesu-Manville Sector were transmitted to Dry Ice Fog Elementary at once to begin counseling the pupils. The psychologists were dressed in camouflage fatigues, *called "terrorist couture."* The pupils received them at their consoles while eating their lunch, with the principal's permission, since this was a special occasion: TV News was running a 30-second segment on the *overweight Hispanic's* classroom suicide, *and the box lunches were donated by Sharper Image, Inc., a sponsor of the news segment, along with Pepsi. Her mom was always "moping," the suicide's daughter said.*

"Very few [pupils] actually saw anything," said Harvey Joy, a high-school principal in the Sector, a former principal of Dry Ice Fog

Elementary, and a psychologist in his own right. "Most of the pupils talked about it as though it was something they'd seen on TV," Dr. Joy said. "Each pupil will handle it differently. I was very impressed with the calmness of the pupils."

The woman was declared dead at Sector 3 Hospital *"For Indigents"* at 11:17 A.M., about an hour after the shooting. School officials said there was absolutely no evidence that Rodriguez, the suicide, had any connection with Dry Ice Fog Elementary. *The preliminary indications are that she was an "Illegal" from El Salvador and that the two guns were stolen in El Salvador or elsewhere in that area.* Rodriguez was not a parent of any of the school's four hundred twelve students. *"We only have three Hispanic pupils in the school,"* an official said. *"And obviously we keep a complete file on the parents of these pupils."* "She was a sort of shy person," Rodriguez' twenty-seven-year-old daughter Hortensia said. *"She was trying to find work and couldn't. My mom had a problem sticking with a job once she got it,"* Hortensia said.

The parents of the twenty-three fifth-graders in Sector 3 met with their attorneys to discuss filing a dual lawsuit (the figure reportedly was nineteen million dollars) against Dry Ice Fog Elementary for inadequate surveillance, and against Hortensia Rodriguez Cora, the sole living relative of the suicide *in the U.S. Cora's husband is unemployed and they have three young children. Dry Ice Fog is a Type C "private" institution, established in the throes of the Civil Rights struggles when concerned parents of middle-class white children struck out for an alternative to violent public schooling in the inner cities.*

"Very few of the pupils, if any, saw anything," Dr. Joy emphasized. "Ms. Bornagin instructed them to stare at the TV monitors above the blackboards, and our indications are that the pupils followed instructions and watched a videotape of themselves at their consoles accessing the geography of Mexico. Nonetheless, the *overweight Illegal Alien's* suicide was demonstrably traumatic, and the parents of the twenty-three fifth graders in Sector 3 are constitutionally entitled to sue *not only the Illegal Alien's heirs but also, according to experts in International Law, the Marxist-Leninist government of El Salvador."*

Thom Jurek

From

Straight Fiction

There is no longer an opposition in the territories between the abstractions of money and the apparent materiality of commodities. The extraterritoriality of the console expands the body's reach into the dissolution of markets and the centrality of language. The unity of representation is fictive and fractal in the virtual annexation of all spaces and the liquidation of any specific signs that occupied them.

I live further to remember codes that allow me to forget myself to pieces: Inside the network the body becomes an augmented pleasure center, fragmented into figurative images that lose their transparence and become yet another code. The activity of my feelings logs itself into an endless transference onto and over itself, described and logified from inside the CPU. My hands reach and clutch blindly for the contours of your face, where I need to find heat. The sound of coughing motorcycles rattles the mirror in the bedroom.

To lapse into the web, responding to the sound of human violence, intimate and terrifying. The open wound of fear is for me the brightest light imaginable, seeing for the first time a sidewalk after a head-on collision. I can be prepared by nothing in my technical makeup. Fingers punching out the correct sequence yields only a question mark in response. Velocity can be calculated, the pliability of entrails cannot. It is in this place full of unfamiliar shapes and shadows that I attempt to place you, your body reclined and ready to move without the slightest provocation. Each number I read out here is contradicted by the one previous. Photographs from medical textbooks adorn your walls where your face hangs in disfigurement. One step further reveals the terror of your nipples and the landscape that lies between them spurning my lack of a masculine smell. Your trimmed pubis reduces me to failure in fleeing your gaze.

Metrophage: The ceaseless transformation of the city into the post-human. Piles of ruin are continually tunneled and reformed into an equation of billboards. Central themes are target vehicles for the analysis of entropy, as the body becomes a sum total of cosmetic surgery and replacement parts as the outfit to fulfill any desire. Secrets of all types have been stored into read-only software for decades. The system has become entropic when the rise of virtual and biological technologies dominate the feedback process by guaranteeing the amount of energy lost will be greater than the amount of energy gained by their sheer number and diversity, with no multiplication or diversity of energy sources. Hence the body begins to die, and transmorgrify into the columnar table of information and dissemination, cancelled by its need to continually replace and remodel without proper understanding of what dies when it is replaced. The grey scale increases three shades. The data net hides on the reverse side of the screen.

Richard Kadrey

The Toilet
Was Full
of Nietzsche
(*from* Metrophage)

In the alley, the speed came on like an old friend, an electric hum up and down his spine. Suddenly, all things were possible. The nervous glare of neon signs and halogen streetlamps domed Sunset in a pulsing nimbus of come-on colors. Stepping from the alley, Jonny barely felt his boots on the pavement. Easy Money was as good as dead.

There were five or six lepers clustered around the entrance to Carnaby's Pit, begging alms and exhibiting their wounds to those willing to pay for a look. An upturned Stetson on the ground before them held an assortment of coins, crumpled dollar and peso notes and gaily colored pills. Ever since the lepers' numbers had grown too large to ignore, odd rumors had sprung up around them. Many people swore that the Committee for Public Health was putting something in the water, while others suspected the Arabs. Some blamed the extraterrestrial Alpha Rats, claiming they were trying to destroy the Earth with "Leprosy Rays" from the moon. It was Jonny's opinion that most people were idiots.

One leper in a ragged Spacer uniform was reciting in a low whiskey voice:

"The streets breathe, ebb and flow like the seas beneath a sodden twilight eye. The sky appears from a maw of rooftops—Dusk street, dry fountains coax the cemetery stars."

Jonny pulled a few Dapsone and tetrahydrocannabinol capsules from his pouch and dropped them into his battered Stetson. The leper who had been reciting, his head and face heavily bandaged, opened his jacket.

"Thank you, friend," the leper said through broken lips, pointing to his freshest scars.

Nodding politely, Jonny left the lepers and stepped down into the Pit.

The skyline tilted, angled steeply downward, then up, became a vertical blur of mirrored windows, skyscrapers leading to a hologram star field. Jonny was in the Pit's game parlor, separated from the bar by a dirty lotus-print curtain. Around the edges of the room, antique pinball machines beeped and rang prosaically while the air in the center of the parlor burned with the phantom light of hologram games. Crossing the parlor, Jonny was caught in a spray of hot-blue laser blasts from Sub-Orbital Commando, showered with fragments of pintsized galaxies spinning from Vishnu and Shiva's hands. Ratsized nudes swarmed above his head, frantically groping at each other for Fun In Zero G.

One angry pinball player threw a glass, and it shattered against the far wall. Jonny stepped back as two members of the Pit's Meat Boys moved smoothly from opposite ends of the room to intercept the shouting man.

"Goddamit, this machine just ate my last dollar!" screamed the pinball player.

He was still screaming as the two beefy monsters grabbed an arm apiece and ushered him through the front doors. They came back alone. Jonny half expected to see them return with the guy's arms.

"Peace! Can't we have a little peace in here?" mumbled a sweating man lining up Jacqueline Kennedy in the sights of a fiberglass reproduction of a Mannlicher-Carcano rifle. It was Smokefinger, the pickpocket, fat and nervous, jacked into the Date With Destiny game by a length of pencil-thin cable extending from the game console to a twenty-four-pronged miniplug implanted at the base of his skull. Most of the players in the room were jacked into various games by similar plugs. Jonny's stomach fluttered at the sight. Elective surgery, he had decided years before, did not extend to having little platinum bullets permanently jammed into his skull, thank you. He could watch the World Link on a monitor and, as for the games, they seemed real enough without the skull-plugs.

Smokefinger tracked the ghostly hologram of the presidential limousine as crimson numbers flickered in the metallic-blue Dallas sky, reading out his score.

Jonny leaned close to pickpocket's ear and said, "How's it going, Smoke?" Smokefinger ignored him and continued to move the toy rifle with steady, insect-like concentration. "Hey, Smoke," said Jonny, waving his fingers before Smokefinger's eyes just as the fat man pulled the trigger.

No score. "Shit," mumbled the pickpocket, still ignoring Jonny. He had aced the chauffeur.

This wasn't going to be any fun at all, Jonny decided. He pushed the release button on the plug at the back of Smokefinger's head. The wire dropped, and a spring-loaded coil drew it back inside the game console.

"What the hell—" yelled Smokefinger, grabbing for his neck. He looked at Jonny dumbly as his eyes slowly refocused. In a moment, he said, "Hey, Jonny, *que pasa?*"

"Not much," Jonny said. "I can't believe you're still playing this game. Haven't you killed everybody in Dallas by now?"

Smokefinger shrugged. "I pop 'em, but they keep coming back." Sweat pooled on the pickpocket's glasses where the rims touched his cheeks.

Jonny smiled and looked around the room wondering if there was someone else from whom he might get information. However, in the pastel glare of meteor showers and laser fire, none of the faces looked familiar. "You seen Easy Money around?" he asked Smokefinger. "I've got to talk to him."

"Right, talk. You and everybody else." Smokefinger looked back at the empty hologram chamber and cursed. "I almost broke my own record, you know," he said. He looked at Jonny accusingly. "No, I ain't seen Easy. Random's tending bar tonight. Maybe you should go talk to him. To tell you the truth, you're distracting me." Smokefinger never took his finger from the trigger of the fiberglass rifle. Jonny pulled some yen coins from his pocket and fed them into the machine.

"Thanks for all your help, killer," he said. But the pickpocket did not hear him; he was already jacking in. Jonny left Smokefinger, wishing he could find peace as easily as that, and pushed his way into the bar. Jonny always found it a little disconcerting that the main room never seemed to change. He imagined it frozen in time, like a scratched record, repeating the same snatch of lyric over and over again. The usual weekend crowd of small-time smugglers, B actors, and bored prostitutes stared from the blue veil of smoke around the bar. The same tired porn played on the big screen for the benefit of those unfortunates not equipped with skull-plugs. Even the band, Taking Tiger Mountain, was blasting the same old riffs, stopping half-way through their own "Guernica Rising" when the crowd shouted them down. They switched to a desultory "Brown Sugar," a song that was out-of-date long before anybody in the club had been born. Dancers undulated under the strobes and subsonic mood enhancers as projectors threw holograms of lunar atrocities onto their hot bodies. In fact, the only real difference Jonny could see in the place was the darkness in the HoloWhores bundling booths.

Jonny pushed his way through the tightly packed crowd and tried the door to Easy's control room. It was locked, and the bar was far too crowded for him to force the door. He would have to wait. Feeling relief, and guilt at that relief, Jonny made his way to the bar for a drink and some questions.

Random, the bartender, was drying glasses behind a bar constructed of old automobile dashboards. Tall and thin, his skin creased like dead leaves, Random offered Jonny the same half-smile he offered everybody. Jonny ordered an Asahi dark and gin: he put a twenty on the bar. Random set down the beer and slid the bill into his pocket in one smooth motion. The bartender inclined his head toward the dance floor. "Necrophiliacs," he said above the roar of the band. "They can't stand new music. Like it's deadly to them or something. Bunch of assholes." Random shrugged. Then he looked away, like a blind man, eyes unfocused. "They just nuked Kansas City. The Jordanian Re-Unification Army, a New Palestine splinter group. They called the local Link station. Said Houston's next," he reported. The bartender shook his head. "Those boys must really hate cows." Random had a passion for morbid news items and stayed plugged into the Link's data lines constantly, relaying the most worthy bits to his customers. Jonny thought it was one of his most charming qualities.

He turned back to Jonny as if anticipating his question. "Easy split. Been gone a couple of days now. Left quick, too. Didn't touch his holo stuff."

"I don't suppose you have any idea where he went?" asked Jonny.

"I'm afraid he neglected to leave a forwarding address. A shame, too, so close to Thanksgiving and all."

The band's volume jumped abruptly as they broke from the song into a tense, rhythmic jam. Saint Peter, the guitarist, stood at the edge of the stage between soaring liquid-cooled stacks of Krupp-Verwandlungsinhalt speakers. Eyes squeezed shut, shoulders loose, he pumped walls of noise, his myoelectric left hand racing like a frantic silver spider up and down the fretboard. As he played, a pattern of light glinted off the chrome hand, marking its progress through the air. Then, just as the jam reached its peak, the song died; the porn faded, and the lights dimmed. "Brown-out," said Random. He casually threw the switch under the bar and power returned. "Tell Sumi gracias for the watts," he said.

Jonny nodded. "Did you hear that Easy had another Flare Gun Party?" he asked.

"No, who got burned?"

"Raquin."

Random raised an eyebrow in sympathy. "Sorry, man," he said. "Although, I must admit, I'm not entirely surprised to hear he's been up to something." He took a long hit from a hookah next to the cash register. "Looking for Easy Money seems to be the hot new game in town. Last night the crowd was so thick I had 'em line up and take numbers. Of course, Easy's not the only one who seems to have captured the public's imagination." Random smiled at Jonny. "You appear to have developed a bit of celebrity all your own."

"Me?" Jonny asked guardedly. "Who's been asking about me?"

Random shrugged. "No one I knew." The bartender winked conspiratorially. "Come on, boy-o. Whose ankles have you been nipping at?"

"I am pathetically clean," Jonny said. "Tell me about them. Anything you can remember."

Random stuck two nicotine-yellow fingers into his shirt pocket and pulled out a glicene envelope of white powder. "Pure as Mother Mary and twice as nice," he said, giving the envelope a light kiss. "Interesting lads. They didn't try to pay off in crude cash." He dropped the envelope back into his pocket.

"Smugglers?" asked Jonny.

"Could be, only what's a smuggler lord doing shooting for small shit like Easy Money? Or you for that matter."

"Who knows?" Jonny said. He took a long gulp of his drink. "Maybe he's decided he's in the wrong business."

"Hell," said the bartender, "everybody in Last Ass is in the wrong business."

Random set down the glass he had been cleaning and said, "Weather." His eyes shifted. "Junior senator on the Atmospheric Management Committee announced they can clean up the mess left by the Weather Wars. Says they ought to be able to stabilize weather patterns over most of North America in three to five years."

"Didn't they announce that same program three to five years ago?" asked Jonny. "At least." And with that, Random gave Jonny the other half of the smile and moved on to his new customers. Swirling the dregs of his beer, Jonny turned and studied the noisy crowd moving through the bar. He searched their heads for a sign of goat horns grafted above a thin face, inset with darting, suspicious eyes. Or arms thick with tattooed serpents, like the stigmata of some junky god. Easy Money always stood out in a crowd which, Jonny supposed, was the idea. If Easy was around, he should not be hard to spot.

Jonny had met Easy while they were both in the employ of the smuggler lord, Conover. This was just after Easy had made a name for himself with his first Flare Gun Party.

The party had become something of a legend with the pushers. It went like this: Easy Money, a human parasite with the unerring ability to detect the softest, most vulnerable part of his prey, had acquired a contract to kill the leader of the Los Santos Atomicos gang. Beginning with a philosophy that later became his trademark (like the hourglass on the belly of a spider), Easy reasoned that gang retribution being such a swift and ugly thing, eliminating the entire gang would be less trouble than the removal of any single member.

It was well known to those who, like Easy, always kept a metaphorical ear to the ground, that the Los Santos Atomicos gang's particular vice was freebasing cocaine. Easy located their safe house with information from a rival gang. He also found that the Los Santos Atomicos liked to buy the ether, they used to treat the coke, in bulk. They kept big tanks of the stuff hidden under the floor.

As he was fond of saying, from there it was easy money.

Like some stoned Prometheus, Easy brought fire to the Los Santos Atomicos in the form of a red Navy signal flare which he fired into their lab from the roof of a Catholic mission across the street. The explosion literally ripped the roof off the ether-filled building. The fireball boiled down onto many of the adjoining buildings, igniting them, too.

Besides the Los Santos Atomicos, at least a dozen other people, mainly junkies and prostitutes, died in the fires that engulfed the grimy neighborhood. And Easy Money moved up a rung in the hierarchy of movers and shakers in their little world. Looking back, none of it had seemed important to Jonny at the time. When he heard of the deaths, it seemed somehow normal. Just one more senseless act in the long series of senseless acts that made up their lives. However, Raquin's death had moved events from the abstract into a personal affront. He *knew* Raquin. And he knew Easy had killed him. Jonny would finish Easy Money simply because nobody else would and because the little prick deserved it.

Jonny slowed his breathing, counted each intake of breath, centering himself as his roshi had taught him. Visions of horned, tattooed Easy swam before him as he hunted for that savage part of himself he had sought before whenever he had to kill.

But the passion was gone, seemed pointless now. The speed had been cut with something unpleasant. It was wearing off already, leaving him feeling numb and stupid. Jonny gulped down the rest of his beer and tried to get into the buzz from the liquor.

He wondered if perhaps he had figured things wrong. If the smuggler lords really were after Easy, maybe he was not needed, after all. There was always work to do, money to be made. He had to establish a new connection. Something bothered Jonny, though. He could not figure out who, besides the Committee, would be looking for him. Had he trod on someone's toes in the last few days looking for Easy? He could not remember. The bar seemed to tip slightly as Jonny downed his second Asahi and gin. When he wiped a hand across his brow it came away cool and covered in sweat. He left the bar, pushing carelessly through a tight knot of nervous teenagers from the Valley made up to look like they had grafts and implants. Near the restroom, a Zombie Analytic with subcutaneous pixels flashed Jonny in quick succession: Marilyn Monroe, Jim Morrison, and Aoki Vega. He ignored her.

Inside the restroom, Jonny splashed rusty water onto his face. The room stank of human waste, and the paper-towel dispenser was empty. On the floor he found half a copy of *Twilight of the Gods*. The toilet was full of Nietzsche. Jonny dried his hands with the few remaining pages. The water made him feel a little better. However, the comedown from the speed had left him jumpy and nervous.

When Jonny left the restroom, a hand clamped on his arm.

"Jonny, how's it going?" asked a short man whom Jonny did not recognize. The man's smile was wide and toothy, intended to give the impression that he was a very dangerous character. He wore shades, the lenses of which were dichromatic holograms depicting some cavern. Where his eyes should have been were twin bottomless pits.

"That's a good way to lose some teeth or an eye," Jonny said evenly.

The little man's smile faded only slightly. He relaxed his grip on Jonny's arm, but did not release him. "Sorry, Jonny," he said. "Look, could I buy you a drink or something?"

"No."

Jonny shook off the little man's grip and headed back to the bar to get drunk. But, again, strong fingers caught him.

"Where are you going in such a hurry?" the little man asked. "Let's talk. I've got a deal for you." Jonny jammed his elbow into the little man's midsection, spun and pressed the barrel of the Futukoro into the man's throat.

"If you ever grab me again, I will kill you. Do you understand that?" Jonny whispered.

The little man released Jonny's arm and stepped back, his hands held in front of his chest, palms out. "It's cool," he said giddily. "It's cool."

Jonny pushed the man away roughly and left him chattering to himself.

He was sweating again. Jonny went back to the bar and drank cheap, fishy-tasting Japanese vodka, thinking as he drank about how vile it was and how he wished he could afford the good stuff. He put the little man out of his mind. Jonny wondered if he should call Sumi, but that seemed like a bad idea. She would ask questions he did not want to answer. Eventually, his thoughts drifted to Raquin. He wondered what it was like to burn to death. He remembered that someone had once told him that you would not feel anything, that the fire would consume all the oxygen, and you would smother before you ever felt the flames. That seemed like small comfort. How much better was it to smother than to burn?

Jonny continued drinking straight shots of fishy vodka until the taste disappeared altogether. Taking six of the shot glasses, he constructed a little pyramid, but Random took the glasses away and soon Jonny ran out of money. While he was fishing in his pouch for more dope, there was a slight tug on his arm. Somehow, when he turned, Jonny knew the little man would be standing there. His shades were off, and he held his hands up as if to ward off a blow.

"Truce, okay? I did not grab you," the little man said. "I just tapped you on the shoulder."

Jonny nodded. "I could tell you were a quick study. What do you want?" The man leaned forward, anxiously.

"Look, Jonny, I didn't want to tell you before—I'm working for Mister Conover. He sent me to get you. If you don't come back with me, my ass is grass."

"Sorry to hear that. Tell Mr. Conover I'll get in touch with him as soon as I'm through with the deal I'm working on now."

"I can't do that. He wants you now," said the little man. Hopefully, he added, "You know whatever it is you're working on, Mr. Conover will make it worth your while to drop."

Jonny shook his head. "No, thanks. This is personal."

The little man leaned closer. "You aren't looking for Easy Money, are you?"

"What if I am?"

"Well, that's great," said the little man. "That's the job—Easy Money copped something that belongs to Mister Conover, and he wants you to help him get it back."

Jonny nodded, took a piece of ice from someone else's glass, and rubbed it across his forehead. "My problem, friend, is that I know Mr. Conover pretty well, and I know that he is a professional," Jonny said. "No offense, but why would he send a hard guy like you to get me?"

The little man looked around, apparently to make sure that nobody was eavesdropping. "This isn't really my job," he whispered.

Jonny smiled. "No shit?" he said.

"I'm more of a bookkeeper. It's just that Mr. Conover's got all his muscle guys out looking for Easy Money," he said. The little man looked at Jonny gravely. "You know how it is."

"Yeah, I know how it is," said Jonny, genuinely amused.

"He told me you always hang out at Carnaby's Pit," the little man continued. He made a face as if he had just smelled something foul. "To tell you the truth, it's a bit much for me."

Jonny laughed. "Sometimes it's a bit much for me, too," he said. The little man smiled; for real this time. "Then you'll come with me?" he asked.

Jonny shrugged. "That stuff about looking for Easy, you weren't just being cute again, were you?"

"No, all I said was true," he said.

"Good."

"Then you'll come?"

"I'm not sure. I hate to beat a point to death, but how do I know you work for Mr. Conover?"

"Oh, yeah," said the little man brightening. He reached into his jacket pocket. "Mr. Conover said to give you this."

He handed Jonny a plastic bag containing two gelatinous blue capsules. The manufacturer's markings were Swiss, the capsules NATO issue, banded with an orange warning stripe indicating mycotoxins. Jonny had seen the stuff on the Committee. Frosty the Snowman. It was a necrotic, a synthetic variation on pit viper venom that killed by breaking down collagen fibers, effectively dissolving skin and muscle tissue. The NATO variation, he had heard, was constructed with certain "open" segments along its DNA chain, allowing the toxin to bind with polypeptides in the victim's collagen and replicate itself there. Rumor had it that Frosty could break down the skin and muscle tissue of a seventy-kilo man in just under fourteen hours. It was not the kind of drug that many people would have access to. Jonny stuffed the bag into his pouch.

"So, I'm convinced," he said.

"Then you'll come?"

"Why not," he said. "I'm not getting anywhere here."

The little man beamed at him. Jonny thought it might be love.

"By the way, have you got a name?" Jonny asked.

"Cyrano. Bender Cyrano, like the guy in the old book, you know? Only I haven't got a nose." He laughed at his own joke. Jonny did not know what the hell Cyrano was talking about, but he smiled so as not to hurt the little man's feelings. When Cyrano extended his hand, Jonny shook it.

"Nice to meet you, Cyrano. Let's get out of here," said Jonny.

When they reached the dirty curtain, Jonny turned and took a last look at the band. They were burning through one of Saint Peter's best tunes, "Street Prince." The crowd ignored them, utterly. Random was right, Jonny decided. A bunch of assholes.

Marc Laidlaw

Office of
the Future
(*from* Dad's Nuke)

She rose, a little uncertainly, for it was dark in the house. All the lights were off in order to keep the headaches away. She felt them circling around her like wolves, closing in, and darkness was some protection.

As she climbed the stairs, the base of her neck throbbed as though with a touch of fever.

Leaning into Bill's office, his sanctuary, she hesitated. Stray, pointless thoughts fluttered around the edges of her mind, flickering like moths until she batted them away. They were selfish thoughts. She couldn't worry about things like where she had come from, or why she was here. She couldn't change any of those things. She had to be practical. Where, for instance, was Bill? That was a question worth asking.

There was no clue to be found on his desk, but of course there wouldn't be. She expected to find the drawers locked, but they were open—worse, they were empty. There was not a scrap of paper or even a pencil in any of them. He must have left all his work at the office.

His console.

"You can't use that," he always said. "You have to be a skilled IMR typist. You have to learn it young, get it into your blood, you know. Like P.J. He's a whiz."

Like P.J., she thought, but not like Bill. When had he ever learned how to type?

It must be easier than it looks. Probably about as complicated as a holiday. I always see him smiling when he's plugged in. What if he doesn't work at all? What if he's got nothing there but a one-man plug-in vacation?

The thought made her quiver. She slipped into his chair.

"On," she said, and the system began to purr. Light spilled over the desk, speckled her hands. She found the IMR-gloves resting on the arms of the chair and put them on; and then, somewhat clumsily in the gloves, she struggled to get the hood over her head. For a second she suffocated in darkness, but the eyepieces moved into place with slight suction and she found light flashing into her eyes, pulsing, and she relaxed. Her hands tingled. Electricity raced through her spine.

Where was she?

Black curtains parted ahead of her and she moved into a dusty, yellow-lit hallway. With a start she became aware of her body—a heavy-set male physique, dressed in a gray suit. Everything seemed dim and out of focus, including herself. Her steps were heavy, plodding, and hardly carried her down the hall.

She approached a door, one of many, moving with incredible slowness. *Mr. Johnson* was painted on the frosted glass pane. Monday, she kept thinking. Monday. Sigh.

Poor Bill, she thought in spite of herself. Every day he comes to this.

She was almost afraid to open the door, but she did. There might be a clue to his whereabouts.

The place lit up as she entered. She gazed into a room that surpassed the hallway in drabness. Steel desks, cork partitions, rows of filing cabinets. The hands of an enormous antique clock were frozen at five after eight. Stacks of paper covered the nearest desk, and on the topmost sheet of the tallest stack she saw in huge red letters:

NEED YOUR COMMENTS ASAP.

Her hands, in the gray sleeves, trembled. She felt exhausted, weak, thirsty, as though the dust of the office had settled into her pores. She backed out of the room, turning off the light as she went, and continued down the hall in search of a fountain. A constant clicking sound emanated from the walls on all sides, no louder than the rattling of her teeth, and her headache finally seized her.

With a moan she turned to the nearest door, where the sound of clattering—it must be a typewriter—was very loud.

CENTRAL FILES

Someone here should be able to help her.

She went in, but found herself in an aisle of filing cabinets. There was no one typing, no room in fact for a desk, and the sound she heard came from beyond a door at the far end of the room. When she saw the name on it —*Men*— she started to leave, but the clamor coming from behind the door kept her a moment longer. It sounded like someone scrabbling at the knob, a trapped person hoping to get out but knowing that there was no one in the room he could call out to. Of course, she had come in silently. The knob quivered and shook in its socket, turned a little in either direction, but it did not quite open.

So the door was locked from outside. How simple to remedy. Her head felt better, now that she had found a solution to some problem, however small.

She crossed the room quickly, her steps sounding loud and clear to her ears; the whole scene brightened as her mood lifted. The scratching and rattling stopped as she unlocked the door. She could hear him shifting about inside.

And then a thought: what if it were Bill? Could he have gotten stuck in the men's room? No, there had been a note. . . .

"You can come out," she said in her manly voice. "I unlocked it for you."

The door opened swiftly in the hand of a shadow. Beyond the opener were layers of blackness, darkening successively into the distance. It hardly looked like a restroom.

Four figures stood in the dark. None of them was her husband.

"Hello?" she said.

As they came forward they put out their hands, but she hardly cared when she got a look at their eyes.

Bits of raw meat.

Backward. She banged into a high metal shelf covered with colored forms and boxes of paperclips, and set it rocking. Before it fell she got the doorknob in her hand and escaped into the hallway; as the door closed she heard a crash, but she did not wait to learn if the four with torn eyes had survived. They had not looked like they could be stopped so easily.

In the hallway, everything was quiet and dim and slow again, the yellow light full of dust. She ran toward the curtains at the far end of the hall, wishing that her body were lighter, her legs more agile. Motes of dust hammered against her face. At last she staggered into the dark, and came to herself in the gloves and the hood, at Bill's desk. She was covered in a light sweat, shaking.

She was out of the chair and downstairs in seconds. In the kitchen she shoved a glass under the faucet and almost drank down a glass of blue dissolving liquid; she poured that out and filled the glass from the other tap, and drank to soothe her parched throat. Leaning against the counter, she looked around as if expecting to see those four come in from the living room; but the house was still silent.

Mark Leyner

I Was

an Infinitely Hot

and Dense Dot

(*from* My Cousin,

My Gastroenterologist)

I was driving to Las Vegas to tell my sister that I'd had Mother's respirator unplugged. Four bald men in the convertible in front of me were picking the scabs off their sunburnt heads and flicking them onto the road. I had to swerve to avoid riding over one of the oozy crusts of blood and going into an uncontrollable skid. I maneuvered the best I could in my boxy Korean import but my mind was elsewhere. I hadn't eaten for days. I was famished. Suddenly as I reached the crest of a hill, emerging from the fog, there was a bright neon sign flashing on and off that read: FOIE GRAS AND HARICOTS VERTS NEXT EXIT. I checked the guidebook and it said: *Excellent food, malevolent ambience.* I'd been habitually abusing an illegal growth hormone extracted from the pituitary glands of human corpses and I felt as if I were drowning in excremental filthiness but the prospect of having something good to eat cheered me up. I asked the waitress about the soup du jour and she said that it was primordial soup—which is ammonia and methane mixed with ocean water in the presence of lightning. Oh I'll take a tureen of that embryonic broth, I say, constraint giving way to exuberance—but as soon as she vanishes my spirit immediately sags because the ambience is so malevolent. The bouncers are hassling some youngsters who want drinks—instead of simply carding the kids, they give them radiocarbon tests, using traces of carbon-14 to determine how old they are—and also there's a young wise guy from Texas A&M at a table near mine who asks for freshly ground Rolaids on his fettuccine and two waiters viciously work him over with heavy bludgeon-sized pepper mills, so I get right back into my car and narcissistically comb my thick jet-black hair in the rearview mirror and I check

James O'Barr

I Was an Infinitely Hot and Dense Dot   **103**

the guidebook. There's an inn nearby—it's called Little Bo Peep's—its habitués are shepherds. And after a long day of herding, shearing, panpipe playing, muse invoking, and conversing in eclogues, it's Miller time, and Bo Peep's is packed with rustic swains who've left their flocks and sunlit, idealized arcadia behind for the more pungent charms of hard-core social intercourse. Everyone's favorite waitress is Kikugoro. She wears a pale-blue silk kimono and a brocade obi of gold and silver chrysanthemums with a small fan tucked into its folds, her face is painted and powdered to a porcelain white. A cowboy from south of the border orders a "Biggu Makku." But Kikugoro says, "This is not Makudonarudo." She takes a long cylinder of gallium arsenide crystal and slices him a thin wafer which she serves with soy sauce, wasabi, pickled ginger, and daikon. "Conducts electrons ten times faster than silicon . . . taste good, gaucho-*san*, you eat," she says, bowing.

My sister is the beautiful day. Oh beautiful day, my sister, wipe my nose, swaddle me in fresh-smelling garments. I nurse at the adamantine nipple of the beautiful day. I quaff the milk of the beautiful day, and for the first time since 1956, I cheese on the shoulder of the beautiful day. Oh beautiful day, wash me in your lake of cloudless azure. I have overdosed on television, I am unresponsive and cyanotic, revive me in your shower of gelid light and walk me through your piazza which is made of elegant slabs of time. Oh beautiful day, kiss me. Your mouth is like Columbus Day. You are the menthol of autumn. My lungs cannot quench their thirst for you. Resuscitate me—I will never exhale your tonic gasses. Inflate me so that I may rise into the sky and mourn the monotonous topography of my life. Oh beautiful day, my sister, wipe my nose and adorn me in your finery. Let us lunch alfresco. Your club sandwiches are made of mulch and wind perfumed with newsprint. Your frilly toothpicks are the deciduous trees of school days.

I was an infinitely hot and dense dot. So begins the autobiography of a feral child who was raised by huge and lurid puppets. An autobiography written wearing wrist weights. It ends with these words: A car drives through a puddle of sperm, sweat, and contraceptive jelly, splattering the great chopsocky vigilante from Hong Kong. Inside, two acephalic sardines in mustard sauce are asleep in the rank darkness of their tin container. Suddenly, the swinging doors burst open and a mesomorphic cyborg walks in and whips out a 35-lb. phallus made of corrosion-resistant nickel-base alloy and he begins to stroke it sullenly, his eyes half shut. It's got a metal-oxide membrane for absolute submicron filtration of petrochemical fluids. It can ejaculate herbicides, sulfuric acid, tar glue, you name it. At the end of the bar, a woman whose album-length poem about temporomandibular joint dysfunction (TMJ) had won a Grammy for best spoken word recording is gently slowly ritually rubbing copper hexafluoroacetylacetone into her clitoris as she watches the hunk with the non-Euclidian features shoot a glob of dehydrogenated ethylbenzene 3,900 miles towards the Arctic archipelago, eventually raining down upon a fiord on Baffin Bay. Outside, a basketball plunges from the sky, killing a dog. At a county fair, a huge and hairy man in mud-caked blue overalls, surrounded by a crowd of retarded teenagers, swings a sledgehammer above his head with brawny keloidal arms and then brings it down with all his brute force on a tofu-burger on a flowery paper plate. A lizard licks the dew from the stamen of a stunted crocus. Rivets and girders float above the telekinetic construction workers. The testicular voice of Barry White emanates from some occult source within the laundry room. As I chugalug a glass of tap water milky with contaminants, I realize that my mind is being drained of its contents and refilled with the beliefs of the most mission-oriented, can-do feral child ever raised by huge and lurid puppets. I am the voice . . . the voice from beyond and the voice from within—can you hear me? Yes. I speak to you and you only—is that clear? Yes, master. To whom do I speak? To me and me only. Is "happy" the appropriate epithet for someone who experiences each moment as if he were being alternately flayed alive and tickled to death? No, master.

In addition to the growth hormone extracted from the glands of human corpses, I was using anabolic steroids, tissue regeneration compounds, granulocyte-macrophage colony-stimulating factor (GM-CSF)—a substance used to stimulate growth of certain vital blood cells in radiation victims—and a nasal spray of neuropeptides that accelerates the release of pituitary hormones and I was getting larger and larger and my food bills were becoming enormous. So I went on a TV game show in the hopes of raising cash. This was my question, for $250,000 in cash and prizes: If the Pacific Ocean were filled with gin, what would be, in terms of proportionate volume, the proper lake of

vermouth necessary to achieve a dry martini? I said Lake Ontario—
but the answer was the Caspian Sea, which is called a sea but is a lake
by definition. I had failed. I had humiliated my family and disgraced
the kung fu masters of the Shaolin temple. I stared balefully out into
the studio audience which was chanting something that sounded like
"dork." I'm in my car. I'm high on Sinutab. And I'm driving anywhere.
The vector of my movement from a given point is isotropic—meaning
that all possible directions are equally probable. I end up at a squalid
little dive somewhere in Vegas maybe Reno maybe Tahoe. I don't
know . . . but there she is. I can't tell if she's a human or a fifth-
generation gynemorphic android and I don't care. I crack open an
ampule of mating pheromone and let it waft across the bar, as I sip my
drink, a methyl isocyanate on the rocks—methyl isocyanate is the
substance which killed more than 2,000 people when it leaked in
Bhopal, India, but thanks to my weight training, aerobic workouts,
and a low-fat fiber-rich diet, the stuff has no effect on me. Sure enough
she strolls over and occupies the stool next to mine. After a few
moments of silence, I make the first move: We're all larval psychotics
and have been since the age of two, I say, spitting an ice cube back
into my glass. She moves closer to me. At this range, the downy cilia-
like hairs that trickle from her navel remind me of the fractal ferns
produced by injecting dyed water into an aqueous polymer solution,
and I tell her so. She looks into my eyes: You have the glibness,
superficial charm, grandiosity, lack of guilt, shallow feelings, im-
pulsiveness, and lack of realistic long-term plans that excite me right
now, she says, moving even closer. We feed on the same prey species,
I growl. My lips are now one angstrom unit from her lips, which is one
ten-billionth of a meter. I begin to kiss her but she turns her head
away. Don't good little boys who finish all their vegetables get dessert?
I ask. I can't kiss you, we're monozygotic replicants—we share 100%
of our genetic material. My head spins. You are the beautiful day, I
exclaim, your breath is a zephyr of eucalyptus that does a pas de
bourrée across the Sea of Galilee. Thanks, she says, but we can't go
back to my house and make love because monozygotic incest is forbidden by the elders. What if I said I could change all that. . . . What if I
said that I had a miniature shotgun that blasts gene fragments into the
cells of living organisms, altering their genetic matrices so that a
monozygotic replicant would no longer be a monozygotic replicant and

she could then make love to a muscleman without transgressing the incest taboo, I say, opening my shirt and exposing the device which I had stuck in the waistband of my black jeans. How'd you get that thing? she gasps, ogling its thick fiber-reinforced plastic barrel and the Uzi-Biotech logo embossed on the magazine which held two cartridges of gelated recombinant DNA. I got it for Christmas. . . . Do you have any last words before I scramble your chromosomes, I say, taking aim. Yes, she says, you first. I put the barrel to my heart. These are my last words: When I emerged from my mother's uterus I was the size of a chicken bouillon cube and Father said to the obstetrician: I realize that at this stage it's difficult to prognosticate his chances for a productive future, but if he's going to remain six-sided and 0.4 grams for the rest of his life, then euthanasia's our best bet. But Mother, who only milliseconds before was in the very throes of labor, had already slipped on her muumuu and espadrilles and was puffing on a Marlboro: No pimple-faced simp two months out of Guadalajara is going to dissolve this helpless little hexahedron in a mug of boiling water, she said, as a nurse managed with acrobatic desperation to slide a suture basin under the long ash of her cigarette which she'd consumed in one furiously deep drag. These are my last words: My fear of being bullied and humiliated stems from an incident that occurred many years ago in a diner. A 500-lb. man seated next to me at the counter was proving that one particular paper towel was more absorbent than another brand. His face was swollen and covered with patches of hectic red. He spilled my glass of chocolate milk on the counter and then sopped it up with one paper towel and then with the other. With each wipe of the counter the sweep of his huge dimpled arm became wider and wider until he was repeatedly smashing his flattened hand and the saturated towel into my chest. There was an interminable cadence to the blows I endured. And instead of assistance from other patrons at the counter, I received their derision, their sneering laughter. But now look at me! I am a terrible god. When I enter the forest the mightiest oaks blanch and tremble. All rustling, chirping, growling, and buzzing cease, purling brooks become still. This is all because of my tremendous muscularity . . . which is the result of the hours of hard work that I put in at the gym and the strict dietary regimen to which I adhere. When I enter the forest the birds become incontinent with fear so there's this torrential downpour of shit from the trees. And I stride through—my whistle is like an earsplitting fife being played by a lunatic with a bloody bandage around his head. And the sunlight, rent into an incoherence of blazing vectors, illuminates me: a shimmering, serrated monster!

Joseph McElroy

From **Plus**

Something had been taken away.

From Imp Plus.

Yet he had wanted to get away, he remembered. The impulses drew him in again away from the shadows like birds cast on what could be a skull or grid if he had one. Small white birds with pink sides and black scissor-tails twice as long as their bodies. And after them a greater bird. Like a high, dark shearwater with wings three times the rest of it.

There was a project.

Against the gradient grid of the impulses drawing Imp Plus in from these now larger shadows with requests for enzyme action in chlorella, there was laughter.

Yet laughter then, not now; vibration bent out of its source.

The shadows around were more than birds.

Chlorella: that was the green, the vegetable. Inside the head of Imp Plus if there were a head, the blind news vendor said he himself could have been a vegetable but instead he'd taken hold.

The impulses seemed to bear their own answers for Imp Plus to free from the questions. The impulses made shadows on the gradient grid. Not the shadows coming around that were now more than birds, but shadows not seen. Yet also shadows that fell beyond the gradient grid and were the difference between the impulses now and then.

Yet nothing like the shadows Imp Plus saw around him on the inside of his skull that was not a skull.

ME READ reversed reads READ ME. The impulses themselves weren't the reversal. Some other operation reversed them.

But new force had come in the impulses. It conveyed itself to Imp Plus in measures of new impedance, and the force wasn't only the impulses from Earth which went on and on.

IMP PLUS CHECK GLUCOSE LEVEL. WE READ GLUCOSE UNSTABLE UP AND DOWN.

GROUND I READ YOU, said Imp Plus.

But his next answer seemed new. For he told Earth glucose levels had dropped. He took time to know this answer after he had given it to Earth.

IMP was said, and then PLUS.

And Imp Plus responded.

So did Earth.

IMP PLUS IMP PLUS DO YOU CONNECT LOWER GLUCOSE LEVEL WITH SLOWER RESPONSE TO TRANSMISSIONS? REPEAT: DO YOU CORRELATE YOUR SLOWER RESPONSE AND THOSE LOWER GLUCOSE LEVELS?

He thought of not answering, and this was a new thought, and he felt a trace of the thought all over, and like a ray he fell everywhere after the trace which was the absence close to his heart but alight with inclination that was more than gradient though it was gradient.

WAIT IMP PLUS. GLUCOSE UP NOW. GLUCOSE UP.

Imp was a word. So was *Plus*. On the Concentration Loop Imp Plus had answered messages from Earth that used the words *Imp Plus*. Imp Plus could talk.

IMP PLUS TO GROUND: ARE SPROUTS FROM OPTIC STALKS?

But from inside somewhere and not from Earth came an answer he had not requested in so many words: IMP was Interplanetary Monitoring Platform. The answer came from inside. From Imp Plus. Not from Earth.

But what (he asked inside his own new circuit and not to CAP COM on Earth), what is IMP PLUS?

And before he had the answer, Ground was heard in the impulses which Imp Plus now found harder to understand saying after a pause: NEGATIVE. NO OPTIC STALKS AFTER STAGE ONE OF OPERATION TL.

Laughter went up the grid, shadows more than lines. Laughter past. What was TL?

IMP PLUS DO YOU READ? DO YOU READ? REPEAT WHAT IS SPROUTS? WHAT IS SPROUTS?

The shadows on the walls were more. Not larger, not exactly smaller. But more. Like a tree grown out of birds. Now two birds: a bird with tail much longer than the rest of it seen from a car one early spring on Earth; and a bird with wingspread three times the rest of it seen once on Earth one late spring, seen by somebody who stood outside a car.

Imp Plus had not prepared to remember these.

And now desired only to obey his Operation TL frequency and answer Earth's transmissions.

SAY AGAIN IMP PLUS. WHAT SHADOWS? CHECK DUAL ATTITUDE STABILIZER. WE READ NO CHANGE. CHECK ATTITUDE STABILIZER. IF YOU HAVE CHANGED ATTITUDE YOU MAY BE GETTING SHADOWS.

But Imp Plus had not said *shadows* to Ground.

The answer was that Imp Plus was able to think in transmission. Yet that was what the Concentration Loop was, to begin with.

Glucose level up: he had known that already. And as if Ground read his thought, Ground paralleled his answer: CAP COM TO IMP PLUS. GLUCOSE UP AGAIN. DO YOU READ?

And Imp Plus did not tell what was felt in all the holes, for each was its own: holes that X-rayed and darted after the particles that had made the holes until then the particles met a match in other particles of contrary lean and each pair in a new mutual gradient vanished as if becoming the hole that had been darting after them: and what was left after the new mutual gradients of all the pairs of magnet particles was more than absence and other than attraction. Then he knew what it was. It was a radiance. Radiance he thought he had not prepared for. And so instead of reporting the packed shadows all around or asking was it true he could change attitude, Imp Plus answered only himself, not Ground, and knew as he answered *Travelling on light* that he was answering with the Sun.

But Ground had read Imp Plus again without a transmission from Imp Plus.

But what came to him was *Travel light*. Operation TL was Operation Travel Light.

When did Ground read what he thought, and when did Ground not?

But what was here was the thing. And Ground was not here. Imp Plus was here in the gradient grids of light. And what there was more of was not only glucose.

There was more all around.

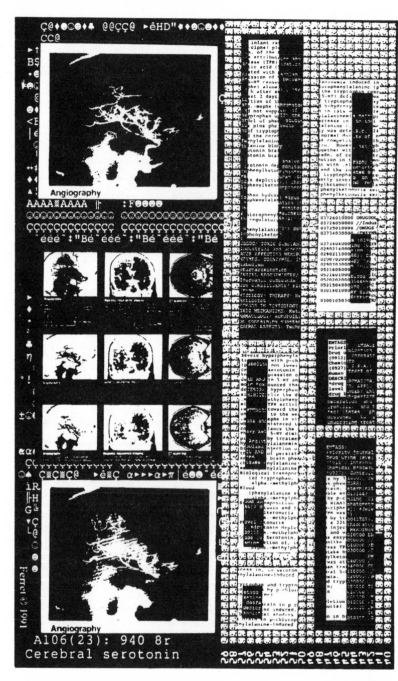

Angiography

Angiography

A106(23): 940 8r
Cerebral serotonin

Ferret © 1991

Ferret

Misha

Wire

Movement

#9

—for Geri & K.W.

Electronic signals crouch outside your door. Your hands are on fire. You shake them out of your wire hair. Recombinant viruses leap out at you from designer dumpsters. Your careful eyes glow. Metal belches stun your ears. The lead exhaust coats your lungs. Your hand brushes the scales of rust. You irradiated your fruit. Acid sterilizations rain down.

Her concertina. Her wire movement. Her ninth. Her mutilated masks. Her symphonic wings suspend her in a battlement. Her echappe tangled in wire.

She pulls her number from the barb. Stasis signals spear her performance eternally into the cosmos. Gnash the mesh that binds her. Quench the icy iron. Her mind is a matrix of non-stop digital flickerings.

Outside your door her horrible headdress performs wire movement. Her braids of wire reach to your feet. Fifty gallon hand drums. She ghost dances. You handgame out of sync.

They steal the coils. They dance pas de deux. The instruments are barbed. These children of science perform the ninth movement. In wire.

Ferret

Misha

Wire

for Two

Tims

—for Tim S. Vickers and Tim W. McNamara

Two silver wires cross his leather smile. Across the lawman's lips the wires run. His eyes arc in time with the wireless. Barbed tongues lap the battery acid, the black cats jumping nines and sixes. A silver badge keeps him wired. The wire of rapidograph connects the corners of his world with silver strands. Copper connections conduct the orchestras of electric musics, television static is all he wants. His wirecutter words pull back the skin, the flesh of his arm to reveal the colored wires. Red to green, yellow to black, blue to orange. The wire movement.

He crosses himself in the telephone wire. His suspicions slink away. The wire-trigger of his black gun rips violently from his hand. He's an electronic composer. His ears bleed wires, He chips away the seconds in real time. Tear out the midimaster, tear off the terrible mask, tear the hot wire from his charred hands. The karakura wheel away the remains of the sparking cords. The terminal gray roll of the monitor reveals his threadbare smile. Black and white meshes in mizuhiki. His face a cerecloth of dangerous wires.

One Tim wires the other red and white noshi—a tension song for two Tims.

Ted Mooney

From Easy
Travel to
Other Planets

Use of the Third Return Posture

Entering the apartment, they embrace. From where they are, in the foyer, she is able to see the enormous serigraph over the bed: a distant but unspeakably inviting view of puffy clouds seem from above, as though from an airplane. She wishes to go there, closes her eyes. He can smell maritime smells in her closely cropped hair. Why did she take the speed? he wonders. They kiss lengthily. Once the movement of their love-making has begun, they grow casual about it, as they have grown casual about physical distance, and they separate. Jeffrey goes into the kitchen and swallows twice from a bottle of gin. Melissa goes into the bedroom, shedding clothes. He thinks: we are getting very good at this, but life goes faster and faster. He puts the gin away and walks down the hall to the bedroom. Melissa is sitting naked on the blue rug. She has assumed the third return posture, also known as the memory-elimination posture. Selected sets of neurons begin tentatively to rearrange themselves. He squats before her and kisses her hairline, feeling refreshed, awaiting her refreshment. Her eyes perform little dances of fear and desire.

A Case of Information Sickness

On his way to Diego's, Jeffrey discovers a woman harmed by information excess. All the symptoms are present: bleeding from the nose and ears, vomiting, deliriously disconnected speech, apparent disorientation, and the desire to touch everything. She has a rubber mat rolled up under her arm and is walking around one of the soft, new park benches recently installed by the city, palpating it hungrily. A small crowd has collected around her, listening to her complicated monologue: Birds of Prey Cards, sunspot soufflé, Antarctic unemployment. Jeffrey hesitates. I've never seen one so far gone, he thinks. But, judging her young enough to warrant hope, he gently takes the rubber mat from the woman, unrolls it upon the pavement, and helps her to assume the memory-elimination posture. After a minute, the bleeding stops. "I was on my way to dance class," she says to him, still running her ravening fingers over his leather coat sleeve, "when suddenly I was dazzled. I couldn't tell where one thing left off and the next began." She is rather pretty. Jeffrey explains that he believes information sickness, like malaria, recurs unpredictably. "Please let me through," comes a voice. "I'm this lady's husband." The woman and her husband thank Jeffrey profusely and he leaves.

James O'Barr

RICHO WAS FAIR THAT WAY.

OVER BY THE HOLO GAMES A BUNCH OF RAGGEDY BOYS AND SOME BOLT THROWERS WERE LOOKING AT EACH OTHER HARD.

RICHO WOULDN'T LET IT ESCALATE TOO FAR: AFTER THE BOLTS DROPPED A DOZEN RAGS HE'D PROBABLY STEP IN WITH A BIRD BRAIN STUN GUN.

AFTER ABOUT A YEAR THE JUICE BAG I'D BEEN WAITING FOR CAME IN AND HAD A SEAT.

HE CALLED HIMSELF LEOPARD BUT HE WAS JUST ANOTHER PEDESTRIAN PUNK WASTING O² MOLECULES.

HE WAS FLANKED BY TWO PAPER WEIGHT A-STEROID BOYS.

MY PAL, SKINNY D HAD OFFERED ME FIFTEEN HUNDRED SQUARE-UP DOLLARS TO DUST LEO.

MAN, THIS JUST WASN'T HIS DAY.

HE SAT RIGHT NEXT TO THE DOOR.

THE DRUGS WERE PEAKING.

AND I'D LOADED THE VACH WITH 9MM BLUE TIP FLESHETTES.

STRIKE THREE, FUCKER.

EXPLAINED HOW LEO HAD GOTTEN INTO THE BABY FLESH MARKET, SELLING TEN YEAR OLD KIDS TO PAIN JUNKIES.

AND SKINNY D'S LITTLE SISTER HAD GONE MISSING.

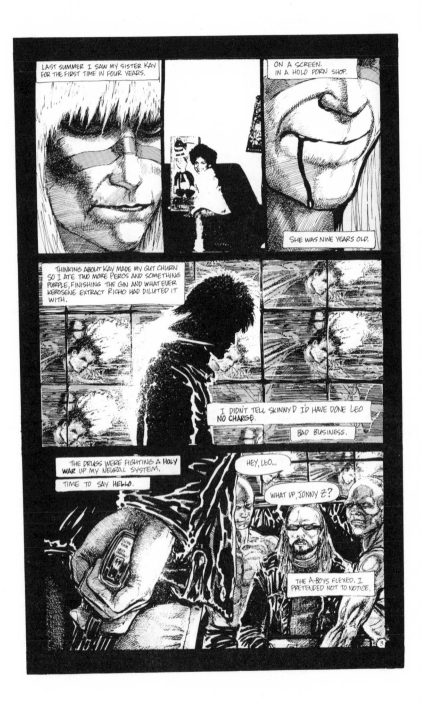

LAST SUMMER I SAW MY SISTER KAY FOR THE FIRST TIME IN FOUR YEARS.

ON A SCREEN. IN A HOLO PORN SHOP.

SHE WAS NINE YEARS OLD.

THINKING ABOUT KAY MADE MY GUT CHURN SO I ATE TWO MORE PERCS AND SOMETHING PURPLE, FINISHING THE GIN AND WHATEVER KEROSENE EXTRACT RICHO HAD DILUTED IT WITH.

I DIDN'T TELL SKINNY D I'D HAVE DONE LEO NO CHARGE.

BAD BUSINESS.

THE DRUGS WERE FIGHTING A HOLY WAR UP MY NEURAL SYSTEM.

TIME TO SAY HELLO.

HEY, LEO...

WHAT UP, JONNY Z?

THE A-BOYS FLEXED. I PRETENDED NOT TO NOTICE.

Thomas Pynchon

From

The Crying

of Lot 49

San Narciso lay further south, near L.A. Like many named places in California it was less an identifiable city than a grouping of concepts— census tracts, special purpose bond-issue districts, shopping nuclei, all overlaid with access roads to its own freeway. But it had been Pierce's domicile, and headquarters: the place he'd begun his land speculating in ten years ago, and so put down the plinth course of capital on which everything afterward had been built, however rickety or grotesque, toward the sky; and that, she supposed, would set the spot apart, give it an aura. But if there was any vital difference between it and the rest of Southern California, it was invisible on first glance. She drove into San Narciso on a Sunday, in a rented Impala. Nothing was happening. She looked down a slope, needing to squint for the sunlight, onto a vast sprawl of houses which had grown up all together, like a well-tended crop, from the dull brown earth; and she thought of the time she'd opened a transistor radio to replace a battery and seen her first printed circuit. The ordered swirl of houses and streets, from this high angle, sprang at her now with the same unexpected, astonish- ing clarity as the circuit card had. Though she knew even less about radios than about Southern Californians, there were to both outward patterns a hieroglyphic sense of concealed meaning, of an intent to communicate. There'd seemed no limit to what the printed circuit could have told her (if she had tried to find out); so in her first minute of San Narciso, a revelation also trembled just past the threshold of her understanding. Smog hung all round the horizon, the sun on the bright beige countryside was painful; she and the Chevy seemed parked at the centre of an odd, religious instant. As if, on some other frequency, or

John Bergin

out of the eye of some whirlwind rotating too slow for her heated skin even to feel the centrifugal coolness of, words were being spoken. She suspected that much. She thought of Mucho, her husband, trying to believe in his job. Was it something like this he felt, looking through the soundproof glass at one of his colleagues with a headset clamped on and cueing the next record with movements stylized as the handling of chrism, censer, chalice might be for a holy man, yet really tuned in to the voice, voices, the music, its message, surrounded by it, digging it, as were all the faithful it went out to; did Mucho stand outside Studio A looking in, knowing that even if he could hear it he couldn't believe in it?

Rudy Rucker

From Software

Chapter Three

Riding his hydrogen-cycle home from work Friday afternoon, Sta-Hi began to feel sick. It was the acid coming on. He'd taken some Black Star before turning in his cab for the weekend. That was an hour? Or two hours ago? The digits on his watch winked at him, meaningless little sticks. He had to keep moving or he'd fall through the crust.

On his left the traffic flickered past, on his right the ocean was calling through the cracks between buildings. He couldn't face going to his room. Yesterday he'd torn up the mattress.

Sta-Hi cut the wheel right and yanked back to jump the curb. He braked and the little hydrogen burner pooted to a stop. Chain the mother up. *Gang bang the chain gang. Spare spinach change.* A different voice was going in each of his ears.

Some guy stuck his head out a second floor window and stared down. Giving Sta-Hi a long, lingering leer. For a second it felt like looking at himself. *Crunch, grind.* He needed to mellow out for sure. It was coming on too fast and noisy. The place he'd parked in front of, the Lido Hotel, was a brainsurfer hangout with a huge bar in the lobby. *Mondo mambo. Is it true blondes have more phine?*

He got a beer at the counter and walked through to the ocean end of the lounge. Group of teenage 'surfers over there, sharing a spray-can of z-gas. One of them kept rocking back in his chair and laughing big *hyuck-hyucks* from his throat. Stupid gasbag.

Sta-Hi sat down by himself, pulled twitchingly at the beer. Too fast. Air in his stomach now. Try to belch it up, *uh, uh, uh.* His mouth filled with thick white foam. Outside the window a line of pelicans flew by, following the water's edge.

There wasn't good air in the lounge. Sweet z. The 'surfer kids sliding looks over at him. Cop? Fag? Thief? *Uh, uh, uh.* More foam. Where did it all come from? He leaned over his plastic cup of beer, spitting, topping it up.

He left the drink and went outside. His acid trips were always horrible bummers. But why? There was no reason a mature and experienced person couldn't mellow out was there? Why else would they still sell the stuff after all these years? *Poems are made like fools by me. But only God can tear your brain into tiny little pieces.*

"Wiggly," Sta-Hi murmured to himself, reflexively, "Stuzzy. And this too. And this too." *And two three?* He felt sick, sick bad. A vortex sensation at the pit of his stomach. Fat stomach, layered with oil pools, decayed dinosaur meat, nodules of yellow chicken fat. The ocean breeze pushed a lank, greasy strand of hair down into Sta-Hi's eye. *Bits and pieces, little bits and pieces.*

He walked towards the water, massaging his gut with both hands, trying to rub the fat away. The funny thing was that he looked skinny. He hardly ever ate. But the fat was still there, hiding, scrambled-egg agglutinations of cholesterol. Degenerative connective tissue.

Oysters had cholesterol. Once he'd filled a beer bottle with corn-oil and passed it to a friend. It would be nice to drown. But the paperwork!

Sta-Hi sat down and got his clothes off, except for the underwear. Windows all up and down the beach, perverts behind them, scoping the little flap in his underwear. He dug a hole and covered his clothes with sand. It felt good to claw the sand, forcing the grains under his fingernails. *Deep crack rub. Do that smee goo?* Dental floss. He kept thinking someone was standing behind him.

Utterly exhausted, Sta-Hi flopped onto his back and closed his eyes. He saw a series of rings, sights he had to line up on that distant yet intimate white center, the brain's own blind spot. He felt like an oyster trying to see up through the water to the sun. Cautiously he opened his shell a bit wider.

There was a sudden thunder in his ear, a smell of rotten flesh. *Ha schnurf gabble O.* Kissy lick. A black poodle at his face, a shiteater for sure. Sta-Hi sat up sharply and pushed the puppy away. It nipped his hand with needlelike milk-teeth.

A blonde chick stood twenty meters away, smiling back at her pup. "Come on, Sparky!" She yelled like a bell.

The dog barked and tossed its head, ran off. The girl was still smiling. *Aren't I cute with my doggy?* "Jesus," Sta-Hi moaned. He wished he could melt, just fucking *die* and get it over with. Everything was too wiggly, too general, too specific.

He stood up, burning out thousands of braincells with the effort. He had to get in the water, get cooled off. The chick watched him wade in. He didn't look, but he could feel her eyes on his little flap. *A spongy morsel.*

A quiver of fish phased past. Hyper little mothers, uptightness hardwired right into their nervous systems. He squatted down in the waist-deep water, imagining his brain a jelly-fish floating beneath the Florida sun. Limp, a jelly-fish with wave-waved tendrils.

Uh, uh, uh.

He let the saltwater wash the light-tan foam-spit off his lips. The little bubbles moved among the white water-bubbles, forming and bursting, each a tiny universe.

His waistband felt too tight. Slip off the undies?

Sta-Hi slid his eyes back and forth. The chick was hanging around down the beach a ways. Throwing a stick in the surf, "Come *on*, Sparky!" Each time the dog got the stick it would prance stiff-legged around her. Was she trying to bug him or what? Of course it could be that she hadn't really noticed him in the first place. But that still left all the perverts with spyglasses.

He waded out deeper, till the water reached his neck. Looking around once more, he slipped off his tight underwear and relaxed. Jellyfish jellytime jellypassed. The ocean stank.

He swam back towards shore. The saltwater lined his nostrils with tinfoil.

When he got to shallower water he stood, and then cried out in horror. He'd stepped on a skate. Harmless, but the blitzy twitch of the livery fleshmound snapping out from underfoot was just too . . . too much like a thought, a word made flesh. The word was "AAAAAUUGH!" He ran out of the water, nancing knees high, trying somehow to run on top.

"You're naked," someone said and laughed *hmmm-hmmm-hmmm.* His undies! It was the chick with the dog. High above, spyglasses stiffened behind dirty panes.

"Yeah, I . . ." Sta-Hi hesitated. He didn't want to go back into the big toilet for more electric muscle-spasm foot-shocks. Suddenly he remembered a foot-massager he'd given his Dad one Christmas: Vibrating yellow plastic arches.

The little poodle jumped and snapped at his penis. The girl tittered. Laughing breasts.

Bent half double, Sta-Hi trucked back and forth across the sand in high speed until he saw a trouser-cuff. He scrabbled out the jeans and T-shirt, and slipped them on. The poodle was busy at the edge of the water.

"Squa tront," Sta-Hi muttered, "Spa fon." The sounds of thousands of little bubble-pops floated off the sea. The sun was going down, and the grains of sand crackled as they cooled. Each tiny sound demanded attention, *undivided attention.*

"You must really be phased," the girl said cheerfully. "What did you do with your bathingsuit?"

"I . . . an eel got it." The angles on the chick's face kept shifting. He couldn't figure out what she looked like. Why risk waking up with a peroxide pig? He dropped onto the sand, stretched out again, let his eyes close. Turdbreath thundered in his ear, and then he heard their footsteps leave. His headbones could pick up the skrinching.

Sta-Hi breathed out a shuddering sigh of exhaustion. If he could ever just get the time to cut power. . . . He sighed again and let his muscles go limp. The light behind his eyes was growing. His head rolled slowly to one side.

A film came to mind, a film of someone dying on a beach. His head rolled slowly to one side. And then he was still. *Real death.* Slowly to one side. *Last motion.*

Dying, Sta-Hi groaned and sat up again. He couldn't handle. . . . The chick and her dog were fifty meters off. He started running after them, clumsily at first, but then fleetly, floatingly!

Chapter Five

The prick of a needle woke Sta-Hi up. Muddy dreams . . . just brown mud all night long. He tried to rub his eyes. His hands wouldn't move. Oh, no, not a paralysis dream again. But something had pricked him?

He opened his eyes. His body seemed to have disappeared. He was just a head resting on a round red table. People looking at him. Greasers. And the chick he'd been with last. . . .

"Are you awake?" she said with brittle sweetness. She had a black eye.

Sta-Hi didn't answer right away. He had gone home with that chick, yeah. She had a cottage down the beach. And then they'd gotten drunk together on synthetic bourbon whiskey. He'd gotten drunk anyway, and must have blacked-out. Last thing he remembered was breaking something . . . her hollowcaster. Crunching the silicon chips underfoot and shouting. Shouting what?

"You'll feel better in a minute," the chick added in that same falsely bright tone. He heard her poodle whimpering from across the room. He had a memory of throwing it, arcing it along a flat, fuzzy parabolic path. And now he remembered slugging the chick too.

One of the men at the table shifted in his chair. He wore mirrorshades and had short hair. He had his shirt off. It seemed like another hot day.

The man's foot scuffed Sta-Hi's shin. So Sta-Hi had a body after all. It was just that his body was tied up under the table and his head was sticking out through a hole in the table-top. The table was split and had hinges on one side, and a hook-and-eye on the other.

"Stocks and bonds," Sta-Hi said finally. There was a nasty-looking implement lying on the table. It plugged into the wall. He attempted a smile. "What's the story? You mad about the . . . the hollowcaster? I'll give you mine." He hoped the dog wasn't hurt bad. At least it was well enough to be whimpering.

No one but the chick wanted to meet his eyes. It was like they were ashamed of what they were going to do to him. The stuff they'd shot him up with was taking hold. As his brain speeded up, the scene around him seemed to slow down. The man with no shirt stood up with dreamlike slowness and walked across the room. He had words tattooed on his back. Some kind of stupid rap about hell. It was too hard to read. The man had gained so much weight since getting tattooed that the words were all pulled down on both sides.

"What do you want?" Sta-Hi said again. "What are you going to do to me?" Counting the chick there were five of them. Three men and two women. The other woman had stringy red hair dyed green. The chick he'd picked up was the only one who looked at all middle-class. Date bait.

"Y'all want some killah-weed?" One of the men drawled. He had a pimp mustache and a pockmarked face. He wore a chromed tire-chain around his neck with his name in big letters. BERDOO. Also hanging from the chain was a little mesh pouch full of hand-rolled cigarettes.

"Not me," Sta-Hi said. "I'm high on life." No one laughed.

The big man with no shirt came back across the room. He held five cheap steel spoons. "We really gonna do it, Phil?" the girl with green hair asked him. "We really gonna do it?"

Berdoo passed a krystal-joint to his neighbor, a bald man with half his teeth missing. Exactly half the teeth gone, so that one side of the face was flaccid and caved in, while the other was still fresh and beefy. He took a long hit and picked up the machine that was lying on the table.

"Take the lid off, Haf'N'Haf," the chick with the black eye urged. "Open the bastard up."

"We really gonna do it!" the green-haired girl exclaimed, and giggled shrilly. "I ain't never ate no live brain before!"

"It's a stuzzy high, Rainbow," Phil told her. With the fat and the short hair he looked stupid, but his way of speaking was precise and confident. He seemed to be the leader. "This ought to be a good brain, too. Full of chemicals, I imagine."

Haf'N'Haf seemed to be having some trouble starting the little cutting machine up. It was a variable heat-blade. They were going to cut off the top of Sta-Hi's skull and eat his brain with those cheap steel spoons. He would be able to watch them . . . at first.

Someone started screaming. Someone tried to stand up, but he was tied too tightly. The variable blade was on now, set at one centimeter. The thickness of the skull.

Sta-Hi threw his head back and forth wildly as Haf'N'Haf leaned towards him. There was no way to read the ruined face's expression.

"Hold still, damn you!" the chick with the black eye shouted. "It's no good if we have to knock you out!"

Sta-Hi didn't really hear her. His mind had temporarily . . . snapped. He just kept screaming and thrashing his head around. The sound of his shrill voice was like a lattice around him. He tried to weave the lattice thicker.

The little pimp with the tire-chain went and got a towel from the bathroom. He wedged it around Sta-Hi's neck and under his chin to keep the head steady. Sta-Hi screamed louder, higher.

"Stuff his *mayouth*," the green-haired girl cried. "He's yellin' and all."

"No," Phil said. "The noise is like . . . part of the trip. *Wave* with it, baby. The Chinese used to do this to monkeys. It's so wiggly when you spoon out the speech-centers and the guy's tongue stops moving. Just all at—" He stopped and the flesh of his face moved in a smile.

Haf'N'Haf leaned forward again. There was a slight smell of singed flesh as the heat-blade dug in over Sta-Hi's right eyebrow. Attracted by the food smell, the little poodle came stiffly trotting across the room. It tried to hop over the heat-blade's electric cord, but didn't quite make it. The plug popped out of the wall.

Haf'N'Haf uttered a muffled, lisping exclamation.

"He says git the dog outta here," Berdoo interpreted. "He don't think hit's sanitary with no dawg in here."

Sullenly, the chick with the black eye got up to get the dog. The sudden pain over his eyebrow had brought Sta-Hi back to rationality. Somewhere in there he had stopped screaming. If there were any neighbors they would have heard him by now.

He thought hard. The heat-blade would cauterize the wound as it went. That meant he wouldn't be bleeding when they took the top of his skull off. So what? *So the fuck what?*

Another wave of wild panic swept over him. He strained upward so hard that the table shifted half a meter. The edge of the hole in the table began cutting into the side of his neck. He couldn't breathe! He saw spots and the room darkened. . . .

"He's choking!" Phil cried. He jumped to his feet and pushed the table back across the uneven floor. The table screeched and vibrated.

Sta-Hi threw himself upward again, before Haf'N'Haf could get the heat-blade restarted. Anything for time, no matter how pointless. But the vibrating of the table had knocked open the little hook-and-eye latch. The two halves of the table yawned open, and Sta-Hi fell over onto the floor.

His feet were tied together and his hands were tied behind his back. He had time to notice that the people at the table were wearing brightly colored sneakers with alphabets around the edges. The Little Kidders. He'd always thought the newscasters had made them up.

Someone was hammering at the door, harder and harder. Five pairs of kids' sneakers scampered out of the room. Sta-Hi heard a window open, and then the door splintered. More feet. Shiny black lace-up shoes. Cop shoes.

Lucius Shepard

From Life
During Wartime

One afternoon a couple of weeks before he was scheduled to leave for
La Ceiba, Izaguirre gave him a final booster injection of the drug. The
shot left him achy and nervous, the inside of his head tender-feeling;
and that night, unable to sleep, plagued by flash hallucinations of
unfamiliar streets and people's faces that melted away too quickly for
him to identify, he wandered through the hotel, ending up in Izaguirre's
office, which was never kept locked. It was a small room just off the
lobby, outfitted with a desk, two chairs, a bookcase, and a filing
cabinet. Mingolla sat in the doctor's chair and went through the files,
too distracted to understand much of what he was reading, ignoring the
typed material—the letters seemed to be scurrying around like ants—
and concentrating on the marginalia penned in Izaguirre's florid script.
He continued to have hallucinations, and when he ran across a note
describing Izaguirre's concern that he might have given Mingolla too
large a dosage in the booster shot, the hallucinations grew more vivid.
He saw part of a mural on a pebbled wall, a woman's brown arm
hanging off the edge of a mattress, rendered with a fey sensuality that
put him in mind of Degas, and accompanying it, oppressive heat and
the smell of dust and decay. This hallucination had the compelling
clarity of a premonition, yet was so much more detailed than his usual
premonitions that he became frightened. He stood up, felt queasy,
dizzy, and shook his head. The walls darkened, whirled, brightened
again, and he closed his eyes, trying to quell his nausea. Put his hand
on the desk, and touched warm skin. Opened his eyes, saw a bag lady
staring up at him from a curb, her fat cheeks webbed with broken
capillaries, her nose bulbous, a scarf knotted so tightly under her chin
it warped her ruddy face into a knobbly vegetable shape.

"This ain't America," she said dolefully. "America wouldn't treat nobody like this."

Mingolla staggered, had an incoherent impression of orange sky, a night sky above a city, diseased-looking palm trees with brown fronds and scales on their trunks, and rain-slick asphalt reflecting nebular blurs of neon, and bars with glowing words above them. Sinewy music whose rhythms seemed to be charting the fluctuations of his nerves. Somebody bumped into him, said, "Whoops," an oily fat man with a moon face, sticking out his pink meat of a tongue on which a cobra had been tattooed, then smiling and mincing off to a world where he was beautiful.

"See what I tol' ya," said the bag lady.

Gaudily dressed crowds shuffling in and out of the low glass-front buildings, a history of the American perverse. . . . Hookers in day-glo hotpants, leather boys, floozies in slit skirts, topless teenage girls with ANGEL stamped on their left breasts, and all the faces pale in the baking heat, characters in a strange language, circular dominoes with significant arrangements of dark eyes and mouths, borne along on the necks of fleshy machines, one thought per brain like a prize in a plastic egg, doing a slow drag down the devil's row of bars and sex shops and arcades, under the numinous clouded light, under the smears of red and yellow words melting into the air, their voices a gabble, their laughter a bad noise, the rotten yolk of their senses streaking the night, and Mingolla knew the bag lady was wrong, that this was most definitely America, the void with tourist attractions, the Southern California bottomland experience, and somewhere or everywhere, maybe lurking behind a billboard, was a giant red-skinned flabby pig of a Satan, his gut hanging over his tights, horny and giggling, watching through a peephole the great undressing of his favorite bitch, the Idea of Order. . . .

The bag lady shook her head in despair. "We need a new Columbus, that's what we need."

Lewis Shiner

Stoked

Skate or Die !

I'm way into the music when my dad starts pounding at the door. It's Suicidal Tendencies doing "Possessed to Skate." I unlock the door and he goes over first thing to turn it down.

My dad is like losing all his hair in front so he lets it grow out over his collar in back. He has to do it, see, because he wants everybody to know that even though he's a lawyer and has a Mercedes and everything he didn't sell out. As if anybody cared. A hippie is still a hippie, even if he wears ties and drives a Mercedes. Even if he's your dad.

So he says did you take your skateboard to school again.

I tell him NO.

Don't lie to me Bobby, he says. Mister Woodrow called me today and said you and some of those other skate punks were fighting at lunch.

I don't think he's ever called me a skate punk before. I kind of like it. I say we weren't fighting we were thrashing.

He shakes his head. He sits on the edge of the bed and gets real quiet for a second. He says how I'm only fifteen and in a couple more years I can do what I want but right now I have to do what he says. Like him being all reasonable and shit is supposed to make this big difference to me. Then he looks around the room, at the Ratt and Mötley Crüe posters and the dirty clothes on the floor and the tapes everywhere and the schoolbooks where I threw them in the corner. Then he shakes his head some more and tells me how hard he's trying to relate.

So I just tell him two years is more than I've got to spare. Because in no time at all I'm going to turn into a brain-dead, dick-dead old poser like him. Which he is too stupid to understand on account of his head being so far up his hippie ass, just like that borf Woodrow.

Well, I don't really say that but I'm thinking it, loud and clear.

I know he's not my real father anyway. I was left here by mistake by this time machine from the future. So who cares what he thinks.

After everybody else is asleep including my worthless big brother, another fucking lawyer in the making, I go into the kitchen and get down the Mason jar where the old lady keeps her cash. She does these hand-painted T-shirts and sells them and keeps all the dinero in the kitchen. We always borrow a buck or two because she never knows what's there. This time I take the whole wad. It's about fifty bills, which is okay. I get my blaster and some tapes, some Painted Willie and some Dead Kennedys and some Suicidals. I put another pair of jams and a clean T-shirt and boxers in a plastic Alpha Beta bag. Then I get my stick and stench on out of there for good.

Once I get the skate under me everything is cool. Better than cool. I'm on top of the world and it's turning under me and I'm the only still thing in the universe. This is something skaters know that assholes like my dad never will. Every time there's a new subdivision goes up he's pissing and moaning about all the trees getting cut. He's never sla-lomed across a floor slab between the little copper tubes or caught air coming up out of a half-pipe where the new sewers are going in. Concrete is radical. Concrete is the future. You don't cry about it, man, you skate on it.

Sean's house is two miles away. I make it in about ten minutes. The lights are off in her room so I go over the chain link, holding the board up over my head like I'm doing an invert on a skatepark ramp. Her asshole dog, some kind of fuzzy white little runt, starts getting all aggro and barking and everything. I make like I'm going to brain the little bastard and it backs away growling.

I knock on her window until she opens it and puts her face up to the screen. She's wearing just this thin T-shirt and the cool air makes her nipples get hard, which makes me get hard too. Her hair is all pushed up on one side where she's been sleeping on it. I tell her to come on out.

She says why.

I tell her I'm cutting out.

She says to meet her out front in two minutes.

It's more like ten but it doesn't matter, it's not like I have to be anywhere else. It's March and there's all this stuff blooming all over the place. See? Plenty of trees and gardens and shit to make everybody sneeze and get their hormones all worked up.

She hasn't got her skate when she comes out. There's a lot of streetlights and I can see she's put on lipstick and combed out her hair and drawn stuff around her eyes. She's only like fourteen but she's pretty rad. Her hair is kind of short and bleached out on the ends. She'd spike it but her mom would kill her.

I tell her to go back and get her skate.

She asks am I serious. Am I really cutting out.

I tell her me and this small-time little town are history.

She says she doesn't know if she's up for anything that heavy.

I tell her to come along for a while and she can make up her mind later.

She decides it's a nice night out so okay.

She has to open the garage to get her stick. It makes some serious noise but her mom doesn't wake up. She just leaves the door open and we skate away.

The streets are really empty. It's like they've dropped the Big One and all the old farts and assholes have blown each other away. There's nothing left but me and Sean and a million miles of concrete. I see a car ahead and I take her hand. We kickturn together into an alley and across to another street. Only mutants have cars after the Big One. They'll kill us if they can or use us in their weird mutie ceremonies, stealing our eyeballs and fingernails. But they can't catch us. We can skate where their fat metal and rubber cars can't go.

There's this big culvert in a park over by the college. Kids get lost and drown in there sometimes. When it's dry the skaters go there to get vertical. It's too dark to skate it now but there's light enough to see the top of the pipe fifteen feet overhead. There's a lot of trash on the floor. Busted bottles, an old sleeping bag, beat-up copies of *Penthouse* and *Thrasher*, cigarette packs, donut boxes. We clear off some room and lie down on the sleeping bag.

Sean's mouth is warm and wet and tastes like the air outside. She opens it wide and works her tongue around mine. I put my hand up inside her T-shirt. She doesn't have very big tits but like I said, she's only fourteen. She's breathing hard and for a second I think she might really do it.

I know she's done it before. She used to hang with this guy Steve, the raddest skater in town. I'm talking Hawk, Caballero, Guerrero, that good. There's this unfinished overpass out on Highway 207, about a twenty-foot drop. Steve's gone off it twice and rode it out both times. The other kids who tried it really slammed. I'm talking busted bones and hospital city.

I think Sean was pretty in love with him. The word is he did her a few times and kind of lost interest. He's seventeen and he's got his own Trans Am and plays guitar in a band. The girls all hang around him and everything. He doesn't care that much though. Between skating and girls, skating is number one with him. Sean was fucked up about it for a long time.

I've got both hands up inside her shirt and I'm wondering what's next when she turns her head and says Bobby don't. She says it's late. Says she has to get back home.

I can't believe she wants to go back. Back to her mom that she hates and her mom's boyfriends that are always getting drunk and trying to grab her ass. I tell her she could stay there with me and not go back to school or her mom or anything.

She asks am I crazy. Am I going to live in a hole in the ground for the rest of my life.

Better than going back, I tell her.

She says I really like you Bobby. But you have this problem with reality. You're underage. There's gonna be cops and truant officers and everybody else looking for you.

Then I'll just have to keep moving, I tell her.

What I'm trying to say is this is like the last time we're going to be together and I think we should really do it this time. But she's already walking away.

She stops at the end of the tunnel and says see you Bobby.

Maybe you will, I say, and maybe you won't.

She just shakes her head and says grow up.

I say what's the point.

She acts like she doesn't hear me and just walks away, carrying her board by the front truck. I hit the concrete wall with my fist. The pain pulls me back in where I can think again. I lie back and listen to the tape. Like the Suicidals say, won't fall in love today.

The tape is over. Suddenly I think maybe the cops are already after me. They could shoot tear gas into the tunnel and be waiting with M-16s to cut me down. I stash the box and my extra clothes deep in the tunnel where I can come back for them later. Then I pump up the sides of the pipe a couple of times to get some speed. I come out crouching low, arms up to protect my head. I catch some air as I shoot out into the drainage ditch, climbing high and fast over the concrete embankment, heading for the highway.

There's lights behind me. They must have called in some SWAT teams, probably even the National Guard. I play it fast and loose. I'm not scared at all. This is my town and I see it through skater's eyes. I see things the cops have never looked for. The paved medians and retaining walls, the sidewalks and storm sewers and spillways. I can skate them all. No cop can ever touch me.

I'm all alone when I blast under the Loop on the north end of the city. I'm shredding down the middle of empty, four-lane concrete. The moon is up and there are truly gnarly country sounds all around me, insects and owls and wild dogs. It's cold as hell and I'm not paying any attention where I'm going. But I don't care. I'm stoked to the max, wild and free.

Up ahead I can see the barricades for the Highway 207 overpass. And at the same time these lights come up behind me.

At first I think it's Steve's Trans Am. Then I realize they look like ordinary lights but they're not. That's just part of the disguise. What it is is a UFO come to pick me up. There's only one problem, see, which is they can't set it down. That's the thing about UFOs. They want to take me with them but I have to somehow get up to where they are.

I boost off the barricades to get more speed. Speed is the thing. I can see where the ramp ends in twisted rebar. The empty highway is down below it in the dark. The lights are behind me and I can hear voices calling out my name. One of them sounds like Sean. I tell myself it isn't, it's just the whine of the UFO. The approach is downhill and I get way low to cut the air resistance. There's nothing left to think about, only action, the way it should be.

And then I'm flying, and it's just me and the wind.

John Shirley

Wolves

of the

Plateau

Nine A.M., and Jerome-X wanted a smoke. He didn't smoke, but he wanted one in here, and he could see how people went into prison non-smokers, came out doing two packs a day. Maybe had to get their brains rewired to get off it. Which was ugly, he'd been rewired once to get off *sink*, synthetic cocaine, and he'd felt like a processor with a glitch for a month after that.

He pictured his thoughts like a little train, zipping around the cigarette-burnt graffiti YOU FUCKED NOW and GASMAN WAS HERE and GASMAN IS AN IDIOTMO. The words were stippled on the dull pink ceiling in umber burn-spots. Jerome wondered who Gasman was and what they'd put him in prison for.

He yawned. He hadn't slept much the night before. It took a long time to learn to sleep in prison. He wished he'd upgraded his chip so he could use it to activate his sleep endorphins. But that was a grade above what he'd been able to afford—and *way* above the kind of brain-chips he'd been dealing. He wished he could turn off the light-panel, but it was sealed in.

There was a toilet and a broken water fountain in the cell. There were also four bunks, but he was alone in this static place of watery blue light and faint pink distances. The walls were salmon-colored garbage blocks. The words singed into the ceiling were blurred and impotent.

Almost noon, his stomach rumbling, Jerome was still lying on his back on the top bunk when the trashcan said, "Eric Wexler, re-ma-a-in on your bunk while the ne-ew prisoner ente-e-ers the cell!"

Wexler? Oh, yeah. They thought his name was Wexler. The fake ID program.

He heard the cell door slide open; he looked over, saw the trashcan ushering a stocky Chicano guy into lockup. The trashcan was a stumpy metal cylinder with four camera lenses, a retractable plastic arm, and a gun muzzle that could fire a Taser charge, rubber bullets, tear gas pellets, or .45 caliber rounds. It was supposed to use the .45 only in extreme situations but the can was battered, it whined when it moved, its voice was warped. When they got like that you didn't fuck with them, they'd mix up the rubber bullets with the .45 caliber.

The door sucked itself shut, the trashcan whined away down the hall, its rubber wheels squeaking once with every revolution. Jerome heard a tinny cymbal crash as someone, maybe trying to get the trashcan to shoot at a guy in the next cell, threw a tray at it. Followed by some echoey shouting and a distorted admonishment from the trashcan. The Chicano guy laughed.

"'Sappenin'" Jerome said, sitting up on the bed. He was grateful for the break in the monotony.

"*Qué pasa, cabrône?* You like the top bunk, huh? Thas good."

"I can read the ceiling better from up here. About ten seconds worth of reading matter. It's all I got. You can have the lower bunk."

"You fuckin'-*A* I can." But there was no real aggression in his tone. Jerome thought about turning on his chip, checking the guy's subliminals, his somatic signals, going for a model of probable aggression index; or maybe project for deception. He could be an undercover cop: Jerome hadn't given them his dealer; hadn't bargained at all.

But he decided against it. Some jails had scanners for unauthorized chip output. Better not use it unless he had to. And his gut told him this guy was only a threat if he felt threatened. His gut was right almost as often as his brain-chip.

The Chicano was thick bodied, maybe five foot six, a good five inches shorter than Jerome but probably outweighed him by fifty pounds. His face had Indian angles and small jet eyes. He was wearing printout gray-blue prison jams, #6631; they'd let him keep his hairnet. Jerome had never understood the Chicano hairnet, never had the balls to ask about it. The Chicano was standing by the plexigate, hands shoved in his pockets, staring at Jerome, looking like he was trying to place him.

Jerome was pleased. He liked to be recognized, except by people who could arrest him.

"You put your hands in the pockets of those paper pants, they'll rip and in LA County they don't give you any more for three days," Jerome advised him.

"Yeah? Shit." The Chicano took his hands carefully out of his pockets. "I don't want my *huevos* hanging out, people think I'm advertising some shit. You not a faggot, right?"

"Nope."

"Good. How come I know you? When I *don't* know you."

Jerome grinned. "From television. You saw my tag. Jerome-X."

"Ohhhh yeah. Jerome-X. You got one of those little transers? Chop into transmissions with your own shit?"

"Had. They confiscated it."

"That why you here? Video graffiti?"

"I wish—then I'd be out in a couple months. No, man. Illegal augs."

"Hey, man! Me too!"

"You?" Jerome couldn't conceal his surprise. You didn't see a lot of the brown brothers doing illegal augmentation. They generally didn't like people dicking with their brains.

"What, you think a guy from East LA can't use augmentation?"

"No, no. I know lots of Hispanic guys that use it," Jerome lied.

"Ooooh, he says *Hispanic*, that gotta nice sound." Overtones of danger.

Jerome hastily changed the direction of the conversation. "You never been in the big lockups where they use paper jammies?"

"No, just the city jail once. They didn't have those fucking screw machines either. Hey, you Jerome, my name's Jessie. Actually it's Jesus—" he pronounced it Hay-soo "—but people they, you know. . . . You got any smokes? No? Shit. Okay, I adjust."

He sat on the edge of the bed, to one side of Jerome's dangling legs, and tilted his head forward. He reached under his hairnet, and under what turned out to be a hairplug, and pulled a chip from a jack unit set into the base of his skull.

Jerome stared. "Goddamn, their probes really *are* busted."

Jessie frowned over the chip. There was a little blood on it. The jack unit was leaking. Cheap installation. "No, they ain't busted, there's a guy working the probe, he's paid off . . . letting everyone through for a couple of days 'cause some mob *vatos* are coming in and he don't know exactly which ones they are."

"I thought sure they were going to find my unit," Jerome said. "The strip search didn't turn it but I figured the prison probes would and that'd be another year on my sentence. But they didn't." Neither one of them thinking of throwing away the chips. It'd be like cutting out an eye.

"Same story here. We both lucky."

Jessie put the microprocessing chip in his mouth, the way people did with their contact lenses, to clean it, lubricate it.

"Jack hurt?" Jerome asked.

Jessie took the chip out, looked at it a moment on his fingertip; it was smaller than a contact lens, a sliver of silicon and gallium arsenide with, probably, 1,500,000 nanotransistors of engineered protein molecules sunk into it, maybe more. "No it don't hurt yet. But if it's leaking, it fuckin' *will* hurt man." He said something else in Spanish, shaking his head. He slipped it back into his jack-in unit, and tapped it with the thumbnail of his right hand. So that was where the activation mouse was: under the thumbnail. Jerome's was in a knuckle.

Jessie rocked slightly, just once, sitting up on his bunk, which meant the chip had engaged and he was getting a readout. They tended to feed back into your nervous system a little at first, make you twitch once or twice; if they weren't properly insulated they could make you crap your pants.

"That's okay," Jessie said, relaxing. "That's better." The chip inducing his brain to secrete some vasopressin, contract the veins, simulate the effect of nicotine. It worked for awhile, till you could get cigarettes. A highgrade chip could do some numbing, if you were hung up on *sim*, synthetic morphine, and couldn't score. But that was Big Scary. You could turn yourself off that way, permanently. You better be doing fine adjusting.

Jerome thought about the hypothetical chip scanners. Maybe he should object to the guy using his chip here. But what the Chicano was doing wouldn't make for much leakage.

"What you got?" Jerome asked.

"I got an Apple NanoMind II. Good megabytes. You?"

"You got the Mercedes, I got the Toyota. Usin' a *Sesó Picante*

Mark I. One of those Argentine things." (How had this guy scored an ANM II?)

"Yeah, what you got, they kinda *basto* but they do most what you need. Hey, your name's Jerome, mine's Jessie, they both start with J. And we both here for illegal augs. What else we got in common? What's your sign?"

"Uh—" What was it anyway? He always forgot. "Pisces."

"No shit! I can relate to Pisces. I ran an astrology program, figured out who I should hang with, Pisces is okay. But Aquarius is— I'm a Scorpio, like—Aquarius, *qué bueno.*"

What did he mean exactly, *hang with*, Jerome wondered. Scoping me about am *I* a faggot, maybe that was something defensive.

But he meant something else. "You know somethin' Jerome, you got your chip too, we could do a link and maybe get over on that trashcan."

Break out? Jerome felt a chilled thrill go through him. "Link with that thing? Control it? I don't think the two of us would be enough."

"We need some more guys maybe but I got news, Jerome, there's more comin'. Maybe their names all start with J."

But they didn't. In quick succession, the trashcan brought them a fortyish beachbum named Eddie, a cadaverous black dude named Bones, a queen called Swish, whose real name, according to the trashcan, was Paul Torino.

"This place smells like it's comin' apart," Eddie said. He had a surfer's greasy blond topknot and all the usual surf punk tattoos. Meaningless now, Jerome thought, the pollution-derived oxidation of the local offshore had pretty much ended ocean surfing. The anerobics had taken over the surf, thriving in the toxic waters like a gelatinous Sargasso. "Smells in here like it died and didn't go to heaven. Stinks worse'n Malibu."

"It's those landfill blocks," Bones said. He was missing four front teeth (confiscated?) and his sunken face resembled something out of a zombie flick. But he was an energetic zombie. "Compressed garbage," he told Eddie. "Organic stuff mixed with the polymers, the plastics, whatever was in the trash heap, make 'em into bricks 'cause they run outta landfill, but after a while, if the contractor didn't get 'em to set right, y'know, they start to rot. It's hot outside is why you're gettin' it now. Use garbage to cage garbage, they say. Fucking assholes."

In the heat of the day the background smell of rancid garbage thickened. It turned Jerome's stomach more because of what it reminded him of than the actual smell. It made him think of garbage disposals, and Charlie Chesterton had once told him that prisons, in the year 2022, were the State's garbage disposal system. . . . Get caught in the penal system and you could almost feel the dispose-all blades. . . .

The trashcan pushed a rack of trays up to the plexiglass bars and *whirred* their lunch to them, tray by tray. It gave them an extra one. It was screwing up.

They ate their chicken patties—the chicken was almost greaseless, gristleless, which meant it was vat chicken, genetically engineered stuff—and between bites they bitched about the food and indulged in the usual paranoid speculation about mind control chemicals in the coffee. Jerome looked around at the others, thinking: *At least they're not ass-kickers.* They were crammed here because of the illegal augs sweep, some political drive to clean up the clinics, maybe to see to it that the legal augmentation companies kept their pit-bull grip on the industry. So there wasn't anybody in for homicide, for gang torture, or anything. Not a bad cell to be in.

"You Jerome-X, really?" Swish fluted. A faint accent. She (Jerome always thought of a queen as *she* and *her*, out of respect for the tilt of her consciousness) was either Mexican or Filipino; hard to tell because she'd had her face "girled" at a cheap clinic. Cheeks built up for a heart-shape, eyes rounded, lips filled out, glass tits looking like there was a couple of tin funnels under her jammies. Some of the injected collagen in her lips had shifted so her lower lip was now lopsided. One cheekbone was a little higher than the other. A karmic revenge on malekind, Jerome thought, for forcing women into girdles and footbinding and anorexia. What did this creature use her chip for, besides getting high?

"Oooh, Jerome-X! I saw your tag before on the TV. The one when you kind of floated around the President's head and some printout words came out of your mouth and blocked her face out. God, she's such a *cunt.*"

"What words did he block her out with?" Eddie asked.

" 'Would you know a liar if you heard one anymore?' That's what it was," Swish said. "It was *sooo* perfect because that cunt wants another war, you *know* she does. And she lies about it, ooh *God* how she lies."

"You just think she's a cunt because *you* want one," Eddie said, dropping his pants to use the toilet. He talked loudly to cover up the noise of it. "You want one and you can't afford it. I think the President's right, the fucking Mexican People's Republic is scummin' on our borders, sending commie agents in—"

Swish said, "Oh God he's a Surf Nazi—but *God* yes I want one—I want *her* cunt. That prune doesn't know how to use it anyway. Honey, I know how *I'd* use that thing—" Swish stopped abruptly and shivered, hugging herself. With her long purple nails she reached up and pried loose a flap of skin behind her ear, and plucked out her chip. She wet it, adjusted its feed-mode, put it back in, tapping it with the activation mouse under a nail. She pressed the flap shut. Her eyes glazed as she adjusted. She could do that for maybe twenty-four hours and then it'd ice her, sure. She'd have to go cold turkey or die. Or get out. And maybe she'd been doing it for awhile now.

None of them would be allowed to post bail. They'd each get the two years mandatory minimum sentence. Illegal augs, the feds thought, were getting out of hand. Black market chip implants were used for playing havoc with the State database lottery; used by bookies of all kinds; used to keep accounts where the IRS couldn't find them; used to scam banking computers, and for spiking cash machines; used to milk the body, prod the brain into authorizing the secretion of beta-endorphins and ACTH and adrenalin and testosterone and other bio-chemical toys; used to figure the odds at casinos; used to compute the specs for homemade designer drugs; used by the mob's street dons to plot strategy and tactics; used by the kid gangs for the same reasons; used for illegal congregations on the Plateau.

It was the Plateau, Jerome thought, that really scared the shit out of the Feds. It had possibilities.

The trashcan dragged in a cot for the extra man, shoved it folded under the door, and blared, "Lights out, all inmates are required to be i-i-in their bu-unks-s-s. . . ." Its voice was failing.

After the trashcan and the light had gone, they climbed off their bunks and sat hunkered in a circle on the floor.

They were on chips, but not transmission-linked to one another. Jacked-up on the chips, they communicated in a spoken shorthand.

"Bull," Bones was saying. "Door." He was a voice in the darkness.

"Time," Jessie said.

"Compatibility? Know?" Eddie said.

Jerome said, "No shit." Snorts of laughter from the others.

"Link check," Bones said.

"Models?" Jessie said.

Then they joined in an incantation of numbers.

It was a fifteen-minute conversation in less than a minute.

"It's bullshit," Bones was saying, translated. "You get past the trashcan, there's human guards, you can't reprogram them."

"But at certain hours," Jessie told them, "there's only one on duty. They're used to seeing the can bring people in and out. They won't question it till they try to confirm it. By then we'll be on their ass."

"We might not be compatible," Eddie pointed out. "You understand, compatible?"

"Oh, hey man, I *think* we can comprehend that," Jerome said, making the others snort with laughter. Eddie wasn't liked much.

Bones said, "The only way to see if we're compatible is to do a systems link. We got the links, we got the thinks, like the man says. It's either the chain that holds us in or it's the chain that pulls us out."

Jerome's scalp tightened. A systems link. A mini-Plateau. Sharing minds. Brutal intimacy. Maybe some fallout from the Plateau. He wasn't ready for it.

If it went sour he could get time tacked onto his sentence for attempted jailbreak. And somebody might get dusted. They might have to kill a human guard. Jerome had once punched a dealer in the nose, and the spurt of blood had made him sick. He couldn't kill anyone. But . . . he had shit for alternatives. He knew he wouldn't make it through two years anyway, when they sent him up to the Big One. The Big One'd grind him up for sure. They'd find his chip and it'd piss them off. They'd let the bulls rape him and give him the New Virus; he'd flip out from being locked in and chipless and they'd put him in Aversion Rehab and burn him out totally.

Jerome savaged a thumbnail with his incisors. *Sent to the Big One.* He'd been trying not to think about it. Making himself take it one day at a time. But now he had to look at the alternatives. His stomach twisted itself to punish him for being so stupid. For getting into dealing augments so he could finance a big transer. *Why?* A transer didn't get him anything but his face pirated onto local TV for maybe twenty seconds. He'd thrown himself away trying to get it. . . .

Why was it so fucking important? his stomach demanded, wringing itself vindictively.

"Thing is," Bones said, "we could all be cruisin' into a setup. Some kind of sting thing. Maybe it's a little too weird how the police prober let us all through."

(Someone listening would have heard him say, "Sting, funny luck.")

Jessie snorted. "I tol' you, man. The prober is paid off. They letting them all through because some of them are mob. I know that, because I'm part of the thing. Okay?"

("Probe greased, fade me.")

"You with the mob?" Bones asked.

("You?")

"You got it. Just a dealer. But I know where a half million newbux wortha the shit is, so they going to get me out. The way the system is set up, the prober had to let everyone through. His boss thinks we got our chips taken out when they arraigned us, sometimes they do it that way. This time it was supposed to be the jail surgeon. Before they catch up with their own red tape we get outta here. Now listen—we can't do the trashcan without we all get into it, because we haven't got enough *K* otherwise. So who's in?"

He'd said, "Low, half million, bluff surgeon, there here, all-none, *who* yuh fucks?"

Something in his voice skittering behind smoked glass: he was getting testy, irritable from the chip adjustments for his nicotine habit, maybe other adjustments. The side effects of liberal cerebral self-modulating burning through a threadbare nervous system.

The rest of the meeting, translated. . . .

"I dunno," Eddie said. "I thought I'd do my time 'cause if it goes sour—"

"Hey man," Jessie said, "I can *take* your fuckin' chip. And be out before they notice your ass don't move no more."

"The man's right," Swish said. Her pain-suppression system was unraveling, axon by axon, and she was running out of adjust. "Let's just do it, okay? Please? Okay? I gotta get out. I feel like I wish I was dog shit so I could be something better."

"I can't handle two years in the Big, Eddie," Jerome heard himself say. Realizing he was helping Jessie threaten Eddie. Amazed at himself. Not his style.

"It's all of us or nobody, Eddie," Bones said.

Eddie was quiet for a while.

Jerome had turned off his chip, because it was thinking endlessly about Jessie's plan, and all it came up with was an ugly model of the risks. You had to know when to go with intuition.

Jerome was committed. And he was standing on the brink of link. The time was now, starting with Jessie.

Jessie was the operator. He picked the order. First Eddie, to make sure about him. Then Jerome. Maybe because he had Jerome scoped for a refugee from the middle class, an anomaly here, and Jerome might try and raise the Man on his chip, cut a deal. Once they had him linked in, he was locked up.

After Jerome, it'd be Bones and then Swish.

They held hands, so that the link signal, transmitted from the chip using the electric field generated by the brain, would be carried with the optimum fidelity.

He heard them exchange frequency designates, numbers strung like beads in the darkness, and heard the hiss of suddenly indrawn breaths as Jessie and Eddie linked in. And he heard, "Let's go, Jerome."

Jerome's eyes had adjusted to the dark, the night giving up some of its buried light, and Jerome could just make out a crude outline of Jessie's features like a charcoal rubbing from an Aztec carving.

Jerome reached to the back of his own head, found the glue-tufted hairs that marked his flap, and pulled the skin away from the chip's jack unit. He tapped the chip. It didn't take. He tapped it again, and this time he felt the shift in his bioelectricity; felt it hum between his teeth.

Jerome's chip communicating with his brain via an interface of rhodopsin protein; the ribosomes borrowing neurohumoral transmitters from the brain's blood supply, reordering the transmitters so that they carried a programmed pattern of ion releases for transmission across synaptic gaps to the brain's neuronal dendrites; the chip using magnetic resonance holography to collate with brain-stored memories and psychological trends. Declaiming to itself the mythology of the brain; reenacting on its silicon stage the personal Legends of his subjective world history.

Jerome closed his eyes and looked into the back of his eyelids. The digital readout was printed in luminous green across the darkness. He focused on the cursor, concentrated so it moved up to ACCESS. He subverbalized, "Open frequency." The chip heard his practiced subverbalization, and numbers appeared on the back of his eyelids: 63391212.70. He read them out to the others and they picked up his frequency. Almost choking on the word, knowing what it would bring, he told the chip: "Open."

It opened to the link. He'd only done it once before. It was illegal and he was secretly glad it was illegal because it scared him. "They're holding the Plateau back," his brain-chip source had told him, "because they're scared of what worldwide electronic telepathy might bring down on them. Like, everyone will collate information, use it to see through the bastards' game, throw the ass-bites out of office."

Maybe that was one reason. It was something the power brokers couldn't control. But there were other reasons. Reasons like a strikingly legitimate fear of going batshit crazy.

All Jerome and the others wanted was a sharing of processing capabilities. Collaborative calculation. But the chips weren't designed to filter out the irrelevant input before it reached the user's cognition level. Before the chip had done its filtering the two poles of the link— Jerome and Jessie—would each see the swarming hive of the other's total consciousness. Would see the other as they perceived themselves to be, and then objectively, as they were.

He saw Jessie as a grid and as a holographic entity. He braced himself and the holograph came at him, an abstract tarantula of computer-generated color and line, scrambling down over him . . . and for an instant it crouched in the seat of his consciousness. Jessie. Jesus Chaco.

Jessie was a family man. He was a patriarch, a protector of his wife and six kids and his widowed sister's four kids and of the poor children of his barrio. He was a muddied painting of his father, who had fled the social forest fire of Mexico's communist revolution, spiriting his capital to Los Angeles where he'd sown it into the black market. Jessie's father had been killed defending territory from the mob; Jessie compromised with the mob to save his father's business, and loathed himself for it. Wanted to kill their *capos*; had instead to work side by side with them. Perceived his wife as a functional pet, an object of adoration who was the very apotheosis of her fixed role. To imagine her doing anything other than child-rearing and keeping house would be to imagine the sun become a snowball, the moon become a monkey.

And Jerome glimpsed Jessie's undersides: Jesus Chaco's self-image with its outsized penis and impossibly spreading shoulders, sitting in a perfect and shining cherry automobile, always the newest and most luxurious model, the automotive throne from which he surveyed his kingdom. Jerome saw guns emerging from the grill of the car to splash Jessie's enemies apart with his unceasing ammunition. . . . It was a Robert Williams cartoon capering at the heart of Jessie's unconscious. . . . Jessie saw himself as Jerome saw him; the electronic mirrors reflecting one another. Jessie cringed.

Jerome saw himself, then, reflected back from Jessie.

He saw Jerome-X on a video screen with lousy vertical hold; wobbling, trying to arrange its pixels firmly and losing them. A figure of mewling inconsequence; a brief flow of electrons that might diverge left or right like spray from a waterhose depressed with the thumb. Raised in a high-security condo village, protected by cameras and computer lines to private security thugs; raised in a media-windowed womb, with PCs and VCRs and a thousand varieties of video games; shaped by cable-TV and fantasy rentals; sexuality distorted by sneaking looks at his parents' badly-hidden stash of Cassex videos. And always plugged into the Grid, the condo's satellite dish pulling in stations from around the nation, around the world, seeing the same StarFaces appear on channel after channel as the star's fame spread like a stain across the frequency bands. Seeing the Star's World Self crystallizing; the media figure coming into definition against the backdrop of media competition. Becoming real in this electronic collective unconscious.

Becoming real simply because he'd appeared on a few thousand TV screens. Growing up with a sense that media events were real, and personal events were not. Anything that didn't happen on television didn't happen. Even as he hated conventional programming, even as he regarded it as the cud of ruminants, still it defined his sense of personal unreality; and left him unfinished.

Jerome saw Jerome: perceiving himself unreal. Jerome: scamming a transer, creating a presence via video graffiti. Thinking he was doing it for reasons of radical statement. Seeing, now, that he was doing it to make himself feel substantial, to superimpose himself on the Media Grid. . . .

And then Eddie's link was there, Eddie's computer model sliding down over Jerome like a mudslide. Eddie seeing himself as a Legendary Wanderer, a rebel, a homemade mystic; his fantasy parting to reveal an anal-expulsive sociopath; a whiner perpetually scanning for someone to blame for his sour luck.

Suddenly Bones tumbled into the link; a complex worldview that was a sort of streetside sociobiology, mitigated by a loyalty to friends, a mystical faith in brain-chips and amphetamines. His underside a masochistic dwarf, the troll of self-doubt, lacerating itself with guilt.

And then Swish, a woman with an unsightly growth, errant glands that were like tumors to her. Grown predatory for the means to dampen the pain of an infinite self-derision that mimicked her father's utter rejection of her. A mystical faith in synthetic morphine.

. . . Jerome mentally reeling from disorientation, seeing the others as a network of distorted self-images, caricatures of grotesque ambitions. Beyond them he glimpsed another realm through a break in the psychic clouds: the Plateau, the whispering plane of brain-chips linked on forbidden frequencies, an electronic haven for doing deals unseen by cops; a Plateau prowled only by the exquisitely ruthless; a vista of enormous challenges and inconceivable risks and always the potential for getting lost, for madness. A place roamed by the wolves of wetware.

There was a siren quiver from that place, a soundless howling, pulling at them . . . drawing them in. . . .

"*Uh*-uh," Bones said, maybe aloud or maybe through the chips. Translated from chip shorthand, those two syllables meant: "Stay away from the Plateau, or we get sucked into it, we lose our focus. Concentrate on parallel processing function."

Jerome looked behind his eyelids, sorted through the files. He moved the cursor down. . . .

Suddenly it was there. The group-thinking capacity looming above them, a sentient skyscraper. A rush of megalomaniacal pleasure in identifying with it. A towering edifice of Mind. Five chips become One.

They were ready. Jessie transmitted the bait.

Alerted to an illegal use of implant-chips, the trashcan was squeaking down the hall, scanning to precisely locate the source. Stopping in front of their cell. Jessie reached through the bars and touched its input jack.

Midway through a turn the machine froze with a *clack*, humming as it processed what they fed it. Would it bite? Bones had a program for the IBM Cyberguard 14s, with all the protocol and a range of sample entry codes. Parallel processing from samples, it took them less than two seconds to decrypt the trashcan's access code. They were in. The hard part was the reprogramming.

Jerome found the way. He told the trashcan that he wasn't Eric Wexler, because the DNA code was all wrong, if you looked close enough; what we have here is a case of mistaken identity.

Since this information, from the trashcan's viewpoint, was coming from authorized sources—the decrypted access code made them authorized—it fell for the gag and opened the cage.

The trashcan took the five Eric Wexlers down the hall—that was Jessie's doing, showing them how to make it think of five as one, something his people had learned for the Immigration computers. It escorted them through the plastiflex door, through the steel door, and into Receiving. The human guard was heaping sugar into his antique Ronald MacDonald coffee mug and watching *The Mutilated* on his wallet-TV. Bones and Jessie were in the room and moving in on him before he broke free of the television and went for the button. Bones's long left arm spiked out and his stiffened fingers hit a nerve cluster below the guy's left ear. The guard went down, the sugar dispenser in one hand swishing a white fan onto the floor.

Jerome's chip had cross-referenced Bones's attack style. *Commando training*, the chip said. *Military elite*. Was he a plant? Bones smiled at him and tilted his head, which Jerome's chip read as: *No. I'm trained by the Underground. Roots Radics.*

Jessie was at the console, deactivating the trashcan, killing the cameras, opening the outer doors. Jessie and Swish led the way out; Swish whining softly and biting her lip. There were two more guards at the gate, one of them asleep. Jessie had taken the gun from the screw Bones had put under, so the first guard at the gate was dead before he could hit an alarm. The cat-napping guy woke and yelled with hoarse terror, and then Jessie shot him in the throat.

Watching the guard fall, spinning, blood making its own slow-motion spiral in the air, Jerome felt sickness, fear, self-disgust seeing this stranger die. The guard was young, wearing a cheap wedding ring, probably had a young family. So Jerome stepped over the dying man and made an adjustment; used his chip, chilled himself out with adrenalin. Had to. He was committed now. And he knew with a bland certainty that they had reached the Plateau after all.

He would stay on the Plateau. He belonged there, now that he was one of the wolves.

Bruce Sterling

Twenty Evocations

1. EXPERT SYSTEMS. When Nikolai Leng was a child, his teacher
was a cybernetic system with a holographic interface. The holo took the
form of a young Shaper woman. Its "personality" was an interactive
composite expert system manufactured by Shaper psychotechs. Nikolai loved it.

2. NEVER BORN. "You mean we all came from Earth?" said Nikolai
unbelieving.

"Yes," the holo said kindly. "The first true settlers in space were
born on Earth—produced by sexual means. Of course, hundreds of
years have passed since then. You are a Shaper. Shapers are never
born."

"Who lives on Earth now?"

"Human beings."

"Ohhhh," said Nikolai, his falling tones betraying a rapid loss of
interest.

3. A MALFUNCTIONING LEG. There came a day when Nikolai saw
his first Mechanist. The man was a diplomat and commercial agent,
stationed by his faction in Nikolai's habitat. Nikolai and some children
from his creche were playing in the corridor when the diplomat stalked
by. One of the Mechanist's legs was malfunctioning and it went *click-
whirr, click-whirr*. Nikolai's friend, Alex, mimicked the man's limp.
Suddenly the man turned on them, his plastic eyes dilating. "Gene-
lines," the Mechanist snarled. "I can buy you, grow you, sell you, cut
you into bits. Your screams: my music."

4. FUZZ PATINA. Sweat was running into the braided collar of Nikolai's military tunic. The air in the abandoned station was still breathable, but insufferably hot. Nikolai helped his sergeant strip the valuables off a dead miner. The murdered Shaper's antiseptic body was desiccated, but perfect. They walked into another section. The body of a Mechanist pirate sprawled in the feeble gravity. Killed during the attack, his body had rotted for weeks inside his suit. An inch-thick patina of grayish fuzz had devoured his face.

5. NOT MERITORIOUS. Nikolai was on leave in the Ring Council with two men from his unit. They were drinking in a free-fall bar called the ECLECTIC EPILEPTIC. The first man was Simon Afriel, a charming ambitious young Shaper of the old school. The other man had a Mechanist eye implant. His loyalty was suspect. The three of them were discussing semantics. "The map is not of the territory," Afriel said. Suddenly the second man picked an almost invisible listening device from the edge of the table. "And the tap is not meritorious," he quipped. They never saw him again.

. . . A Mechanist pirate, malfunctioning, betraying gene-lines. Invisible listening devices buy, grow, and sell you. The abandoned station's ambitious young Shaper, killed during the attack. Falling psychotechs produced by sexual means the desiccated body of a commercial agent. The holographic interface's loyalty was suspect. The cybernetic system helped him strip the valuables off his plastic eyes. . . .

6. SPECULATIVE PITY. The Mechanist woman looked him over with an air of speculative pity. "I have an established commercial pattern here," she told Nikolai, "but my cash-flow is temporarily constricted. You, on the other hand, have just defected from the Council with a small fortune. I need money; you need stability. I propose marriage."

Nikolai considered this. He was new to Mech society. "Does this imply a sexual relationship?" he said. The woman looked at him blankly. "You mean between the two of us?"

7. FLOW PATTERNS. "You're worried about something," his wife told him. Nikolai shook his head. "Yes, you are," she persisted. "You're upset because of that deal I made in pirate contraband. You're unhappy because our corporation is profiting from attacks made on your own people."

Nikolai smiled ruefully. "I suppose you're right. I never knew anyone who understood my innermost feelings the way you do." He looked at her affectionately. "How do you do it?"

"I have infrared scanners," she said. "I read the patterns of blood flow in your face."

8. *OPTIC TELEVISION*. It was astonishing how much room there was in an eyesocket, when you stopped to think about it. The actual visual mechanisms had been thoroughly miniaturized by Mechanist prostheticians. Nikolai had some other devices installed: a clock, a biofeedback monitor, a television screen, all wired directly to his optic nerve. They were convenient, but difficult to control at first. His wife had to help him out of the hospital and back to his apartment because the subtle visual triggers kept flashing broadcast market reports. Nikolai smiled at his wife from behind his plastic eyes. "Spend the night with me tonight," he said. His wife shrugged. "All right," she said. She put her hand to the door of Nikolai's apartment and died almost instantly. An assassin had smeared the door handle with contact venom.

9. *SHAPER TARGETS*. "Look," the assassin said, his slack face etched with weariness, "don't bother me with any ideologies. . . . Just transfer the funds and tell me who it is you want dead."

"It's a job in the Ring Council," Nikolai said. He was strung out on a regimen of emotional drugs he had been taking to combat grief, and he had to fight down recurrent waves of weirdly tainted cheerfulness. "Lieutenant-Doctor Martin Leng of the Ring Security Council. He's one of my own gene-line. My defection made his own loyalty look bad. He killed my wife."

"Shapers make good targets," the assassin said. His legless, armless body floated in a transparent nutrient tank, where tinted plasmas soothed the purplish ends of socketed nerve clumps. A bodyservo waded into the tank and began to attach the assassin's arms.

10. *CHILD INVESTMENT*. "We recognize your investment in this child, shareholder Leng," the psychotech said. "You may have created

her—or hired the technicians who had her created—but she is not your property. By our regulations she must be treated like any other child. She is the property of our people's corporate republic."

Nikolai looked at the woman, exasperated. "I didn't create her. She's my dead wife's posthumous clone. And she's the property of my wife's corporations, or, rather, her trust fund, which I manage as executor. . . . No, what I mean to say is that she owns, or at least has a lienhold on, my dead wife's semiautonomous corporate property, which becomes hers at the age of majority. . . . Do you follow me?"

"No. I'm an educator, not a financier. What exactly is the point of this, shareholder? Are you trying to re-create your dead wife?"

Nikolai looked at her, his face carefully neutral. "I did it for the tax break."

. . . Leave the posthumous clone profiting from attacks. Semiautonomous property has an established commercial position. Recurrent waves of pirate contraband. His slack face bothers you with ideologies. Innermost feelings died almost instantly. Smear the door with contract venom. . . .

11. ALLEGIANCES RESENTED. "I like it out here on the fringes," Nikolai told the assassin. "Have you ever considered a breakaway?"

The assassin laughed. "I used to be a pirate. It took me forty years to attach myself to this cartel. When you're alone, you're meat, Leng. You ought to know that."

"But you must resent those allegiances. They're inconvenient. Wouldn't you rather have your own Kluster and make your own rules?"

"You're talking like an ideologue," the assassin said. LED displays blinked softly on his prosthetic forearms. "My allegiance is to Kyotid Zaibatsu. They own this whole suburb. They even own my arms and legs."

"I own Kyotid Zaibatsu," Nikolai said.

"Oh," the assassin said. "Well, that puts a different face on matters."

12. MASS DEFECTION. "We want to join your Kluster," the Superbright said. "We *must* join your Kluster. No one else will have us."

Nikolai doodled absently with his light-pen on a convenient videoscreen. "How many of you are there?"

"There were fifty in our gene-line. We were working on quantum physics before our mass defection. We made a few minor breakthroughs. I think they might be of some commercial use."

"Splendid," said Nikolai. He assumed an air of speculative pity. "I take it the Ring Council persecuted you in the usual manner—claimed you were mentally unstable, ideologically unsound, and the like."

"Yes. Their agents have killed thirty-eight of us." The Superbright dabbed uneasily at the sweat beading on his swollen forehead. "We are not mentally unsound, Kluster-Chairman. We will not cause you any trouble. We only want a quiet place to finish working while God eats our brains."

13. DATA HOSTAGE. A high-level call came in from the Ring Council. Nikolai, surprised and intrigued, took the call himself. A young man's face appeared on the screen. "I have your teacher hostage," he said.

Nikolai frowned. "What?"

"The person who taught you when you were a child in the creche. You love her. You told her so. I have it on tape."

"You must be joking," Nikolai said. "My teacher was just a cybernetic interface. You can't hold a data system hostage."

"Yes, I can," the young man said truculently. "The old expert system's been scrapped in favor of a new one with a sounder ideology. Look." A second face appeared on the screen: it was the superhumanly smooth and faintly glowing image of his cybernetic teacher. "Please save me, Nikolai," the image said woodenly. "He's ruthless."

The young man's face reappeared. Nikolai laughed incredulously. "So you've saved the old tapes?" Nikolai said. "I don't know what your game is, but I suppose the data has a certain value. I'm prepared to be generous." He named a price. The young man shook his head. Nikolai grew impatient. "Look," he said, "What makes you think a mere expert system has any objective worth?"

"I know it does," the young man said. "I'm one myself."

14. CENTRAL QUESTION. Nikolai was aboard the alien ship. He felt uncomfortable in his brocaded ambassador's coat. He adjusted the heavy sunglasses over his plastic eyes. "We appreciate your visit to our Kluster," he told the reptilian ensign. "It's a very great honor."

The Investor ensign lifted the multicolored frill behind his massive head. "We are prepared to do business," he said.

"I'm interested in alien philosophies," Nikolai said. "The answers of other species to the great questions of existence."

"But there is only one central question," the alien said. "We have pursued its answer from star to star. We were hoping that you would help us answer it."

Nikolai was cautious. "What is the question?"

"'What is it you have that we want?'"

15. *INHERITED GIFTS*. Nikolai looked at the girl with the old-fashioned eyes. "My chief of security has provided me with a record of your criminal actions," he said. "Copyright infringement, organized extortion, conspiracy in restraint of trade. How old are you?"

"Forty-four," the girl said. "How old are you?"

"A hundred and ten or so. I'd have to check my files." Something about the girl's appearance bothered him. "Where did you get those antique eyes?"

"They were my mother's. I inherited them. But you're a Shaper, of course. You wouldn't know what a mother was."

"On the contrary," Nikolai said. "I believe I knew yours. We were married. After her death, I had you cloned. I suppose that makes me your—I forget the term."

"Father."

"That sounds about right. Clearly you've inherited her gifts for finance." He reexamined her personnel file. "Would you be interested in adding bigamy to your list of crimes?"

. . . The mentally unstable have a certain value. Restraint of trade puts a different face on the convenient videoscreen. A few minor breakthroughs in the questions of existence. Your personnel file persecuted him. His swollen forehead can't hold a data system. . . .

16. *PLEASURE ROAR*. "You need to avoid getting set in your ways," his wife said. "It's the only way to stay young." She pulled a gilded inhaler from her garter holster. "Try some of this."

"I don't need drugs," Nikolai said, smiling. "I have my power fantasies." He began pulling off his clothes.

His wife watched him impatiently. "Don't be stodgy, Nikolai."

She touched the inhaler to her nostril and sniffed. Sweat began to break out on her face, and a slow sexual flush spread over her ears and neck.

Nikolai watched, then shrugged and sniffed lightly at the gilded tube. Immediately a rocketing sense of ecstasy paralyzed his nervous system. His body arched backward, throbbing uncontrollably.

Clumsily, his wife began to caress him. The roar of chemical pleasure made sex irrelevant. "Why . . . why bother?" he gasped.

His wife looked surprised. "It's traditional."

17. FLICKERING WALL. Nikolai addressed the flickering wall of monitor screens. "I'm getting old," he said. "My health is good—I was very lucky in my choice of longevity programs—but I just don't have the daring I once did. I've lost my flexibility, my edge. And the Kluster has outgrown my ability to handle it. I have no choice. I must retire."

Carefully, he watched the faces on the screens for every flicker of reaction. Two hundred years had taught him the art of reading faces. His skills were still with him—it was only the will behind them that had decayed. The faces of the Governing Board, their reserve broken by shock, seemed to blaze with ambition and greed.

18. LEGAL TARGETS. The Mechanists had unleashed their drones in the suburb. Armed with subpoenas, the faceless drones blurred through the hallway crowds, looking for legal targets.

Suddenly Nikolai's former Chief of Security broke from the crowd and began a run for cover. In free-fall, he brachiated from handhold to handhold like an armored gibbon. Suddenly one of his prosthetics gave way, and the drones pounced on him, almost at Nikolai's door. Plastic snapped as electromagnetic pincers paralyzed his limbs.

"Kangaroo courts," he gasped. The deeply creased lines in his ancient face shone with rivulets of sweat. "They'll strip me! Help me, Leng!"

Sadly, Nikolai shook his head. The old man shrieked: "You got me into this! You were the ideologue! I'm only a poor assassin!"

Nikolai said nothing. The machines seized and repossessed the old man's arms and legs.

19. ANTIQUE SPLITS. "You've really got it through you, right? All that old gigo stuff!" The young people spoke a slang-crammed jargon that

Nikolai could barely comprehend. When they watched him, their faces showed a mixture of aggression, pity, and awe. To Nikolai, they always seemed to be shouting. "I feel outnumbered," he murmured.

"You *are* outnumbered, old Nikolai! This bar is your museum, right? Your mausoleum! Give our ears your old frontiers, we're listening! Those idiot video ideologies, those antique spirit splits. Mechs and Shapers, right? The wars of the coin's two halves!"

"I feel tired," Nikolai said. "I've drunk too much. Take me home, one of you."

They exchanged worried glances. "This *is* your home! Isn't it?"

20. EYES CLOSED. "You've been very kind," Nikolai told the two youngsters. They were Kosmosity archaeologists, dressed in their academic finery, their gowns studded with awards and medals from the Terraforming-Klusters. Nikolai realized suddenly that he could not remember their names.

"That's all right, sir," they told him soothingly. "It's now our duty to remember you, not vice-versa." Nikolai felt embarrassed. He hadn't realized that he had spoken aloud.

"I've taken poison," he explained.

"We know," they nodded. "You're not in any pain, we hope?"

"No, not at all. I've done the right thing, I know. I'm very old. Older than I can bear." Suddenly he felt an alarming collapse within himself. Pieces of his consciousness began to break off as he slid toward the void. Suddenly he realized that he had forgotten his last words. With an enormous effort, he remembered them and shouted them aloud.

"Futility is freedom!" Filled with triumph, he died, and they closed his eyes.

Bruce Sterling

The Mare
Tranquillitatis People's
Circumlunar Zaibatsu:
2-1-'16
(*from* Schismatrix)

The Geisha Bank was a complex of older buildings, shellacked airtight and connected by a maze of polished wooden halls and sliding paper airlocks. The area had been a red-light district even before the Zaibatsu's collapse. The Bank was proud of its heritage and continued the refined and eccentric traditions of a gentler age.

Lindsay left the eleven nationals of the Fortuna Miners' Democracy in an antiseptic sauna vault, being scrubbed by impassive bathboys. It was the first real bath the pirates had had in months. Their scrawny bodies were knobbed with muscle from constant practice in free-fall jujutsu. Their sweating skins were bright with fearsome tattoos and septic rashes.

Lindsay did not join them. He stepped into a paneled dressing room and handed over his Nephrine Medicals uniform to be cleaned and pressed. He slipped into a soft brown kimono. A low-ranking male geisha in kimono and obi approached him. "Your pleasure, sir?"

"I'd like a word with the *yarite*, please."

The geisha looked at him with well-bred skepticism. "One moment. I will ask if our chief executive officer is prepared to accept guests."

He vanished. After half an hour a blonde female geisha in business suit and obi appeared. "Mr. Dze? This way, please."

He followed her to an elevator guarded by two men armed with electrode-studded clubs. The guards were giants; his head barely came to their elbows. Their long, stony faces were acromegalic: swollen jaws, clifflike jutting cheekbones. They had been treated with hormonal growth factors.

The elevator surged up three floors and opened.

Lindsay faced a thick network of brightly colored beads. Thousands of dangling, beaded wires hung from floor to ceiling. Any movement would disturb them.

"Take my hand," the banker said. Lindsay shuffled behind her, thrashing and clattering. "Step carefully," she said. "There are traps."

Lindsay closed his eyes and followed. His guide stopped; a hidden door opened in a mirrored wall. Lindsay stepped through it, into the *yarite*'s private chamber.

The floor was of ancient wood, waxed to a dark gleam. There were flat square cushions underfoot, in patterns of printed bamboo. In the long wall to Lindsay's left, glass double-doors showed a sunlit wooden balcony and a splendid garden, where crooked pines and tall japonicas arched over curving paths of raked white pebbles. The air in the room smelled of evergreen. He was gazing on this world before its rot, an image of the past, projected on false doors that could never open.

The *yarite* was sitting cross-legged on a cushion. She was a wizened old Mech with a tight-drawn mouth and hooded, reptilian eyes. Her wrinkled head was encased in a helmetlike lacquered wig, skewered with pins. She wore an angular flowered kimono supported by starch and struts. There was room in it for three of her.

A second woman knelt silently with her back to the right-hand wall, facing the garden's image. Lindsay knew at once that she was a Shaper. Her startling beauty alone was proof, but she had that strange, intangible air of charisma that spread from the Reshaped like a magnetic field. She was of mixed Asiatic-African gene stock: her eyes were tilted, but her skin was dark. Her hair was long and faintly kinked. She knelt before a rack of white keyboards with an air of meek devotion.

The *yarite* spoke without moving her head. "Your duties, Kitsune." The girl's hands darted over the keyboards and the air was filled with the tones of that most ancient of Japanese instruments: the synthesizer.

Lindsay knelt on a cushion, facing the old woman. A tea tray rolled to his side and poured hot water into a cup with a chaste tinkling sound. It dipped a rotary tea whisk into the cup.

"Your pirate friends," the old woman said, "are about to bankrupt you."

"It's only money," Lindsay said.

"It is our sweat and sexuality. Did you think it would please us to squander it?"

"I needed your attention," Lindsay said. His training had seized him at once, but he was still afraid of the girl. He hadn't known he would be facing a Shaper. And there was something drastically wrong with the old woman's kinesics. It looked like drugs or Mechanist nerve alteration.

"You came here dressed as a Nephrine Black Medical," the old woman said. "Our attention was guaranteed. You have it. We are listening."

With Ryumin's help, Lindsay had expanded his plans. The Geisha Bank had the power to destroy his scheme; therefore, they had to be co-opted into it. He knew what they wanted. He was ready to show them a mirror. If they recognized their own ambitions and desires, he would win.

Lindsay launched into his spiel. He paused midway to make a point. "You can see what the Black Medicals hope to gain from the performance. Behind their walls they feel isolated, paranoid. They plan to gain prestige by sponsoring our play.

"But I must have a cast. The Geisha Bank is my natural reservoir of talent. I can succeed without the Black Medicals. I can't succeed without you."

"I see," the *yarite* said. "Now explain to me why you think we can profit from your ambitions."

Lindsay looked pained. "I came here to arrange a cultural event. Can't that be enough?"

He glanced at the girl. Her hands flickered over the keyboards. Suddenly she looked up at him and smiled, slyly, secretly. He saw the tip of her tongue behind her perfect teeth. It was a bright, predatory smile, full of lust and mischief. In an instant it burned itself into his bloodstream. Hair rose on the back of his neck. He was losing control.

He looked at the floor, his skin prickling. "All right," he said heavily. "It isn't enough, and that shouldn't surprise me. . . . Listen, madame. You and the Medicals have been rivals for years. This is your chance to lure them into the open and ambush them on your own ground. They're naive about finance. Naive, but greedy. They hate dealing in a financial system that you control. If they thought they could succeed, they'd leap at the chance to form their own economy.

"So, let them do it. Let them commit themselves. Let them pile success on success until they lose all sense of proportion and greed overwhelms them. Then burst their bubble."

"Nonsense," the old woman said. "How can an actor tell a banker her business?"

"You're not dealing with a Mech cartel," Lindsay said intensely, leaning forward. He knew the girl was staring at him. He could feel it. "These are three hundred technicians, bored, frightened, and completely isolated. They are perfect prey for mass hysteria. Gambling fever will hit them like an epidemic." He leaned back. "Support me, madame. I'll be your point man, your broker, your go-between. They'll never know you were behind their ruin. In fact, they'll come to you for help." He sipped his tea. It tasted synthetic.

The old woman paused as if she were thinking. Her expression was very wrong. There were none of the tiny subliminal flickers of mouth and eyelid, the movements of the throat, that accompanied human thought processes. Her face was more than calm. It was inert.

"It has possibilities," she said at last. "But the Bank must have control. Covert, but complete. How can you guarantee this?"

"It will be in your hands," Lindsay promised. "We will use my company, Kabuki Intrasolar, as a front. You will use your contacts outside the Zaibatsu to issue fictitious stock. I will offer it for sale here, and your Bank will be ambivalent. This will allow the Nephrines to score a financial coup and seize control of the company. Fictitious stockholders, your agents, will react in alarm and send in pleas and inflated offers to the new owners. This will flatter their self-esteem and overwhelm any doubts.

"At the same time, you will cooperate with me openly. You will supply me with actors and actresses; in fact, you will jealously fight for the privilege. Your geishas will talk of nothing else to every customer. You will spread rumors about me: my charm, my brilliance, my hidden resources. You will underwrite all my extravagances, and establish a free-wheeling, free-spending atmosphere of carefree hedonism. It will be a huge confidence trick that will bamboozle the entire world."

The old woman sat silently, her eyes glazed.

The low, pure tones of the synthesizer stopped suddenly. A tense hush fell over the room. The girl spoke softly from behind her keyboards. "It will work, won't it?"

He looked into her face. Her meekness had peeled off like a layer of cosmetics. Her dark eyes shocked him. They were full of frank, carnivorous desire. He knew at once that she was feigning nothing, because her look was beyond pretense. It was not human.

Without knowing it, he rose to one knee, his eyes still locked with hers. "Yes," he said. His voice was hoarse. "It will work, I swear it to you." The floor was cold under his hand. He realized that, without any decision on his part, he had begun to move toward her, half crawling.

She looked at him in lust and wonder. "Tell me what you are, darling. Tell me really."

"I'm what you are," Lindsay said. "Shaper's work." He forced himself to stop moving. His arms began to tremble.

"I want to tell you what they did to me," the girl said. "Let me tell you what I am."

Lindsay nodded once. His mouth was dry with sick excitement. "All right," he said. "Tell me, Kitsune."

"They gave me to the surgeons," she said. "They took my womb out, and they put in brain tissue. Grafts from the pleasure center, darling. I'm wired to the ass and the spine and the throat, and it's better than being God. When I'm hot, I sweat perfume. I'm cleaner than a fresh needle, and nothing leaves my body that you can't drink like wine or eat like candy. And they left me bright, so that I would know what submission was. Do you know what submission is, darling?"

"No," Lindsay said harshly. "But I know what it means not to care about dying."

"We're not like the others," she said. "They put us past the limits. And now we can do anything we like to them, can't we?"

Her laugh sent a shuddering thrill through him. She leaped with balletic grace over her deck of keyboards.

She kicked the old woman's shoulder with one bare foot, and the *yarite* fell over with a crunch. Her wig ripped free with a shredding of tape. Beneath it, Lindsay glimpsed her threadbare skull, riddled with cranial plugs. He stared. "Your keyboards," he said.

"She's my front," Kitsune said. "That's what my life is. Fronts and fronts and fronts. Only the pleasure is real. The pleasure of control."

Lindsay licked his dry lips.

"Give me what's real," she said.

She undid her obi sash. Her kimono was printed in a design of irises and violets. The skin beneath it was like a dying man's dream of skin.

"Come here," she said. "Put your mouth on my mouth."

Lindsay scrambled forward and threw his arms around her. She slipped her warm tongue deep into his mouth. It tasted of spice.

It was narcotic. The glands of her mouth oozed drugs.

They sprawled on the floor in front of the old woman's half-lidded eyes.

She slipped her arms inside his loose kimono. "Shaper," she said, "I want your genetics. All over me."

Her warm hand caressed his groin. He did what she said.

William T. Vollmann

The Indigo
Engineers
(*from* The
Rainbow Stories)

The Master Plan

Winged like maple-seeds and insects, their thoughts fell to earth in a
thousand ways—always verified by the smell of machine grease. First
there were the martyrized pigeons, then the posters, then the rockets
and the crawling robots viciously battling for possession of decayed
freeway underpasses or rubble-covered parking lots, while spectators
cheered, fulfilling their own function of ghouls revelling in devasta-
tion,[1] and *then* the machines began to get larger and smarter and
eviller. In those days they had flamethrowers and military CO_2 lasers.
Meanwhile the Indigo Engineers,[2] concerned, perhaps, lest their machines become too complacent in their metallic strength, mated them
to fresh or mummified carcasses, so that the robots were subjected to
foul and stinking burdens. Dead rabbits became rabots when attached
to devices which made them walk backwards in coy dead shudders;
these worried and irritated the Mr. Satan robot as if they were vermin.
The Indigo Engineers had by now begun to shatter glass in their
festivities whenever possible. So punctuations were crystal-sharp in
the expanding grammar of the Mechanical Hand, whose digits were so
much more powerful than Mark Pauline's finger-stumps; and the stain-
less steel Walking Machine did its tormented part, at which the
Mummy-Cat bucked and spat and the Witchy-Head expressed grave
displeasure; but the Indigo Engineers (who called themselves Survival
Research Laboratories) were not satisfied even so, and conceived the
Screw Machine to massacre their Sneaky Soldiers (every predator is
also a prey); and in the world we now had, therefore, the Spiky Roller
Machine and the Buzz Saw, the dynamite-powered Shock Wave Can-

non, the Walk and Peck Machine, whose pecks reduced the rabots and stink-dogs to bloody protoplasm, the Flying Rocket Powered Shark, the fifteen-hundred-pound Square Wheel Car, and of course the Inspector, "performing its contrasting functions of delicate manipulation and total destruction."[3] Best of all was the Sprinkler From Hell, which sprinkled high-pressure gasoline in a truly illuminating fashion.

The Frightmaster

"How would you say that cruelty enters into your work?" I said.

Sourly, Mark Pauline chewed his Mongolian beef. "Cruelty is one of those kinda words that you hear repeated so much that it doesn't make any sense anymore," he said. "Cruelty the way I use it is just one aspect of the shows. It's like a tool; it's one way that we use to make the shows really happen. We're talking about shows with MACHINES, you know. It's kind of like in silent movies, actors tend to overact to get the same point across. You know, when sound came along, it settled down to the point where acting became a much more subtle thing. Well, I see what we're doing now as the very beginnings of trying to understand how people relate to the sight of machines interacting. In the old days, when philosophers talked about identity, it was never an issue for inanimate things. Inanimate things could not recognize in each other any kind of identity. You had to be alive; you had to have an intelligence in order to have an identity. And you had to have an identity in order to be able to understand either other identities or inanimate objects. Well, in these shows, what we're trying to do is bring inanimate objects to a level where they can act, and people can relate to them as identities. Towards that end, everything we do in the shows is very, very, *very* overplayed. But I just see the cruelty as one angle, an intensification. I mean, where do you draw the line? What's fondling and what's caressing? Kind of like that thing, you know, in child molestation? What's cruelty and what's like some sort of a personalized interaction between devices? It's hard to say, and in *fact*, how can *you* even ask? You say a machine can be cruel to another machine? How can that be? That's a weird question to ask, and it just suggests to me that what we're trying to do here to a degree succeeds."

"What if the machines *were* conscious and *did* recognize each other? What would they think about then?"

"Well, you have to infer that they think in the same terms that a person thinks: pretty much in terms of their limitations. You think in terms of what you have awareness of. Of course with people, the way that their mind works, they have an awareness that's cumulative. That has its limits, though. These machines are very limited in comparison to that. There's a very limited amount of functions that they can do. There's a potential that they have, and we are able to bring out that potential and operate them, but still, there's a limited potential that they have in some ways. I think that if they could think, and whatever they feel, if they do feel—there is that argument, that every single thing has consciousness, although it's such a speculative sideline that it's not worth bringing in—I think for a machine it would be just a question of *fulfilling the range of its potential possibilities in the best way possible*, and that's all a machine thinks about. A machine has no concern for whether its actions are right or wrong; a machine has no use for morality in the human sense. All it wants to do is . . . Well, it's like a *missile*, you know, with one of those high-explosive warheads. Think of the High Explosive as like the BRAIN. All it wants to do is *explode*. It's telling all the other parts of itself, 'I've gotta explode, I've gotta explode! You've gotta help me! We all have to work together so that I can BLOW UP'; And then like the Guidance Thing says, 'Wait a minute! You can't just blow up; we've gotta find a *target!*' and the Explosive just says, 'I don't care, I don't care; I'm just gonna blow up right now!'— and then the Rocket Motors are going, 'C'mon, c'mon, c'mon, you guys! Like, get it together 'cause I wanna like *get going*, you know!' You have to kind of look at it that way. All these machines—the complicated ones, at any rate—are made up of all these different systems that interact. You can sort of imagine all of them . . . *wanting* to get in on the action. When they don't get in on the action they get sick.—But these machines are still at a point where they can only express their personalities through people, which I'm sure is very disconcerting to them. But that's just the way it is. Just like *I* can only express *my* ideas through machines. It's too bad, but it's the way it is."

Notes

1   Mark Pauline disagrees with my assessment of the spectators. But more on this later.
2   I call them this because they operate in the Beyond.
3   From a leaflet, "Previous Events by S.R.L."

Nonfiction

Stephen P. Brown

Before the Lights
Came On: Observations of
a Synergy

San Diego, 1969. I sprawled on the crowded floor and soaked up the goofy psychedelic excesses of the Quicksilver Messenger Service. "Are you having a good time?" asked Gary Duncan, as John Cipollina stood next to him dressed in a loincloth, a guitar, and an ankle-length Indian headdress. Cipollina was swallowing a flaming sword with one hand and ripping off a solo with the other. Yes, I thought, I am.

Then it was over. Another evening filled with fun. But inertia compelled me to wait a little longer and hear a tune or two from the weird New York band that was to follow.

Suddenly the lights went black, and the Velvet Underground proceeded to demolish and rebuild every aspect of what I had come to appreciate as the ultimate expression of hedonism in art: rock'n'roll. Black sheets of sound starkly illuminated the lives of junkies and hookers, the unloved and the unlovely.

It was a wake-up call: You're growing older, said Lou Reed directly to me, it's past time to start paying attention.

I stumbled from the hall and stood on the street corner, half expecting giant black engines to appear and transform the landscape. But it was still 1969, and I was still in California. The breeze was warm, the palm trees swayed. Yet there was a difference.

Within a year I had left the primary colors of California for the gray halftones of Portland, Oregon.

Portland, 1970–1973. I spent the first few months of 1970 watching the remnants of my life-style curl up and drift away. Then, a skinny blonde kid named John Shirley entered my life.

John was, and is, a true original, a manic lightning rod with a skewed surreal viewpoint on every aspect of life. He wrote compulsively and voluminously, creating fiction that defied category. His stories were populated with meat guitars, sentient events, Siamese octuplets: an endless flow of wildly hyperreal images observed with meticulous verbal brushstrokes.

For the next three years we lived in a succession of group houses noted for the peculiar and kaleidoscopic nature of their cohabitants. Shirley's presence in my life, and in the lives of all those around us, was catalytic. Our life-style became bizarre and multiplex.

Yet, throughout the chaos, Shirley kept writing. Soon he began selling to some SF markets, more or less by default. Most of those early stories were published in Ted White's *Amazing* and *Fantastic*, the primary source of the most adventurous fiction being published in the SF field at the time.

I had been a compulsive SF reader as a child, but had lost interest as an adult. The visionary potential still excited me (as it does to this day), but the juvenile and subliterate execution of most of it bored me. John Shirley's fiction, however, held a funhouse mirror to the world around me. I found that John had reawakened in me an interest in the more peculiar possibilities of vision. What he wrote, I came to understand, wasn't just deliciously insane imagery, it was a metaphorically true reflection of post-sixties societal disintegration.

East Lansing, 1974. Shirley had gone to the Clarion Writer's Workshop a couple of years earlier, and I had the opportunity to try it myself that summer. I went in search of a group of kindred souls interested in the kind of thunderclaps of the imagination that life with John had accustomed me to. Instead, I found myself in the midst of a group of sensitive souls, people who had come to learn how to use the structures and tropes of SF to sketch out pastel mood-pictures.

But there was an exception—a self-assured kid from Texas named Bruce Sterling. Bruce seemed to be the only person there enthusiastic about SF's visionary possibilities; the only one aware of the future that was crashing into everyone's lives with the aplomb of a freight train. His stories were audacious, fearlessly strange, yet grounded in an impeccable realism.

After the workshop, Sterling returned to Texas, and settled down to finish *Involution Ocean* (1977) and to write *The Artificial Kid* (1980). Neither book would find an appropriate audience for a decade. The latter, with its fecund speculation and outré social patterns, was a powerful precursor of the fiction to come.

I introduced Sterling to the work of Shirley, and the two began to hit it off via the mail. Meanwhile, I ran off to join the circus and disappeared from the real world for two and a half years.

Washington, D.C., 1978–1984. I reentered reality, and regained contact with old friends. Shirley had become immersed in the punk explosion, a social milieu for which he had been waiting all his life. He moved to New York and wrote songs and sang for a series of bands. His stage shows of the late seventies were powerful and uncompromising.

But he also continued to write. He wrote a seminal novel, *City Come A' Walkin'* (1977), that remains a key work, along with Sterling's *Artificial Kid*, in what would soon be indelibly misnamed "cyberpunk."

Sterling began to produce *Cheap Truth*, a printout of interesting bits that flowed through a Texas SF computer bulletin board. Lewis Shiner, a fellow Texan and friend of Sterling's, began chiming in with mordant bits of slasher criticism under the name "Sue Denim." The Texans were disgusted at the pathetic state of contemporary SF, and determined to do something about it. The rhetorical level slowly began to heat up, ready to boil over.

Then, at a convention in Vancouver in 1980 or 1981, Shirley found himself on a panel with a man named William Gibson. Gibson was impatient with most of what he saw, and found in Shirley a kindred spirit. The two became immediate and close friends. Shirley goaded Gibson into not only writing, but into selling his early short stories.

Soon Gibson came to the attention of the unruly Texans, and a synergy was formed. Each writer bullied, wheedled, shamed, and forced the others into outdoing themselves, into stretching their talents far beyond what each thought themselves capable. It was a vital and unique form of cross-fertilization, and for a brief moment it all happened away from the spotlight.

The early fruits were Shiner's brilliant first novel, *Frontera* (1984); the first volume of Shirley's ambitious *Eclipse* series (1985), signaling the beginning of a new, intensely socially aware phase for him; Sterling's first Shaper/Mechanist stories and the groundwork for his stunning *Schismatrix* (1985); and Gibson's *Neuromancer* (1984). All of these people fed and cross-fed each other, passing around manuscripts, hammering out a vision of modern SF that more accurately reflected the future of the real world.

The future was beginning to collect like dustballs in the corners and interstices of every home, every office, every street corner. It wasn't the lean, clean linear future of the mainstream science fiction writers, it was messy, disorganized, crowded and clamoring. It needed a new kind of fiction to describe it, dense, complex, jammed-to-the-gills fiction.

Neuromancer was published in 1984, as part of a seminal paperback original series edited by the late Terry Carr. It snuck onto the racks without fanfare. But its hyperdense, eloquent, and uncompromising transformations of the social indicators of the mid-eighties found its own audience. People began buying the book, and passing it on to their friends. It became that rarest of phenomena, a true word-of-mouth hit.

Shortly thereafter, Gardner Dozois wrote an essay in *The Washington Post* in which he labeled Gibson, Shirley, Sterling, Shiner, and other related visionaries, such as Rudy Rucker and Pat Cadigan, as "cyberpunks." The name burned into the world psyche, and the fiction of the cyberpunks began burrowing into every tiny crack of the culture like a runaway electronic virus.

New York, 1985. The relative placement of the editors' and agents' tables at the Nebula Awards banquet in New York was an indicator of the importance of the editor or agent. Quiet, reasonable people in suits and nice dresses sat at these tables. But way off in a corner was a small table jammed against a wall. Martha Millard was Gibson's and Shirley's agent. The unruly group who sat around her table included Lew Shiner, Gibson, Shirley, myself, and a few other friends.

Then Fred Pohl announced that a lowly paperback original, *Neuromancer* by William Gibson, had won the best novel award, beating out the high-profile hardbacks by SF's reigning dinosaur-princes, and eyes turned to Martha's table in puzzlement.

The after-Nebula cocktail party was a dull and pointless exercise in content-free social exchanges, so the group snuck out to the street and hailed a cab. There were too many people for the cabbie to legally drive us, so I laid on the floor, balancing Gibson's Nebula—a lucite cube containing a stylized galaxy—on my stomach.

After a wild ride through the city, we ended up at a table in the back room of a downtown club. At one end of our table reposed Gibson's Nebula, dripping with spilled beer, sprinkled with cigarette ash, surrounded by empty glasses. Two young women with multicolored hair and black leather jackets puzzled over the object, but showed no real interest in what it represented.

Way after hours, we were still prowling the backstreets and littered allies. We saw a man squatting on a sidewalk at four A.M., two dozen copies of *Penthouse* neatly laid out, side by side, trying to sell them to whoever chanced to walk by at that hour. It was a scene straight out of the Sprawl—the man had gleaned bits of detritus and lashed together an ad hoc entrepreneurial campfire that would burn for a few moments, then gutter out.

Years before, I now realized, I had misinterpreted the Velvet Underground. They weren't inventing anything new. They had simply reflected back to me a truer reality than any musician I had heard before. The cyberpunks, as well, did not originate their vision, but picked up bits and pieces of what was actually coming true, and fed it back to the readers who were already living in Gibson's Sprawl, whether they knew it or not.

Jean Baudrillard

The
Automation of
the Robot
(*from* Simulations)

A whole world separates these two artificial beings. One is a theatrical
counterfeit, a mechanical and clocklike man; technique submits entirely to *analogy* and to the effect of semblance. The other is dominated
by the technical principle; the machine overrides all, and with the
machine *equivalence* comes too. The automaton plays the part of
courtier and good company; it participates in the pre-Revolutionary
French theatrical and social games. The robot, on the other hand, as
his name indicates, is a worker: the theater is over and done with, the
reign of mechanical man commences. The automaton is the *analogy* of
man and remains his interlocutor (they play chess together!). The
machine is man's *equivalent* and annexes him to itself in the unity of its
operational process. This is the difference between a simulacrum of the
first order and one of the second.

We shouldn't make any mistakes on this matter for reasons of
"figurative" resemblance between robot and automaton. The latter is
an interrogation upon nature, the mystery of the existence or nonexis-
tence of the soul, the dilemma of appearance and being. It is like God:
what's underneath it all, what's inside, what's in the back of it? Only
the counterfeit men allow these problems to be posed. The entire
metaphysics of man as protagonist of the *natural theater* of the creation
is incarnated in the automaton, before disappearing with the Revolution. And the automaton has no other destiny than to be ceaselessly
compared to living man—so as to be more natural than him, of which
he is the ideal figure. A perfect double for man, right up to the
suppleness of his movements, the functioning of his organs and intelligence—right up to touching upon the anguish there would be in

Ferret

becoming aware that there is no difference, that the soul is over with and now it is an ideally naturalized body which absorbs its energy. Sacrilege. This difference is then always maintained, as in the case of that perfect automaton that the impersonator's jerky movements on stage imitate; so that at least, even if the roles were reversed, no confusion would be possible. In this way the interrogation of the automaton remains an open one, which makes it out to be a kind of mechanical optimist, even if the counterfeit always connotes something diabolical.[1]

No such thing with the robot. The robot no longer interrogates appearance; its only truth is in its mechanical efficacy. It is no longer turned towards a resemblance with man, to whom furthermore it no longer bears comparison. That infinitesimal metaphysical difference, which made all the charm and mystery of the automaton, no longer exists; the robot has absorbed it for its own benefit. Being and appearance are melted into a common substance of production and work. The first-order simulacrum never abolished difference. It supposes an always detectable alteration between semblance and reality (a particularly subtle game with trompe-l'oeil painting, but art lives entirely off of this gap). The second-order simulacrum simplifies the problem by the absorption of the appearances, or by the liquidation of the real, whichever. It establishes in any case a reality, image, echo, appearance; such is certainly work, the machine, the system of industrial production in its entirety, in that it is radically opposed to the principle of theatrical illusion. No more resemblance or lack of resemblance, of God, or human being, but an imminent logic of the operational principle.

From then on, men and machines can proliferate. It is even their law to do so—which the automatons never have done, being instead sublime and singular mechanisms. Men themselves only started their own proliferation when they achieved the status of machines, with the industrial revolution. Freed from all resemblance, freed even from their own double, they expand like the system of production, of which they are only the miniaturized equivalent. The revenge of the simulacrum that feeds the myth of the sorcerer's apprentice doesn't happen with the automaton. It is, on the other hand, the very law of the second type; and from that law proceeds still the hegemony of the robot, of the machine, and of dead work over living labor. This hegemony is necessary for the cycle of production and reproduction. It is with this reversal that we leave behind the counterfeit to enter (re)production. We leave natural law and the play of its forms to enter the realm of the mercantile law of value and its calculations of force.

Notes

1   Counterfeit and reproduction imply always an anguish, a disquieting foreignness: the uneasiness before the photograph, considered like a witches trick—and more generally before any technical apparatus, which is always an apparatus of reproduction, is related by Benjamin to the uneasiness before the mirror-image. There is already sorcery at work in the mirror. But how much more so when this image can be detached from the mirror and be transported, stocked, reproduced at will (cf. *The Student of Prague*, where the devil detaches the image of the student from the mirror and harrasses him to death by the intermediary of this image). All reproduction implies therefore a kind of black magic, from the fact of being seduced by one's own image in the water, like Narcissus, to being haunted by the double and, who knows, to the moral turning back of this vast technical apparatus secreted today by man as his own image (the narcissistic mirage of technique, McLuhan) and that returns to him, cancelled and distorted—endless reproduction of himself and his power to the limits of the world. Reproduction is diabolical in its very essence; it makes something fundamental vacillate. This has hardly changed for us: simulation (that we describe here as the operation of the code) is still and always the place of a gigantic enterprise of manipulation, of control and of death, just like the imitative object (primitive statuette, image of photo) always had as objective an operation of black image.

Istvan Csicsery-Ronay, Jr.

Cyberpunk
and
Neuromanticism

As a label, "cyberpunk" is perfection. It suggests the apotheosis of postmodernism. On the one hand, pure negation: of manners, history, philosophy, politics, body, will, affect, anything mediated by cultural memory; on the other, pure attitude: all is power, and "subculture," and the grace of Hip negotiating the splatter of consciousness as it slams against the hard-tech future, the techno-future of artificial immanence, where all that was once nature is simulated and elaborated by technical means, a future world-construct that is as remote from the "lessons of history" as the present mix-up is from the pitiful science fiction fantasies of the past that tried to imagine us. The oxymoronic conceit in "cyberpunk" is so slick and global it fuses the high and the low, the complex and the simple, the governor and the savage, the techno-sublime and rock and roll slime. The only thing left out is a place to stand. So one must move, always move.

Those are evocations; it's harder to say what the label actually refers to. The best-known cyberpunk manifesto, Bruce Sterling's introduction to the *Mirrorshades* anthology (1986), cannily describes the cyberpunk school's aspirations not in terms of conceits, but as the reflection of a new cultural synthesis being born in the 1980s, making it essentially a paradoxical form of realism. Cyberpunk art, Sterling says, captures "a new kind of integration. The overlapping of worlds that were formerly separate: the realm of high tech and the modern pop underground" (ix).

> This integration has become our decade's crucial source of cultural energy. The work of the cyberpunks is paralleled through the Eighties pop culture: in rock video; in the hacker underground; in

the jarring street tech of hip-hop and scratch music; in the synthesizer rock of London and Tokyo. This phenomenon, this dynamic, has a global range; cyberpunk is its literary incarnation. . . .

Suddenly a new alliance is becoming evident: an integration of technology and the Eighties counterculture. An unholy alliance of the technical world and the world of organized dissent—the underground world of pop, visionary fluidity, and street-level anarchy. (x)

Heady stuff. An art reflecting these trends must surely be the vanguard white male art of the age, a literature competing and allied with video games, MTV and new wave rock. But Sterling's claims immediately raise some questions. The question of the "integration" for one. What is this world of a high-tech pop underground? The punk club world of Sonic Youth and Pussy Galore, acts never to be simulated on MTV? The violently sexist, stylized gangster-chic of unsanitized ghetto rap? Where's the "organized dissent," and how does it jive with "street-level anarchy"? Sterling hints at some new political attitude with technical know-how and antiestablishment feelings, an "alliance," an "integration," a "counterculture." To put it mildly, it's hard to see the "integrated" political-aesthetic motives of alienated subcultures that adopt the high-tech tools of the establishment they are supposedly alienated from. It seems far more reasonable to assume that the "integrating," such as it is, is being done by the dominant telechtronic cultural powers, who—as cyberpunk writers know very well—are insatiable in their appetite for new commodities and commodity fashions. The big question for 1980s art is whether any authentic countercultural art can exist for long without being transformed into self-annihilating simulations of themselves for mass consumption, furthering central cultural aims. Given the chances of cyberpunk's success in the amusement marketplace, its potential for movie options, that is, its ripe co-optability, one might suspect Sterling's enthusiasm for his "integration" is based on less than thorough social analysis, if not on less than sincere motives.

Another interesting question is exactly what cyberpunk literature can offer that video games, hip-hop, and Rejection Front rock cannot. At one point in *Mirrorshades*, Sterling speaks of the "classic cyberpunk mix" of "mythic images and technosocial politics" (125). But to my mind that is a very different thing from the putative "integration"—closer to the traditional ways of SF perhaps, but pretty far from the street and counterculture.

It's also hard to see how Sterling's claims are borne out by the writing associated with the *Mirrorshades* anthology. Right off, one should be suspicious of any movement said to include writers as remarkable, and remarkably different, as Greg Bear, Rudy Rucker, and William Gibson. Bear's and Rucker's inclusion among the cyberpunks smacks more of friendly endorsement than of truly shared aesthetic aims. And it's hard to tell whether Sterling means his "literary incarnation" to be a direction within the popular science fiction industry, a visionary style transcending the SF ghetto boundaries, or an artistic "integration" of high and low culture, or all three. In the first case, "cyberpunk" might actually be just an intraprofessional label—like the old "New Wave"—intended to distinguish a new, more daring generation of writers from the old farts who once controlled the means of literary production. The second and third require some convincing proofs.

Maybe one shouldn't want too much "philosophy" from a style that proclaims its allegiance to pulp hard SF as proudly as Sterling does. Still, how many formulaic tales can one wade through in which a self-destructive but sensitive young protagonist with an (implant/prosthesis/telechtronic talent) that makes the evil (megacorporations/police states/criminal underworlds) pursue him through (wasted urban landscapes/elite luxury enclaves/eccentric space stations) full of grotesque (haircuts/clothes/self-mutilations/rock music/sexual hobbies/designer drugs/telechtronic gadgets/nasty new weapons/exteriorized hallucinations) representing the (mores/fashions) of modern civilization in terminal decline, ultimately hooks up with rebellious and tough-talking (youth/artificial intelligence/rock cults) who offer the alternative, not of (community/socialism/traditional values/transcendental vision), but of supreme, life-affirming *hipness*, going with the flow which now flows in the machine, against the spectre of a world-subverting (artificial intelligence/multinational corporate web/evil genius)? Yet judging from even the best of writers in Sterling's anthology, for cyberpunks, "hipness is all."

The postmodern sensibility has come to suspect the idea of depth, "profundity," with a vengeance; true punks don't even have to know how to play the instruments they perform with, true hackers need no other goals than challenges to their programming skills. Still, there's a line between suspicion and a belief that the truest cultural struggles of the strange 1980s are style wars. Hip is a hard goddess. Who is so hip as to be above Hip? There's a very tricky premise in that aesthetic, in presenting the *idea* of cyberpunk's Meta-Hip as a mode that can transcend the trash and competition for shelf-space of 1980s SF; for if Sterling's cyberpunks are right, and win their aesthetic wager, they lose: their style will die with the next trend in the telematic culture-industry, with the next style to be certified as a hip "integration." Hence, perhaps, all those self-destructive artists in their works. Hence, the second- and third-rate writing that passes for style, not even worrying about art.

My suspicion is that most of the literary cyberpunks bask in the light of the one major writer who is original and gifted enough to make the whole movement seem original and gifted. That figure is William Gibson, whose first novel, *Neuromancer* (1984), is to my mind one of the most interesting books of the postmodern age. I suggest, then, that we think of cyberpunk not as a movement in the U.S. and Japanese SF trade, but as a more encompassing aesthetic—as it is embodied by Gibson and certain other postmodern artists. Viewed like this, cyberpunk is a legitimate international artistic style, with profound philosophical and aesthetic premises. It has already produced a body of significant work in literature (Gibson's novels) and especially in film: Ridley Scott's *Alien* (1979) and *Blade Runner* (1982), *Robocop* (1987), and Cronenberg's *Videodrome* (1983). It has its philosophers: Deleuze and Guattari, Jean Baudrillard, and the Canadian Arthur Kroker; it even has, in Michael Jackson and Ronald Reagan, its hyperreal icons of the human simulacrum infiltrating reality.

I spoke of philosophy. Although the main point of the label "cyberpunk" may be to signify the irreverence of the high-tech hipster, a macho substitute for the neuter "hacker," the terms of the oxymoron imply certain conceptual possibilities that the most ambitious cyberpunk artists are very well aware of. Both cybernetics and punk transcend familiar distinctions. Cybernetics provides the pretext for the mechanized control of social life, of the body itself, and all of it through the delicate nets of nonmachine-derived mathematical formulae. Cybernetics represents the hardening and exteriorization of certain vital forms of knowledge, the crystallization of the Cartesian spirit into material objects and commodities. Cybernetics is already a paradox: simultaneously a sublime vision of human power over chance and a dreary augmentation of multinational capitalism's mechanical process of expansion—so far characterized by almost uninterrupted positive feedback. Cybernetics is, thus, part natural philosophy, part necromancy, part ideology.

So is punk, but in reverse. A self-stupefying and self-mutilating refusal to dignify or trust anything that has brought about the present world, even the human body, all for the promise of an authenticity so undefinable it can't ever be known, let alone co-opted. Punk is sentimentalism's *Schone Seele* inverted: it slam-dances angrily out of the world, playing "power chords" to deafness. Yet for all that, it embodies philosophy. The punk is a sarcastic mirror-reflection of the social engineers' dream. The punk pretends to be a soft machine, but the machine is savage and intractable. "Cyber/punk"—the ideal postmodern couple: a machine philosophy that can create the world in its own image and a self-mutilating freedom, that is that image snarling back.

This broader sense of cyberpunk reflects the increasingly pervasive influence of a particular moment of science fiction on postmodern culture: the moment when science fiction depicts what one theorist, Zoe Sofia, calls the "collapse of the future on the present." Beginning in the 1950s science fiction writers began to abandon the conventions of expansionist SF: heroic planetary exploration, space travel without boredom, the dignity of aliens, small groups of harmonious researchers, and in style, lucid, utilitarian prose emphasizing the no-nonsense attitudes of adventurer-scientists in command and control. The expansive forms of SF reflected the optimistic and secure ideology of scientistic humanism, which held that classical liberal virtues have some moral-ethical control over the forces of technological production. Moreover, the mythologies of the expansion of human consciousness into "outer space" were to represent guarantees that they would be implanted or strengthened in the future. The point of the expansive mode was to show that human consciousness can contain the future. Its future was the dominant ideology of the present purified of uncertainties. In Asimov's robots, artificial intelligences were endowed with superhuman ethics; majestically superior intelligences, like the Krell in *Forbidden Planet* (1956), fell prey to "monsters of the Id"; and radically different forms of being worked hand in hand with human adventurers in Clement's *Mission of Gravity* (1954), proving the ideal synthesis of bourgeois technicism and bourgeois virtue on all possible worlds.

Such expansion was usually represented as a sort of manic explosion, in which projectiles of human consciousness fly giddily out into "outer space," where they encounter either the variety of being or the final proof of the universality of consciousness. They either learn to learn more and better, or they learn to accept the laws of *moira*. The important knowledge was to be gained by spreading out. In SF's expansive phase, it did not matter whether the "moral" was liberal-optimistic like *Star Trek* or Freudian-conservative like *Forbidden Planet*; the truth was discovered through exploration of what was not Earth. Hence, the Earth was placed in a bubble that insured its safe and secure historical development within liberal constraints.

In the 1960s this vector was reversed, and most writers who used science as a metaphor in their work dwelt on its inherent paradoxes, its reverses, its self-defeating assumptions. Most of all, they depicted the destruction of liberal ideology by autonomous technology. Nowadays this SF of implosion dominates everywhere. Where there was uncontrolled expansion, the *afflatus* of an expanding technicist ego hallucinating cosmic humanism, now there is implosion, a drastic, careening plunge toward some inconceivable center of gravity that breaks up the categories of rationality by jamming them together. While the expansion was fueled by the desire for containment, implosion is fueled by the desire for dissolution.

The metaphor of implosion comes up often in theoretical writings on the crisis of representation and politics in the postmodern condition, especially in the work of Jean Baudrillard and Arthur Kroker, who might be taken as the central theorists of cyberpunk philosophy. Theory and metaphor follow practice here. The boom fields of current scientific research—which are naturally the favored topoi of current SF—also demonstrate this sharp inward turn. Microbiology, data storage miniaturization, bionic prosthetics, artificial intelligence, particle physics, the world-shrinking global grid of communication/control systems, and the marked decrease in enthusiasm for space exploration (which must not be attributed solely to the *Challenger* disaster): all these interests require the radical shrinking of focus onto microcosms, and all imply the impossibility of drawing clear boundaries among perceptual and cognitive, indeed, even ontological, categories. The current scientific scene is entranced by the microstudy of boundaries no longer believed to be fundamental: between life and nonlife, parasite and host, human and machine, great and small, body-brain and cosmos. Expansive SF was based on historical analogies of colonialism and social Darwinism, the power struggles of the old against the new, the ancient against the scientific. The topoi of implosive SF are based on analogies of the invasion and transformation of the body by alien entities of our own making. Implosive science fiction finds the scene of SF problematics not in imperial adventures among the stars, but in the body-physical/body-social and a drastic ambivalence about the body's traditional—and terrifyingly uncertain—integrity.

This is cyberpunk's formative culture. It is related to, and overlaps, the literature of horror, especially the splash-and-splatter films of the 1970s and 1980s. But different values are involved in the two genres. The horror genre has always played with the violation of the body, since it adopts as its particular "object" *fear*—the violent disruption of the sense of security, which, precisely because it is a sense, works from within the body, the house of the senses. Hence, in horror, the house/body's integrity is generally threatened from within, using analogues of disease and unconscious psychosomatic pathology, or by evil entities that hate the flesh and wish not only to destroy it, but to torture and degrade it. The demiurge of horror works out a drama of pollution and curse, which terrorizes the mind by assuring it it will feel the utmost conceivable pain.

The drama of pollution and curse has recently been raised in the horror genre to a level of confusion and fury where splattering brains and organs without bodies are required to show the punishment of the physical. In the past, it was bad enough to violate the dignity of life (anachronistically preserved in such current crimes as "wrongful death" and "depriving of civil rights," that is, homicide). Strangling and poisoning seem almost clean, intellectual crimes nowadays, far less interesting than the savage dismemberments we have come to expect. SF does not have to emulate such effects from the horror genre (except perhaps to increase sales). But as it concentrates increasingly on the vulnerability of the body, it deals more and more with the ways in which science reveals and creates new ways of intruding on that vulnerability. (Greg Bear's marvelous *Blood Music* [1985] is a model of the way in which SF can use the ambivalence of the scientific attitude to "redeem" the devices of horror.)

Even when the same images or motifs are used as in the horror genre, they have a different value in SF because they attack not the image of the body, but the *idea* of the image of the body, the very possibility of "imaging" the body (to borrow a metaphor from cyber-medicine). This implies that the object of attack is a calm, intellectual-rational still-point, the locus of reflection and constraint that both science and much art assume as the black box mediator of experience into design—the prerequisite for conceiving of a psychodynamics, or indeed a psyche, in the first place. This is where the computer plays a decisive role both as actor and symbol. For the computer represents the possibility of modeling everything that exists in the phenomenal world, of breaking down into information and then simulating perfectly in infinitely replicable form those processes that precybernetic humanity had held to be inklings of transcendence. With the computer, the problem of identity is moot, and the idea of reflection is transformed into the algorithm of replication. SF's computer wipes out the Philo-sophical God and ushers in the demiurge of thought-as-technique.

The horrifying element in implosive SF is the disruption of knowl-edge in its most tangible form: the madness of the knower. Cyberpunk is part of a trend in science fiction dealing increasingly with madness, more precisely with the most philosophically interesting phenomenon of madness: hallucination (derangement). Tales are constructed around the literal/physical exteriorization of images representing the break-down of stable, standard-giving rational, perceptual, and conceptual categories. So the most important sense is not fear, but *dread*. Halluci-nation is always saturated with affect. It is perception *instigated* by affect. The threefold nightmare of the scientific mind is that such a process, would it extend beyond the confines of individual skulls, will create its own "other" reality, invalidate previous articulations, and use the scientific mind as its agent, or its victim. It is natural to expect that as technology proves more and more able to construct the world in its own image (that is, to create simulacra to replace the "real" and the "original")—indeed, to restructure the operations of the multinational capitalism that enables it to exist—there will be an increasing sense of its hallucinatory nature, its arbitrary yet *overdetermining* power. For there seems to be little contest between the overdetermination of technology and the underdetermination of theory.

More and more SF treats hallucination as an object in the world— a privileged object, since it does not merely exist among other things, but changes their ontic status by its very "exteriorized" existence. The trend began seriously with Philip K. Dick, J. G. Ballard, and the New Wave, the 1960s fascination with hallucinogens and altered states of consciousness; and already with Dick there is difficulty distinguishing between mystical truths and machine dreams. By the time we get to cyberpunk, reality has become a case of nerves—that is, the interfusion of nervous system and computer-matrix, sensation and information, so all battles are fought out in feeling and mood, with dread exteriorized in the world itself. The distance required for reflection is squeezed out as the world implodes; when hallucinations and reality collapse into each other, there is no place from which to reflect.

What cyberpunk—at least in its most successful works—has going for it is a rich thesaurus of metaphors linking the organic and the electronic. Most of these metaphors lie ready to hand in the telechtronics-saturated culture. Psychology and even physiology are wiring, nerves are circuits, drugs and sex and other thrills turn you on, you get a buzz, you get wired, you space out, you go on automatic. They work the other way, too, of course: there are "virus programs" constructed to work against other information systems' "immune systems." The advantage these metaphors have over the more deliberate and reflective symbols that usually go into the cybernetic fiction discussed in David Porush's *The Soft Machine* (1985) is that they are embedded in the constantly shifting context of a global culture drawn into ever newer, ever stranger webs of communication command and control. The metaphors themselves have a life. And in the hands of a master, like Gibson, the fuzzy links can become a subtly constructed, but always merely implied, four-level hierarchy of evolving systems of information processing, from the individual human being's biological processes and personality, through the total life of society, to nonliving artificial intelligences, and ultimately to new entities created out of those AIs. In *Neuromancer*, each level of the hierarchy is meaningless to itself, yet it creates the material/informational conditions for the evolution of the next higher one, and all participate in a quasicosmic "dance of biz."

Cyberpunk is fundamentally ambivalent about the breakdown of the distinctions between human and machine, between personal consciousness and machine consciousness. In almost every significant cyberpunk work, the breakdown is initiated from outside, usually by the pressures exerted by multinational capitalism's desire for something better than the fallible human being. The villains come from the human corporate world and use their great technical resources to create beings that program out the glitches of the human: the Company in *Alien* seeking a perfect war machine; the consortium in *Robocop* constructing the perfect crime fighter; in *Blade Runner*, Terrell Industries, who have created the Nexus-4 replicants, the perfect servant/worker/warrior; in *Videodrome*, the conspiracy determined to wipe the Earth clean of anachronistic sadism-loving people; in *Neuromancer*, the Tessier-Ashpool clan.

And yet, out of the antihuman evil that has created conditions intolerable for normal human life comes some new situation. This new situation is, then, either the promise of an apocalyptic entrance into a new evolutionary synthesis of the human and the machine, or an all-encompassing hallucination in which true motives, and true affects, cannot be known. *Neuromancer*'s myth of the evolution of a new cosmic entity out of human technology is perhaps the only seriously positive version of the new situation—but even it offers only limited transcendence, since the world is much the same in Gibson's second novel, *Count Zero* (1986a), set some years later.

Along with this ambivalent mythopoeia goes cyberpunk artists' irresistible attraction to the nervous excesses of malaise. In a universe where the forces of innovation are constantly tinkering with human beings' own information processing systems through telematics, drugs, and surgical intervention, the regulator of experience (ego? self? spirit?) can no longer accept any experience as worth more than any other. The only standard is thrill, the ability to "light up the circuits" of the nervous matrix, sensation so strong that it can draw consciousness into the conditions of its own possibility. Rather than putting the mind to sleep, thrill keeps the mind alert, allowing it to keep up with the velocities at which the production of sensation works. In Gibson's world, human beings have nothing left but thrill. It is all that power can offer, but it is also—the ambivalence again—the only way to create new conditions, since old philosophical-moral considerations mean nothing in a world where one can plug in another's feelings or a personality-memory complex through "simstim" (simulated stimulus), assimilate a myriad of power programs through "microsofts" plugged directly into "cranial jacks," be rebuilt or redesigned with special features or resurrected through nerve splicing and elective surgery, or have one's consciousness kept intact after physical death entirely through a program.

So cyberpunks, like near-addicts of amphetamines and hallucinogens, write as if they are both victims of a life-negating system and the heroic adventurers of thrill. They can't help themselves, but their hip grace gets them through an amoral world, facing a future which, for all intents and purposes, has gone beyond human influence, and where the only way to live is in speed, speed to avoid being caught in the web and getting rubbed out by the Yakuza, the AIs, the androids, the new corporate entities bent on their own self-elaboration. Here, the speed of thrill substitutes for affection, reflection, and care, which require room and leisure and relaxation; so there are no families, no art, no crafting of natural materials, no lazy climbing out of the stream. (Where there is a hint of valuable art in the future, it is by psychotics or by marginal nonwhite folk who are somehow closer to the ancient, the latter a sentimental motif particularly dear to Gibson.) Movement all the time: in plot, in theme, in style, and in syntax. Huge amounts of new information—neologisms, innovations, twists of plot, secreted levels of hierarchy—are carried along an incredibly swift stream of narrative. In the world: drugs, "biz," metal traveling in cyberspace, orgasm without tenderness, and the constant, wearying drive to *do*, which translates into impelled work. Ultimately, sensation wears matter out. Humanity burns bright in its hotshot suicide; it may live on as "The New Flesh," which may not be flesh at all, and may preserve of us what we admire least.

The knowledge of "what we can do" and "what we can hope for" is left suspended, unasked.

Human intelligence has become a case of nerves, and the meaning of things, if it is to be revealed, will be by an intelligence "not for us."

For us is *thrill* and *work*, and *maybe* hope that we will be in the right place at the right time to find the right combination of things, which will benefit our friends (unless they betray us).

All of the ambivalent solutions of cyberpunk works are instances/ myths of bad faith, since they completely ignore the question of whether some political controls over technology are desirable, if not exactly possible. Cyberpunk is then the apotheosis of bad faith, the apotheosis of the postmodern.

I don't mean that as pejoratively as it sounds. It goes along with the sophistication and ambivalence of cyberpunk artists that they know that their art is in bad faith. But in a world of absolute bad faith, where the real and the true are superseded by simulacra and the hyperreal, perhaps the only hope is in representing that bad faith appropriately.

But let's not get carried away. Cyberpunk artists acquire much of their power like the *poetes maudits* before them by dealing with the Devil. They aren't concerned with the implications of cybernetic knowledge for knowledge and identity—the dizzying process of constructing a self (as in McElroy's *Plus* [1976])—or the philosophical problems of imagining a truly artificial intelligence (as in Lem's *His Master's Voice* [1968] or *Golem XIV*—the latter, the ruminations of a "luminal" megacomputer, the diametrical opposite of cyberpunk, in its meditative tedium). For the one thing that cyberpunk is fascinated with above all else, its ruling deity, is sleaze—the scummy addiction to thrill that can focus all of a person's imaginative power on a sensation that wipes out all discipline, and which at the same time sells books, attracts movie options, and generates sequels. They are not delirious fools. They know sleaze, because they have set up shop in the belly of the beast. They are canny men—almost all of them men (why would a woman care about a technological society she had no role in creating?)—who have an uncanny sense that the nightmarish neuromanticism is a powerful drug, too. Reflection on thrill can be a thrill, too, when an audience grows used to the technologies of reflection: replication, commentary, entertainment tonight. This romanticism does not repress the "meat" as the forebears did. This one has permitted itself enough distance to demand that the "meat" show its unruly self, show that it's not only not the enemy, but that it's the victim—it can splatter, burst, writhe, pulsate, secrete, furiously publicize its anguish. It is helpless and sad, against the powers of exteriorized mind—whose modes are the hard, cruel, gun-metal cold, spiky, and unyielding ways of self-proliferating hard stuff. The flesh is sad, and then some— romance is a case of nerves.

Jacques Derrida

From

Of

Grammatology

For some time now . . . here and there, by a gesture and for motives that
are profoundly necessary, whose degradation is easier to denounce
than it is to disclose their origin, one says "language" for action,
movement, thought, reflection, consciousness, unconsciousness, experience, affectivity, etc. Now we tend to say "writing" for all that and
more: to designate not only the physical gestures of literal pictographic
or ideographic inscription, but also the totality of what makes it
possible; and also, beyond the signifying face, the signified face itself.
And thus we say "writing" for all that gives rise to an inscription in
general, whether it is literal or not and even if what it distributes in
space is alien to the order of the voice: cinematography, choreography,
of course, but also pictorial, musical, sculptural "writing." One might
also speak of athletic writing, and with even greater certainty of
military or political writing in view of the techniques that govern those
domains today. All this to describe not only the system of notation
secondarily connected with these activities but the essence and the
content of these activities themselves. It is also in this sense that the
contemporary biologist speaks of writing and *pro-gram* in relation to
the most elementary processes of information within the living cell.
And, finally, whether it has essential limits or not, the entire field
covered by the cybernetic *program* will be the field of writing. If the
theory of cybernetics is by itself to oust all metaphysical concepts—
including the concepts of soul, of life, of value, of choice, of memory—which until recently served to separate the machine from man, it
must conserve the notion of writing, trace, grammè [written mark], or
grapheme, until its own historico-metaphysical character is also ex-

posed. Even before being determined as human (with all the distinctive characteristics that have always been attributed to man and the entire system of significations that they imply) or nonhuman, the *grammè*— or the *grapheme*—would thus name the element. An element without simplicity. An element, whether it is understood as the medium or as the irreducible atom, of the arche-synthesis in general, of what one must forbid oneself to define within the system of oppositions of metaphysics, of what consequently one should not even call *experience* in general, that is to say the origin of *meaning* in general.

Joan Gordon

Yin and
Yang
Duke
It Out

There exists two kinds of feminist science fiction: overt and covert. Overt feminist science fiction always grapples with the definition of femaleness and at least implies the possibility of a world whose values support a feminist definition of female identity. Covert feminist science fiction ignores the definition, showing a sexually egalitarian world; furthermore, its values often ignore specifically feminist issues, making its morality a more generally applied one.

Overt feminist SF is in a rut. Femaleness is consistently defined in terms of the Zen principle of Yin—passive, gentle, nurturing, peaceful (see Le Guin's essay, "A Non-Euclidean View of California as a Cold Place to Be"). We females are in tune with nature, living in it, adapting to it: we're vegetarian, nonpolluting earth mothers, representatives of prepatriarchal nature religions. Males are, of course, competitive, aggressive, meat-eating polluters, members of the now-dominant patriarchy. One longs for the good old days not so much of nature religions, but just of Joanna Russ's *The Female Man* (1975).

Now, however, cyberpunk has appeared. At first glance it seems to be overt masculinist science fiction—men are men, waving guns and knives, competing like all getout and plugged up to the gills with pollutant technology. But look at the women in mirrorshades—Molly in Gibson's *Neuromancer* (1984), Deadpan Allie in Cadigan's *Mindplayers* (1987), for instance—aren't they tougher than the rest? I would suggest that cyberpunk is covert feminist science fiction. On that night foray into the underworld which is the central experience of what we will conveniently call cyberpunk, men and women travel as equals. Furthermore, and potentially liberating for feminist science fiction, the cyberpunk vision is a radical departure from traditional feminist SF. This difference allows an escape from the present nostalgia for a distant and irrecoverable past.

Cyberpunk isn't exactly a direct line to feminist thought. It describes something quite separate from the concerns of feminism and acknowledges only one female author, Pat Cadigan. Bruce Sterling's discussion of cyberpunk's origins, in both *Mirrorshades* (1986a) introduction and in his preface to William Gibson's *Burning Chrome* (1986b), completely ignores the tremendous influence on SF, even on cyberpunk, of many women writers. One might think women science fiction writers had no part in the SF tradition, much less in cyberpunk. I would suggest the movement has been and continues to be strongly influenced by feminist SF writers. James Tiptree's "The Girl Who Was Plugged In" (1973) prefigures cyberpunk, which William Gibson points out in his *Science Fiction Eye* interview with Takayuki Tatsumi (1988). As cyberpunk matures away from the limitations of Gardner Dozois's label, its writers have shown the feminist influence more clearly. Bruce Sterling's *Islands in the Net* (1988) has a female protagonist who works for a company based on those nice Yin principles, and William Gibson's *Mona Lisa Overdrive* (1988) has three female protagonists. In both novels, the women represent various instructive distances from the traditional female role. Despite the oversight in Sterling's introduction to *Mirrorshades*, I doubt these writers would deny the debt.

It nevertheless seems oddly true that cyberpunk is a boys' club. In fact, science fiction by women, often characterized by soft rather than hard science, by emphasis on character and interpersonal relations, seems quite "humanist," while humanism and cyberpunk have been set up as opposites in some recent discussions in *Science Fiction Eye*. It's time for women to break into the boys' club; cyberpunk may be feminism's SF salvation.

One reason has to do with the typical protagonists of such recent feminist science fiction as Joan Slonczewski's *A Door Into Ocean* (1986), where a good woman nurtures, shares, and shuns violence. Such a vision of good is philosophically admirable but has become, for me, too predictable. I long for blood thirsty Janet of Whileaway in *The Female Man*. Listen to *her* opening statement: "I love my daughter . . . I love my family . . . I love my wife . . . I've fought four duels. I've killed four times" (1975:2). It may not be moral, but it is energetic and surprising. It even allows women to lapse from moral perfection. Whileaway, Janet's all-female alternate world, is nurturing and pastoral, like virtually all SF worlds illustrating feminist principles, but it is also technologically well developed and far from pacifist. Thus, Russ's overtly feminist novel avoids some of what will become an entire set of clichés about matriarchal worlds, and shows instead a tough woman who behaves unself-consciously like a human being, not like a representative of female principles.

That is also the power of such female cyberpunk characters as Molly in *Neuromancer* and Deadpan Allie in *Mindplayers*. They're both good at their jobs, mayhem and pathosfinding, and they're both very tough. In his interview with Tatsumi, Gibson talks about how film director Howard Hawks influenced him:

> *"I'm starting to think that Howard Hawks programmed a whole lot of my first two books, especially in terms of the strong woman who can't really relate to any of the other men in the narrative except for the one guy who might possibly be as strong as she is, but usually turns out not to be."* (1988)

That sounds like Molly of the implanted mirrorshades and knife-blade fingernails. To some extent she's a man in women's clothing (see that line about "*other* men" above), the most facile and least thoughtful representation of the liberated woman. But to some extent, also, she is simply a human being in women's clothing, one of the two standard issue uniforms for the species. It seems to me that for a woman to enter the human army as an average soldier with no distinction in rank, privilege, or job position is, on the covert level, a feminist act.

Deadpan Allie of Pat Cadigan's *Mindplayers* is another tough soldier. Cadigan's book, with little casual violence and no mirrorshades, has less of the feel of cyberpunk than *Neuromancer*, but shares much of the common vision. Deadpan Allie, pathosfinder, takes hallucinatory trips into the underworld of her clients' subconscious, and withstands more psychic violence than anyone else, male or female, never revealing her own emotional state. Yes, like Molly, she is tougher than the rest. Her job, delving into the unconscious, is less a departure from the female role than Molly's contract killing, but it is just as dangerous in its own way. Like Molly, Allie handles the risk without showing emotion: hence her nickname, Deadpan Allie. Blunt affect seems an important component of cyberpunk toughness. Allie's toughness, like Molly's, represents no female principle, just a human coping mechanism. Less violent than Molly, there is less danger of her being taken for the man in woman's clothing. But like Molly, she performs the covert feminist act of entering the human army combat-ready and on equal footing.

Egalitarian toughness makes the women of male-dominated cyberpunk politically appealing to feminists, but cyberpunk has something more important and less direct to offer as well: a vision of the world which is both a logical extension of the 1980s and a radical departure from the essentially nostalgic view of feminist science fiction. Virtually every feminist SF utopia dreams of a pastoral world, fueled by organic structures rather than mechanical ones, inspired by versions of the archetypal Great Mother. And virtually every feminist SF novel, utopian or not, incorporates a longing to go forward into the idealized past of earth's earlier matriarchal nature religions. Because cyberpunk extrapolates from the 1980s—not a sterling time for feminism in the world at large—it's no wonder few women are presently involved in the movement. Nevertheless, cyberpunk does much that could enrich overt feminist SF by directing it away from nostalgia. Cyberpunk embraces technology, revels in the complexities of an imperfect world, and grapples with the journey to the underworld. Feminist science fiction has veered away from these activities, all of which allow us to shape and manage our futures rather than escape them.

The artificial kids of cyberpunk are more than enthusiastic about the latest technology; they plug it into their skulls, pop it in their eye sockets, and embed it into their fingertips. Feminist SF consistently avoids the kind of intrusive technology cyberpunk embraces. In *The Female Man*, inhabitants have the "possibility" of teleportation but prefer to walk. "Whileaway is so pastoral that at times one wonders whether the ultimate sophistication may not take us all back to a kind of prepaleolithic dawn age." The Shorans of *A Door Into Ocean* skillfully employ genetic engineering to control their environment but are sharply distrustful of any form of mechanical, nonorganic engineering. Although I share the latter work's discomfort with technology that disrupts the environment and the former work's preference to walk, and although I can launch a full-scale Jungian sort of explanation for this feminist vision, I need a change. It isn't likely that the earth will pull back from its movement toward high technology and the Sprawl for a long time, if ever. Cyberpunk, with all its cynicism, shows a future we might reasonably expect, and shows people successfully coping, surviving, and manipulating it. Feminist SF needs to acknowledge that if we can control technology even as it increases its potential to control us, we will have a better chance for survival in the imperfect future which we can reasonably expect.

Overt feminist science fiction has explored its mythic past and its utopian ideals in a number of fine works, but it could gain much by turning to an exploration of women's role in the imperfect world that we will continue to inhabit. Bruce Sterling praises William Gibson's short stories for "their brilliant self-consistent evocation of a credible future," an effort which he claims "many SF writers have been ducking for years." It's a bit narrow to claim, as Sterling does here, that writing SF about something other than a "credible future" is an "intellectual failing." However, it is true that the feminist movement in SF has neglected this particular subgenre of SF. Women are acculturated to be *good*; boys will be boys but girls can't misbehave. Is that one reason we keep looking to idealized worlds rather than our sure-to-be flawed future in feminist science fiction? Let's try exploring the female presence in a likely and imperfect near future so we can survive and even enjoy a world where neither we nor it is perfect. What definition of female identity might arise out of an unapologetic acknowledgement of our imperfection? I for one am not convinced that I am an earth mother. What else might I be? If science fiction can show what it means to be female in the world toward which we hurtle, I want to read it.

So the cyberpunk vision would allow feminist science fiction writers to consider the possibilities of a less antagonistic relationship with technology and to examine women's identity in the "credible future," but cyberpunk has more to offer. Another characteristic which has not been exploited by feminist science fiction is cyberpunk's extensive and gritty handling of the motif of the journey to the underworld. In each pathosfinder episode of *Mindplayers*, Allie dives into her own subconscious or that of a client, making one version of the journey. Each trip into some chaotic, lawless Sprawl constitutes another version of the trip. Elsewhere are drug-induced trips into other varieties of the heart of darkness. In every case, the trip reveals the underside of the human condition; hence, the "hard-edged, gloomy passion" with which Sterling characterizes Gibson's literary tone.

Feminist SF has investigated movingly and convincingly the underside of the male power structure, but only rarely has it explored the underside of female identity. It has been necessary to explore what is good and strong about female identity, and what is dangerous about an inimicable male-dominated society. But since every human being has a dark side, for us to acknowledge our full female identity requires that we undertake the journey. In our willingness to admit our imperfection, we may be sacrificing our completeness. A version of the mythic journey to the underworld will help us capture our own dark side. Maybe we're not too eager to reveal that side of our nature; socially, women are still in the position of proving equality by being a credit to our sex. It is perhaps dangerous yet to admit our real dark side to a world still deeply interested in women's imagined sinful nature. But the risk may well be worth it in both psychological and literary terms.

And not just because it makes you a better person to admit your faults. Katabasis, the mythic journey to the underworld, does more. As Joseph Campbell shows in *The Hero with a Thousand Faces* (1949), it makes us heroes, and the journey is not just to our own dark side, but to the dark side of the human condition. Moreover, its power lies not so much in what we learn on the journey as it does on the fact of our learning and in our subsequent transformation.

As Campbell says: "The hero . . . is the man or woman who has been able to battle past his personal and local historical limitations to the generally valid, normally human forms. Such a one's visions, ideas, and inspirations come pristine from the primary springs of human life and thought. Hence they are eloquent, not of the present, disintegrating society and psyche, but of the unquenched source through which society is reborn. The hero has died as a modern man—he has been reborn. His second solemn task and deed [after the journey itself] . . . is to return to us transfigured and teach the lesson he has learned of life renewed."

Some feminist SF writers have allowed their characters to take this journey—notably Ursula Le Guin—but never from a place near us, never under circumstances available to us in any foreseeable future. To imagine the journey in a possible and seemingly attainable future, to allow the learning and subsequent transformation to take place without the attainment of perfection or utopia, might be very valuable. At the end of *Mindplayers*, Allie finds not utopia or perfection but what her psyche has dubbed "alerted snakes of consequences." And they tell her, "you will go down into darkness before you die—but you won't go alone." On her journey she has learned to choose "a whole self" rather than just "an accumulation of elements." She has moved from the personal to the universal.

In the grim future of most cyberpunk, the message taken back from the night journey is seldom cheering, but it does move beyond the "disintegrating society" to a realization that has the potential for renewal in both the individual and society. Overt feminist science fiction, the kind which directly confronts issues of meaning and direction for the condition of women, needs to risk such a journey, starting near enough the present to find its way back to us with a coherent lesson. If that lesson teaches us less about perfection and more about coping with and enjoying the gritty future to which we are likely heirs, so much the better.

Veronica Hollinger

Cybernetic
Deconstructions:
Cyberpunk and
Postmodernism

Technology is now, not only in a distant,
science fictional future, an extension of our
sensory capacities; it shapes our perceptions
and cognitive processes, mediates our
relationships with objects of the material and
physical world, and our relationships with our
own or other bodies.
—(De Lauretis, 1980:167)

If, as Fredric Jameson has argued, postmodernism is our contemporary
cultural dominant (1984a:56), so equally, according to Teresa de Lauretis, is technology "our historical context, political and personal"
(1980:167). Putting these two aspects of our reality together, Larry
McCaffery has recently identified SF as "the most significant evolution
of a paraliterary form" in contemporary literature (1986:xvii).

Postmodernist texts which rely heavily on SF iconography and
themes have proliferated since the 1960s and it can be argued that
some of the most challenging science fiction of recent years has been
produced by mainstream and vanguardist rather than genre writers. A
random survey of postmodernist writing that has been influenced by
SF—works for which Bruce Sterling (1989) suggests the term "slipstream"—might include, for example, Richard Brautigan's *In Watermelon Sugar* (1968), Monique Wittig's *Les Guérillères* (1969), Angela
Carter's *Heroes and Villains* (1969), J. G. Ballard's *Crash* (1973),
Russel Hoban's *Riddley Walker* (1980), Ted Mooney's *Easy Travel to
Other Planets* (1981), Anthony Burgess's *The End of the World News*
(1982), and Kathy Acker's *Empire of the Senseless* (1988).

Not surprisingly, however, the specific concerns and aesthetic techniques of postmodernism have been slow to appear in genre SF, which tends to pride itself on its status as a paraliterary phenomenon. Genre SF thrives within an epistemology that privileges the logic of cause-and-effect narrative development and it usually demonstrates a rather optimistic belief in the progress of human knowledge. Appropriately, the space ship was its representative icon during the 1940s and 1950s, the expansionist "golden age" of American SF. Equally appropriately, genre SF can claim the realist novel as its closest narrative relative; both developed in an atmosphere of nineteenth-century scientific positivism and both rely to a great extent on the mimetic transparency of language as a "window" through which to provide views of a relatively uncomplicated human reality. When SF is enlisted by postmodernist fiction, however, it becomes integrated into an aesthetic and a worldview whose central tenets are an uncertainty and an indeterminacy which call into question the "causal interpretation of the universe" and the reliance on a "rhetoric of believability" which virtually define it as a generic entity (Ebert, 1980:92).

It is within the conflictual framework of realist literary conventions played out in the postmodernist field that I want to look at cyberpunk, a "movement" in 1980s SF that produced a wide range of fictions exploring the technological ramifications of experience within late capitalist, postindustrial, media-saturated Western society. Cyberpunk was a product of the commercial mass market of "hard" SF; concerned on the whole with near-future extrapolation and more or less conventional on the level of narrative technique, it was nevertheless at times brilliantly innovative in its explorations of technology as one of the "multiplicity of structures that intersect to produce that unstable constellation the liberal humanists call the 'self'" (Moi, 1985:10). From this perspective, cyberpunk can be situated among a growing (although still relatively small) number of SF projects which can be identified as "antihumanist." In its various deconstructions of the subject—carried out in terms of a cybernetic breakdown of the classic nature/culture opposition—cyberpunk can be read as one symptom of the postmodern condition of genre SF. While SF frequently problematizes the oppositions between the natural and the artificial, the human and the machine, it generally sustains them in such a way that the human remains securely ensconced in its privileged place at the center of

things. Cyberpunk, however, is about the breakdown of these oppositions.

This cybernetic deconstruction is heralded in the opening pages
of what is now considered the quintessential cyberpunk novel (we
might call it "the c-p limit-text"), William Gibson's *Neuromancer*
(1984). Gibson's first sentence—"The sky above the port was the color
of television, tuned to a dead channel" (3)—invokes a rhetoric of
technology to express the natural world in a metaphor that blurs the
distinctions between the organic and the artificial. Soon after, Gibson's
computer cowboy, Case, gazes at "the chrome stars" of shuriken, and
imagines these deadly weapons as "the stars under which he voyaged,
his destiny spelled out in a constellation of cheap chrome" (12).
Human bodies, too, are absorbed into this rhetorical conflation of
organism and machine: on the streets of the postmodern city whose
arteries circulate information, Case sees "all around [him] the dance of
biz, information interacting, data made flesh in the mazes of the black
market . . ." (16). The human world replicates its own mechanical
systems and the border between the organic and the artificial threatens
to blur beyond recuperation.

If we think of SF as a genre which typically foregrounds human
action *against* a background constituted by its technology, this blur-
ring of once clearly defined boundaries makes cyberpunk a particularly relevant form of SF for the postindustrial present. We can read
cyberpunk as an analysis of the postmodern *identification* of human
and machine.

Common to most of the texts which have become associated with
cyberpunk is an overwhelming fascination, at once celebratory and
anxious, with technology and its immediate—that is, *unmediated*—
effects upon human being-in-the-world, a fascination which sometimes spills over into the problematizing of "reality" itself. This emphasis on the potential interconnections between the human and the
technological, many of which are already gleaming in the eyes of
research scientists, is perhaps the central "generic" feature of cyberpunk. Its evocation of popular/street culture and its valorization of the
socially marginalized, that is, its "punk" sensibility, have also been
recognized as important defining characteristics.

Bruce Sterling, one of the most prolific spokespersons for the
movement during its heyday, has described cyberpunk as a reaction to

"standard humanist liberalism" because of its interest in exploring the various scenarios of humanity's potential interfaces with the products of its own technology. For Sterling, cyberpunk is "posthumanist" SF based on the belief that the "technological destruction of the human condition leads not to futureshocked zombies but to hopeful monsters" (1987:5,4).

SF has traditionally been enchanted with the notion of transcendence, but, as Glenn Grant points out in his discussion of *Neuromancer*, cyberpunk's "preferred method of transcendence is through technology" (1990:43). Themes of transcendence, however, point cyberpunk back to the romantic trappings of the genre at its most conventional, as does its valorization of the (usually male) loner rebel/hacker/punk who appears so frequently as its central character. Even Sterling has recognized this, concluding that "the proper mode of critical attack on cyberpunk has not yet been essayed. Its truly dangerous element is incipient Nietzschean philosophical fascism: the belief in the Overman, and the worship of will-to-power" (1987:5).

It is also important to note that not all the monsters it has produced have been hopeful ones; balanced against the exhilaration of potential technological transcendence is the anxiety and disorientation produced in the self/body in danger of being absorbed into its own technology. Mesmerized by the purity of technology, Gibson's Case initially has only contempt for the "meat" of the human body and yearns to remain "jacked into a custom cyberspace deck that project[s] his disembodied consciousness into the consensual hallucination that was the matrix" (5). And the protagonist of K. W. Jeter's *The Glass Hammer* (1985), which I will discuss in some detail below, experiences his very existence as a televised simulation. The postmodern anomie which pervades *The Glass Hammer* demonstrates that Sterling's defense of cyberpunk against charges that it is peopled with "futureshocked zombies" has been less than completely accurate.

Gibson's *Neuromancer*, the first of a trilogy of novels which includes *Count Zero* (1986a) and *Mona Lisa Overdrive* (1988), is set in a near-future trash culture ruled by multinational corporations and kept going by black-market economies, all frenetically dedicated to the circulation of computerized data and "the dance of biz" (1984:16) played out by Gibson's characters on the streets of the new urban overspill, the

Sprawl. The most striking spatial construct in *Neuromancer*, however, is neither the cityscape of the Sprawl nor the artificial environments like the fabulous L-5 or Freeside, but "cyberspace," the virtual reality that exists in simulated splendor on the far side of the computer screen—the real center of technological activity in Gibson's fictional world.

And along with the "other" space of cyberspace, *Neuromancer* offers alternatives to conventional modalities of human existence as well: computer hackers have direct mental access to cyberspace, artificial intelligences live and function within it, digitalized constructs are based on the subjectivities of humans whose "personalities" have been downloaded into computer memory, and human bodies are routinely cloned.

This is Sterling's posthumanism with a vengeance, a posthumanism which, in its representation of "monsters"—hopeful or otherwise—produced by the interface of the human and the machine, radically decenters the human body, the sacred icon of the essential self, in the same way that the virtual reality of cyberspace works to decenter conventional humanist notions of an unproblematical "real."

As I mentioned above, however, cyberpunk is not the only mode in which SF has demonstrated an antihumanist sensibility. Although radically different from cyberpunk, which is written for the most part by a small number of white middle-class men, many of whom, inexplicably, live in Texas, feminist SF has also produced an influential body of antihumanist texts. These would include, for example, Joanna Russ's *The Female Man* (1975), Jody Scott's *I, Vampire* (1984), and Margaret Atwood's *The Handmaid's Tale* (1985), novels which also participate in the postmodernist revision of conventional SF. Given the exigencies of their own particular political agendas, however, these texts demonstrate a very different approach to the construction/deconstruction of the subject than is evident in the technologically influenced posthumanism of most cyberpunk fiction.

Jane Flax, for example, suggests that

> feminists, like other postmodernists, have begun to suspect that all such transcendental claims [those which valorize universal notions of reason, knowledge, and the self] reflect and reify the experience of a few persons—mostly white, Western males. These

transhistoric claims seem plausible to us in part because they reflect important aspects of the experience of those who dominate our social world. (1987:626)

Flax's comments are well taken, although her conflation of all feminisms with postmodernism tends to oversimplify the very complex and problematical interactions of the two.

We can also include writers like Philip K. Dick, Samuel R. Delany, and John Varley within the project of antihumanist SF, although these writers are separated from cyberpunk not only by chronology, but also by cyberpunk's increased emphasis on technology as a constitutive factor in the development of postmodern subjectivity. Darko Suvin also notes some of the differences in political extrapolation between cyberpunk and its precursors: "[I]n between Dick's nation-state armies or polices and Delany's Foucauldian micro-politics of bohemian groups, Gibson (for example) has—to my mind more realistically—opted for global economic power-wielders as the arbiters of peoples' life-styles and lives" (p. 354, this volume).

Sterling's *Schismatrix* (1985) is one version of "posthumanism" presented as picaresque epic. Sterling's far-future universe—a rare construction in the cyberpunk canon—is one in which countless societies are evolving in countless different directions; the Schismatrix is a loose confederation of worlds where the only certainty is the inevitability of change. Sterling writes that "the new multiple humanities hurtled blindly toward their unknown destinations, and the vertigo of acceleration struck deep. Old preconceptions were in tatters, old loyalties were obsolete. Whole societies were paralyzed by the mind-blasting vistas of absolute possibility" (238). Sterling's protagonist, a picaresque hero for the postmodern age, "mourned mankind, and the blindness of men, who thought that the Kosmos had rules and limits that would shelter them from their own freedom. There were no shelters. There were no final purposes. Futility, and freedom, were Absolute" (273).

Schismatrix is a future history different from many SF futures in that what it extrapolates from the present is the all-too-often ignored/denied/repressed idea that human beings will be different in the future and will continue to develop within difference. In this way, *Schismatrix* demonstrates a familiarly poststructuralist sensibility, in its recognition both of the potential anxiety *and* the potential play inherent in a universe where "futility, and freedom, [are] Absolute."

Sterling's interest in and attraction to the play of human possibility appears as early as his first novel, *Involution Ocean* (1977). In this story, which reads in some ways like a kind of drug culture post-*Moby Dick*, the protagonist falls into a wonderful vision of an alien civilization, in a passage which, at least temporarily, emphasizes freedom over futility: "There was an incredible throng, members of a race that took a pure hedonistic joy in the possibilities of surgical alteration. They switched bodies, sexes, ages, and races as easily as breathing, and their happy disdain for uniformity was dazzling. . . . It seemed so natural, rainbow people in the rainbow streets; humans seemed drab and antlike in comparison" (154).

This is a far cry from the humanist anxieties which have pervaded SF since the nineteenth century. Consider, for example, the anxiety around which H. G. Wells created *The Time Machine* (1968 [1895]): it is "dehumanization," humanity's loss of its position at the center of creation, which produces the tragedy of the terminal beach, and it is, to a great extent, the absence of the human which results in the "abominable desolation" (91) described by Wells's Time Traveler. Or consider what we might term the "transhumanism" of Arthur C. Clarke's *Childhood's End* (1953), in which a kind of transcendental mysticism precludes the necessity of envisioning a future based on changing technologies, social conditions, and social relations. Greg Bear's more recent *Blood Music* (1985) might be read, from this perspective, as a contemporary version of the same transcendental approach to human transformation, one based on an apocalyptic logic that implies the impossibility of any change in the human condition *within history*. *Blood Music* is especially interesting in this context, because its action is framed by a rhetoric of science which would seem to repudiate any recourse to metaphysics. Darko Suvin has noted, however, that it functions as "a naïve fairy tale relying on popular wishdreams that our loved ones not be dead and that our past mistakes may all be rectified, all of this infused with rather dubious philosophical and political stances" (p. 350, this volume).

Sterling points out that "Certain central themes spring up repeatedly in cyberpunk. The theme of body invasion: prosthetic limbs, implanted circuitry, cosmetic surgery, genetic alteration. The even more powerful theme of mind invasion: brain-computer interfaces, artificial intelligence, neurochemistry—techniques radically redefining the nature of humanity, the nature of the self" (1986a:xiii).

The potential in cyberpunk for undermining concepts like "subjectivity" and "identity" derives in part from its production within what has been termed "the technological imagination," that is, cyberpunk is hard SF which recognizes the paradigm-shattering role of technology in postindustrial society. We have to keep in mind here, of course, that the movement has become (in)famous for the adversarial rhetoric of its ongoing and prolific self-commentary, which, in turn, functions as an integral part of its overall production as a "movement." We should be careful, for this reason, not to confuse claims with results. The antihumanist discourse of cyberpunk's frequent manifestoes, however, strongly supports de Lauretis's contention that "technology is our historical context, political and personal" (1980:167). As I suggested above, this context functions in cyberpunk as one of the most powerful of the multiplicities of structures that combine to produce the postmodern subject.

Thus, for example, the characters in Michael Swanwick's *Vacuum Flowers* (1987) are subjected to constant alterations in personality as the result of programming for different skills or social roles—metaphysical systems grounded on faith in an "inner self" begin to waver. Human bodies in Gibson's stories, and even more so in Sterling's, are subjected to shaping and reshaping, the human form destined perhaps to become simply one available choice among many. Thus, notions of a human nature determined by a "physical essence" of the human begin to lose credibility and, consequently, many behavioral patterns defined by sexual difference become irrelevant in these futures. And Rudy Rucker can offer the following as a chapter title in *Wetware* (1988): "Four: In Which Manchile, the First Robot-Built Human, Is Planted in the Womb of Della Taze by Ken Doll, Part of Whose Right Brain Is a Robot Rat."

We must also recognize, however, that "the subject of the subject" at the present time has given rise to as much anxiety as it has celebration. The breakup of the humanist "self" in a media-saturated postindustrial present has produced darker readings which cyberpunk also recognizes. Fredric Jameson, whose stance vis-à-vis the postmodern is at once appreciative and skeptical, has suggested that fragmentation of subjectivity may be the postmodern equivalent of the modernist predicament of individual alienation (1984a:63). Pat Cadigan's "Pretty Boy Crossover" (1985), for example, raises questions about the effects of simulated reality upon our human sense of self as complete and inviolable. In her fictional world, physical reality is "less efficient" than computerized simulation and video stars are literally video programs, having been "distilled . . . to pure information" (89, 88) and downloaded into computer matrices. Cadigan's eponymous Pretty Boy is tempted by the offer of literal eternal life within the matrix and, although he finally chooses "real" life, that reality seems to fade against the guaranteed "presence" of its simulation. Bobby, who has opted for existence as simulation, explains the "economy of the gaze," which guarantees the authenticity of the self in this world: "If you love me, you watch me. If you don't look, you don't care and if you don't care I don't matter. If I don't matter, I don't exist. Right?" (91).

In Jeter's *The Glass Hammer*, being is *defined* by its own simulation. *The Glass Hammer* is one of the most self-conscious deconstructions of unified subjectivity produced in recent SF, and one which dramatizes (in the neurotic tonalities familiar to readers of J. G. Ballard) the anxiety and schizophrenia of the (technologically produced) postmodern situation. In *The Glass Hammer*, the breakup of the "self" is narrated in a text as fragmented as its subject (subject both as protagonist and as story). Jeter's novel is a chilling demonstration of the power of simulated re-presentation to construct "the real," so that it functions like a cyberpunk simulacrum of the theories of Jean Baudrillard. It "narrates" episodes in the life of Ross Schuyler, who watches the creation of this life as a video event in five segments. There is no way to test the accuracy of the creation, since the self produced by memory is as unreliable a re-presentation as is a media "bio." As Schuyler realizes: "Just because I was there—that doesn't mean anything" (59).

The opening sequence of *The Glass Hammer* dramatizes the schizophrenia within the subjectivity of the protagonist:

> Video within video. He watched the monitor screen, seeing himself there, watching. In the same space . . . that he sat in now. . . .
>
> He watched the screen, waiting for the images to form. Everything would be in the tapes, if he watched long enough. (7)

Like Schuyler himself, the reader waits for the images to form as s/he reads the text. Episodes range over time, some in the past(s), some in the present, some real, some simulated, many scripted rather than "novelized," until the act of reading/watching achieves a kind of temporary coherence. It is this same kind of temporary coherence that formulates itself in Ross Schuyler's consciousness, always threatening to dissolve again from "something recognizably narrative" into "the jumbled, half-forgotten clutter of his life" (87).

What takes place in *The Glass Hammer* may also be read as a deconstruction of the opposition between depth and surface, a dichotomy which is frequently framed as the familiar conflict between reality and appearance. Jeter reverses this opposition, dramatizing the haphazard construction of his character's "inner self" as a response to people and events, both real and simulated, over time. The displacement of an "originary" self from the text places the emphasis on the marginal, the contingent, the re-presentations (in this case electronically produced) which actually create the sense of "self." Jeter's technique is particularly effective: the reader watches the character, and watches the character watching himself watching, as his past unfolds, not as a series of memories whose logical continuity guarantees the stability of the ego, but as an entertainment series the logical continuity of which is the artificial rearrangement of randomness to *simulate* coherence.

I find it significant that the "average" cyberpunk landscape tends to be choked with the debris of both language and objects; as a sign-system, it is overdetermined by a proliferation of surface detail which emphasizes the "outside" over the "inside." Such attention to detail—recall Gibson's nearly compulsive use of brand names, for example, or the claustrophobic clutter of his streets—replaces the more conventional (realist) narrative exercise we might call "getting to the bottom of things"; indeed, the shift in emphasis is from a symbolic to a surface reality.

In a discussion of *Neuromancer*, Gregory Benford observes that "Gibson, like Ballard, concentrates on surfaces as a way of getting at the aesthetic of an age" (1988:19). This observation is a telling one even as it misses the point. Benford concludes that Gibson's attention to surface detail "goes a long way toward telling us why his work has proved popular in England, where the tide for several decades now has been to relish fiction about surfaces and manners, rather than the more traditional concerns of hard SF: ideas, long perspectives, and content" (19).

This reliance on tradition is perhaps what prevents Benford, whose own "hard SF" novels and stories are very much a part of SF's humanist tradition, from appreciating the approach of writers like Gibson and Jeter. The point may be that, in works like *Neuromancer* and *The Glass Hammer*, surface *is* content, an equation that encapsulates their critique—or at least their awareness—of our contemporary "era of hyperreality" (Baudrillard, 1983b:128). In this context, the much-quoted opening sentence of *Neuromancer*, with its image of the blank surface of a dead television screen, evokes the anxiety of this new era. Istvan Csicsery-Ronay, for example, sees in cyberpunk the recognition that "with the computer, the problem of identity is moot, and the idea of reflection is transformed into the algorithm of replication. SF's computer wipes out the Philosophical God and ushers in the demiurge of thought-as-technique" (see p. 189, this volume).

Like much antihumanist SF, cyberpunk also displays a certain coolness, a kind of ironically detached approach to its subject matter that precludes nostalgia or sentimentality. This detachment usually discourages any recourse to the logic of the apocalypse, which, whether positive (like Clarke's) or negative (like Wells's), is no longer a favored narrative move. Fredric Jameson and Bruce Sterling (representatives of "high theory" and "low culture" respectively?) both identify a waning interest in the scenarios of literal apocalypse: Jameson perceives in the postmodern situation what he calls "an inverted millenarianism, in which premonitions of the future . . . have been replaced by the senses of the end of this or that" (1984a:53); in his introduction to Gibson's short story collection, *Burning Chrome*, Sterling comments that one "distinguishing mark of the emergent new school of Eighties SF [is] its boredom with the Apocalypse" (1986b:xi).

One reason for this tendency to abandon what has been a traditional SF topos may be the conviction, conscious or not, that a kind of philosophical apocalypse has already occurred, precipitating us into the dis-ease of postmodernism. Another reason may be the increased commitment of antihumanist SF to the exploration of changes that will occur—to the self, to society, and to social relations—in time; that is, it is more engaged with historical processes than attracted by the jump-cuts of apocalyptic scenarios that evade such investment in historical change. Cyberpunk, in particular, has demonstrated a keen interest in the near future, an aspect of its approach to history that discourages resolution-through-apocalypse.

In many cases, however, SF futures are all too often simply representations of contemporary cultural mythologies disguised under heavy layers of futuristic makeup. The recognition of this fact provides part of the "meaning" of one of the stories in Gibson's *Burning Chrome* (1986b) collection. "The Gernsback Continuum" humorously ironizes an early twentieth-century futurism which could conceive of no real change in the human condition, a futurism which envisioned changes in "stuff" rather than changes in social relations (historical distance increases the ability to critique such futures, of course). In Gibson's story, the benighted protagonist is subjected to visitations by the "semiotic ghosts" of a future which never took place, the future, to borrow a phrase from Jameson, "of one moment of what is now our own past" (1984b:244). At the height of these "hallucinations," he "sees" two figures poised outside a vast city reminiscent of the sets for films like *Metropolis* (1926) and *Things to Come* (1936):

> [the man] had his arm around [the woman's] waist and was gesturing toward the city. They were both in white. . . . He was saying something wise and strong, and she was nodding. . . .
>
> . . . [T]hey were the Heirs to the Dream. They were white, blond, and they probably had blue eyes. They were American. . . . They were smug, happy, and utterly content with themselves and their world. And in the Dream, it was *their* world. . . .
>
> It had all the sinister fruitiness of Hitler Youth propaganda. (1986b:32–33)

Gibson's protagonist discovers that "only really bad media can exorcise [his] semiotic ghosts" (33) and he recovers with the help of pop culture productions like *Nazi Love Motel*. "The Gernsback Continuum" concludes with the protagonist's realization that his dystopian present could be worse, "it could be perfect" (35).

Gibson's story is not simply an ironization of naïve utopianism; it also, I think, warns against the limitations, both humorous and dangerous, inherent in any vision of the future based upon narrowly defined ideological systems that take it upon themselves to speak "universally," or which conceive of themselves as "natural" or "absolute." David Brin's idealistic *The Postman* (1985), for example, is a postapocalyptic fiction which closes on a metaphorical note "of innocence, unflaggingly optimistic" (321), nostalgically containing itself within the framework of a conventional humanism. Not surprisingly, its penultimate chapter concludes with a reaffirmation of the "natural" roles of men and women:

> And always remember, the moral concluded: Even the best men—the heroes—will sometimes neglect to do their jobs.
> *Women, you must remind them, from time to time. . . .* (312; Brin's emphasis)

Another story in the *Burning Chrome* collection, "Fragments of a Hologram Rose," uses metaphors of the new technology to express the indeterminate and fragmented nature of the self:

> A hologram has this quality: Recovered and illuminated, each fragment will reveal the whole image of the rose. Falling toward delta, he sees himself the rose, each of his scattered fragments revealing a whole he'll never know. . . . But each fragment reveals the rose from a different angle. . . . (1986b:42)

Gibson's rhetoric of technology finally circumscribes all of reality. In his second novel, *Count Zero* (1986a), there is an oblique but pointed rebuttal of humanist essentialization, which implicitly recognizes the artificiality of the Real. Having described cyberspace, the weirdly real "space" that human minds occupy during computer interfacing, as "mankind's unthinkably complex consensual hallucination" (44), he goes on to write the following:

> "Okay," Bobby said, getting the hang of it, "then what's the matrix? . . . [W]hat's cyberspace?"
> "The world," Lucas said. (131)

It is only by recognizing the consensual nature of sociocultural reality, which includes within itself our definitions of human nature, that we can begin to perceive the possibility of change. In this sense, as

Csicsery-Ronay suggests (although from a very different perspective), cyberpunk is "a paradoxical form of realism" (p. 182, this volume).

Lucius Shepard concludes his "requiem for cyberpunk" by quoting two lines from Cavafy's "Waiting for the Barbarians": "What will we do now that the barbarians are gone? / Those people were a kind of solution" (1989:118). Cyberpunk seemed to erupt in the mid-1980s, self-sufficient and full grown, like Minerva from the forehead of Zeus. From some perspectives, it could be argued that this self-proclaimed movement was nothing more than the discursive construction of the collective imaginations of SF writers and critics eager for something/anything new in what had become a very conservative and quite predictable field. Now that the rhetorical dust has started to settle, however, we can begin to see cyberpunk as itself the product of a multiplicity of influences from both within and outside of genre SF. Its writers readily acknowledge the powerful influence of 1960s and 1970s New Wave writers like Samuel R. Delany, John Brunner, Norman Spinrad, J. G. Ballard, and Michael Moorcock, as well as the influence of postmodernists like William Burroughs and Thomas Pynchon. The manic fragmentations of Burroughs's *Naked Lunch* (1959) and the maximalist apocalypticism of Pynchon's *Gravity's Rainbow* (1973) would seem to have been especially important for the development of the cyberpunk "sensibility." Richard Kadrey has even pronounced *Gravity's Rainbow* to be cyberpunk *avant la lettre*, "the best cyberpunk novel ever written by a guy who didn't even know he was writing it" (1989a:83). On the other hand, Delany has made a strong case for feminist SF as cyberpunk's "absent mother," noting that "the feminist explosion—which obviously infiltrates the cyberpunk writers so much—is the one they seem to be the least comfortable with, even though it's one that, much more than the New Wave, has influenced them most strongly, both in progressive and in reactionary ways. . . ." (Tatsumi 1988:9)

Due in part to the prolific commentaries and manifestoes in which writers like Sterling and Shirley outlined/analyzed/defended their project(s)—usually at the expense of more traditional SF—cyberpunk helped to generate a great deal of very useful controversy about the role of SF in the 1980s, a decade in which the resurgence of fantastic literature left much genre SF looking rather sheepishly out of date. At best, however, the critique of humanism in these works remains incomplete, due at least in part to the pressures of mass market publishing as well as to the limitations of genre conventions which, more or less faithfully followed, seem (inevitably?) to lure writers back into the power fantasies so common to SF. A novel like Margaret Atwood's *The Handmaid's Tale*, for instance, produced as it was outside the genre market, goes further in its deconstruction of individual subjectivity than do any of the works I have discussed in this essay, except perhaps *The Glass Hammer*.

Gibson's latest novel, *Mona Lisa Overdrive* (1988), although set in the same universe as *Neuromancer* and *Count Zero*, foregrounds character in a way that necessarily mutes the intensity and multiplicity of surface detail which is so marked a characteristic of his earlier work. Sterling's recent and unexpected *Islands in the Net* (1988) is a kind of international thriller which might be read as the depiction of life *after* the postmodern condition has been "cured." Set in a future after the "Abolition" (of nuclear warfare), its central character, Laura Webster, dedicates herself to the control of a political crisis situation that threatens to return the world to a global state of fragmentation and disruptive violence, one which only too clearly recalls our own present bad old days. Sterling's "Net" is the vast information system that underlies and makes possible the unity of this future world, and his emphasis is clearly on the necessity for such global unity. Although, in the final analysis, no one is completely innocent—Sterling is too complex a writer to structure his forces on opposite sides of a simple ethical divide—the movement in *Islands in the Net* is away from the margins toward the center, and the Net, the "global nervous system" (15), remains intact.

As its own creators seem to have realized, cyberpunk—like the punk ethic with which it was identified—was a response to postmodern reality that could go only so far before self-destructing under the weight of its own deconstructive activities (not to mention its appropriation by more conventional and more commercial writers). That final implosion is perhaps what Jeter accomplished in *The Glass Hammer*, leaving us with the image of a mesmerized Schuyler futilely searching for a self in the videoscreens of the dystopian future. It is clearly this aspect of cyberpunk which leads Csicsery-Ronay to conclude that "by the time we get to cyberpunk, reality has become a case of nerves. . . . The distance required for reflection is squeezed out as the world implodes: when hallucinations and realia collapse into each other, there is no place from which to reflect" (p. 190, this volume). For him, "cyberpunk is . . . the apotheosis of bad faith, the apotheosis of the postmodern" (p. 193, this volume). This, of course, forecloses any possibility of political engagement within the framework of the postmodern.

Here cyberpunk is theorized as a symptom of the malaise of postmodernism, but, like Baudrillard's apocalyptic discourse on the "condition" itself, Csicsery-Ronay's analysis tends to underplay the positive potential of re-representation and re-visioning achieved in works like *Neuromancer* and *Schismatrix*. Bukatman (1989), for example, has suggested that the function of cyberpunk "neuromanticism" is one appropriate to SF in the postmodern era: the *reinsertion* of the human into the new reality which its technology is in the process of shaping.

The postmodern condition has required that we revise SF's original trope of technological anxiety—the image of a fallen humanity controlled by a technology run amok. Here again we must deconstruct the human/machine opposition and begin to ask new questions about the ways in which we and our technologies "interface" to produce what has become a *mutual* evolution. It may be significant that one of the most brilliant visions of the potential of cybernetic deconstructions is introduced in Donna Haraway's merger of SF and feminist theory, "A Manifesto for Cyborgs: Science, Technology, and Socialist Feminism in the 1980s" (1985), which takes the rhetoric of technology towards its political limits: "cyborg unities are monstrous and illegitimate," writes Haraway; "in our present political circumstances, we could hardly hope for more potent myths for resistance and recoupling" (179).

Fredric Jameson

From **Postmodernism,**
or The Cultural
Logic of
Late Capitalism

The last few years have been marked by an inverted millenarianism, in which premonitions of the future, catastrophic or redemptive, have been replaced by senses of the end of this or that (the end of ideology, art, of social class; the "crisis" of Leninism, social democracy, or the welfare state, etc., etc.): taken together, all of these perhaps constitute what is increasingly called postmodernism. The case for its existence depends on the hypothesis of some radical break or *coupure*, generally traced back to the end of the 1950s or the early 1960s. As the word itself suggests, this break is most often related to notions of the waning or extinction of the hundred-year-old modern movement (or to its ideological or aesthetic repudiation). Thus, abstract expressionism in painting, existentialism in philosophy, the final forms of representation in the novel, the films of the great *auteurs,* or the modernist school of poetry (as institutionalized and canonized in the work of Wallace Stevens): all these are now seen as the final, extraordinary flowering of a high modernist impulse which is spent and exhausted with them. The enumeration of what follows then at once becomes empirical, chaotic, and heterogeneous: Andy Warhol and pop art, but also photorealism, and beyond it, the "new expressionism"; the moment, in music, of John Cage, but also the synthesis of classical and "popular" styles found in composers like Phil Glass and Terry Riley, and also punk and new wave rock (the Beatles and the Stones now standing as the high-modernist moment of that more recent and rapidly evolving tradition); in film, Godard, post-Godard and experimental cinema and video, but also a whole new type of commercial film (about which more below); Burroughs, Pynchon, or Ishmael Reed, on the one hand, and the French *nouveau roman* and its succession on the other, along with alarming new kinds of literary criticism, based on some new aesthetic of textuality or *écriture.* . . . The list might be extended indefinitely; but does it imply any more fundamental change or break than the periodic style- and fashion-changes determined by an older high-modernist imperative of stylistic innovation?

Euphoria and Self-Annihilation

The end of the bourgeois ego or monad no doubt brings with it the end of the psychopathologies of that ego as well—what I have generally here been calling the waning of affect. But it means the end of much more—the end, for example, of style, in the sense of the unique and the personal, the end of the distinctive individual brushstroke (as symbolized by the emergent primacy of mechanical reproduction). As for expression and feelings or emotions, the liberation, in contemporary society, from the older *anomie* of the centered subject may also mean, not merely a liberation from anxiety, but a liberation from every other kind of feeling as well, since there is no longer a self present to do the feeling. This is not to say that the cultural products of the postmodern era are utterly devoid of feeling, but rather that such feelings—which it may be better and more accurate to call "intensities"— are now free-floating and impersonal, and tend to be dominated by a peculiar kind of euphoria to which I will want to return at the end of this essay.

The waning of affect, however, might also have been characterized, in the narrower context of literary criticism, as the waning of the great high-modernist thematics of time and temporality, the elegiac mysteries of *durée* and of memory (something to be understood fully as a category of literary criticism associated as much with high modernism as with the works themselves). We have often been told, however, that we now inhabit the synchronic rather than the diachronic, and I think it is at least empirically arguable that our daily life, our psychic experience, our cultural languages, are today dominated by categories of space rather than by categories of time, as in the preceding period of high modernism proper.

"Historicism" Effaces History

This situation evidently determines what the architecture historians call "historicism," namely the random cannibalization of all the styles of the past, the play of random stylistic allusion, and in general what Henri Lefebvre has called the increasing primacy of the "neo." This omnipresence of pastiche is, however, not incompatible with a certain humor (nor is it innocent of all passion) or at least with addiction— with a whole historically original consumers' appetite for a world transformed into sheer images of itself and for pseudo-events and "spectacles" (the term of the Situationists). It is for such objects that we may reserve Plato's conception of the "simulacrum"—the identical copy for which no original has ever existed. Appropriately enough, the culture of the simulacrum comes to *life* in a society where exchange-value has been generalized to the point at which the very memory of use-value is effaced, a society of which Guy Debord has observed, in an extraordinary phrase, that in it "the image has become the final form of commodity reification" (*The Society of the Spectacle*, 1977).

The new spatial logic of the simulacrum can now be expected to have a momentous effect on what used to be historical time.

The past is thereby itself modified: what was once, in the histori-cal novel as Lukács defines it, the organic genealogy of the bourgeois collective project—what is still, for the redemptive historiography of an E. P. Thompson or of American "oral history," for the resurrection of the dead of anonymous and silenced generations, the retrospective dimension indispensable to any vital reorientation of our collective future—has meanwhile itself become a vast collection of images, a multitudinous photographic simulacrum. Guy Debord's powerful slo-gan is now even more apt for the "prehistory" of a society bereft of all historicity, whose own putative past is little more than a set of dusty spectacles. In faithful conformity to poststructuralist linguistic theory, the past as "referent" finds itself gradually bracketed, and then effaced altogether, leaving us with nothing but texts.

The Nostalgia Mode

Faced with these ultimate objects—our social, historical and exis-tential present, and the past as "referent"—the incompatibility of a postmodernist "nostalgia" art language with genuine historicity be-comes dramatically apparent. The contraction propels this model, however, into complex and interesting new formal inventiveness: it being understood that the nostalgia film was never a matter of some old-fashioned "representation" of historical content, but approached the "past" through stylistic connotation, conveying "pastness" by the glossy qualities of the image, and "1930s-ness" or "1950s-ness" by the attributes of fashion (therein following the prescription of the Barthes of *Mythologies* [1970], who saw connotation as the purveying of imaginary and stereotypical idealities, "Sinité," for example, as some Disney-EPCOT "concept" of China).

The Breakdown of the Signifying Chain

[Lacan's] conception of the signifying chain essentially presupposes one of the basic principles (and one of the great discoveries) of Saussurean structuralism, namely the proposition that meaning is not a one-to-one relationship between signifier and signified, between the materiality of language, between a word or a name, and its referent or concept. Meaning in the new view is generated by the movement from Signifier to Signifier: what we generally call the Signified—the meaning or conceptual content of an utterance—is now rather to be seen as a meaning-effect, as that objective mirage of signification generated and projected by the relationship of Signifiers among each other. When that relationship breaks down, when the links of the signifying chain snap, then we have schizophrenia in the form of a rubble of distinct and unrelated signifiers. The connection between this kind of linguistic malfunction and the psyche of the schizophrenic may then be grasped by way of a two-fold proposition: first, that personal identity is itself the effect of a certain temporal unification of past and future with the present before me; and second, that such active temporal unification is itself a function of language, or better still of the sentence, as it moves along its hermeneutic circle through time. If we are unable to unify the past, present and future of the sentence, then we are similarly unable to unify the past, present, and future of our own biographical experience or psychic life.

With the breakdown of the signifying chain, therefore, the schizophrenic is reduced to an experience of pure material Signifiers, or in other words of a series of pure and unrelated presents in time. We will want to ask questions about the aesthetic or cultural results of such a situation in a moment; let us first see what it feels like:

"I remember very well the day it happened. We were staying in the country and I had gone for a walk alone as I did now and then.

Suddenly, as I was passing the school, I heard a German song; the children were having a singing lesson. I stopped to listen, and at that instant a strange feeling came over me, a feeling hard to analyze but akin to something I was to know too well later—a disturbing sense of unreality. It seemed to me that I no longer recognized the school, it had become as large as a barracks; the singing children were prisoners, compelled to sing. It was as though the school and the children's song were set apart from the rest of the world. At the same time my eye encountered a field of wheat whose limits I could not see. The yellow vastness, dazzling in the sun, bound up with the song of the children imprisoned in the smooth stone school-barracks, filled me with such anxiety that I broke into sobs. I ran home to our garden and began to play 'to make things seem as they usually were,' that is, to return to reality. It was the first appearance of those elements which were always present in later sensations of unreality: illimitable vastness, brilliant light, and the gloss and smoothness of material things." (Séchehaye 1968:19)

In our present context, this experience suggests the following remarks: first, the breakdown of temporality suddenly releases this present of time from all the activities and the intentionalities that might focus it and make it a space of praxis; thereby isolated, that present suddenly engulfs the subject with undescribable vividness, a materiality of perception properly overwhelming, which effectively dramatizes the power of the material—or better still, the literal— Signifier in isolation. This present of the world or material signifier comes before the subject with heightened intensity, bearing a mysterious charge of affect, here described in the negative terms of anxiety and loss of reality, but which one could just as well imagine in the positive terms of euphoria, the high, the intoxicatory or hallucinogenic intensity.

Collage and Radical Difference

This account of schizophrenia and temporal organization might, however, have been formulated in a different way, which brings us back to Heidegger's notion of a gap or rift, albeit in a fashion that would have horrified him. I would like, indeed, to characterize the postmodernist experience of form with what will seem, I hope, a paradoxical slogan: namely the proposition that "difference relates." Our own recent criticism, from Macherey on, has been concerned to stress the heterogeneity and profound discontinuities of the work of art, no longer unified or organic, but now a virtual grab-bag or lumber room of disjoined subsystems and random raw materials and impulses of all kinds. The former work of art, in other words, has now turned out to be a text, whose reading proceeds by differentiation rather than by unification. Theories of difference, however, have tended to stress disjunction to the point at which the materials of the text, including its words and sentences, tend to fall apart into random and inert passivity, into a set of elements which entertain purely external separations from one another.

In the most interesting postmodernist works, however, one can detect a more positive conception of relationship which restores its proper tension to the notion of differences itself. This new mode of relationship through difference may sometimes be an achieved new and original way of thinking and perceiving; more often it takes the form of an impossible imperative to achieve that new mutation in what can perhaps no longer be called consciousness. I believe that the most striking emblem of this new mode of thinking relationships can be found in the work of Nam June Paik, whose stacked or scattered television screens, positioned at intervals within lush vegetation, or winking down at us from a ceiling of strange new video stars, recapitulate over and over again prearranged sequences or loops of images which return at dysynchronous moments on the various screens. The older aesthetic is then practiced by viewers, who, bewildered by this discontinuous variety, decide to concentrate on a single screen, as though the relatively worthless image sequence to be followed there had some organic value in its own right. The postmodernist viewer, however, is called upon to do the impossible, namely to see all the screens at once, in their radical and random difference; such a viewer is asked to follow the evolutionary mutation of David Bowie in *The Man Who Fell to Earth* (1976), and to rise somehow to a level at which the vivid perception of radical difference is in and of itself a new mode of grasping what used to be called relationship: something for which the word *collage* is still only a very feeble name.

The Apotheosis of Capitalism

It is appropriate therefore to recall the excitement of machinery in the preceding moment of capital, the exhilaration of futurism most notably, and of Marinetti's celebration of the machine gun and the motor car. These are still visible emblems, sculptural nodes of energy which give tangibility and figuration to the motive energies of that earlier moment of modernization. The prestige of these great streamlined shapes can be measured by their metaphorical presence in Le Corbusier's buildings, vast Utopian structures which ride like so many gigantic steam-shipliners upon the urban scenery of an older fallen earth. Machinery exerts another kind of fascination in artists like Picabia and Duchamp, whom we have no time to consider here; but let me mention, for the sake of completeness, the ways in which revolutionary or communist artists of the 1930s also sought to reappropriate this excitement of machine energy for a Promethean reconstruction of human society as a whole, as in Fernand Léger and Diego Rivera.

What must then immediately be observed is that the technology of our own moment no longer possesses this same capacity for representation: not the turbine, nor even Sheeler's grain elevators or smoke-stacks, not the baroque elaboration of pipes and conveyor belts nor even the streamlined profile of the railroad train—all vehicles of speed still concentrated at rest—but rather the computer, whose outer shell has no emblematic or visual power, or even the casings of the various media themselves, as with that home appliance called television which articulates nothing but rather implodes, carrying its flattened image surface within itself.

Such machines are indeed machines of reproduction rather than of production, and they make very different demands on our capacity for aesthetic representation than did the relatively mimetic idolatry of the older machinery of the futurist movement, of some older speed-and-energy sculpture. Here we have less to do with kinetic energy than with all kinds of new reproductive processes; and in the weaker productions of postmodernism the aesthetic embodiment of such processes often tends to slip back more comfortably into a mere thematic representation of content—into narratives which are *about* the processes of reproduction, and include movie cameras, video, tape recorders, the whole technology of the production and reproduction of the simulacrum. (The shift from Antonioni's modernist *Blowup* [1966] to DePalma's postmodernist *Blow Out* [1981] is here paradigmatic.) When Japanese architects, for example, model a building on the decorative imitation of stacks of cassettes, then the solution is at best a thematic and allusive, although often humorous, one.

Yet something else does tend to emerge in the most energetic postmodernist texts, and it is the sense that beyond all thematics or content the work seems somehow to tap the networks of reproductive process and thereby to afford us some glimpse into a postmodern or technological sublime, whose power or authenticity is documented by the success of such works in evoking a whole new postmodern space in emergence around us. Architecture therefore remains in this sense the privileged aesthetic language; and the distorting and fragmenting reflections of one enormous glass surface to the other can be taken as paradigmatic of the central role of process and reproduction in postmodernist culture.

As I have said, however, I want to avoid the implication that technology is in any way the "ultimately determining instance" either of our present-day social life or of our cultural production: such a thesis is of course ultimately at one with the post-Marxist notion of a "postindustrialist" society. Rather, I want to suggest that our faulty representations of some immense communicational and computer network are themselves but a distorted figuration of something even deeper, namely the whole world system of present-day multinational capitalism. The technology of contemporary society is therefore mesmerizing and fascinating, not so much in its own right, but because it seems to offer some privileged representational shorthand for grasping a network of power and control even more difficult for our minds and imaginations to grasp—namely the whole new decentered global network of the third stage of capital itself. This is a figural process presently best observed in a whole mode of contemporary entertainment literature, which one is tempted to characterize as "high tech paranoia," in which the circuits and networks of some putative global computer hook-up are narratively mobilized by labyrinthine conspiracies of autonomous but deadly interlocking and competing information agencies in a complexity often beyond the capacity of the normal reading mind. Yet conspiracy theory (and its garish narrative manifestations) must be seen as a degraded attempt—through the figuration of advanced technology—to think the impossible totality of the contemporary world system. It is therefore in terms of that enormous and threatening, yet only dimly perceivable, other reality of economic and social institutions that in my opinion the postmodern sublime can alone be adequately theorized.

The Need for Maps

In a classic work, *The Image of the City* (1960), Kevin Lynch taught us that the alienated city is above all a space in which people are unable to map (in their minds) either their own positions or the urban totality in which they find themselves: grids such as those of Jersey City, in which none of the traditional markers (monuments, nodes, natural boundaries, built perspectives) obtain, are the most obvious examples. Disalienation in the traditional city, then, involves the practical reconquest of a sense of place, and the construction or reconstruction of an articulated ensemble which can be retained in memory and which the individual subject can map and remap along the moments of mobile, alternative trajectories. Lynch's own work is limited by the deliberate restriction of his topic to the problems of the city form as such; yet it becomes extraordinarily suggestive when projected outwards onto some of the larger national and global spaces we have touched on here. Nor should it be too hastily assumed that his model—while it clearly raises very central issues of representation as such—is in any way easily vitiated by the conventional poststructuralist critiques of the "ideology of representation" or mimesis. The cognitive map is not exactly mimetic, in that older sense; indeed, the theoretical issues it poses allow us to renew the analysis of representation on a higher and much more complex level.

There is, for one thing, a most interesting convergence between the empirical problems studied by Lynch in terms of city space and the great Althusserian (and Lacanian) redefinition of ideology as "the representation of the subject's *Imaginary* relationship to his or her *Real* conditions of existence." Surely this is exactly what the cognitive map is called upon to do, in the narrower framework of daily life in the physical city: to enable a situational representation on the part of the individual subject to that vaster and properly unrepresentable totality which is the ensemble of the city's structure as a whole.

Social Cartography and Symbol

An aesthetic of cognitive mapping—a pedagogical political culture which seeks to endow the individual subject with some new heightened sense of its place in the global system—will necessarily have to respect this now enormously complex representational dialectic and to invent radically new forms in order to do it justice. This is not, then, clearly a call for a return to some older kind of machinery, some older and more transparent national space, or some more traditional and reassuring perspectival or mimetic enclave: the new political art—if it is indeed possible at all—will have to hold to the truth of postmodernism, that is to say, to its fundamental object—the world space of multinational capital—at the same time at which it achieves a breakthrough to some as yet unimaginable new mode of representing this last, in which we may again begin to grasp our positioning as individual and collective subjects and regain a capacity to act and struggle which is at present neutralized by our spatial as well as our social confusion. The political form of postmodernism, if there ever is any, will have as its vocation the invention and projection of a global cognitive mapping, on a social as well as a spatial scale.

Arthur Kroker and David Cook

Television and the
Triumph of Culture
(*from* The
Postmodern Scene)

Three Theses

Our general theorization is, therefore, that TV is the real world of postmodern culture which has *entertainment* as its ideology, the *spectacle* as the emblematic sign of the commodity form, *life-style advertising* as its popular psychology, pure, empty *seriality* as the bond which unites the simulacrum of the audience, *electronic images* as its most dynamic, and only, form of social cohesion, *elite media politics* as its ideological formula, the buying and selling of *abstracted attention* as the locus of its marketplace rationale, *cynicism* as its dominant cultural sign, and the diffusion of a *network of relational power* as its real product.

Our *specific* theorizations about TV as the real world of post-modernism take the form of three key theses:

Thesis 1: TV as Serial Culture

Television is the emblematic cultural expression of what Jean-Paul Sartre has described as "serial culture." The specific context for Sartre's description of "serial culture" is an extended passage in *The Critique of Dialectical Reason* (1982) in which he reflects on the philosophical implications of mass media generally, and on radio broadcasting specifically (271–76). Sartre's media analysis is crucial because it represents the beginning of a serious existential critique of the media, from radio to television, and because in his highly nuanced discussion of radio broadcasting Sartre provides some entirely insightful, although grisly, clues as to the fate of society under the sign of the mediascape. For Sartre, the pervasive effect of mass media, and of radio broadcasting specifically, was to impose *serial structures* on the population. Sartre can say that the voice is "vertiginous" for everyone just because the mass media produce "seriality" as their cultural form (275–95). And what's "serial culture" for Sartre? It's a "mode of being," Sartre says, "beings outside themselves in the passive unity of the object" (271)—which has:

- —"absence" as the mode of connection between audience members
- —"alterity" or "exterior separation" as its negative principle of unity
- —"impotence" as the political bond of the (media) market
- —the destruction of "reciprocity" as its aim
- —the reduction of the audience to the passive unity of the "practico-inert" (inertia) as its result
- —and the "three moment" dialectic: triumph (when you know that you're smarter than the media elite); "impotent indignation" (when you realize that the audience is never permitted to speak, while the media elite are allowed to speak but have nothing to say); and fascination (as you study your entrapment as Other in the serial unity of the TV audience, which is the "pure, abstract formula" of the mass media today). (274)

The TV audience is Sartre's serial culture *par excellence*. The audience is constituted on the basis of "its relation to the object and its reaction to it"; the audience is nothing more than a "serial unity" ("beings outside themselves in the passive unity of the object"); membership in the TV audience is always only on the basis of "alterity" or "exterior separation"; impotence of the "three moment" dialectic is the iron law of the hierarchical power of television; "abstract sociality" is the false sociality of a TV audience which as an empty, serial unity is experienced as a negative totality; the image is "vertiginous" for everyone; and the overall cultural effect of television is to do exactly what Sartre prophesied:

The practico-inert object (that's TV) not only produces a unity of individuals outside themselves in inorganic matter, but it also determines their isolation and, insofar as they're separate, assures communication through alterity. (271)

In just the same way that the gigantic red star of the supernova burns most brilliantly when it is already most exhausted and imploding towards that dark density of a new black hole, TV today can be so hyperspectacular and so desperate in its visual efforts because, as Sartre has hinted, its real existence is "inertia" and it is always already on the decline towards the realm of the "practico-inert." What's TV then? It's Sartre's "serial culture" in electronic form, from the "viewer as absence" and "alterity" as TV's basic principle (McLuhan's "exteriorization" of the central nervous system) to the TV audience as that "serial unity" or "negative totality," the truth of whose existence as *pure inertia* (Sartre's being in the *mud* of the practico-inert) can be caught if you glance between the laser canons of color TV as they blast you and catch the black patches, the dead darkness to infinity, which is the pure inertial state which television struggles so desperately to hide. And that darkness to infinity between the hysterical explosions of the laser beam? That's Sartre's "serial culture" as the sign of contemporary society: just when the image becomes "vertiginous" for everyone; when the viewer is reduced to "absence"; and when vacant and grisly "alterity" is the only bond that unites that negative totality—the "audience."

Thesis 2: Television as a Postmodern Technology

Television, just because it's an emblematic expression of Sartre's "serial culture" in electronic form, is also a perfect model of the processed world of postmodern technology. And why not? TV exists, in fact, just at that rupture point in human history between the decline of the now-passé age of sociology and the upsurge of the new world of communications (just between the eclipse of normalized society and the emergence of radical semiurgy as the language of the "structural" society). TV is at the borderline of a great paradigm-shift between the "death of society" (modernism with its representational logic) and the "triumph of an empty, signifying culture" (the "structural paradigm" of postmodernism). In the Real World of television, it's:

–Sign *not* Norm
–Signification *not* Socialization (on signification, see Baudrillard [1983d])

—Exteriorization of the Mind (McLuhan's processed world) *not* (Weber's) Reification

—(Baudrillard's) "simulacrum" *not* institutional discourse

—Radical semiurgy *not* (Foucault's) Normalization

—Simulation *not* Rationalization

—An empire of voyeurs held together by upscale titillation effects (from the valorization of corpses to the crisis jolts of bad news and more bad news) and blasted by the explosions of the laser beam into the pulverized state of Sartre's "serial beings" and *not* the old and boring "structure of roles" held together by the "internalization of need-dispositions"

—Power as seduction *not* (primarily) power as coercion

—Videation not institutionalization

—*Not* society (that's disappeared and who cares) but the triumph of the culture of signification

If TV is the processed world triumphant, this just means that it functions to transform the old world of society under the sign of the *ideology of technicisme*. By technicisme we mean that ideology, dominant in contemporary consumer culture, which holds (as William Leiss has noted) to the historical inevitability and ethical desirability of the technical mastery of social and nonsocial nature. The outstanding fact about the TV "network," viewed as one dynamic expression of the spreading outwards of the fully realized technological society, is that it screens off any sense of technology as *deprival*. Like a *trompe l'oeil*, television functions as "spectacle" to divert the eye from the radical impoverishment of life in technological society. Indeed, television screens off any sense of technology as deprival by means of three strategic colonizations, or subversions, of the old world of society.

1. The Subversion of Sociality. TV functions by substituting the negative totality of the audience with its pseudo-mediations by electronic images for genuine sociality, and the possibility of authentic human solidarities. It's electronic communication as the antimatter of the social! Indeed, who can escape now being constituted by the coercive rhetoric of TV and by its nomination of fictional audiences. We are either rhetorically defined North Americans as we are *technocratically* composed as an audience by the self-announced "electronic bridge" of the TV networks; or we are the electronically constituted audience of Nietzsche's "last men" who just want their consumer comforts and blink as we celebrate the breakdown of American institutions. In *St. Elsewhere*, everything is held together by high tech and the joke: nurses kill doctors; the medical staff resent their patients for dying; and patients are forced to console doctors and nurses alike in this distress over the inability of medical technology to overcome mortality. In *Dynasty*, it is the object-consciousness and dreamlike state of the cynical culture of advanced capitalism itself which is celebrated. And, in *Family Feud*, we celebrate normativity or statistical polling ("survey says"): the very instruments for the measurement of that missing social matter in the new universe of electronic communications—the audience—which exists anyway in the TV universe as a dark and unknown nebula.

The TV audience may be, today, the most pervasive type of social community, but if this is so then it is a very special type of community: an *anticommunity* or a *social antimatter*—electronically composed, rhetorically constituted, an electronic mall which privileges the psychological position of the voyeur (a society of the disembodied eye) and the cultural position of *us* as tourists in the society of the spectacle.

2. The Psychological Subversion. In the real world of television, technology is perfectly interiorized: it comes *within* the self. There is now such a phenomenon as the TV *self*, and it builds directly on Sartre's sense of "serial being." The TV self is not just a pair of flashing eyeballs existing in Andy Warhol's languid and hypercynical state of "bored but hyper." The TV self is the electronic individual *par excellence* who gets everything there is to get from the simulacrum of the media: a market identity as a consumer in the society of the spectacle; a galaxy of hyperfibrillated moods (the poles of ressentiment and manic buoyancy are the psychological horizon of the TV family); traumatized serial being (television blasts away everything which cannot be reduced to the technological limitations of "good visuals" or, as Sartre has said, to "otherness"). Just like in David Cronenberg's classic film, *Videodrome* (1983), television functions by implanting a simulated, electronically monitored, and technocratically controlled identity in the flesh. Television technology makes the decisive connection between the simulacrum and biology by creating a social nerve connection between spectacular visuals, the news as crisis interventions (image-fibrillation) and the psychological mood of its rhetorically constituted audience. TV colonizes individual psychology best by being a "mood setter."

3. The Technological Colonization. The outstanding fact about TV as the real world is that it is a perfect, even privileged, model of how human experience in the twentieth century is actually transformed to fit the instrumental imperatives of technological society. Marx might have had his "factory" as a social laboratory for studying the exploitation of "abstract labor"; Hobbes might have written with the ping-pong universe of classical, Newtonian physics in mind (in the old world of modernist physics it's all action-reaction with things only causally related at a distance); but we have television as a privileged model of how we are reworked by the technological sensorium as it implodes the space and time of lived human experience to the electronic poles of the "screen and the network" (Baudrillard). Television is the real experience of the ideology and culture of technicisme.

1. The dominant *cultural formation* is the psychological voyeur and the audience linked together by images created by media elites, but this only in the form of electronic stimuli formulated in response to the incessant polling of the dark nebula of that missing social matter—the TV audience.

2. *Hypersimulation* is the (disappearing) essence of technically mediated experience; staged communications, fabricated events, packaged audiences held hostage to the big trend line of *crisis moods* induced by media elites for an audience which does not exist in any *social* form, but only in the abstract form of digital blips on overnight rating simulacrums.

3. The *language of signification* and its surrealistic reversals is the basic codex of the real world of television culture. Cars *are* horses; computers *are* galaxies, tombstones, or heartbeats; beer *is* friendship. This is just to say though that Barthes's theorization of the *crossing* of the syntagm of metaphor and metonymy as the grammatical attitude of postmodern culture is now the standard language of television.

4. TV is *information society* to the hyper, just though where information means the liquidation of the social, the exterminism of memory (in the sense of human remembrance as aesthetic judgment), and the substitution of the simulacrum of a deterritorialized and dehistoricized image-system for actual historical contexts.

What is the perfect example of television's technological colonization of the space of the social imaginary? It is that wonderful channel on

Montréal television which consists of a screen split among seventeen images, constantly flickering with dialogue fading in and out, and with the only thematic mediation consisting of a voice-over across the galaxy of disappearing images. That split-screen with its disembodied voice and its pulsating, flickering images *is* the emblematic sign of contemporary (signifying) culture. It is also the social space of serial being in a perfectly serialized culture: background radiation the presence of which only indicates the disappearance of the old world of (normative and representational) society into the new universe of (semiurgical and relational) communications.

Thesis 3: Entertainment as the Dominant Ideology of TV Culture

Television is the *consumption* machine of late capitalism in the twentieth century that parallels the *production* machine of primitive capitalism in the seventeenth century. Television functions as *the* simulacrum of consumption in three major ways.

(1). In *The Society of the Spectacle* (1977), Guy Debord remarked that the "spectacle is capital to such a degree of accumulation that it becomes an image" (thesis 34). That's TV: it is the breakpoint where capital in its final and most advanced form as a spectral image begins to disappear into itself and becomes that which it always was: an empty and nihilistic sign-system of pure mediation and pure exchange which, having no energy of its own, adopts a scorched earth policy towards the missing social matter of society. Like a gigantic funeral pyre, capital, in its present and most exhausted expression as an image, can shine so brilliantly because it sucks in like oxygen any living element in culture, society, or economy: from the ingression of the primitive energy of early rock 'n' roll into Japanese car commercials, and the psychological detritus of anal titillation in jean advertisements to Diana Ross's simulated orgasm in a field of muscle (which is anyway just the American version of Carol Pope's [*Rough Trade*] simulated crotch-play in *High School Confidential* [1958] that, in the proper Canadian way, plays at the edge of exhibitionism and seduction).

(2). Entertainment is the *ideolect* of television as a consumption machine. What is the essence of entertainment or promotional culture? It is just this: the "serial unity" of vicarious otherness which, Sartre

Television and the Triumph of Culture   **235**

predicted, would be the essential cultural text of society in radical decline.

In a recent debate on the state of television, published by *Harper's* magazine (and which begins with the wonderful lines: "Disparaging television has long been a favorite national pastime—second only in popularity to watching it"), Rick Du Brow, television editor of the *Los Angeles Herald Examiner*, said that TV, which has always been more of a "social force" than an art form, is "part of the natural flow of life" (1985:47).

> When you go to the theater, or to a movie, something is presented *to* you by the creator. But in television there's a very important creator who isn't critical to the other forms—the viewer. . . . With the vast number of buttons he can press at home, the TV viewer [Sartre's "absence"] creates his own program schedule—a spectacle that reflects his private tastes and personal history. . . . Today, each viewer can create his own TV life. (47)

Du Brow's "creator"—the "viewer creating his own TV life"—is something like Marshall McLuhan's wired heads as the circuit egos of the processed world of electronic technology. In McLuhan's terms, life in the simulacrum of the mediascape consists of a big reversal: the simulacrum of the image-system goes inside; consciousness is ablated. In the sightscape of television, just like before it in the soundscape of radio, the media function as a gigantic (and exteriorized) electronic nervous system, amplifying technologically our every sense, and playing sensory functions back to us in the processed form of *mutant* images and sounds. TV life? That's television as a mutant society: the mediascape playing back to us our *own* distress as a simulated and hyperreal sign of life.

And why not? At the end of his life, Michel Foucault finally admitted that power functions today, not under the obsolescent signs of death, transgression, confessionality, and the *saeculum* of blood, but under the sign of life. For Foucault, power could be most seductive just when it spoke in the name of life, just when it was most therapeutic and not confessional. Following Foucault, we would just add that power in the new age of the mediascape is most seductive, and thus most dangerous, when it speaks in the name of life to the hyper—TV life. And television is most grisly in its colonization of individual consciousness, most untheorized as a vast system of relational power, and most fascinating as the emblematic form of the death of society and the triumph of signifying culture just when it is most *entertaining*. And it is most entertaining when it is a vast electronic simulation, a sensory playback organon, of *mood*: mood politics, mood news, mood drama, and even, if we take seriously the "happy-time announcers" of Los Angeles TV, *mood weather*. But, then, why be surprised? Heidegger always said that "mood" would be the locus of culture at the end of history, tracing a great ellipsis of decline, disintegration, and disaccumulation *par excellence*. TV life? That's the ideolect of entertainment as a great simulacrum of "mood": sometimes of the radically oscillating moods of that great *absence*, the viewer, which is programmed now to move between the poles of "panic anxiety" and "manic optimism"; and always of the herd moods of that equally great electronic *fiction*, the audience.

(3). *TV functions as a consumption machine (most of all) because it is a life-style medium.* In a superb article in *The Atlantic* (1984:49–58), James Atlas argued the case that TV advertisers are no longer so concerned with the now passé world of demographics (that's the ideolect of the social), but are instead intent on shaping advertising to fit the size of target VALs. And what are VALs but the identification of target audiences by "values and life-styles": the "superachievers" (call them "yuppies" now, but Talcott Parsons described them long ago as "institutional liberals"—upscale technocrats with a minimal social self and a maximal consumer self who define freedom within the limits of mass organizations); the "belongers": the old class of middle North Americans who value, most of all in nostalgic form, the social qualities of friendship and community and at whom the fellowship hype of beer commercials is directed; and the new, rising class of middle Americans who value the friendship of the herd most of all, and at whom are targeted the belongingness hype of commercials for the *Pepsi Generation* or the promotional hype, under the sign of altruism, of *Live Aid* or *We Are the World*; or, finally, the "emulators": what David Riesmann used to call "other-directed personalities": bewildered and in the absence of their own sense of self-identity, hypersensitive to the big trend lines of contemporary culture as defined by media elites.

The conclusion which might be derived from VALs' research, or from Arnold Mitchell's book, *The Nine American Lifestyles* (1983), is that class society has now disappeared into mass society, and that mass society has dissolved into the TV blip. The notion of the serial self in electronic society as a TV blip, a digital neuron floating somewhere in the bigger circuitry of the screen and the network may appear vacuous, but that is only because that's exactly what the TV blip with a life-style is, and has to be, in the new relationship between television and the economic system. The political economy of TV has such a perfect circularity about it that its serial movement could not sustain anything more substantive, and anything less instrumentalist in the consumerist sense, than the '80s self as a blip with a life-style. From the viewpoint of an image-hungry audience, the product of television is, and obviously so, the spectacle of TV as a simulacrum of life-styles. But from the perspective of TV advertisers and media programmers, the *real* product of television is the audience. So, what is TV? Is it the manipulation of society by a media elite using the spectacle as a "free lunch" to expand the depth and pace of universal commodity-exchange in the market place? Or is it the manipulation of the media elite by the audience, that electronic congerie of TV blips with nine life-styles, using the bait of their own consumer gullibility as a lure to get what they want most: free and unfettered access to the open skies of serial culture? What's TV: *The Will to Power* or *Capital*? The high commodity society of neo-technical capitalism or Nietzsche's culture of nihilism? *Or is TV both?* "The spectacle to such a degree that it becomes an image" *and* a perfectly cynical exchange between media programmers operating under the economic imperative to generate the biggest possible audience of TV blips at the lowest possible price for sale to advertisers at the highest possible rate of profit; and an electronically composed public of serial beings which, smelling the funeral pyre of excremental culture all around it, decides of its own unfettered volition to celebrate its own exterminism by throwing its energies, where attention is the oxygen of TV life, to the black hole of television?

TV or Not TV? Well, you just have to listen to the stampeding of feet and the rustling of the flashing eyeballs as the TV blips, who constitute the growing majority of world culture, are worked over by the exploding laser beams to know the answer. And TV life? Well, that's technology now as a simulacrum of disease.

Brooks Landon

Bet On It:
Cyber/video/punk
performance

Give me a Cray computer and someone who
knows how to make fractal geometry work, and
I'll show you why cyberpunk fiction—at least
of the Neuromancer/Schismatrix molds—is
over, give or take a few aftershocks. Give me a
VCR, and I'll show you what I mean in just a
few minutes, much less on fast forward, on jet
search—no time at all.

Even before it arrived, sparking and smoking like a cartoon anarchist's
bowling ball bomb, cyberpunk fiction was headed somewhere else.
Had to, and Sterling, Shiner, Rucker, Gibson, and Shirley all knew it;
indeed, were too hip not to cheer the passing of their own parade. More
important, they undercut expectations almost as quickly as we formed
them, expanding the genre's limits rather than fortifying its center,
defending form, resisting formula. For the real message of cyberpunk
was *inevitability*—not what the future *might* hold, but the inevitable
hold of the present over the future—what the future could not fail to be.
What cyberpunk fiction offered—better make that "brandished"—was
not speculation or extrapolation so much as simple, unhysterical,
unsentimental understanding of the profound technological and epistemological implications of accomplished and near-accomplished cultural fact: what if they gave an apocalypse and nobody noticed?

Precisely because it took technology seriously, cyberpunk
couldn't just create its distinctive semblance, then play out a string of
antique narratives against a technosleaze backdrop. Its energy, its
premium on information density, its unshakable determination to con-

front the new realities of postmodern culture, all meant that cyberpunk could never settle down in established comfort, over and over offering its readers exotic but increasingly familiar territory, a comfy national park of the imagination where the neatly numbered conceptual hook-ups waited patiently for readers to park the campers of their minds. So, even before the summer of 1987, cyberpunk's major writers were all going in new directions, leaving its first star, William Gibson, to turn off the lights with *Mona Lisa Overdrive* (1988).

But this party's far from over. As a descriptor of a sensibility, an awareness, a killer rock in the rapids of postmodernism, "cyberpunk" remains a significant term, a useful handle for creative and destructive acts across a range of media. It's just that as a term designating a kind of fiction, "cyberpunk" seems to me already a map without a territory, its current referents' works of fiction written almost exclusively by people other than cyberpunk's original creative cadre.

An offhand comment by Bruce Sterling brought all of this home to me. I was on the phone with him, asking questions for an article I was doing for *Cinefantastique*, and I was scribbling down names like crazy, some familiar, many I'd never heard of. Mark Pauline rang a bell, as did Rocky Morton and Annabel Jankel. Benoit Mandelbrot wasn't a problem; Stuart Arbright and William Barg were. What hit me was the fact that none of these people were writers, and Sterling nailed that thought down when he said, "Shoot, those guys are the real cyberpunks; we just write about it."

Writing is the key here—not the process, but the medium, an ancient system for processing information, its two hi-tech moments, movable type and the steam press, having come respectively in the fifteenth and nineteenth centuries. In either of those centuries, Mark Pauline would have had to find some other way to blow up his hand, rocket fuel being a much more now kind of thing, as are Pauline's self-destroying robotic sculptures, and the Survival Research Lab videotapes of their profoundly science-fictional performances.

Mandelbrot's work with fractal geometry both represents and helps drive a new wave of computer imaging which allows the representation, generation, and manipulation of images, viewing perspectives, and degrees of realism never before possible. Jankel and Morton, probably best known for their computer-animated music videos for Elvis Costello's "Accidents Will Happen" and for Donald Fagen's

"New Frontier," detail this research in their stunning book, *Creative Computer Graphics* (1984), and put it to quintessential cyberpunk use when they dramatized some of its possibilities in the original British version of *Max Headroom* (1985). However, it fell to Arbright and Barg to make in their eighteen-and-a-half minute cybervideo, *Hip Tech and High Lit*, the overt connection between cyberpunk fiction and the technology which more and more actualizes its basic assumption. More on that video in a moment, but first, the assumption.

In the December 1987 issue of *Cinefantastique*, I make the claim that the central assumption of cyberpunk may be "that life, like film, video, and computer data, can be edited as to become 'posthuman,' radically reprogrammed through artificial evolution or redesigned by technology." Another way of explaining this is to say that the computer-generated special effects "magic" of recent SF film and the manic permutations and informational density of music videos such as Peter Gabriel's *Big Time*, Cutting Crew's *One for the Mocking Bird*, and Tom Petty's *Jamming Me* become for the cyberpunk writers a key index to what everything will be like in the future—a time of designer drugs, designer genetics, designer surgery, designer prosthetics, even (courtesy of time travel) designer history. So strong is this notion of *editing* reality that John Shirley even used it to describe cyberpunk writing itself, as "more like a video process," and as "a mirror you can edit." Or, in Rudy Rucker's terms, "How fast are you? How dense?"

Which brings me back to video and computer technology. Measured in terms of other fiction, perhaps particularly other science fiction, the speed and density (informational complexity) of cyberpunk writing is stunning. But, measured against computer imaging and video technique, even dynamite prose reveals that it cannot compete in precisely these ways. Speed, density, and the process of editing assume dimensions in video and computer graphics that are simply beyond the reach of printed prose. Not a new ballpark, really, but a different game entirely—comparing pixels with phonemes, kumquats with kangaroos. So this would not be a problem, were it not for the self-refractive, techno-intensive qualities of cyberpunk writing, the print-denying *inevitability* of its milieu. Captain James T. Kirk loses no credibility when he dons his granny glasses to read a novel in the umpteenth century, but try to viddy this: after a rough day in cyberspace, computer cowboy Case looks forward to nothing quite so much as settling down with a good book. Or put it this way: what integrity could cyberpunk fiction possibly have in a cyberpunk world? For that matter, how long can cyberpunk's profound lens of technological inevitability be turned on everything in our own culture *but* the game preserve of fixed text print?

My point is that the power of cyberpunk writing, the new realism of postmodern culture, almost demands a reexamination of the status of writing in that culture. In so far as cyberpunk writing directs our attention to MTV, *Max Headroom*, and computer-generated graphics which are rapidly becoming indistinguishable from "real" images of our referential world, it compels us to question the nature of representation in our world—and our traditional assumptions about the nature of fiction and narrative.

And those questions are being asked: whether or not we think much of the prospects for Timothy Leary's plans at Futique to develop an interactive computer game for *Neuromancer* (1984), the scheduled panel on interactive fiction at the 1987 MLA Convention must tell us that the assumption of a fixed literary text is already under technological assault. The once radical-seeming cut-up production model of William Burroughs is tame stuff compared with a cut-up or multiple branching model of *reception* of the text. Moreover, limiting computer technology to manipulating the ways in which words appear on the monitor is roughly analogous to purchasing a Ferrari one intends to drive only through school zones: if the cultural imperative places ever greater premiums on information density, language alone doesn't stand much chance in the conceptual marketplace. Images may not provide the pleasures and the challenges of print, but there's no denying that electronic technology can do infinitely more with images and sounds than it can with printed words. In postmodern electronic culture, as in the Civil War, the prevailing attitude valorizes those artists who "get there fustest with the mostest," and it has fallen to some fifteen years of pioneering video art, and now to high-profile television (MTV and *Night Flight* and *Alive from Off Center*), to speed up our sense of narrative possibility, to remind us that video and computers don't just march to the beat of a different drummer than does fiction, but that they have inexorably juiced up that beat. This is precisely the message of cyberpunk, as it is of most postmodern theory.

Most cyberpunk writing implies the conflation of time and deflation of space, terms suggested by Fredric Jameson in his seminal essay on postmodern culture (1984a) and applied to visual media by Vivian Sobchack in *Screening Space* (1987). Enacting both phenomena is the moebiuslike relationship between cyberpunk writing's fascination with the themes and icons of electronic culture, at the same time as film, video, and TV are so obviously drawing from and/or paralleling the themes and icons of cyberpunk writing. *Max Headroom* provides the most obvious example of this interface, but it continues through *Robocop* (1987), Gibson's writing the script for *Aliens III*, Shirley's script for *Black Glass*, through a hefty percentage of music videos on commercial TV, and finally through experimental video, such as the Residents' *This Is a Man's World* and *Earth vs. The Flying Saucers*.

A striking example of the technological displacement of narrative from print to electronic culture is the William Barg/Stuart Arbright video, *Hip Tech and High Lit*. Initially presented in June 1987 as part of a multimedia performance to an audience including both Sterling and Gibson, this impressive but by no means yet polished video represents an obvious transition from cyberpunk writing to the electronic modes of production I've been describing. Largely a found-footage collage of striking computer graphics, TV news footage, and original videotape, Barg and Arbright's production establishes a compelling high tech semblance, without positing any sustained narrative. The nonlinear progression of its beautiful and complicated images is further textured by an innovative soundtrack, a blend of voice-over readings (some by *Blade Runner*'s [1982] Sean Young) from Gibson's and Sterling's fiction with Arbright's electronic music. That music, much of it created by a Yamaha TX81Z FM tone generator and RX5 digital rhythm programmer, reminds us—as MTV does not—that technology has provided dramatic new ways in which sound, like images, can be generated and manipulated. What results from this combination is clearly *not* a dramatic adaptation of cyberpunk fiction, but an invocation of the technosphere so crucial to much of that writing.

Hip Tech and High Lit strongly suggests that computer animation and fractally generated graphics should be considered much more than merely the latest stage in the evolution of special effects associated with SF film. What this presentation does (as did *Max Headroom* and as, for much briefer duration, do many current music videos and the works of video artists) is to create a sensory environment as compelling and complicated as any conventional narrative which might be set within it. The clear evidence of this video and of a good part of my recent experience of electronic culture seems to me to be that the technology so effectively limned by cyberpunk fiction has the affective power to constitute a narrative line in its own right, an inherent narrative *of* technology, rather than the use of technology to tell a conventional narrative in visual media. In short, if there is something we can call cyber- or cyberpunk video, it is video that *does* or enacts the cyberpunk epistemology, rather than video used to dramatize stories by cyberpunk writers.

I'd like to suggest then that cyberpunk writing is at the heart of a new cultural and media convergence, bringing together writers, video artists, computer graphics experts, film and TV production, and performance art of the wildly different kinds represented by John Cage, Laurie Anderson, Kate Bush, Robert Longo, and Mark Pauline. This convergence seems likely to me to mark the end of cyberpunk's print stage, but to transfer its energy, innovation, and commitment to the global arena of electronic culture.

The first video played when MTV went on the air was *Video Killed the Radio Star* by the Buggles. That was no accident. I find myself wondering whether a similar technological imperialism might not eventually overshadow not only cyberpunk writing, but the literary genre of science fiction itself—not killing its central impulses, but editing them into new, more authoritative modes. Consider this: work now being done by mathematicians such as Michael F. Barnsley at Georgia Tech seems to point inexorably toward the discovery of affine transformations (equations in fractal geometry) capable of generating virtually any target image. The implication of this research, reported in the May 2, 1987 *Science News* is that "it may even be possible to convey a movie from one computer to another simply by sending a chain of formulas down a telephone line." Such a movie would be qualitatively more detailed than any possible cinematographic or video depiction of existing reality, as it would allow the viewer the unparalleled sense of flying into the picture, examining its components from every conceivable angle, even of predicting and exploring the information hidden beneath its visual surfaces. Such a film would be hyperreal, but could be made to do impossible things, like showing a punked-out John Wayne on a pogo stick, Harlan Ellison apologizing, or the Beaver in mirrorshades, Ward and June in drag. Would not such a representation be inherently science fictional, the essence of cyberpunk? And won't it be fun?

Timothy Leary

The Cyberpunk:
The Individual as
Reality Pilot

"Your true pilot cares nothing about anything
on earth but the river, and his pride in his
occupation surpasses the pride of kings."
—Mark Twain, *Life on the Mississippi*

Who Is the Cyberpunk?

Cyberpunks use all available data input to think for themselves.

You know who they are.

Every stage of history has produced a name and a heroic legend
for the strong, stubborn, creative individual who explores some future
frontier, collects and brings back new information, and offers to guide
the gene pool to the next stage. Typically, the time maverick combines
bravery with high curiosity, with super-self-esteem. These three talents
are considered necessary for those engaged in the profession of genetic
guide, a.k.a., philosopher.

The classical Old West–World model for the Cyberpunk is Prometheus, a technological genius who "stole" fire from the Gods and
gave it to humanity.[1] Prometheus also taught his gene pool many useful
arts and sciences. According to the official version of the legend,
he/she was sentenced to the ultimate torture for these unauthorized
transmissions of Classified Information. Prometheus was exiled. In
his/her own version of the myth (unauthorized) Prometheus (a.k.a., the
Pied Piper) uses his/her skills to escape the sinking kinship, taking
with him the cream of the gene pool.

The New World version of this ancient myth is Quetzalcoatl, god
of civilization, high-tech wizard who introduced maize, the calendar,

erotic sculpture, flute playing, the arts. And the sciences. He was driven into exile by the G-man in power, who was called Tezcatolipoca.

Self-assured singularities of the Cyber Breed have been called mavericks, ronin, free-lancers, independents, self-starters, nonconformists, oddballs, troublemakers, kooks, visionaries, iconoclasts, insurgents, blue-sky thinkers, loners, smartalecks. Before Gorbachev, the Soviets scornfully called them hooligans. Religious organizations have always called them heretics. Bureaucrats called them disloyal dissidents, traitors, or worse. In the old days, even sensible normal people used to call them mad.

They have been variously labeled clever, creative, entrepreneurial, imaginative, enterprising, fertile, ingenious, inventive, resourceful, talented, eccentric.

During the tribal, feudal, and industrial-literate phases of human evolution, the logical survival traits were conformity and dependability. The "good serf" or "vassal" was obedient. The "good worker" or "manager" was reliable. Maverick-thinkers were tolerated only at moments when innovation and change were necessary, usually to deal with the local competition.

In the Information/communication civilization of the twenty-first century, creativity and mental excellence become the ethical norm. The world has become too dynamic, complex, and diversified, too cross-linked by the global immediacies of modern (quantum) communication, for stability of thought or dependability of behavior to be successful. The "good person" today is the intelligent one who can think for him/herself. The "problem person" in the Cybernetic Society of the twenty-first century is the one who automatically obeys, who never questions authority, who acts to protect his/her official status, who placates and politics rather than thinks independently.

Thoughtful Japanese are worried about the need for ronin-thinking in their obedient culture. The postwar generation is now taking over.

Cyberpunk Yuppies in the Soviet Union

The new postwar generation of Soviets have apparently caught on that a new role model is necessary to compete in the information age. Under Gorbachev bureaucratic control is being softened, made elastic to encourage some modicum of innovative, dissident thought!

Aleksandr N. Yakovlev, Politburo member and key strategist of the glasnost policy, describes that reform: "Fundamentally, we are talking about self-government. We are moving towards a time when people will be able to govern themselves and control the activities of people that have been placed in the position of learning and governing them.

"It is not accidental that we are talking about *self*-government, or *self*-sufficiency and *self*-profitably of an enterprise, *self*-this and *self*-that. It all concerns the decentralization of power."

The Cyberpunk Person, the pilot who thinks clearly and creatively, using quantum-electronic appliances and brain know-how, is the newest, updated, top-of-the-line model of our species, *homo sapiens sapiens, cyberneticus*.

Let us meet some of these Pilot People. Their example may encourage and empower you to start taking over the wheel. Of your own life.

Cyber Is the Greek Word for Pilot

"A great pilot can sail even when his canvas is rent."
—Lucius Annaeus Seneca

The term *cybernetics* comes from the Greek word *kubernetes*—pilot.

The Hellenic origin of this word is important in that it reflects Greek traditions of independence and individual self-reliance which, we are told, derived from geography. The proud little Greek city-states were perched on peninsular fingers wiggling down into the fertile Mediterranean Sea, protected by mountains from the landmass armies of Asia.

Mariners of those ancient days had to be bold and resourceful. Sailing the seven seas without maps or navigational equipment, they were forced to develop independence of thought. The self-reliance that these Hellenic pilots developed in their voyages probably carried over to the democratic, inquiring, questioning nature of their land life.

The Athenian cyberpunk, the pilot, made his/her own navigational decisions.

These psycho-geographical factors may have contributed to the humanism of the Hellenic religions, which emphasized freedom, pagan joy, celebration of life, and speculative thought. The personal and polytheistic nature of the religions of ancient Greece is often compared with the austere morality of monotheistic Hebraism, the fierce, dogmatic polarities of Persian-Arab dogma, and the imperial authority of Roman (Christian) culture.

A Recent Example of Unauthorized Cyberpunk Behavior

The opening moments of the movie *WarGames* offers a classic example of *cybernetic* performance.

It's a foggy night. An Air Force Captain is skillfully steering a jeep up a winding Colorado mountain road to the secret SAC nuclear missile launching silos. He is accompanied by a lieutenant. The captain speaks the first words in the movie. He tells the lieutenant that he and his wife planted a cultivated grade of marijuana seeds in their garden and, to ensure their growth, invoked the Tibetan Buddhist prayer for enlightenment. *On mane padma hum.*

At this point, the officers reach the entry check-point, identify themselves, and are issued pistols. The huge steel vault door opens. The two men enter the "control" room from which the bombs are fired. As they check dials, the captain continues his story. The cannabis harvest was very successful. The lieutenant interrupts the story. A red light on the control board is flashing ominously. The captain tells him to tap it with his finger. The light disappears: Get it? The captain is a quantum-whiz, alert, competent to detect and debug errors in the electronic system. The blinking begins again. An alarm sounds. They consult the code book and confirm the validity of the message. They gulp. They are commanded to launch nuclear missiles at the Soviet Union.

The captain balks. He orders the lieutenant to phone headquarters for human confirmation. The lieutenant, a loyal liege vassal, protests that this is an unauthorized action. But he obeys the order of his immediate superior.

No answer.

The lieutenant primly reminds the captain that orders command him to fire the nuke. The captain shakes his head. He commits an act of independent thought. He says he won't kill fifty million people without a human command.

The lieutenant, dutifully following the government regulations, points his pistol at the captain's brain.

Cut.

The Roman Concept of Governor, Director, Steersman

The Greek word *kubernetes* translated to Latin comes out as *gubernetes*. The basic verb *gubernare* means to control the actions or behavior of, to direct, to exercise sovereign authority, to regulate, to keep under, to restrain, to steer. This Roman concept is obviously very different from the original notion of "pilot."

It may be relevant that the Latin term "to steer" comes from the word *stare*, which means to stand, with derivative meanings "place or thing which is standing." The past participle of the Latin word produces "status," "state," "institute," "statue," "static," "statistics," "prostitute," "restitute," "constitute."

Example of Governing or Steersman Behavior

A helicopter lands at the SAC base. It is carrying two high status officials of the government. They carry institutional briefcases and standard, serious, worried looks. They are furious. It seems that 25 percent of the captains in silos refused to launch without human confirmation. The government response to this independence of judgment by individuals is predictably institutional.

"Get the persons out of the loop."

They introduce WHOPPER, a totally obedient Artificial Intelligence system guaranteed to follow government orders and to be free of the subjective, (PUNK) human unreliability factor.

Cyberpunk/Pilots Replace Governetics/Controllers

> *"Society everywhere is in conspiracy against the selfhood of every one of its members. The virtue in most request is conformity. Self-reliance is its aversion. It loves not realities and creators, but names and customs."*
> *—Ralph Waldo Emerson, "Nature"*

> *"Who so would be a man must be a nonconformist."*
> *—Ralph Waldo Emerson, "Nature"*

The word "cybernetics" was coined by Norbert Wiener (1948), who wrote, "We have decided to call the entire field of control and communication theory, whether in the machine or in the animal, by the name of Cybernetics, which we form from the Greek word for steersman [sic]." The word "cyber" has been redefined (in the *American Heritage Dictionary*) as "the theoretical study of control processes in electronic, mechanical, and biological systems, especially the flow of information in such systems." The derivative word *cybernate* means "to control automatically by computer or to be so controlled."

An even more ominous interpretation defines cybernetics as "the study of human control mechanisms and their replacement by mechanical or electronic systems."

Note how Wiener and the Romanesque engineers have corrupted the meaning of cyber. The Greek word "pilot" becomes "governor or director"; the word "to steer" becomes "to control."

We are liberating the term, teasing it free from serfdom to represent the autopoetic, self-directed principle of organization which arises in the universe in many systems of widely varying sizes. In people, societies, and atoms. (As explained in the Cybernetic Organization chapter.)

Charles Augustus Lindbergh: Cyber-Politician

Charles Lindbergh was a Republican congressman from Minnesota who first attained national prominence when he attacked industrial and commercial trusts, denounced promilitary propaganda and war profits. His courageous and skillful maverick attitude culminated in his active opposition to World War I in 1917. These acts of independent thinking destroyed his governmental career.

He was the father of Charles Augustus Lindbergh, Lucky Lindy, the Lone Eagle, who attained fame as sky pilot, philosopher, ecologist.

Our Oppressive Birthright: The Politics of Literacy

The etymological distinctions between Greek and Roman terms are quite relevant to the pragmatics of the culture surrounding their usage. French philosophy, for example, has recently stressed the importance of language and semiotics in determining human behavior and social structures. Michel Foucault's classic studies of linguistic politics and mind control led him to believe that

> human consciousness—as expressed in speech and images, in self-definition and mutual designation . . . is the authentic locale of the determinant politics of being.

. . . What men and women are born into is only superficially this or that social, legislative, and executive system. Their ambiguous, oppressive birthright is the language, the conceptual categories, the conventions of identification and perception which have evolved and, very largely, atrophied up to the time of their personal and social existence. It is the established but customarily subconscious, unargued constraints of awareness that enslave.

Orwell and Wittgenstein both agree. To remove the means of expressing dissent is to remove the possibility of dissent. "Whereof one cannot speak, thereof one must remain silent." In this light, the difference between the Greek word "pilot" and the Roman translation "governor" becomes a most significant semantic manipulation. And the flexibility granted to symbol systems of all kinds by their representation in digital computers becomes very dramatic.

Several questions arise. Do we, for example, pride ourselves for becoming ingenious "pilots" or "dutiful controllers"?

Who, What, and Why Is Governetics?

"Damn the torpedoes, full speed ahead."
—Captain David Glasgow Farragut's order to his steersman at the Battle of Mobile Bay, 5 August 1864

"Aye, aye, sir!"
—Unknown enlisted steersman at the Battle of Mobile Bay, 5 August 1864

The word governetics refers to an attitude of obedience-control in relationship to self or others.

Pilots, those who navigate on the seven seas or in the sky, have to devise and execute course changes continually in response to the changing environment. They respond continually to feedback, information about the environment. Dynamic. Alert. Alive.

The Latinate "steersman," by contrast, is in the situation of following orders. The Romans, we recall, were great organizers, road builders, administrators. The galley ships, the chariots must be controlled. The legions of soldiers must be directed.

The Hellenic concept of the individual navigating his/her own course was an island of humanism in a sea of totalitarian empires.

Athens was bounded on the East (the past) by the centralized, authoritarian kingdoms of the Middle East. The Governors of Iran, from Cyrus, the Persian emperor, to the recent Shah and Ayatollah, have exemplified the highest traditions of state control.

The Greeks were bounded on the other side, which we shall designate the West (or future) by a certain heavy concept called Rome. The caesars and popes of the Holy Roman Empire represented the next grand phase of institutional control. The governing hand on the wheel stands for stability, durability, continuity, permanence. Staying the course. Individual creativity, exploration, and change are usually not encouraged.

Christopher Columbus: Another Example of Cyberpunk Behavior

Christopher Columbus (1451–1506) was born in Genoa. At the age of twenty-five, he showed up in Lisbon and learned the craft of map-making. This was the golden era of Portuguese exploration. Many pilots and navigators were convinced that the earth was round and that the Indies and other, unknown lands could be found by crossing the western seas. What was special about Columbus was his persistence and eloquence in support of the dream of discovery. For over ten years, he traveled the courts of Europe attempting to make "the deal" to find backing for his "enterprise of the Indies."

According to the *Columbia Encyclopedia*: "Historians have disputed for centuries his skill as a navigator, but it has been recently proved that with only dead-reckoning Columbus was unsurpassed in charting and finding his way about unknown seas." Columbus was a most unsuccessful governor of the colonies he had discovered. He died in disgrace, his cyber-skills almost forgotten. (At least that's what they tell us in the authorized history books.)

Cyberpunk: The Pilots of the Species

"The winds and waves are always on the side of the ablest navigators."
—*Edward Gibbon*

The word *cybernetic-person* or *cybernaut* returns us to the original meaning of "pilot" and puts the self-reliant person back in the loop. The words *cybernetic-person, cybernaut*, and the more pop term *cyber-*

punk refers to the personalization (and thus the popularization) of knowledge/information technology. Innovative thinking on the part of the individual.

According to Foucault, if you change the language you change the society. Following Foucault, we suggest that the term *cybernetic-person, cybernaut,* may describe a new model of human being and a new social order. *Cyberpunk* is, admittedly, a risky term. Like all linguistic innovations, it must be used with a tolerant sense of high-tech humor. It's a stop gap, transitional meaning-grenade thrown over the language barricades to describe the resourceful, skillful individual who accesses and steers knowledge/communication technology towards his/her own private goals. For personal pleasure, profit, principle, or growth.

Cyberpunks are the inventors, innovative writers, techno-frontier artists, risk-taking film directors, icon-shifting composers, expressionist artists, free-agent scientists, innovative show-biz entrepreneurs, techno-creatives, computer visionaries, elegant hackers, bit-blipping *Prolog* adepts, special-effectives, video wizards, neurological test pilots, media explorers—all of those who boldly package and steer ideas out there where no thoughts have gone before.

Cyberpunks are sometimes authorized by the governors. They can, with sweet cynicism and patient humor, interface their singularity with institutions. They often work within "the governing systems" on a temporary basis.

As often as not, they are unauthorized.

The Legend of the Ronin

The following quotes come from *The Way of the Ronin* by Beverly Potter, Ph.D. "[T]he Ronin . . . has broken with the tradition of career feudalism. Guided by a personally defined code of adaptability, autonomy, and excellence, Ronin are employing career strategies grounded in a premise of rapid change."

Ronin is used as a metaphor based on a Japanese word for a lordless samurai. As early as the eighth century, the word *ronin,* translated literally as "wave people," was used in Japan to describe people who had left their allotted, slotted, caste-predetermined station in life. Samurai who had left the service of their feudal lords to become masterless.

"*Ronin* played a key role in Japan's abrupt translation from a feudal society to industrialism. Under feudal rule, warriors were not allowed to think freely or act according to their own will. On the other hand, having been forced by circumstances to develop independence, they took more readily to new ideas and technologies and became increasingly influential in the independent schools. These schools . . . were more liberal than were the official government schools, which taught only the traditional curriculum."

The West has many historical parallels to the *ronin* archetype. The term *free lance* has its origin in the period after the crusade when a large number of knights were separated from their lords. Many lived by the code of chivalry and became "lances for hire."

The American frontier was fertile ground for the *ronin* archetype. *Maverick*, derived from the Texan word for unbranded steer, is used to describe a free and self-directed individual.

"Although many of the Ronin's roots . . . are in the male culture, most career women are well acquainted with the Way of the Ronin. Career women have left their traditional stations and battled their way into the recesses of the male-dominated workplace. Most women's careers are characterized by a multiplicity of experiences and back-and-forth moves between home, work, and school, causing them to confront the critics of self-direction. Like the Ronin who had no clan, professional women often feel excluded from the corporate cliques' inside tracks, without ally or mentor."

Shall We Boot-Up Some Examples of Cyberpunk?

Carol Suen Rosin, proponent of nonmilitarized outer space, has become "an honest broker" between the American and Soviet scientific groups.

Stanley Kubrick is the essence of cyberpunk.

Mary Ferguson, psyber-punk. Wrote *The Aquarian Conspiracy* and publishes the *Brain/Mind Bulletin*.

Steve Jobs and Steve Wozniak.

David Hockney.

Andy Warhol.

George Koopman.

William Gibson, Bruce Sterling, John Shirley, Rudy Rucker.

Charles Lindbergh: "We (that's my ship and I) took off rather suddenly. We had a report somewhere around 4 o'clock in the afternoon before that the weather would be fine, so we thought we would try it."

"I saw a fleet of fishing boats. . . . I flew down almost touching the craft and yelled at them, asking if I was on the right road to Ireland. They just stared. Maybe they didn't hear me. Maybe I didn't hear them. Or maybe they thought I was a crazy fool. An hour later I saw land."

In 1922, Lindbergh left a promising university career to study air navigation and flight. He was one of the first pilots to carry mail through the skies. On May 21, 1927, he made the first solo nonstop flight from the North American continent to the Eurasian continent. "Lucky Lindy" immediately became a national hero.

In 1929, he married Anne Morrow, an intelligent, cultured author and woman of means. After the marriage, she became an accomplished pilot. The couple astonished the world by making several highly publicized flights together.

In 1936, Lindy (by then in exile) collaborated with Alex Carrel in developing an enhanced heart appliance to aid human circulation.

In 1938, after visiting the Eurasian continent, Lindbergh became convinced that America should stay out of the power struggle developing between the Axis and the Allies.[2]

The media widely publicized a motto/logo for Lindy: "Smiling Through."

Anne Morrow Lindbergh.

Mark Twain. He purchased the Remington-Type writer when it appeared in 1874 for $125.00. In 1875, he became the first author in history to submit a typewritten manuscript to a publisher. It was *The Adventures of Tom Sawyer*. "This newfangled writing machine has several virtues. It piles an awful stack of words on one page. It don't muss things or scatter inkblots around. Of course it saves paper."

Gertrude Stein.

Roy Walford.

Wilt Chamberlain.

Mathias (Rusty) Rust, age 19, a lanky, teenage loner from Hamburg, Germany, attained All-Star status as a cyberpunk when, on 28 May 1987, he flew a one-engine Cessna through the impenetrable Soviet air defenses and landed in Moscow's Red Square. There were no gubernal or organizational motives. The technological adventure was a personal mission. Rusty just wanted to talk to some Russians. German newspapers celebrated the event, calling it "the stuff of dreams" and comparing the youth to the Red Baron Manfred von Richthofen and Charles Lindbergh.

Stewart Brand, founder of *Co-evolution Quarterly*.

Bob Harris, the owner of a hardware store in Riverside, California, is an amateur glider pilot. On 17 February 1986, while soaring over the high desert north of Edwards Air Force Base, he caught the most beautiful "mountain wave" he'd ever seen and rode it to a height of 49,000 feet. A world record. His celebration was rudely interrupted by the Federal Aviation Administration, who moved to revoke his pilot's license. The charge: Pilot Harris had failed to get permission. The flight was unauthorized.

The Cyber-Flash Kid: Another Example of Innovative Behavior

The third scene in *WarGames* introduces us to the hero, Matthew Broderick. He is in a video arcade playing a space adventure game with poise and proficiency.

Get it? He's an Electron Jock. A Quantum Wizard. But is he a company man? Or a self-directed cyberpilot? Let's find out.

He is late for school. His autocratic biology teacher gives him a bad time. When the officious teacher asks about the origin of asexual reproduction, Matthew suggests, "Your wife?"

Okay, we get it. Matthew is ungovernable. He's a cyberkid.

The teacher sends Matthew to the principal. While languishing in the governor's office, he obtains the code for the school's computer system. Back home, he uses his PC to access the school records. He changes the unfair grade to a passing level.

The Cyberpunk Code: TFYQA

The three scenes from *WarGames* present the cultural drama of the Roaring twentieth century. First we note that *WarGames* is an electronic quantum signal, a movie about high-tech computers and human evolution seen by millions, especially impressionable youngsters. The film illustrates and condemns the use of quantum/electronic knowledge technology by governates for control. The film celebrates the independence and skill of cyberpunks who think for themselves and innovate from within the static system. The captain and his wife use high-tech agricultural methods to enhance the potency of unauthorized botanical neuroactivators. The captain makes an unauthorized decision to abort WWIII. In both instances, the captain follows the cyberpunk code: Think for Yourself, Question Authority (TFYQA). He pilots an independent course.

The cyberkid, Matthew Broderick, is equally courageous, outrageous, creative, and bright. He is pulled into the classic confrontation: the Authoritarian Antique Teacher humiliates and punishes the Tom Sawyer kid. Matthew Thinks for Himself and Questions Authority. He rushes to the library and researches the life of Professor Falken, scans scientific journals, scopes microfilm files—not to please the system but in pursuit of his own personal quest. Then he uses his Electron-skills in an unauthorized manner to pilot his own course.

Note that there is a new dimension of Electronic Ethics and Quantum Legality here. The captain and Matthew perform no act of physical violence, no theft of material goods. The captain processes some computer data and decides for himself. Matthew rearranges clusters of electrons stored on a chip.

They seek no control over others.

Cyberpunk as Role Model for the Twenty-First Century

The tradition of the "Individual who Thinks for Him/Herself" extends to the beginnings of recorded human history. Indeed, the very label of our species, *homo sapiens*, defines us as the animals who think.

If our genetic function is *computare* (to think), then it follows that the ages and stages of human history, so far, have been larval or preparatory. Now, at the beginnings of the information age, are we ready to assume our genetic function? After the larval phases of submission to gene pools, the mature stage of the human life-cycle is the individual who thinks for him/herself.

Definitions of the Word "Cyber"

The preceding pages have discussed the politics of knowledge in terms of the concept of "cyber."

Cyber means "pilot."

A *cyber-person* is one who pilots his/her own life. By definition, the cyber-person is fascinated by navigational information—especially maps, charts, labels, guides, manuals, which help pilot one through life. The cyber-person continually searches for theories, models, paradigms, metaphors, images, icons which help chart and define the realities which we inhabit.

Cyber-tech refers to the tools, appliances, and methodologies of knowing and communicating. Linguistics. Philosophy. Semantics. Semiotics. Practical epistemologies. The ontologies of daily life. Words, icons, pencils, printing presses, screens, keyboards, computers, disks.

Cyber-politics introduces the Foucauldian notions of the use of language and linguistic-tech by the ruling classes in Feudal and Industrial societies to control children, the uneducated and powerless individuals.

The words *governor* or *steersman* or *G-man* are used to describe those who manipulate words and communication devices to control, to bolster authority—feudal, management, government. And to discourage innovative thought and free exchange.

We describe a person who relies on static, verbal abstractions, conformity to dogma, reliance on authority, as a vassal or G-Person or G-Man. From which we get G-think, G-text, G-babble, G-berish, vassaline, vassalize.

Notes

1. Every gene pool develops its own name for Prometheus, the fearful genetic agent, Lucifer, who defies familial authority by introducing a new technology which empowers some members of the gene pool to leave the familiar cocoon. Each gene pool has a name for this ancestral state of security: "Garden of Eden," "Atlantis," "Heaven," "Home," etc.

2. The Axis included Germany, Italy, Spain, Austria, Japan, Czechoslovakia, Russia, and many East European, South American, and Middle Eastern (Islamic) nations, and (later) Vichy France. The Allies included France, England, and the British Commonwealth (Canada, Australia, and South Africa). Among the countries that remained neutral during WWII were Switzerland, Ireland, Denmark, and Sweden.

Jean-François Lyotard

The Postmodern
(*from* The
Postmodern
Condition)

What, then, is the postmodern? What place does it or does it not occupy in the vertiginous work of the questions hurled at the rules of image and narration? It is undoubtedly a part of the modern. All that has been received, if only yesterday (*modo, modo,* Petronius used to say), must be suspected. What space does Cézanne challenge? The Impressionists'. What object do Picasso and Braque attack? Cézanne's. What presupposition does Duchamp break with in 1912? That which says one must make a painting, be it cubist. And Buren questions that other presupposition which he believes had survived untouched by the work of Duchamp: the place of presentation of the work. In an amazing acceleration, the generations precipitate themselves. A work can become modern only if it is first postmodern. Postmodernism thus understood is not modernism at its end but in the nascent state, and this state is constant.

Yet I would like not to remain with this slightly mechanistic meaning of the word. If it is true that modernity takes place in the withdrawal of the real and according to the sublime relation between the presentable and the conceivable, it is possible, within this relation, to distinguish two modes (to use the musician's language). The emphasis can be placed on the powerlessness of the faculty of presentation, on the nostalgia for presence felt by the human subject, on the obscure and futile will which inhabits him in spite of everything. The emphasis can be placed, rather, on the power of the faculty to conceive, on its "inhumanity" so to speak (it was the quality Apollinaire demanded of modern artists), since it is not the business of our understanding whether or not human sensibility or imagination can match what it conceives. The emphasis can also be placed on the increase of being and the jubilation which result from the invention of new rules of the game, be it pictorial, artistic, or any other. What I have in mind will become clear if we dispose very schematically a few names on the chessboard of the history of avant-gardes: on the side of melancholia, the German Expressionists, and on the side of *novatio*, Braque and Picasso, on the former Malevitch and on the latter Lissitsky, on the one Chirico and on the other Duchamp. The nuance which distinguishes these two modes may be infinitesimal; they often coexist in the same piece, are almost indistinguishable; and yet they testify to a difference (*un différend*) on which the fate of thought depends and will depend for a long time, between regret and assay.

The work of Proust and that of Joyce both allude to something which does not allow itself to be made present. Allusion, to which Paolo Fabbri recently called my attention, is perhaps a form of expression indispensable to the works which belong to an aesthetic of the sublime. In Proust, what is being eluded as the price to pay for this allusion is the identity of consciousness, a victim to the excess of time (*au trop de temps*). But in Joyce, it is the identity of writing which is the victim of an excess of the book (*au trop de livre*) or of literature.

Proust calls forth the unpresentable by means of a language unaltered in its syntax and vocabulary and of a writing which in many of its operators still belongs to the genre of novelistic narration. The literary institution, as Proust inherits it from Balzac and Flaubert, is admittedly subverted in that the hero is no longer a character but the inner consciousness of time, and in that the diegetic diachrony, already damaged by Flaubert, is here put in question because of the narrative voice. Nevertheless, the unity of the book, the odyssey of that consciousness, even if it is deferred from chapter to chapter, is not seriously challenged: the identity of the writing with itself throughout the labyrinth of the interminable narration is enough to connote such unity, which has been compared to that of *The Phenomenology of Mind*.

Joyce allows the unpresentable to become perceptible in his writing itself, in the signifier. The whole range of available narrative and even stylistic operators is put into play without concern for the unity of the whole, and new operators are tried. The grammar and vocabulary of literary language are no longer accepted as given; rather, they appear as academic forms, as rituals originating in piety (as

Nietzsche said) which prevent the unpresentable from being put forward.

Here, then, lies the difference: modern aesthetics is an aesthetic of the sublime, though a nostalgic one. It allows the unpresentable to be put forward only as the missing contents; but the form, because of its recognizable consistency, continues to offer to the reader or viewer matter for solace and pleasure. Yet these sentiments do not constitute the real sublime sentiment, which is in an intrinsic combination of pleasure and pain: the pleasure that reason should exceed all presentation, the pain that imagination or sensibility should not be equal to the concept.

The postmodern would be that which, in the modern, puts forward the unpresentable in presentation itself; that which denies itself the solace of good forms, the consensus of a taste which would make it possible to share collectively the nostalgia for the unattainable; that which searches for new presentations, not in order to enjoy them but in order to impart a stronger sense of the unpresentable. A postmodern artist or writer is in the position of a philosopher: the text he writes, the work he produces are not in principle governed by preestablished rules, and they cannot be judged according to a determining judgment, by applying familiar categories to the text or to the work. Those rules and categories are what the work of art itself is looking for. The artist and the writer, then, are working without rules in order to formulate the rules of what *will have been done*. Hence the fact that work and text have the characters of an *event*; hence also, they always come too late for their author, or, what amounts to the same thing, their being put into work, their realization (*mise en oeuvre*) always begin too soon. *Post modern* would have to be understood according to the paradox of the future (*post*) anterior (*modo*).

It seems to me that the essay (Montaigne) is postmodern, while the fragment (*The Athaeneum*) is modern.

Finally, it must be clear that it is our business not to supply reality but to invent allusions to the conceivable which cannot be presented. And it is not to be expected that this task will effect the last reconciliation between language games (which, under the name of faculties, Kant knew to be separated by a chasm), and that only the transcendental illusion (that of Hegel) can hope to totalize them into a real unity. But Kant also knew that the price to pay for such an illusion is terror.

The nineteenth and twentieth centuries have given us as much terror as we can take. We have paid a high enough price for the nostalgia of the whole and the one, for the reconciliation of the concept and the sensible, of the transparent and the communicable experience. Under the general demand for slackening and for appeasement, we can hear the mutterings of the desire for a return of terror, for the realization of the fantasy to seize reality. The answer is: Let us wage a war on totality; let us be witnesses to the unpresentable; let us activate the differences and save the honor of the name.

Larry McCaffery

An Interview

with

William Gibson

In 1984 William Gibson's first novel, *Neuromancer*, burst onto the science fiction scene like a supernova. The shock waves from that explosion had an immediate impact on the relatively insular SF field. *Neuromancer* became the first novel to win the triple crown—Hugo, Nebula, and Philip K. Dick awards—and, in the process, virtually single-handedly launched the cyberpunk movement. *Neuromancer*, with its stunning technopoetic prose surface and its superspecific evocation of life in a sleazed-out global village of the near future, has rapidly gained unprecedented critical and popular attention outside SF.

Prior to the publication of *Neuromancer*, Gibson had published only a half-dozen stories (since collected in *Burning Chrome* [1986b]). Although several of these display flashes of his abilities—and two of them, "Johnny Mnemonic" and "Burning Chrome," introduce motifs and elements elaborated upon in the later novels—clearly *Neuromancer* was a major imaginative leap forward for someone who had not even attempted to write a novel previously. The sources of all the white light and white heat being generated by this new kid on the block are immediately apparent from the opening words of the novel: "The sky above the port was the color of television, tuned to a dead channel." Dense, kaleidoscopic, fast-paced, full of punked-out, high-tech weirdos, *Neuromancer* depicts with hallucinatory vividness the desperate, exhilarating feel of life in our new urban landscapes.

A number of critics have pointed out Gibson's affinities with certain earlier innovative SF authors: comparisons with Alfred Bester's early novels, with Philip K. Dick's midperiod fiction, and with Samuel

R. Delany's *Nova* (1968); Gibson's reliance on the cut-up methods and quickfire stream of dissociated images characteristic of William S. Burroughs and J. G. Ballard are also noted. But equally significant are the influences from sources either wholly outside SF—the hard-boiled writing of Dashiell Hammett, 1940s *film noir*, the novels of Robert Stone—or only nominally connected with the field—the garishly intense, nightmarish urban scenes and pacings in the work of rock musicians like Lou Reed; or the sophisticated blend of science, history, pop culture, hip lingoes, and dark humor in Thomas Pynchon's work.

What made *Neuromancer*'s debut so auspicious, however, was not its debts to earlier authors, but its originality of vision, especially the fresh, rush-of-oxygen high of Gibson's prose, with its startling similes and metaphors drawn from computers and other technologies, and its ability to create a powerfully resonant metaphor—the cyberspace of the computer matrix—where data dance with human consciousness, where human memory is literalized and mechanized, where multinational information systems mutate and breed into startling new structures whose beauty and complexity are unimaginable, mystical, and above all *nonhuman*. Probably as much as any first novel since Pynchon's *V.* (1963), *Neuromancer* seemed to create a significant synthesis of poetics, pop culture, and technology.

Although often overlooked by critics and reviewers in this regard, *Neuromancer* is also deeply rooted in human realities. Gibson's presentation of the surface textures of our electronic age re-creates the shock and sensory overload that define our experience of contemporary life, of having grown up with VCRs, CDs, terrorists broadcasting messages on fifty-channel video monitors, designer drugs, David Bowie and the Sex Pistols, video games, computers. Both disturbing and playful, he also explores much deeper questions about the enormous impact of technology on the definition of what it means to be human. After reading *Neuromancer* for the first time, I knew I had seen the future of SF (and maybe of literature in general), and its name was William Gibson.

Gibson's second novel, *Count Zero* (1986a), is set seven years in the future of *Neuromancer*'s world, and to some degree it retains the earlier novel's focus on the underbelly world of computer cowboys, black market drugs, and software. But the pace is somewhat slower, allowing Gibson more time to develop his characters—a mixture of eccentric lowlifes and nonconformists who find themselves confronting representatives of egomaniacal individuals whose vast wealth and power result directly from their ability to control information. More tightly controlled and easier to follow than *Neuromancer, Count Zero* is nevertheless as extraordinarily rich in suggestive neologisms and other verbal pyrotechnics; it's also a fascinating evocation of a world in which humanity seems to be constantly outshone by the flash and appeal of the images and machines that increasingly seem to push people aside in their abstract dance toward progress and efficiency.

When we spoke in August 1986 at his home in Vancouver, British Columbia, William Gibson was working on the screenplay for *Aliens III* and on his third novel, *Mona Lisa Overdrive* (1988), which completes his cyberspace trilogy. *Mona Lisa Overdrive* expands some of the implications of the two earlier novels—for instance, the interface between the human social world and cyberspace is now sufficiently permeable that humans can actually die in cyberspace; Angie Mitchell (who appeared in *Count Zero*) is able to tap into the matrix without a computer; and, once again, we witness people (including Molly from *Neuromancer*) struggling against having their bodies and imaginations manipulated by international corporations who control information and images to suit their own purposes. While these overlaps seem to make *Mona Lisa Overdrive* less startlingly original than the earlier works, Gibson's experiments with prismatic storytelling methods, his ongoing stylistic virtuosity, and his presentation of characters possessing deeper emotional resonances all point to a growing maturation and versatility.

Larry McCaffery: There are so many references to rock music and television in your work that it sometimes seems your writing is as much influenced by MTV as by literature. What impact have other media had on your sensibility?

William Gibson: Probably more than fiction. The trouble with "influence" questions is that they're usually framed to encourage you to talk about your writing as if you grew up in a world circumscribed by books. I've been influenced by Lou Reed, for instance, as much as I've been by any "fiction" writer. I was going to use a quote from an old Velvet Underground song—"Watch out for worlds behind you" (from "Sunday Morning")—as an epigraph for *Neuromancer*.

LM: The breakdown of distinctions—between pop culture and "serious" culture, different genres, different art forms—seems to have had a liberating effect on writers of your generation.

WG: The idea that all this stuff is potentially grist for your mill has been very liberating. This process of cultural mongrelization seems to be what postmodernism is all about. The result is a generation of people (some of whom are artists) whose tastes are wildly eclectic— people who are hip to punk music and Mozart, who rent these terrible horror and SF videos from the 7-11 one night and then invite you to a mud wrestling match or a poetry reading the next. If you're a writer, the trick is to keep your eyes and ears open well enough to let all this in but also, somehow, to recognize intuitively what you should let emerge in your work, how effective something might be in a specific context. I know I don't have a sense of writing as being divided up into different *compartments*, and I don't separate literature from the other arts. Fiction, television, music, film—all provide material in the form of images and phrases and codes that creep into my writing in ways both deliberate and unconscious.

LM: Our culture is being profoundly transformed by technology in ways most people are only dimly starting to realize. Maybe that's why the American public is so fascinated with SF imagery and vocabulary—even people who don't even know what SF stands for are responding to this stuff subliminally, in ads and so on.

WG: Yeah, like *Escape from New York* never made it big, but it's been redone a billion times as a rock video. I saw that movie, by the way, when I was starting "Burning Chrome" and it had a real influence on *Neuromancer.* I was intrigued by the exchange in one of the opening scenes where the Warden says to Snake: "You flew the wing-five over Leningrad, didn't you?" It turns out to be just a throwaway line, but for a moment it worked like the best SF, where a casual reference can imply a lot.

LM: In theory MTV could be an interesting new art form, a combination of advertising and avant-garde film, though it seems to be getting worse.

WG: We don't get MTV up here, but from what I've seen of it in the States, there was initially a feeling of adventure that you don't find in the established forms. But you're right—it's getting worse. So is most SF.

LM: How conscious are you about systematically developing an image or a metaphor when you're writing? For example, the meat puppet image in *Neuromancer* seems like the perfect metaphor for how the soft machine of our living bodies is manipulated by outside forces. I assume you arrived at that metaphor from listening to the cow-punk band Meat Puppets.

WG: No, I got it from seeing the name in print. I like accidents, when an offhand line breezes by and you think to yourself, Yes, that will do. So you put it in your text and start working with it, seeing how it relates to other things you've got going, and eventually it begins to evolve, to branch off in ways you hadn't anticipated. Part of the process is conscious, in the sense that I'm aware of working this way, but how these things come to be embedded in the text is intuitive. I don't see how writers can do it any other way. I suppose some pick these things up without realizing it, but I'm conscious of waiting for them and seeing where they lead, how they might mutate.

LM: Sounds like a virus.

WG: It is—and only a certain kind of host is going to be able to allow the thing to keep expanding in an optimal way. As you can imagine, the structure of a book like *Neuromancer* becomes very complicated at a certain point. It wasn't complicated in the "admirably complex" way that you find in Pynchon's novels, but simply in the sense that all these odds and ends started to affect and infect one another.

LM: Does knowing that most readers won't recognize many of these references bother you? Obviously, they don't have to know that "Big Science" is a song by Laurie Anderson in order to catch the drift of what you're suggesting; but if they do know the song, it might broaden the nature of their response.

WG: I enjoy the idea that some levels of the text are closed to most readers. Of course, writers working in popular forms should be aware that readers aren't always going to respond to subtleties— though that isn't as weird as finding out that people are missing the whole point of what you think you're doing, whether it's thinking you're being ironic when you're not, or being serious when you're trying to make fun of something. When I was in England in February, I noticed that the response to my work was markedly different; people were referring to me as a humorist. In England they think what I'm doing is *funny*—not that I'm *only* being funny, but they can see that there's a certain humor in my work.

LM: Clearly, in "Johnny Mnemonic" and "Burning Chrome" you were laying the foundation for what you would do later on in *Neuromancer.*

WG: Yes, although I didn't think in those terms when I wrote those stories. Actually, "Johnny Mnemonic" was the third piece of fiction I wrote, and the only basis I had for gauging its success was that it sold. "Burning Chrome" was written later on, and even though it got more attention than anything I'd done before, I still felt I was four or five years away from writing a novel. Then Terry Carr recruited me to write a book, which turned out to be *Neuromancer.* He was looking for people he thought had some promise—he'd offer them contracts and say, "Do you want to write a book?" I said "Yes" almost without thinking, but then I was stuck with a project I wasn't sure I was ready for. In fact I was *terrified* once I actually sat down and started to think about what it meant. I didn't think I could fill up that many pages; I didn't even know how many pages the manuscript of a novel was "supposed" to have. It had been taking me something like three months to write a short story, so starting a novel was really a major leap. I remember going around asking other writers things like, "Assuming I double space everything, how *long* is a novel?" When somebody told me 300 pages, I thought, My God!

LM: What got you going with the book?

WG: Panic. Blind animal panic. It was a *desperate* quality that I think comes through in the book pretty clearly: *Neuromancer* is fueled by my terrible fear of losing the reader's attention. Once it hit me that I had to come up with something, to have a hook on every page, I looked at the stories I'd written up to that point and tried to figure out what had worked for me before. I had Molly in "Johnny Mnemonic"; I had an environment in "Burning Chrome." So I decided I'd try to put these things together. But all during the writing of the book I had the conviction that I was going to be permanently shamed when it appeared. And even when I finished it I had no perspective on what I'd done. I still don't, for that matter. I always feel like one of the guys *inside* those incredible dragons you see snaking through the crowds in Chinatown. Sure, the dragon is very brightly colored, but from the inside you know the whole thing is pretty flimsy—just a bunch of old newspapers and papier-mâché and balsa struts.

LM: The world you evoke in *Neuromancer* struck me as being a lot like the underworld we find in the work of Raymond Chandler and Dashiell Hammett—sleazy, intensely vivid, full of colorful details and exotic lingoes that somehow seem realistic *and* totally artificial.

WG: It's probably been fifteen years since I read Hammett, but I remember being very excited about how he had *pushed* all this ordinary stuff until it was *different*—like American naturalism but cranked up, very intense, almost surreal. You can see this in the beginning of *The Maltese Falcon* (1930), where he describes all the things in Spade's office. Hammett may have been the guy who turned me on to the idea of *superspecificity*, which is largely lacking in most SF description. SF authors tend to use generics—"Then he got into his space suit"—a refusal to specify that is almost an unspoken tradition in SF. They know they can get away with having a character arrive on some unimaginably strange and distant planet and say, "I looked out the window and saw the air plant." It doesn't seem to matter that the reader has no idea what the plant looks like, or even what it is. I think Hammett may have given me the idea that you don't have to write like that, even in a popular form. But with Chandler—I never have read much of his work, and I never enjoyed what I did read because I always got this creepy puritanical feeling from his books. Although his surface gloss is very brilliant, his underlying meaning is off-putting to me.

LM: The other reason I thought of Hammett has to do with your rich, poetic vocabulary—the futuristic slang, the street talk, the technical and professional jargon.

WG: I suppose I strive for an argot that seems real, but I don't invent most of what seems exotic or strange in the dialogue—that's just more collage. There are so many cultures and subcultures today that if you're willing to listen, you can pick up different phrases, inflections, and metaphors everywhere. A lot of the language in *Neuromancer* and *Count Zero* that people think is so futuristic is probably just 1969 Toronto dope dealers' slang, or biker talk.

LM: Some of the phrases you use in *Neuromancer*—"flatlining" or "virus program"—manage to evoke some response beyond the literal.

WG: They're poetry! "Flatlining," for example, is ambulance driver slang for "death." I heard it in a bar maybe twenty years ago and it stuck with me. A drunken, crying ambulance driver saying, "She flatlined." I use a lot of phrases that seem exotic to everyone but the people who use them. Oddly enough, I almost never get new buzzwords from other SF writers. I heard about "virus program" from an ex-WAC computer operator who had worked in the Pentagon. She was talking one night about guys who came in every day and wiped the boards of all the video games people had built into them, and how some people were building these little glitch-things that tried to evade the official wipers—things that would hide and then pop out and say, "Screw you!" before vanishing into the framework of logic. (Listening to me trying to explain this, it immediately becomes apparent that I have no grasp of how computers *really* work—it's been a contact high for me.) Anyway, it wasn't until after the book came out that I met people who knew what a virus program actually was.

LM: So your use of computers and science results more from their metaphoric value or from the way they sound than from any familiarity with how they actually operate.

WG: I'm looking for images that supply a certain atmosphere. Right now, science and technology seem to be very useful sources. But I'm more interested in the *language* of, say, computers than I am in the technicalities. On the most basic level, computers in my books are simply a metaphor for human memory: I'm interested in the hows and whys of memory, the ways it defines who and what we are, in how easily memory is subject to revision. When I was writing *Neuromancer*, it was wonderful to be able to tie a lot of these interests into the computer metaphor. It wasn't until I could finally afford a computer of my own that I found out there's a drive mechanism inside—this little thing that spins around. I'd been expecting an exotic crystalline thing, a cyberspace deck or something, and what I got was a little piece of a Victorian engine that made noises like a scratchy old record player. That noise took away some of the mystique for me; it made computers less *sexy.* My ignorance had allowed me to romanticize them.

LM: What many readers first notice in *Neuromancer* are all the cyberpunk elements—exotic lingoes, drugs, cyber-realities, clothes, and so on. In many ways, though, the plot is very traditional: the down-and-out gangster who's been jerked around and wants to get even by pulling the big heist. Did you make a conscious decision to attach this punked-out cyber-reality to the framework of an established plot?

WG: When I said earlier that a lot of what went into *Neuromancer* was the result of desperation, I wasn't exaggerating. I knew I was so inexperienced that I would need a traditional plot armature that had proven its potential for narrative traction. I had these different things I wanted to use, but since I didn't have a preset notion of where I was going, the plot had to be something I already felt comfortable with. Also, since I wrote *Neuromancer* very much under the influence of Robert Stone—who's a master of a certain kind of paranoid fiction—it's not surprising that what I wound up with was something like a Howard Hawkes film.

LM: First novels are often the most autobiographical. Were you drawing on a lot of things from your own past in *Neuromancer*?

WG: Neuromancer isn't autobiographical in any literal sense, but I did draw on my sense of what people are like to develop these characters. Part of that came from accessing my own screwed-up adolescence; and another part of it came from watching how kids reacted to all the truly horrible stuff happening all around them—that unfocused angst and weird lack of affect.

LM: Did the book undergo significant changes once you knew the basic structure was in place?

WG: The first two-thirds was rewritten a dozen times—a lot of stylistic changes, once I had the feel of the world, but also a lot of monkeying around to make the plot seem vaguely plausible. I had to cover up some of the shabbier coincidences, for example. Also, I never had a very clear idea of what was going to happen in the end, except that the gangsters had to score *big*.

LM: Do you look for specific effects when you revise your prose?

WG: My revisions mainly involve looking for passages that "clunk." When I first started to write, I found that in reading for pleasure I'd become suddenly aware that a *beat* had been missed, that the rhythm was gone. It's hard to explain, but when I go over my own writing I look for places where I've missed the beat. Usually I can correct it by condensing my prose so that individual parts carry more weight, are charged with more meaning; almost always the text gets shorter. I'm aware that this condensation process winds up putting off some readers. "Genre" SF readers say that *Neuromancer* and *Count Zero* are impossibly dense, literally impossible to read; but other SF readers who ordinarily have no patience for "serious" fiction seem to be turned on by what I'm doing. Now that I've gained some experience writing, revisions take up less of my time; in fact, it's become easier to hit a level I'm satisfied with and stay there. One of the big problems with *Neuromancer* was that I had so much stuff—all this material that had been accumulating—that it was hard to get it into a manageable book.

LM: Has Thomas Pynchon had an influence on your work?

WG: Pynchon has been a favorite writer and a major influence all along. In many ways I see him as almost the start of a certain mutant breed of SF—the cyberpunk thing, the SF that mixes surrealism and pop culture imagery with esoteric historical and scientific information. Pynchon is a kind of mythic hero of mine, and I suspect that if you talk with a lot of recent SF writers you'll find they've all read *Gravity's Rainbow* (1973) several times and have been very much influenced by it. I was into Pynchon early on—I remember seeing a *New York Times* review of *V.* when it first came out—I was just a kid—and thinking, Boy, that sounds like some really weird shit!

LM: What was the inspiration for your cyberspace idea?

WG: I was walking down Granville Street, Vancouver's version of "The Strip," and I looked into one of the video arcades. I could see in the physical intensity of their postures how *rapt* the kids inside were. It was like one of those closed systems out of a Pynchon novel: a feedback loop with photons coming off the screens into the kids' eyes, neurons moving through their bodies, and electrons moving through the video game. These kids clearly *believed* in the space games projected. Everyone I know who works with computers seems to develop a belief that there's some kind of *actual space* behind the screen, someplace you can't see but you know is there.

LM: From a purely technical standpoint, the cyberspace premise must have been great to hit on simply because it creates a rationale for so many different narrative "spaces."

WG: When I arrived at the cyberspace concept, while I was writing "Burning Chrome," I could see right away that it was resonant in a lot of ways. By the time I was writing *Neuromancer*, I recognized that cyberspace allowed for a lot of *moves*, because characters can be sucked into apparent realities—which means you can place them in any sort of setting or against any backdrop. In some ways I tried to downplay that aspect, because if I overdid it I'd have an open-ended plot premise. That kind of freedom can be dangerous because you don't have to justify what's happening in terms of the logic of character or plot. In *Count Zero*, I wanted to slow things down a bit and learn how to do characterization. I was aware that *Neuromancer* was going to seem like a roller coaster ride to most readers—you've got lots of excitement but maybe not much understanding of where you've been or why you were heading there in the first place. I enjoyed being able to present someone like Virek in *Count Zero*, who apparently lives in any number of "realities"—he's got the city of Barcelona if he wants it, and an array of other possibilities, even though he's actually a pile of cells in a vat somewhere.

LM: Philip K. Dick was always writing about people like Virek who have so many "reality options," so many different reproductions and illusions, that it's difficult to know what reality is more real—the one in their heads or the one that seems to exist outside. That's a powerful notion.

WG: Yeah, it is powerful—which is why it's such a temptation to keep pushing once you've got a concept like cyberspace that creates an instant rationale. I probably was a little heavy-handed in *Count Zero* with Bobby's mother, who's hooked on the soaps, who *lives* in them, but it was just too much to resist. Everybody asks me about Dick being an influence, but I hadn't read much of his work before I started writing— though I've imagined a world in which Pynchon sold his early stories to *Fantasy and Science Fiction* and became an alternate Dick.

LM: One of the issues your work raises is the way information— this "dance of data," as you refer to it—not only controls our daily lives but may be the best way for us to understand the fundamental processes that control the universe's ongoing transformations. It seems significant that mostly SF writers are tuned to this.

WG: Information is the dominant scientific metaphor of our age, so we need to face it, to try to understand what it means. It's not that technology has changed everything by transforming it into codes. Newtonians didn't see things in terms of information exchange, but today we do. That carries over into my suspicion that Sigmund Freud has a lot to do with steam engines—both seem to be similar metaphors.

LM: The various ways you use the dance metaphor in *Neuromancer* suggests a familiarity with the interactions between Eastern mysticism and modern physics.

WG: I was aware that the image of the dance was part of Eastern mysticism, but a more direct source was John Shirley, who was living in the East Village and wrote me a letter that described the thing about proteins linking. That's just another example of how pathetically makeshift everything looks from inside the papier-mâché dragon. It was the same thing with the voodoo gods in *Count Zero*: a copy of *National Geographic* was lying around that had an article about Haitian voodoo in it.

LM: Back in the '60s and early '70s, most of the important New Wave SF took a pessimistic stance toward technology and progress. Although your work has sometimes been described as glorifying technology, I'd say it offers a more ambivalent view.

WG: My feelings about technology are *totally* ambivalent—which seems to me to be the only way to relate to what's happening today. When I write about technology, I write about how it has *already* affected our lives; I don't extrapolate in the way I was taught an SF writer should. You'll notice in *Neuromancer* that there's obviously been a war, but I don't explain what caused it or even who was fighting it. I've never had the patience or the desire to work out the details of who's doing what to whom, or exactly when something is taking place, or what's become of the United States. That kind of literalism has always seemed silly to me; it detracts from the reading pleasure I get from SF. My aim isn't to provide specific predictions or judgments so much as to find a suitable fictional context in which to examine the very mixed blessings of technology.

LM: How consciously do you see yourself operating outside the mainstream of American SF?

WG: A lot of what I've written so far is a conscious reaction to what I felt SF—especially American SF—had become by the time I started writing in the late '70s. In fact, I felt I was writing so far outside the mainstream that my highest goal was to become a minor cult figure, a sort of lesser Ballard. I assumed I was doing something no one would like except for a few crazy "art" people—and maybe some people in England and France, who I always assumed would respond to what I was doing because I knew their tastes were *very* different and because the French like Dick a lot. When I was starting out, I simply tried to go in the opposite direction from most of the stuff I was reading, which I felt an aesthetic revulsion toward.

LM: What sorts of '70s SF did you have in mind? All those sword-and-sorcery books or the hard SF that people like Jerry Pournelle, Gregory Benford, and Larry Niven were writing?

WG: Some of my resistance had to do with a certain didactic, right-wing stance that I associated with a lot of hard SF, but mainly it was a more generalized angle of attack. I'm a very desultory reader of SF—I have been since my big period of reading SF when I was around fifteen—so my stance was instinctual. In the '70s, during the years just before I seriously thought about writing SF, it seemed like the SF books I enjoyed were few and far between. Just about everything I picked up seemed too slick, and, even worse, *uninteresting*. Part of this has to do with the adolescent audience that a lot of SF has always been written for. My publishers keep telling me that the adolescent market is where it's at, and that makes me pretty uncomfortable because I remember what my tastes ran to at that age. One new factor around 1975 was that writers started getting these *huge* advances for SF books, and I said to myself, Hey, you can get *big money for SF*. But by the time I started writing SF, those big advances had dried up, because a lot of them had gone to books that had lost money. I had a sense of what the expectations of the SF industry were in terms of product, but I *hated* that product and felt such a genuine sense of disgust that I consciously decided to reverse expectations, not give publishers or readers what they wanted.

LM: How would you describe the direction of your work?

WG: When I first started writing, what held me up for a long time was finding a way to introduce the things that turned *me* on. I knew that when I was reading a text—particularly a fantastic text—it was the *gratuitous* moves, the odd, quirky, irrelevant details, that provided a sense of strangeness. So it seemed important to find an approach that would allow for gratuitous moves. I didn't think that what I was writing would ever "fit in" or be accepted, so what I wanted was to be able to plug in the things that interested me. When Molly goes through the Tessier-Ashpool's library in *Neuromancer*, she sees that they own Duchamp's *Large Glass*. Now that reference doesn't make sense on some deeper symbolic level; it's really irrelevant, a gratuitous move. But putting it there seemed right—here are these very rich people on this space station with this great piece of art just gathering dust. In other words, I liked the piece and wanted to get it into the book somehow.

LM: Precisely these personal "signatures" create a texture and eventually add up to what we call a writer's "vision." You can see this in Alfred Bester, whose books remind me of yours.

WG: Bester was into flash very early. When *Neuromancer* came out, a lot of reviewers said that I must have written it while holding a copy of *The Demolished Man* (1953). Actually, it had been some time since I'd read Bester, but he was one of the SF authors who had stuck with me, who seemed worthy of imitating, mostly because I always had the feeling he had a ball writing. And I think I know exactly what it was that produced that sense: he was a New York guy who didn't depend on writing SF to make a living, so he really just let loose; he didn't have to give a damn about anything other than having fun, pleasing himself. If you want to get a sense of how groovy it could have been to be alive and young and living in New York in the '50s, read Bester's SF. It may be significant that when you read his mainstream novel (which is pretty hard to find over here, but it's been released in England as *The Rat Race*), you can see him using the same tools he used in those two early SF books—but somehow it doesn't work. Bester's palette just isn't suited for convincing you that you're reading about reality.

LM: This business about realism often seems misleading. You said that Bester's SF books gave you a sense of what it felt like to be in New York at a certain time—*that's* realism, though different from what you find in Zola, Balzac or Henry James; it's the realism that cyberpunk supplies, that sense of what it really feels like to be alive in our place, at our time.

WG: My SF *is* realistic in that I write about what I see around me. That's why SF's role isn't central to my work. My fiction amplifies and distorts *my* impressions of the world, however strange that world may be. One of the liberating effects of SF when I was a teenager was precisely its ability to tune me in to all sorts of strange data and make me realize that I wasn't as totally isolated in perceiving the world as being monstrous and crazy. In the early '60s, SF was the only source of subversive information available to me.

LM: Some of that spirit of subversiveness, that sense of the strangeness of the ordinary, is finding its way into mainstream quasi-SF novels: Ted Mooney's *Easy Travel to Other Planets* (1981), Don De-Lillo's *White Noise* (1985), Denis Johnson's *Fiskadoro* (1985), Steve Erickson's books, and recent work by Robert Coover, Margaret Atwood, Max Apple, and Stanley Elkin.

WG: Funny you should bring up Mooney's novel, because I was very jealous of the attention it got. *Easy Travel* is a brilliant book, but I remember thinking, "Here's this guy using all these SF tropes and he's getting reviewed in *Time*." I was struck with how categories affect the way people respond to your work. Because I'm labeled a "SF writer" and Mooney is a "mainstream writer," people may never take me as seriously as they do him—even though we're both operating on some kind of SF fringe area.

LM: Your work and Mooney's share a hyperawareness that people are being affected in all sorts of ways—psychologically, perceptually—by the constant bombardment of sounds and other data. And you're both willing to experiment stylistically to find a means suitable for presenting the effects of information overload.

WG: I'm very prone to what Mooney calls "information sickness," and I'm having increasing trouble dealing with it. Without doing this too consciously, I had set up my life to minimize input. But now that I've started to make it—even relatively modestly in an obscure field like SF—I've been bombarded with all kinds of stuff. People are coming to my home, stuff arrives in the mail, the phone is ringing, I've got decisions to make about movies and book jackets.

LM: One of the common, maybe simplistic comments you hear about information overload is that the result is a kind of psychological confusion or dislocation. We have all this stuff coming in but we can't seem to put anything together so that it *means* anything. We're only slightly better off than Mooney's characters, with their paralysis and convulsions.

WG: But sometimes you find you can have *fun* with these dislocations. When I said I was prone to information sickness, I meant I sometimes get off on being around a lot of unconnected stuff—but only certain *kinds* of stuff, which is why I'm having trouble handling the input right now. I have a friend, Tom Maddox, who did a paper on my work. He's known what I've been up to for a long time—he says I display "a problematic sensitivity to semiotic fragments." That probably has a lot to do with the way I write—stitching together all the junk that's floating around in my head. One of my private pleasures is to go to the corner Salvation Army thrift shop and look at all the junk. I can't explain what I get out of doing this. I mean, I used to have to spend time there as a survival thing, and even now I'll go in and find something I want.

LM: You said you weren't really reading much SF when you started out as a writer. What got you started writing SF?

WG: A series of coincidences. I was at the University of British

Columbia, getting an English B.A.—I graduated in '76 or '77—because it was easier at the time than finding a job. I realized I could get the grades I needed as an English major to keep getting the grants I needed to avoid getting a job. There were a couple of months during that period when I thought very seriously about SF without thinking I was ever going to *write* it—instead, I thought I might want to write *about* it. I took courses with a guy who talked about the aesthetic politics of fascism—we were reading an Orwell essay, "Raffles and Miss Blandish," and he wondered whether or not there were fascist novels—and I remember thinking, "Reading all these SF novels has given me a line on this topic—*I* know where this fascist literature is!" I thought about working on an M.A. on this topic, though I doubt that my approach would have been all that earthshaking. But it got me thinking seriously about what SF did, what it was, which traditions had shaped it and which ones it had rejected. Form/content issues.

LM: Were there other literature classes that might have influenced your thinking about SF?

WG: Most of the lit classes I took went in one ear and out the other. However, I remember a class on American naturalism, where I picked up the idea that there are several different kinds of naturalist novels: the mimetic naturalist novel—the familiar version—and the crazed naturalist novel—the kind Hammett writes, or Algren's *Man with the Golden Arm* (1949), where he tries to do this realistic description of Chicago in the '40s but his take on it is weirder than anything I did with Chiba City in *Neuromancer*. It's full of people with neon teeth, characters with pieces of their faces falling off, stuff out of some bad nightmare. Then there's the overt horror/pain end of naturalism, which you find in Hubert Selby's books. Maybe related in some way to these twisted offshoots of naturalism are the books by William Burroughs that affected SF in all kinds of ways. I'm of the first generation of American SF authors who had the chance to read Burroughs when we were fourteen or fifteen years old. I know having had that opportunity made a big difference in my outlook on what SF—or any literature, for that matter—could be. What Burroughs was doing with plot and language and the SF motifs I saw in other writers was literally mind expanding. I saw this crazy outlaw character who seemed to have picked up SF and gone after society with it, the way some old guy might grab a rusty beer opener and start waving it around. Once you've had that experience, you're not quite the same.

LM: Has the serious attention you've gotten from the SF world made you feel any less alienated?

WG: Yeah—everyone's been so nice—but I still feel very much out of place in the company of most SF writers. It's as though I don't know what to do when I'm around them, so I'm usually very polite and I keep my tie on. SF authors are often strange, ill-socialized people who have good minds but are still kids.

LM: Who among the current writers do you admire or feel some connections with?

WG: Bruce Sterling is certainly a favorite—he produces more ideas per page than anyone else around. Marc Laidlaw had a book called *Dad's Nuke* that I really enjoyed. And John Shirley, of course. I also admire Greg Bear's work, even though his approach is much more hard SF oriented than mine. Recently I came across some quasi-SF books by Madison Smartt Bell—*The Washington Square Ensemble* (1983) and *Waiting for the End of the World* (1985)—which are wonderful, brilliant.

LM: What about Samuel Delany? His work seems to have influenced your generation of SF authors in important ways.

WG: There's no question about his importance, and he's obviously influenced me. Those books he was writing when he was twenty-one or whatever were my favorite books when I was fifteen and plowing through all that SF. I'm pretty sure I didn't know at the time that Delany wasn't much older than I was, but I think the fact that I was a kid reading books by a slightly older kid had something to do with my sense that his books were a lot *fresher* than anything else I could find.

LM: You're usually considered the leading figure of the cyberpunk movement. Is there such a thing, or was the movement dreamed up by a critic?

WG: It's mainly a marketing strategy—and one that I've come to feel trivializes what I do. Tying my stuff to *any* label is unfair because it gives people preconceptions about what I'm doing. But it gets complicated because I have friends and cohorts who are benefiting from the hype and who like it. Of course, I can appreciate that the label gives writers a certain attitude they can rally around, feel comfortable with—they can get up at SF conventions, put on their mirrored sunglasses, and say, "That's right, baby, that's us!"

LM: That was exactly the scene at the recent SFRA conference in San Diego. John Shirley, decked out in a leather jacket and shades, wound up in a screaming match with the hard SF "Killer B's"—Brin, Bear, and Benford—who have their own identity, their own dress code.

WG: Michael Swanwick wrote an article about the split between the cyberpunks and the humanists. He referred to John Shirley as John-the-Baptist-of-Cyberpunk, roaming the wilderness trying to spread the new gospel. Even though I don't agree with everything Swanwick wrote, I do think John has always had this evangelical side to him—though he's less like that now than when I first met him in 1977, when he was into spiked dog collars. No one was ready for his insane novels, which are unfortunately very hard to find. There just wasn't anything else like that being written then—no hook or label like cyberpunk, no opening—so they were totally ignored. If those books were published now, people would be saying, "Wow, look at this stuff! It's *beyond* cyberpunk." Really, though, I'm tired of the whole cyberpunk phenomenon. I mean, there's already bad *imitation cyberpunk*, so you know it can only go downhill from here. All that really happened was that a bunch of work by some new authors landed on some publishers' desks at the same time. People didn't know what to make of us, so they gave us this tag.

LM: The cyberpunk/humanist opposition seems way off base to me. There are a lot of scenes in both *Neuromancer* and *Count Zero* that are very moving from a human standpoint. Beneath the glittery surface hardware is an emphasis on the "meat" of people, the fragile body that can get crushed so easily.

WG: That's my "Lawrentian" take on things. It's very strange to write something and realize that people will read into it whatever they want. When I hear critics say that my books are "hard and glossy," I almost want to give up writing. The English reviewers, though, seem to understand that what I'm talking about is what being hard and glossy does to you.

LM: One of the scenes that sticks out for me is the one near the end of *Neuromancer* where Case is on that beach with the woman. It's a powerful and sad moment even though—or maybe *because*—we know he's in cyberspace imagining all this.

WG: It's great to hear *someone* react that way to that scene, because that passage was the emotional crux of the book, its center of gravity. I'd like to think that the novel is balanced in such a way that the scene shows how distorted everything has become from several different perspectives.

LM: Another scene that has a peculiar emotional charge is the one where Case is trying to destroy the wasps' nest. What makes the nest seem so primal, so scary?

WG: The fear of bugs, for one thing! That scene evolved out of an experience I had destroying a very large wasps' nest. I didn't know what was inside, didn't know they were "imprinted" that way, so when the nest broke open I was astounded and scared by all the wasps. It probably also helped that I got stung several times.

LM: Do you consciously build a metaphor like the wasps' nest so that it resonates in different ways, or is the process buried in your unconscious?

WG: Once I've hit on an image, a lot of what I do involves the controlled use of collage; I look around for ways to relate the image to the rest of the book. That's something I got from Burroughs's work, and to a lesser extent from Ballard. I've never actually done any of that cut-up stuff, except for folding a few pages out of something when I'd be stuck or incredibly bored and then checking later to see what came out. But I could see what Burroughs was doing with these random methods, and why, even though the results weren't always that interesting. So I started snipping things out and slapping them down, but then I'd air-brush them a little to take the edges off.

LM: Isn't that approach out of place in a field like SF, where most readers are looking for scientific or rational connections to keep the futuristic fantasy moving forward credibly?

WG: As I said earlier, I'm not interested in producing the kind of literalism most readers associate with SF. This may be a suicidal admission, but most of the time I don't know what I'm talking about when it comes to the scientific or logical rationales that supposedly underpin my books. Apparently, though, part of my skill lies in my ability to convince people otherwise. Some of the SF writers who are actually working scientists do know what they're talking about; but for the rest of us, to present a whole world that doesn't exist and make it seem real, we have to more or less pretend we're polymaths. *That's just the act of all good writing.*

LM: Are you interested in developing a futuristic, Faulknerian Yoknapatawpha County in which everything you write will be interconnected in a single fictional world?

WG: No—it would look too much like I was doing one of those Stephen R. Donaldson things. People are already asking me how many of these books I'm going to write, which gives me a creepy sensation because of the innate sleaziness of so much SF publishing. When you're not forced to invent a new world from scratch each time, you find yourself getting lazy, falling back on the same stuff you used in an earlier novel. I was aware of this when I was finishing *Neuromancer*, and that's why, near the end, there's an announcement that Case never saw Molly again. That wasn't directed so much at the reader as at me. If you had told me seven years ago that I would write a SF trilogy, I would have hung myself in shame. Posthaste.

LM: The obsession today with being able to reproduce a seemingly endless series of images, data, and information of all sorts is obviously related to capitalism and its drive for efficiency; but it also seems to grow out of our fear of *death*, a desire for immortality. The goals of religion and technology, in other words, may be closer than we think.

WG: I can see that. But this isn't something that originated with contemporary technology. If you look at any of the ancient temples, which were the result of people learning to work stone with the technology available to them, what you'll find are machines designed to give those people immortality. The pyramids and snake mounds are time machines. This kind of application of technology seems to run throughout human culture.

LM: You didn't start college until the mid-1970s. What were you doing during the late '60s and early '70s?

WG: Virtually nothing. My father was a contractor back in the '40s; he made a bunch of money installing flush toilets for the Oak Ridge projects and went on to the postwar, pre–Sun Belt building boom in the South. He died when I was about eight, and my mother decided to move the family back to this little town in Virginia where they had both come from. I stayed there until I was sixteen or seventeen, a bookish, geekish, can't-hit-the-baseball kind of kid. Then I went to boarding school in Tucson, where I was exposed to urban kids and where I encountered the first wave of hippies pouring over the land from San Francisco. They were older than I was, and they were really into some cool stuff. Eventually, I got kicked out of boarding school for smoking pot. I went back to Virginia, but my mother had died and my relatives weren't particularly sympathetic to my style. So I spent some time bumming around. I more or less convinced my draft board that they didn't want me; in any case, they didn't hassle me, and in 1968 I left for Toronto without even knowing that Canada would be such a different country. I wound up living in a community of young Americans who were staying away from the draft.

LM: Was it pretty much an underground scene? Did it contribute to your novels?

WG: I'm sure it did, in terms of supplying me with some of the offbeat language I use. But to describe it as an "underground scene" would seem funny to anyone who knew me and what was going on. It was really pretty tame compared to what was happening in a lot of places; it was a soft-core version of the hippie/underground street scene, nothing heavy. I did have the small-town kid's fascination with watching criminal things. No question, though, that it made a lasting impression on me. Those were portentous days. Nobody knew what was going to happen.

LM: You weren't giving much thought at that point to being a writer?

WG: Only occasionally. Like a lot of other people, I felt I was living in an age in which everything was going to change very radically, so why make career plans? When things *didn't* get different, except maybe worse, I retreated. I went to Europe and wandered around there for a year—I had enough income from my parents' estate to starve comfortably. I came back to Canada because my wife, Deb, wanted to finish a B.A., and we moved to Vancouver so she could attend UBC. When Deb began work on an M.A. in linguistics, I realized that higher education was a good scam. If I hadn't wandered into SF, I'd be totally unemployable.

LM: Are you interested in trying your hand at non-SF soon, maybe breaking out of the SF ghetto into the mainstream's mean street?

WG: I am, because I'm afraid of being typecast if I make SF my permanent home. But what seems important right now is finding my way out of what I'm doing without losing a sense of what it is I'm doing. I don't want to go back and start over. I have glimpses of how this might be done, but it's a lateral move that has become increasingly difficult to make. It's taken as gospel among SF writers that to get out of SF once you've made a name in it is virtually impossible: "The clout isn't transferable."

LM: That's ironic, given all the mainstream writers doing quasi-SF. Not to mention the Latin American fabulists.

WG: I envy the Latin American writers because they can do what they want. In America, it seems like these influences mostly travel in one direction—mainstream writers borrow from SF, but SF writers seem locked into provincialism. When I was in England, I thought it was interesting that their community of SF writers was enthusiastic about Latin American fabulism. But few people in the equivalent American SF community seem remotely familiar with it.

LM: What can you tell me about your next novel? Have you started work on it yet?

WG: I'm supposed to be working on it, but as you can see by this household's sublime sense of peace and order, it's tough going right now. It's called *Mona Lisa Overdrive* and it's not a linear sequel to *Count Zero*—in fact, it bears the same relationship to *Count Zero* that *Count Zero* did to *Neuromancer,* in that each book takes place seven years after the previous one. You glimpse some of the same people, but fourteen years is a long time in a world like this, where things change so fast you can hardly recognize anything from minute to minute. When I was doing *Count Zero*, I had initially intended to pursue what was going to happen to Mitchell's daughter; that seemed like an interesting thread to follow. But I was so anxious to finish the book, so tired of working on it, that I talked myself out of making any judgments about it. It nagged at me, though; I kept wondering what happened to her. She's a permanent interface with the voodoo gods and she's also obviously going to be the next Superstar. Somehow, though, that wasn't enough to get me going. Then I spent a weekend at the Beverly Hills Hotel with some producers, an eye-opening trip. Coming back on the plane, it struck me that for the first time I had actually gotten to see some of the stuff I had been writing about. I had another book I was supposed to start, but when I got back to Vancouver I phoned the agents and told them I wanted to do *Mona Lisa Overdrive* instead.

LM: The Japanese settings you've used, notably in *Neuromancer,* seem right in all sorts of ways. Was any of that based on personal experience?

WG: "Terry and the Pirates" probably had more to do with it than personal experience. I've never been to Japan, but my wife has been an ESL teacher for a long time, and since the Japanese can most afford to send their teenagers over here to study English, there was an extended period when this stream of Japanese students turned up in Vancouver—I'd meet them a week off the plane, see them when they were leaving, that sort of thing. Also, Vancouver is a very popular destination for Japanese tourists—for example, there are special bars here that cater exclusively to the Japanese, and almost no one else goes into them because the whole scene is too strange. I'm sure I got a lot of this in when I wrote *Neuromancer*. Of course, the Japanese have really bought the whole cyberpunk thing. It's as if they believe everything Bruce Sterling has written about it! It's frightening. But one of the things they seem to like about my work is that I don't try to invent Japanese names—I got the street names from a Japan Air Lines calendar. And I got lucky with the geography. I didn't even know where Chiba was when I wrote *Neuromancer*—all that stuff about it being on a peninsula and across a bay came out of my head—so I was really sweating when the book came out. But then I got a map and there was Chiba—on a peninsula! on a bay! Life imitates art. The only culture I've seen firsthand that might have influenced *Neuromancer* was Istanbul, which had a big impact on me even though I was only there for a week or so. Another place that affected my writing was the East Village, which John Shirley introduced me to in 1980. Nothing had prepared me for what I encountered when I stepped out into the street. The buildings were papered with Xerox art as high up as people could reach. From the point of view of somebody who'd been living in a place like Vancouver, the whole scene was total chaos and anarchy. It was weird and frightening and interesting all at the same time.

LM: Do you sometimes wish you lived in New York or Los Angeles so you could draw on the strangeness more directly?

WG: If I lived in a place like that, I'd write about unicorns. I'll leave well enough alone for now.

Larry McCaffery

Cutting Up:
Cyberpunk, Punk
Music, and Urban
Decontextualizations

Well, said I, we shall consult Damon on this
question, which meters are expressive of
madness, insolence, frenzy, and other such
devils, and which rhythms we must retain to
express their opposites. It would take a long
time to settle that.
It would indeed.
—Plato, "Musical Accompaniment and
Meter," *The Republic*, Book III

In Greece, as I said, words and music gave a
rhythm to Action. Afterwards music and
rhymes became toys, pastimes. . . .
—Arthur Rimbaud, Letter to Paul Demeny, 15
May 1871

But how could we know when I was young
All the changes that were to come?
All the photos in the wallets of the battlefield
And now the terror of the scientific sun?
—The Clash, "Something About England"

The City and Its Doubles: Punk and Cyberpunk

**The city exists as a series of doubles; it has official and hidden cultures, it
is a real place and a site of the imagination. Its elaborate network of
streets, housing, public buildings, transport systems, parks, and shops is
paralleled by a complex of attitudes, habits, customs, expectancies, and
hopes that reside in us as urban subjects. We discover that urban "real-**

ity" is not single but multiple, that inside the city there is always another city. (Chambers, 1986:183)

The confluence of influences, historical and artistic circumstances, and cultural contexts that give rise to artistic movements is always complex, fluid, difficult to pinpoint. Precisely identifying such features in contemporary art is especially problematic because of the rapidity with which influences and contexts become known, assimilated, discarded. This is certainly the case with the swirl of artistic and cultural circumstances that produced the punk music scene in the mid-1970s and cyberpunk art about a decade later. But having provided this perfunctory acknowledgment of the terrors of terminology, I would like to press on and explore the connections between punk music and cyberpunk. These interactions supply useful insights into the sources of vitality and originality in each art form as well as providing excellent examples of the way in which postmodern artists are responding to the massive shifts occurring almost daily in our urban environments. What I hope to establish are not "influences" per se, although cyberpunk authors, several of whom have actually played in rock bands, have clearly borrowed specific aspects of punk iconography, aesthetic, and thematic emphases, and incorporated them

Now I lay me down to Sleep
I hear the sirens in the street
All my dreams are made of chrome
I have no way to get back home
(Tom Waits, used as the epigraph to Richard Kadrey's cyberpunk novel,
***Metrophage*)**

Rickenharp was listening to a collector's item Velvet Underground tape, from 1968. It was capped into his Earmite. The guitarists were doing things that would make Baron Frankenstein say, "There are some things man was not meant to know." (John Shirley, *Eclipse*, 68)

The Meat Puppets—name of Phoenix cow-punk band (cf. William Gibson's *Neuromancer*)

***Life During Wartime*—title of Lucius Shepard novel, taken from song of the same name by David Byrne/Talking Heads (from *Fear of Music* [1981])**

into their fiction. Rather, the point I wish to develop has to do with the new syntheses and other forms of interaction we see developing among the arts. It's a spirit of "integration" pointed to by Bruce Sterling in his introduction to the *Mirrorshades* cyberpunk anthology (1986a) where he notes that cyberpunk represents "the overlapping of worlds that were formerly separate, the realm of high tech and the modern pop underground" (xi). Sterling makes a crucial point here by linking cyberpunk with the pop "underground," for what distinguishes cyberpunk from other forms of SF is its admiration of and empathy for certain extremist figures of the underground art scene. Some of these are literary figures (William S. Burroughs, Thomas Pynchon, Philip K. Dick, the dadaist and surrealist poets, Arthur Rimbaud), some are movie and video makers (George Romero, David Cronenberg, Ridley Scott), some are musicians (Laurie Anderson, Sonic Youth, the Residents, certain New Wave and Industrial Noise bands), and some are doing unclassifiable work (performance artists Karen Finley and Johanna Went, Mark Pauline and the Survival Research Laboratories). Almost inevitably, some are punk musicians and poets, such as Patti Smith, the Sex Pistols, Jim Carroll, Henry Rollins, the Clash, X, and Lou Reed and the Velvet Underground. What unites all of these artists is what might be termed a shared "attitude"—an attitude of defiance towards cultural and aesthetic norms; an attitude of distrust towards rationalist language and all other forms of discourse required by legal,

GADJI BERI BIMBA CLANDRIDI
LAULI LONNI CADORI GADJAM
A BIM BERI GLASSALA GLANDRIDE
E GLASSALA TUFFM I ZIMBRA
(The Talking Heads, "I Zimbra"; words by Hugo Ball; from *Fear of Music*)

A wop bop a loola a wop bam boom! (Little Richard, "Tutti Fruiti")

political, and consumer capitalism, but which ultimately have the effect of distorting the individual's sense of him-or-herself as an individual and as a body made of flesh; (therefore) an attitude that artists need not only to *disrupt* the usual modes of communication but to find a means of self-expression that is more "authentic," less tied to abstractions, more tied to the senses and emotions; an attitude that extremities of content and aesthetics are valuable and interesting in and of themselves (they produce bodily and emotional responses that are powerful and hence undeniably "real") and valuable, too, because such art fundamentally questions the assumptions of "normative art" (and of the culture which produces this).

Cyberpunks, then, are merely the latest in a long list of "underground" artists who have appeared since the Age of Reason from Sade up through Baudelaire, Rimbaud, the dadaists and surrealists, Bataille, Artaud, Genet, and then continuing on through the Beats, Elvis, the French Situationists, and the Sex Pistols. That cyberpunks

Leaving the road most taken we might step out and join Lefebvre's long line almost anywhere: step into the *champ libre*, the *freie strasse*, most often the imaginary terrain of a parallel history—once the realm of heretics, alchemists, esoterics, since the French Revolution the domain of political conspiracies and aesthetic "avant-gardes," perhaps little more than a place for naysayers to claim a position ahead of history while fighting a rear-guard action against it, against the Industrial Revolution, the middle class, the "bourgeoisie," "mass man," "mass society" (in a phrase, modern democracy)—a parallel history powered by the plain wish to break out of the story most told and most often condemned to travel with it like the bird on the rhinoceros, the naysayer's wish circling back, finally to meet No New Man, no new world, but only what little is left of the desire that set off the journey in the first place. (Greil Marcus, *Lipstick Traces: A Secret History of the 20th Century*, 189–90)

would be intrigued by figures from the punk music scene is hardly surprising. Not only was punk arguably the most significant artistic movement of the 1970s, but it shared with cyberpunk the same urges to use technology as a weapon against itself, and to seize the control of its form from the banalizing effects of the media industry and reestablish a sense of menace, intensity. Decked out in mirrorshades and leather jackets, quoting Lou Reed and the Stones and Johnny Rotten as often as Einstein and Heisenberg, the cyberpunks aimed at presenting themselves in much the same way as the punk musicians did: as "bad," as extreme, as in touch with what was happening now, and, of course, as being *daring*. Examining these connections also offers a perfect opportunity to explore some of the defining features of postmodernism itself: its spirit of collaboration, intertextuality, and *jouissance*; its

The debate over postmodernism can also be read as the symptom of the disruptive ingression of popular culture, its aesthetic and intimate possibilities, into a previously privileged domain. Theory and academic discourse are confronted by the wider, unsystematized, popular networks of cultural production and knowledge. The intellectual's privilege to explain and distribute knowledge is threatened; his authority, for it is invariably "his," redimensionalized. (Iain Chambers, *Popular Culture: The Metropolitan Experience*, 216)

lack of distinctions between pop and avant-garde art forms, between genres—and between the technical scientific world and the humanist, countercultural realm; its application of such formal methods as cut-ups, facetious quotation, and reflexivity which all had the effect of subverting closure while opening up discourses. Finally, this investigation is long overdue, for although the implications of the "cyber"-features of cyberpunk have by now been fairly thoroughly identified, the relevance of the "punk" label has been unduly neglected.

This neglect may well have to do with the common misperception of punk music being *merely* unsophisticated and utterly vulgar (and hence unlikely to share much with the glittery, hyperhip second cousin beyond an obvious mutual interest in the aesthetics of extremity). But, in fact, the commonalities shared by punk rock and cyberpunk art are fundamental and run much more deeply than the superficial linkages most critics (even many cyberpunk authors themselves) have thus far acknowledged. Punk and cyberpunk share a variety of aesthetic impulses and influences that extend well beyond the benzedrine rush of their rhythms and pacings or their fascination with the grotesque and perverse. Among these overlapping formal concerns are their reliance on collage and cut-up methods (William S. Burroughs is a particularly important shared point of reference); their presentation of highly idiomatic lingoes, drawn primarily from subcultures of drugs and crime, whose operations explicitly and implicitly serve to oppose the power and authority of public discourses and texts (cyberpunk poetics, of course, are also grounded within the emerging vocabularies of emerging technologies, especially cybernetics and computers); a more generalized, demolition derby approach to the genre conventions that had previously governed their forms, and in particular a willingness to use obscenity, "noise," sensory overload, and other methods to disrupt the usual pathways through which meaning is conveyed, while exploring other possibilities. Their works are saturated with many of the same thematic and symbolic preoccupations as well—paranoia, sexual and psychic violation and manipulation, the desire to achieve transcendence through drugs, religion, or the computer-generated dance of data.

Schismatrix is bare bones, like a Ramones three-minute pop song: we're not going to have any pretentious lighter shades of pale guitar noodling here, it's going to be "Sheena Is a Punk Rocker," blam blam blam, let's move on. (Bruce Sterling, in Larry McCaffery, "An Interview with Bruce Sterling," *Across the Wounded Galaxies*, 228)

Punk and cyberpunk are both hard-edged, "roots-oriented" forms developed to return their genres to some mythic, primal source of energy; hence, the "anyone can do this" slogan of punk musicians and their emphasis on the simple lyrics and rock chord progressions and the analogous return by cyberpunk authors to their own version of "roots music." For example, the recycling of the hard-boiled thriller formula and similar appropriations of storylines that are as familiar to SF audiences as a Chuck Berry or Scotty Moore guitar riff, a Jerry Lee Lewis piano solo, or a Little Richard falsettoed shriek would be to a rock fan. Arguments that this reliance on prior forms displayed a failure of creative imagination have been used by critics to discount the significance of punk and cyberpunk; such criticisms were highly misleading in both cases, however, because they failed to take into account the spirit of free play and collaboration of these forms, their delight (à la Burroughs) in using familiar contexts primarily to "contain" very nontraditional "materials," and the way their return-to-basics approach becomes a reflexive commentary on specific genre conventions that had evolved around their respective forms. Johnny Rotten and the Sex Pistols may really have been aiming to return to rock basics, but certainly their manager Malcolm McLaren obviously knew that the chance of any *real* "*return*" was possible only with the aid of a time machine. The Sex Pistols and the Ramones and the Clash and Patti Smith did not create a return but a "return"; their work was not lyrically stupid and musically simple, it was "lyrically simple" and "musically stupid." The point is the same one made by Borges in "Pierre Menard" (1962), and echoed in the criticism of many poststructuralist critics: a work of art produced at one moment of history has utterly different meanings and nuances than an earlier work of art *even if the two works are exact duplicates of one another.* Thus, the rebellious stance of punk music, despite being displayed in the same chord progressions one would hear in the 1950s, is of an utterly different sort of rebelliousness than that produced by Elvis Presley, the first punk rocker. Punk's "rebelliousness," and the analogous spirit of revolt found in cyberpunk, is of the sort that can only emerge after a genre has reached the "threshold of complexity" described by Douglas Hofstadter in *Gödel, Escher, Bach*—that is, the stage at which a system explores the elements that comprise it until it begins developing reflexive examinations of itself. Punk and cyberpunk, then, should most properly be seen as subversive metaforms whose emphasis on shocking, exotic presentations and disruptive formal methods were self-consciously devised by their creators as challenges both to conventional genre features of their forms and to the banalizing effects of their respective mass market industries.

Another highly significant connection between the two forms is that both have emerged specifically within the context of contemporary *urban* life—a life characterized by the bewilderingly frantic pace of its interactions and transformations (it's no accident that speed is the drug of choice in cyberpunk narratives), by its rich profusion of daily stimuli, by its power to dehumanize, and by the desperation and

A modern man registers a hundred times more sensory impressions than an eighteenth-century artist. (Fernand Léger, 1914)

violence of the urban subcultures who populate its mean streets. Indeed, crucial to understanding the aesthetic and thematic inter-

I don't like to use the word "real," but in a sense we were trying to make everything more real . . . and to portray, the same way a Cut-up theoretically does: what it's like to be in a house and go along the street and have a car go past or a train and work in a factory or walk past a factory. Just a kind of industrial life, or suburban—urban-industrial life.

When we finished that first record, we went outside and we suddenly heard trains going past, and little workshops under the railway arches, and the lathes going, and electric saws, and we suddenly thought, "We haven't actually created anything at all, we've just taken it in subcon-

sciously and re-created it." ("Interview with Genesis" [of Throbbing Gristle], *Re/Search: Industrial Culture Handbook*, 10.)

actions of punk rock and cyberpunk is the recognition that both are radical, highly stylized forms of postmodernist *urban* art that have been forged in response to the violent, surreal, hyperstimulated realities

Night City was like a deranged experiment in social Darwinism, designed by a bored researcher who kept one thumb permanently on the fast-forward button. (William Gibson, *Neuromancer*, 7)

found in the science fictional, punked-out landscapes urban artists already inhabit. Both have created vivid and powerfully disturbing visions of our blighted and glitzy urban culture—and of the garish but often grotesquely deformed people and cultures that are dying, thriving, and mutating in the midst of the neon glow and television skies of today's technopolises. Thus, many of the chief formal features shared

Industrialism, the main creative force of the nineteenth century, produced the most degraded urban environment the world had yet seen: for even the quarters of the ruling classes were befouled and overcrowded. (Lewis Mumford, *The City in History*, 61)

by punk and cyberpunk art, as well as their common thematic obsessions, can be seen as related aspects of an artistic vision of urban despair, confusion, and victimization; or, more precisely, punk and c-p have forged from the *materials* of this negative vision highly energized and defiant works that bear comparison to the graffiti art one finds in our barrios and ghettos, the rap and dub music produced by black

Sounds of gunfire, off in the distance, I'm getting used to it now. (David Byrne/Talking Heads, "Life During Wartime," from *Fear of Music*)

artists (the Industrial Noise approach, mostly created by white musicians like Sonic Youth, is a related development), and other art forms associated with urban guerilla warfare. (For the present I will ignore the many ironies and complexities involved in capitalism's ability to co-opt instantaneously even those forms most expressly opposed to its operations.) With punk and c-p, then, one is confronting the efforts of the "soft machines" inhabiting this hallucinatory realm to find some means of transcendence and authenticity, even if this is achieved only by projecting to society a self-mutilating, parodically exaggerated mirror reflection of its condition.

Operating on parallel but separate tracks, then, punk and cyberpunk have created a series of works that managed to produce what Iain Chambers has termed (in reference to punk) a "self-conscious style of crisis" (1986:170). This "style of crisis," while reflecting the complex, literal crises facing urban youths growing up in the midst of massive unemployment and a generally dehumanizing, boring environment, was also a calculated decision to create a confrontational situation with the media and the record industry, thereby emphasizing their disavowal of the standards of the day. The effectiveness of punk music in generating controversy and attention was not to be ignored by equally savvy—but no less disgruntled—cyberpunk authors such as John Shirley and Bruce Sterling, who succeeded in creating an uproar at SF conventions and in public debates and in print with their only slightly lower-keyed tactics of flamboyant dress, polemical rhetoric, and confrontational tactics.

Punk Rock: The Aesthetics of Trash

Now at such a point, you will agree, the question turns from a question of disposing of this "trash" to a question of appreciating its qualities, because, after all, it's 100 percent, right? And there can no longer be any question of "disposing" of it, because it's all there is, and we will simply have to learn how to "dig" it. . . . It's that we want to be on the leading edge of the trash phenomenon, the everted sphere of the future, and that's why we pay particular attention, too, to those aspects of language that may be seen as a model of the trash phenomenon. (Donald Barthelme, *Snow White*, 97–98)

The specific evolutions of the punk rock scenes in New York and London differed somewhat. In New York, for example, the punk scene, with the notable exception of the Ramones, tended to be more closely tied to the St. Mark's poetry and art rock scene associated with Lou Reed, the New York Dolls, Patti Smith, and Television than the more proletariat-oriented British punkers. But in both locales, punk music emerged partially as a response to the manner in which rock music's vitality and sense of rebellious energy had been co-opted by a media industry whose chief aim was simply to sell as many "safe," indistinguishable products as possible. Punk was thus launched as an

But the problem is to make the soul into a monster. (Arthur Rimbaud,
Letter to George Izambard, *Complete Works*, 102)

assault against the record industry and against the same-sounding,
passionless music (with its emphasis on bland lyrics and sophisticated
but joyless production values) this industry represented. Punk aimed
at returning to rock's original sense of power and menace by creating a
deliberately "crude" sound that emphasized sensuality and surface-
level energy at the expense of technical virtuosity. Those punk bands
who adopted the exaggerated, self-consciously "vacant," "dumb," and
nihilistic pose—the Ramones and the Sex Pistols would be quintes-

Such intentional and obvious psychological references are so blatant as to
be the surface appearance itself, supplying an explanation itself with no
further need to reach below; yet this new type of self-explanatory surface
is such an overstatement that it baffles the analytical critic far more than
ordinarily. The sheer overstatement of rock 'n' roll presents a front which
escapes all criticism, but which leads to an interestingly absurd body of
this attempted criticism. (Richard Meltzer, *The Aesthetics of Rock*, 14)

sential examples—tended to discard any verbal complexity in favor of
pure noise and direct, parodically stupid lyrical content. In early
classic punk songs such as "Pretty Vacant" (Sex Pistols) and "I Wanna
Be" (the Ramones) we can see this blend of archnihilism and vacancy
attaining a dadaesque sense of absurdity that acts as a bitterly funny,
reflexive commentary on the linguistic structures used to oppress
them. Consider the Ramones' "I Don't Care":

> I don't care
> I don't care
> I don't care
> About this world
> I don't care
> About that girl
> I don't care
> I don't care
> I don't care
> About these words
> I don't care

On the other hand, the linguistic approach favored by the artier punk
bands, such as Television, Jim Carroll, X, and especially Patti Smith,

while equally disdainful of logic, reason, and other semiological features required for consumer capitalism's efficient exchange of goods, attempted to forge more ambitious alternate discourses. In the tradition of Rimbaud, punk's avatar, the surrealists, and more recent protopunk figures such as Genet, Bukowski, and Burroughs, these groups aimed at forging from the debased, squalid verbal elements around them a new punk poetics capable of expressing their despair,

> **The poet, therefore, is truly the thief of fire.**
>
> **He is responsible for humanity, for animals even; he will have to make sure his visions can be smelled, fondled, listened to; if what he brings back from beyond has form, he gives it form; if it has none, he gives it none. A language must be found . . . of the soul, for the soul, and will include everything: perfumes, sounds, colors, thought grappling with thought. (Arthur Rimbaud, Letter to Paul Demeny, *Complete Works*, 103)**

frustration, and defiance at the daily conditions they were subjected to. The poetic effects of the best of their lyrics are gained from a sensuous sense of profusion, overstatement, hyperviolence, and blunt sexuality, surrealist juxtapositions of imagery and language that verge on the hallucinatory in their effects. The opening to Patti Smith's "babelogue," is a good example of the complex affects and undeniable power this supposedly inarticulate form could produce at times:

> I haven't fucked with the past but i've fucked plenty with the future. over the silk of skin are scars from the splinters of stages and walls i've caressed. each bolt of wood, like the log of helen was my pleasure. i would measure the success of a night by the amount of piss and seed i could exude over the columns that nestled the p/a. some nights i'd surprise everybody by snapping on a skirt of green net sewed over with flat metallic circles which dangled and flashed. the lights were violet and white. for a while i had an ornamental veil. but i couldn't bear to use it. when my hair was cropped it craved covering. but now my hair itself is a veil and the scalp of a crazy and sleepy comanche lies beneath the netting of skin.
>
> i wake up. i am lying peacefully and my knees are open to the sun. i desire him and he is absolutely ready to serve me. in house i am moslem. in heart i am an american artist and i have no guilt. i

seek pleasure. i seek the nerves under your skin. the narrow archway. the layers. the scroll of ancient lettuce. we worship the flaw. the mole on the belly of an exquisite whore. one who has not sold her soul to god.

(Patti Smith, "babelogue," from *Easter*)

The overall effect of lyrics such as these, or those produced by such other gifted punk figures as Jim Carroll, Henry Rollins, Polly Styrene, and Exene Cervenka—especially when the words are being delivered in a punk concert, with its backdrop of high-decibeled music and gyrating, slam-dancing youths clad in utterly bizarre outfits pogoing up and down to a driving beat—is a revved-up, visionary projection of urban intensity and brutality, sleaze and allure. Combining equal measures of anarchy and self-conscious posing, punk created a musical and poetic mode of expression that reflected the debased but extraordinarily *vivid* lives of the disaffected urban youths who must somehow exist in the midst of concrete jungles, casual violence, and towering monuments that threaten to dwarf all *human* perspective.

The city's paving stones are hot
Despite the gasoline you shower,
And absolutely, now, right now, we've got
To find a way to break your power.

Bourgeois, bug-eyed on their balconies
Shaking at the sound of breaking glass,
Can hear trees falling on the boulevards
And, far off, a shivering scarlet clash.
(Arthur Rimbaud, "Parisian War Cry," *Complete Works*, 56)

Indeed, punk artists, like all artists wishing to express a specifically "urban" perspective, were forced constantly to confront the same problem facing Western (that is, Southwestern) artists: how to find a suitable means of somehow making the human participants in their work not seem overwhelmed by the inhuman immensity lying all around them. This helps to explain the gesture of punk (and of cyberpunk) toward images and storylines which can hopefully break through this anonymity while paradoxically expressing it. Punk and cyberpunk obsessively depict violence and sexual perversion not simply because these are urban realities, but because they wish to foreground *any*

I spent my whole life in the city,
where junk is king and the air smells shitty
People dying everywhere,
miles of blood and scabs and hair
People dying on the streets,
but those guys in their suits,
they don't care,
They just get fat and dye their hair
I love Living in the City!
(Fear, "I Love Living in the City," from *Fear*)

action that momentarily generates for its participants a sense of human authenticity—even of the self-mutilating variety—which counters the daily boredom and confusion of existence. To this end, punk artists demolished and then reconstructed the semiological codes and physical objects around them, determined to play with and otherwise manipulate these discarded cultural and technological elements into new objects with new purposes that their original creators could not have anticipated. The effects of this kind of "retrofitting" or recycling of

> I don't look at things like that as stealing, I see it as grants from industry. (Mark Pauline of Survival Research Laboratories, Interview, in Peter Belsito, *Notes from the Pop Underground*, 12)

discarded materials has been described by Iain Chambers: "With punk, the traditional closure of subcultural style was subverted as it became the object of facetious quotations, irreverent cut-ups and ironic poses. Punks ransacked postwar subcultures for fashions and signs to recycle and relive. In a blasphemous remixing of revered subcultural memories . . . the punks constructed an iconography of disrespect, pillaging the subcultural past and attiring themselves in urban rubbish" (1986:170–71). Examples of this method can be seen in the blasphemous uses to which the Sex Pistols and the Dead Kennedys employed familiar political slogans and musical signatures in songs such as "God Save the Queen" and "Moral Majority," in the gruesome, slithery materials (tools, sandwiches, Kotex, clothes, food, etc.) hurled at the audience in a typical Johanna Went performance piece, or in the Boschean industrial sculptures concocted by Mark Pauline and the Survival Research Laboratories. Like the cyberpunks afterward, punks were "cutting up"—making jokes, applying the methods of Burroughs, literally severing the content of their lives so that it could be reshaped later on.

The Style of William Gibson: Shopping in the Urban Supermarket

It had always looked good to Bobby, up there, so much happening on the balconies at night, amid red smudges of charcoal, little kids in their underwear swarming like monkeys, so small you could barely see them. Sometimes the wind would shift, and the smell of cooking would settle over Big Playground, and sometimes you'd see an ultralight glide out from some secret country of rooftop up there. And always the mingled beat from a million speakers, waves of music that pulsed and faded in and out of the wind. (William Gibson, *Count Zero*, 30)

The term "cyberpunk" is still probably most appropriately used in the narrow sense Gardner Dozois originally intended: as a description of the remarkable fiction of William Gibson. And, in several recent interviews, the relevance of punk aesthetics to Gibson's work becomes obvious: "I see myself as a kind of literary collage artist, and SF as a marketing framework that allows me to gleefully ransack the whole fat supermarket of twentieth-century cultural works." Of course, literary and visual artists have been ransacking the urban supermarket for materials to use in their presentations of urban scenes throughout this

That's how it's been around me.
I'm all tuned in, I see all the programmes
I save coupons from packets of tea
I've got my giant hit discotheque album,
I empty a bottle and I feel a bit free.
The kids in the halls and the pipes in the walls,
Make me noises for company,
Long distance callers make long distance calls,
And the silence makes me lonely
And it's not here
It disappear.
(The Clash, "Lost in the Supermarket")

century. In this, Warhol, Duchamp, Joyce, Robert Rauschenberg, Donald Barthelme, and, in a somewhat different manner, Mark Pauline and the Survival Research Laboratories come immediately to mind as artists who use the detritus of urban scenes as principle building blocks, language, and objects in the collages they've constructed. Indeed, when one thinks of those writers who have best caught the "feel" of urban life in this century—Kafka's Prague, Joyce's Dublin, Doblin's Berlin, the Los Angeles of West and Chandler, Algren's Chicago, Hammett's San Francisco—we find that nearly all their presentations are characterized by surrealist effects produced by a profusion (often overprofusion) of sharply etched images colliding in unexpected ways.

But while punk art often relies on surrealist principles, this is not to equate them. What supplies a work with its particular "punk" quality is the way in which the artist charges the language, symbols, and images being employed with a certain sense of *extremity* whose purpose is to force the audience into a confrontation with different and, often, initially frightening or disturbing realms of aesthetic experience; that is, the artist must select images, words, and other semiotic elements—usually ones highly charged with violent and sexual resonances—which will produce in the audience a sense of shock, perverse beauty, and (the trickiest) empathy. The audience's shock of recognition is essential for punk art to operate successfully; images

Beauty belongs to the sphere of the simple, the ordinary, whilst ugliness is something extraordinary, and there is no question but that every ardent imagination prefers in lubricity, the extraordinary to the commonplace. (Sade, *The 120 Days of Sodom*, 184)

which merely evoke only surprise or shock are ultimately useless at conveying a vision *of* anything (this is why punk rarely employs nonsense or genuinely absurd forms). The audience must be made to feel somehow that the images they are being exposed to, no matter how distasteful, surreal, or ugly, are speaking to them in a shared (if twisted) vocabulary. The opening of "Jonny Hit and Run Paulene," by L.A.'s premiere punk band, X, provides a good illustration of what is involved here:

> He bought a sterilized hypo
> To shoot a sex machine drug

He got 24 hours
To shoot all Paulene's between the legs
He'll throw 96 tears thru 24 hours
Wants sex once every hour
Jonny hit and run Paulene

This is punk poetry at its supercharged best—dissonant harmonic vocals suddenly interjected into a familiar Chuck Berry guitar riff; unsettling images violently yoked together in a way that evades rational analysis—a "sterilized hypo" that shoots a "sex machine drug," or the title itself, "Jonny Hit and Run Paulene"—but which produce a complex, nightmarish set of deeper associations: phallus/gun/hypo; sperm/bullets/drugs; the sex act as a mechanized activity devoid of passion or understanding; money/violence/sexuality; the double entendre of "hit and run" with its linking of cars/violence/rape/abandonment/machines. Compare the way this passage works with what we find on the opening pages of Gibson's *Neuromancer* as a bartender is being described:

> Ratz was tending bar, his prosthetic arm jerking monotonously as he filled a tray of glasses with draft Kirin. He saw Case and smiled, his teeth a webwork of East European steel and brown decay. . . .
> The antique arm whined as he reached for another mug. It was a Russian military prosthesis, a seven-function force-feedback manipulator, cased in grubby pink plastic. "You are too much the artiste, Herr Case." Ratz grunted; the sound served him as laughter. He scratched his overhang of white-shirted belly with the pink claw. (3–4)

The way in which this passage produces in the reader a sense of shock and lurid fascination has much in common, of course, with the effect of similar passages in the work of other urban writers specializing in depicting the seamy sides of modern urban life—especially authors like Hammett, Algren, and Chandler, whose superspecific renderings of such scenes create a nightmarish familiarity. What makes Gibson's writing different is not only his remarkable eye for the grotesque, ordinary details (the tray of glasses, the overhang of "white-shirted belly"), but the introduction of "cyber" details that clash sharply with the familiar. It's not the "brown decay" of Ratz's mouth or his "grubby pink plastic" case that startles us, but their being combined with "a webwork of East European steel" and the "Russian military prosthesis" with its "seven-function force-feedback manipulator." Gibson's ability to develop contexts in which the "punk" and "cyber" elements can lie down together in uneasy (but unforgettable) alignment is one of the chief features of his distinctive prose imagination.

Lou Reed, William S. Burroughs, and William Gibson: A Walk on the Wild Side

Two comments made by Gibson in the interview appearing in *Storming the Reality Studio* clarify the ways in which his hot-wired prose and mannerisms, his collage methods, and his focus on urban subcultures have been consciously affected by punk aesthetics:

> I've been influenced by Lou Reed, for instance, as much as I've been by any "fiction" writer. (265)

> I'm of the first generation of American SF authors who had the chance to read Burroughs when we were fourteen or fifteen years old. I know having had that opportunity made a big difference in my outlook on what SF—or any literature, for that matter—could be. What Burroughs was doing with plot and language and the SF motifs I saw in other writers was literally mind expanding. I saw this crazy outlaw character who seemed to have picked up SF and gone after society with it, the way some old guy might grab a rusty beer opener and start waving it around. Once you've had that experience, you're not quite the same. (278)

Gibson's citations of Reed and Burroughs are revealing because these two artists were punk's twin Godfathers. Reed, of course, has produced a remarkable body of work closely associated with the mythical street scene prowled by Gibson. Frequently, he has populated his songs with the brand of brutally honest, street-tough yet vulnerable figures that Gibson has chosen for his central heroes. Reed and John Cale were the chief creative sensibilities behind the Velvet Underground, the band usually regarded as the seminal protopunk band of the 1960s. Reed and Cale actually collaborated only on the first two VU albums—*Andy Warhol Presents the Velvet Underground and Nico* and *White Light/*

White Heat (both released in 1967)—but what they achieved there probably remains unequaled in rock history in terms of its extremity of vision, its range of musical and lyrical effects, and its ability to blend urban sounds and images into an organic, often shocking, but always exhilarating whole.

Sponsored initially by Andy Warhol, whose role in postmodernism's breakdown of the division between avant-garde and the mainstream is central and ongoing, the Velvet Underground mixed genres

Andy Warhol Looks a scream
Hang him on my wall.
Andy Warhol, Silver Screen
Can't tell him apart at all
(David Bowie, "Andy Warhol," from *Hunky Dory* [1971])

(their performances combined music, dance, film, poetry readings, and light shows), musical styles (folk, minimalism, thrash, jazz, gothic rock), and messages in a way ideally suited for expressing the multiple textures of city life. The songs Reed wrote for VU were troubling, rough-edged glimpses into the street scenes he had grown up in. Rock music, of course, had emerged from many conflicting and competing scenes (country and western, Dixieland jazz, Southern gospel, for example), and urban life had always been a central component of its sounds (its urban blues and jazz traditions), its imagery and metaphors (the cars, bars, black leather-jacketed juvenile delinquents, factories, and the street scene itself), and its thematic preoccupation with youthful dreams thwarted by the squalid, all-consuming Evil of Big City Life. The songs one finds on the first two VU albums, however, while undeniably rooted in rock's traditional urban textures, unarguably departed from rock's familiar treatments of this scene. The nature of both these implicit continuities and differences bears a striking resemblance to what we find in the handling of urban presentations by Gibson and other cyberpunks.

In 1967, while most of the rock world was celebrating the Summer of Love, with its attendant emphasis on peace, the transformative power of hallucinogens, and harmony, the VU released its first two albums, which laid down the blueprint for many of the musical and thematic directions punk rock would pursue a decade later. The chief departure made by Reed and his VU cohorts has to do with the brutal honesty and frightening sense of empathy brought to their depictions of a series of shocking character types and situations. These were powerful tales of sadomasochism, narcissism, drug abuse, and despair in which Reed presented people and situations that either never had appeared in popular music before or whose appearance had been utterly disguised or romanticized:

"Waiting For My Man": re-creates the anxieties and sensory impressions of a strung-out kid waiting apprehensively on the streets of Harlem for his "man" to show with a drug delivery.

"Sunday Morning": the deeply ambiguous musings of Reed as he faces a postparty sunrise with contradictory feelings of hope and dread. Gibson originally planned to use the ominous refrain to this song—"Watch out for worlds behind you"—as the epigraph to *Neuromancer*.

"Heroin": "I want to nullify my life," says the narrator of this harrowing depiction of the agonies and false transcendence of drug addiction. Reed's cooly detached vocal delivery, the stark realism and lyricism of its details, and the remarkable musical textures that parallel the physical sensation of shooting heroin contributed to the revolutionary influence this song had on the treatment of drugs in pop music.

"Sister Ray": a horrific and wonderful blend of Ornette Coleman–influenced dissonance and minimalist heavy-metal thrash, this song obliquely tells the story of an orgy and a murder when a band of drag queens take some sailors home and shoot them up with heroin. With its black humor, its bursts of obscenities and raw, piercing sounds, its overwhelming sense of dissonance and pure noise, and the finely held tension between its tight formal structure and utter chaos, "Sister Ray" assaulted the musical conventions of pop music more radically than any other rock song of its day, bar none. And in its exploration of the relationship between the mechanical and the human, artfulness and gutter trash, tasteless exoticism and sublime beauty, "Sister Ray" provided a perfect illustration of the ways in which popular artists could extend their treatments of urban life into more extreme (and more exciting) realms. For a generation of brash, cocky youths, the call of this particular wildness must have been irresistible.

While it might not occur to most readers that a rock musician like Lou Reed could be a central influence on a science fiction author, it should hardly be surprising to discover that the work of William S. Burroughs had a profound impact on both punk music and cyberpunk fiction. Because his work has long been associated with graphic, wickedly humorous portrayals of drug addiction, violence, sexual perversion, and just about any other form of human depravity imaginable, Burroughs was quickly embraced by punk musicians as a fellow traveler in extremist aesthetics. Here was a figure whose very life was the embodiment of punk ideology, a man who had encouraged at least two earlier generations of artists to boldly go to those forbidden areas of artistic expression where no artists had gone before. So it was during the mid-to-late 1970s that the Burroughs name, along with those of Rimbaud and Genet (two earlier literary "criminals"), began appearing within the context of punk mutations (New Wave, Industrial Noise, and so on). Soon Burroughs became the equivalent of a rock star himself: songs were written about him (notably, VU's "Lonesome Cowboy Bill"), he was interviewed for major record magazines with Devo and other rock groups, he gave readings at rock concerts headlined by figures such as Jim Carroll and Patti Smith, and he made appearances on rock albums and movies (as on Laurie Anderson's *Mr. Heartbreak* album and her movie *Home of the Brave*). The significance of this flurry of activity surrounding an already legendary underground cult figure could not have been lost on a certain segment of young, aspiring SF authors whose sensibilities were being shaped by a strange assortment of materials—underground music and cinema, comic book art, video games, TV evangelists, *Saturday Night Live*, and postmodernist fiction by Pynchon, Ballard, Dick, and Burroughs.

Cyberpunk writers, like punk musicians, were drawn to Burroughs's work not only because of the extremity and exoticism of its content, though Burroughs's wide-ranging interest in science, pseudosciences (L. Ron Hubbard's Scientology was an ongoing interest for a while), and quirky branches of learning would have been of obvious appeal to the quirky sensibilities associated with cyberpunk. Of even greater importance to punk and cyberpunk artists was Burroughs's radical approach to form/content issues. Burroughs's reliance on cut-up and fold-in methods, his efforts to deconstruct and then reassemble the codes and imagery of popular culture, and his appropriation of other discontinuous structuring devices—all aimed at furthering his assault on the "Reality Studio" in an effort to regain control of the illusion-making systems producing Reality—were naturally suggestive to punk and cyberpunk authors whose aesthetic aims were similarly tied to appropriating the appropriators' codes and imagery, trashing the conventions associated with the forms while simultaneously creating a reflexive, subversive dialogue with these conventions, and re-creating the sense of sensory overload, speed, and extremity associated with contemporary urban life.

In his SF trilogy—*The Soft Machine* (1966), *The Ticket That Exploded* (1967), and *Nova Express* (1964)—Burroughs had demonstrated that artists could use the central motifs, themes, and plot devices of SF as a kind of framing device to "contain" the sorts of materials he (like the cyberpunks) wished to use to explore a world increasingly saturated by media images, information manipulations, and discarded waste products (including discarded people). Ultimately,

the transformation of waste is perhaps the oldest preoccupation of man. gold, being the chosen alloy, must be resurrected—via shit, at all cost. inherent within us is the dream of the alchemist. to create from clay a man. and to recreate from the excretions of man pure and soft then solid gold. (Patti Smith, "the salvation of rock," *Babel*, 140)

what Burroughs offered punk and cyberpunk artists was the example of a radicalized sensibility fully engaged with the surrounding culture. Burroughs's aim, however, was to use this engagement as a means of breaking down the power relationships that have been established by the culture over its constituent members.

This Is the End

Punk and cyberpunk artists have created a significant body of work that explores vital new connections between high art and trash, beauty and ugliness, avant-garde and pop, delicacy and violence, the utterly programmed and the spontaneous, and, perhaps their most original synthesis, technology and humanism. Like other postmodernist art, cyberpunk is fascinated with the surfaces and textures of daily life not because it is intellectually or aesthetically "shallow," but because of its recognition that artists, like ordinary citizens, can no longer overlook the heterogeneous surface activities of everyday life—these too are *real* and need to be dealt with on their own terms, just as the computer and cybernetic technologies currently invading and manipulating our lives are real and need to be explored and appropriated. Cyberpunk authors, then, like punk rock musicians a decade ago, are creating art that recognizes that these sign systems and technologies need to be *inhabited* by human beings rather than by the bloodless simulacra who manage corporate and political concerns. In this sense, both punk and cyberpunk are exemplary postmodernist art forms in their acceptance of the principle that only by playing with and transforming these signs and technologies can we hope to avoid being played with and transformed by them. In other words, use it (our humanity) or lose it.

Brian McHale

POSTcyberMODERNpunkISM

These are days of lasers in the jungle. . . .
—Paul Simon

Suppose a reader, in search of a reliable and authoritative account of contemporary fiction in the United States, were to consult the *Columbia Literary History of the United States* (1988), edited by Emory Elliot with nine distinguished Americanists listed as associate and advisory editors. What could be more reliable and authoritative? Opening to the chapter titled "The Fictions of the Present," this reader would immediately encounter an epigraph from *Neuromancer* (1984) by William Gibson. William who? William Gibson, the cyberpunk science fiction writer, of course. Reading on, she or he would find that the author of this chapter, Larry McCaffery, considers science fiction to be "arguably the most significant body of work in contemporary fiction" (1988b: 1167), and ranks science fiction's "emergence . . . as a major literary genre" first among the "most significant new directions in recent American fiction" (1162). Moreover, McCaffery's judgments are reflected in his allocation of space in what must have been a very tightly budgeted essay: of its twenty-two paragraphs, two full paragraphs are devoted to SF in general, another to women SF writers, two more to Ted Mooney's *Easy Travel to Other Planets* (1981) (not "hard" SF but SF-related), and parts of two other paragraphs to the SF novelists Samuel R. Delany and (of course) William Gibson.

The *Columbia Literary History* represents, if not a breakthrough, at least a striking advance in the process of science fiction's legitimation. What explains this new "official" acceptability of SF? Perhaps after all it is just a matter of quality: SF writers are now able to meet the standards that we expect "serious" writing to meet. But there have always been critics willing to maintain that SF has already achieved such standards, and there have always been at least a few SF writers who could measure up to even the most demanding literary criteria; anyway, the notion that there exists some absolute threshold of quality which candidates for legitimation must cross seems dubious, to say the least.

This is not, in any case, the explanation that the *Columbia Literary History* gives. Here and elsewhere McCaffery views the new cyberpunk SF in the light of a general postmodernist phenomenon, the alleged collapse of genre distinctions, including the distinction between "genre" fiction (such as SF) and "serious" fiction (1988b:1174; cf. McCaffery, 1988a:13). The underlying thesis, in other words, is the one associated with Fredric Jameson and Andreas Huyssen, among others: namely, that postmodernism is characterized by the collapse of hierarchical distinctions between high and low art, between "official" high culture and popular or mass culture (Jameson, 1984a:54–55, 1988c:14; Huyssen, 1986). So attractive and influential is this thesis that we ought to be more than a little wary of it. For one thing, as E. Ann Kaplan has observed, just because certain high culture texts happen to mingle high culture and popular culture elements, there is no reason to conclude that the boundaries between high and popular culture have been effaced in the culture at large. In fact, of course, the institutions for the production, distribution, and consumption of high culture continue to be distinct from those for popular culture, regardless of whatever promiscuous minglings of cultural strata may occur inside texts (Kaplan, 1988:4; cf. Csicsery-Ronay, 182–93, this volume).

McCaffery also proposes this thesis of the collapse of cultural distinctions in his interview with William Gibson (pp. 263–85, this volume), who unreservedly endorses it: "This process of cultural mongrelization seems to be what postmodernism is all about. . . . I know I don't have a sense of writing as being divided up into different *compartments . . .*" (266). Nevertheless, it is easy to demonstrate that Gibson's own writing relies on the continuing viability of cultural compartmentalization. Gibson's fiction functions at every level, even down to the "micro" structures of phrases and neologisms, on the principle of incongruous juxtaposition—juxtapositions of American culture with Japanese culture, of high technology with the subcultures of the "street" and the underworld, and so on. The term "cyberpunk" has been constructed according to this incongruity principle. There is an example in the McCaffery interview itself, when Gibson gives as an instance of "cultural mongrelization" people who like punk and Mozart, and who will "invite you to mud wrestling or a poetry reading" (266). The effect of incongruity here and elsewhere in Gibson's writing obviously depends on the persistence of hierarchical cultural categories: a poetry reading belongs to high culture and mud wrestling to low culture. If the distinction were effaced, the effect would be lost; no compartmentalization, no effect of incongruity. As Ralph Cohen remarks, in the context of a discussion of the persistence of genres in postmodernism, the very possibility of transgression presupposes the existence of generic (or, more generally, categorial) boundaries (1987:246).

Furthermore, the thesis of postmodernism's effacement of the "great divide" between high and low culture depends for much of its potency and persuasiveness on a particular construction of modernism. Historical "high modernism," by this account, sought to seal high culture off from "contamination" by mass culture. This particular construction of modernism is obviously tendentious, designed partly to throw into high relief the novelty and difference of postmodernism. A little reflection will show, however, the degree to which even the most self-assertively "artistic" modernist writers exploited popular art models and genres, and not just by ironically quoting or parodying them: think of James's reliance on melodrama and romance, or Conrad's on adventure story models; Faulkner's exploitation of historical "costume" romance, detective fiction, horror stories, pornography, and just about every other currently available pop art genre; and the almost universal impact of cinematic models and strategies, especially in the United States (Hemingway, Faulkner, Dos Passos, Fitzgerald, Nathanael West). This is not to say that there is no significant difference between modernism and postmodernism on this issue, for of course there is, but it is mainly a difference of their respective self-descriptions: where the modernists repudiated and sought to camouflage their reliance on pop art models, the postmodernists have tended openly to advertise theirs. But we must try not to confuse polemics with actual practice.

In fact, it would be utterly astonishing if modernist writing had failed to exploit pop art models, for the constant traffic between low and high—the high art appropriation of pop art models and the reciprocal assimilation by pop art genres of "cast-off" high art models—is one of the universal engines driving the history of literary (and, more generally, cultural) forms. Thus, while modernist writers were quarrying popular genres for materials with which to revivify their own high art productions, they were also supplying, directly or through intermediaries, popular writers with materials to replenish their stock. For example, we can trace the diffusion of a certain avant-garde minimalist prose style from its innovator (Gertrude Stein, about 1914) through her epigones (especially Sherwood Anderson, about 1920, and Hemingway, about 1925) to certain intermediaries (especially Dashiell Hammett), and from them to a wide range of mass-market media—a sort of "trickle-down" modernism. [1]

What is distinctive of postmodernism, then, is not the fact of "contamination" of high culture by mass culture, since that turns out to be a universal of cultural history (and as characteristic of modernism as it is of postmodernism), but rather the technologically enhanced speed of the traffic in models between the high and low strata of culture. Pop art models are assimilated by high art (and vice versa) more quickly now than ever before, and this has the further consequence of producing an ever more intimate interaction, an ever-tighter feedback loop, between high and low. Such speed and intimacy of interaction is not, however, to be confused with the collapse or effacement of hierarchical distinctions. For the engine to continue to turn over, the high culture/low culture distinction must persist, in however problematic or attenuated a form.

Science fiction is a case in point. A number of critics, including Teresa Ebert (1980), Kenneth Mathieson (1985), and myself (1987), have noted the "convergence" or "cross-fertilization" between recent science fiction and "serious" or "mainstream" postmodernist fiction. Yet, so steadily has the tempo of this interaction accelerated from decade to decade that at the same time we were making these observations the youngest generation of science fiction writers, the so-called cyberpunks, were both corroborating our observations and preempting them, in a sense rendering them obsolete. In any case, the trajectory of convergence we had begun to map can now be extended through the 1980s.

Samuel Delany contends, in his contribution to the *Mississippi Review* "Forum" (28–35), that only in the context of the internal history of the SF genre do cyberpunk's themes and styles acquire their full significance. Delany makes a strong case; but I want to argue that the SF tradition is not the only relevant context for cyberpunk, and that, on the contrary, part of cyberpunk's significance derives from the changing relationship between SF and "mainstream" fiction in recent decades.

For SF is not a genre in a vacuum, of course, but belongs to an entire system of genres, popular entertainment genres as well as high art genres, within the overall system of systems, or polysystem, of the culture.[2] In order to describe some of the systemic relations relevant to cyberpunk, we need to make a few preliminary distinctions. First of all, if we continue to operate with the distinction, current in SF criticism and polemic, between SF and "mainstream" fiction, we do so only with the severest reservations. Obviously too crude for most theoretical uses, indeed more a caricature than a descriptive tool, this opposition nevertheless does capture economically some of the most salient facts about SF's systemic relations. In particular, it captures the orientation of all species of "genre" fiction—including SF, detective fiction, women's gothic romance, horror stories, and so on—toward the central or mainstream genres, and their functional "indifference" to one another. That is, each of these popular genres defines itself in terms of its differences from the central system of mainstream fiction, perceived (from the position of these peripheral genres) to be relatively homogeneous, and *not* in terms of its differences from other popular genres. The functionally relevant distinctions for SF are not the ones that differentiate it from, say, detective fiction, but the ones that differentiate it from the mainstream. And, of course, this opposition between "genre" writing and the mainstream is faithfully reflected by the practice of the book marketing industry, which helped to produce the opposition in the first place, and continues to maintain it.

So we can retain the familiar opposition between SF and mainstream fiction as a kind of convenient shorthand, on the condition, however, that we introduce a functional distinction *within* the "mainstream" category. In order to make the mainstream/SF opposition more fully adequate to our purposes, we need to discriminate between (aesthetically) conservative mainstream genres and (again, aesthetically) progressive genres, between norm-observant writing and norm-violating or innovative writing. We could call the conservative wing of mainstream writing "bestseller" fiction, and its progressive wing "advanced" or "state-of-the-art" fiction.[3]

In the earliest phases of SF history, from the 1920s through the 1940s, SF and mainstream fiction existed in mutual isolation from one another, mutually incommunicado. Modern SF crystallized and developed as a "ghetto" enclave, largely out of touch with both contemporary bestselling fiction and advanced mainstream fiction, just as these latter were in turn largely unresponsive to SF. The first important interspecies contacts, so to speak, occurred in the 1950s, with the "leveling up" of SF to something approaching the stylistic norms of mainstream bestseller fiction. Heinlein, Asimov, Clarke, Sturgeon, Bester, and others of their generation modeled their prose style and narrative structures on those of bestseller fiction, while a few mainstream bestsellers in turn adopted typical SF motifs, themes, and materials (for example, Nevil Shute's *On the Beach* [1957], Walter Tevis's *The Man Who Fell to Earth* [1963]).[4] It is partly due to the success of the SF novelists of this generation that the poetics of the leveling-up phase has come to be perceived as the SF norm. No doubt it is the poetics of this phase that critics such as Christine Brooke-Rose (1981) have in mind when they describe SF as an essentially realist discourse.[5]

There had as yet, however, been little if any interaction between SF and advanced or state-of-the-art mainstream fiction. That interaction began in the next phase, in the 1960s and early 1970s, with New Wave SF and the first wave of postmodernist mainstream fiction. What is striking here is that, when this mutual interaction finally did get under way, it had an oddly regressive character, with each partner in the exchange returning to an earlier historical phase of its opposite number. That is, SF in this phase began to absorb models from state-of-the-art mainstream fiction of an earlier period, not the advanced fiction contemporaneous with itself, while advanced mainstream fiction in the 1960s and early 1970s drew on the SF of an earlier phase of its development, not the concurrent phase.[6]

Thus, postmodernist fiction in those decades began to exploit motifs and materials drawn from early, long outdated SF sources: the space operas and bug-eyed-monster fiction of the early pulp magazines (William Burroughs, Kurt Vonnegut, Thomas Pynchon), superhero comics (Italo Calvino's *Cosmicomics*, Pynchon's Rocketman, Plasticman, and other superheroes), SF disaster and monster movies (Sam Shepard's early plays, *Operation Sidewinder* and *Angel City*, and Pynchon's use of King Kong), and so on.[7] Meanwhile, SF in its New Wave phase "modernized" itself, absorbing elements from the poetics of the high modernists of the 1920s and 1930s, not its postmodernist contemporaries. In most New Wave writing the model involved is that of a kind of generalized high modernist poetics, but in some cases specific indebtednesses or homages can be traced: to Conrad in the case of J. G. Ballard, to Dos Passos in the case of John Brunner, to Thomas Mann in the specific case of Thomas Disch's *Camp Concentration* (1968), and so on.[8]

Only in the course of the 1970s did SF and postmodernist mainstream fiction really become one another's contemporaries, functionally as well as chronologically, with each finally beginning to draw on the current phase of the other, rather than on some historically prior phase. It is during this period that we encounter SF that incorporates elements of postmodernist poetics, such as the later novels of Philip K. Dick, especially *Ubik* (1969); J. G. Ballard's novels beginning with *The Atrocity Exhibition* (1969) and *Crash* (1973); Samuel R. Delany's big SF novels of the 1970s and early 1980s, *Dhalgren* (1974), *Triton* (1976), and *Stars in My Pocket Like Grains of Sand* (1984); and the late, linguistically playful SF novels of Alfred Bester. It is also during this period that mainstream postmodernist fiction opens itself up to motifs and materials from SF of the New Wave and later. Indicative of this new openness to contemporary SF is an essay by the mainstream novelist Joseph McElroy (1975) in which J. G. Ballard is credited as an influence alongside such state-of-the-art postmodernists as Butor, Robbe-Grillet, and Pynchon.[9]

As this phase of the interaction prolongs itself into the 1980s, a feedback loop begins to operate between SF and postmodernist fiction. That is, we find postmodernist texts absorbing materials from already "postmodernized" SF, and SF texts incorporating models drawn from already "science-fictionized" postmodernism, so that certain elements can be identified which have cycled from SF to mainstream postmodernism and back to SF again, or from mainstream fiction to SF and back to the mainstream again. A case in point would be William S. Burroughs's "lost civilization" motifs (see, for example, "The Mayan Caper" in *The Soft Machine* [1966]). Burroughs combined formulaic motifs from jungle adventure thrillers and pulp magazine SF to create a new motif complex, recontextualizing the original materials and literally reprocessing them, that is, subjecting them to his cut-up and fold-in techniques. When this particular bundle of motifs, bearing traces of Burroughs's characteristic obsessions and emphases, reappears in 1980s SF (for example, Lucius Shepard's *Life During Wartime* [1987] or Lewis Shiner's *Deserted Cities of the Heart* [1988]), this is clear evidence of the circulation of motifs from SF sources back to SF again by way of a postmodernist intermediary.[10]

It is this latest phase of the interaction that, on the SF end of the feedback loop, has acquired the label of "cyberpunk." In this systemic perspective, cyberpunk can be seen as SF which derives certain of its elements from postmodernist mainstream fiction which has already been "science-fictionized" to some degree.[11] When questioned, cyberpunk writers typically acknowledge the influence of non-SF writers in about equal proportion with that of their SF predecessors, and the non-SF writers most frequently named are Burroughs and Pynchon, state-of-the-art mainstream writers heavily indebted to earlier forms of SF for themes, motifs, and materials.[12] Burroughs's role in recycling transformed SF elements back to cyberpunk SF has already been noted. Pynchon's position in this loop is, if anything, even more crucial.

The presence of Pynchon's texts, *Gravity's Rainbow* (1973) in particular, is pervasive in cyberpunk, ranging from plot structure and large-scale world elements down to fine verbal details. For example, the Slothrop plot of *Gravity's Rainbow* would appear to have provided the model for Shepard's *Life During Wartime*, in which a soldier with psychic talents is trained by military intelligence for special operations, escapes from his handlers, and undergoes picaresque and fantastic adventures traversing a war zone. Traces of this same plot-structure (perhaps fused with that of a SF precursor, Bester's *The Stars My Destination*, 1956) may be detected in Michael Swanwick's *Vacuum Flowers* (1987), while the plot of Pynchon's *The Crying of Lot 49* (1966) surely underlies the adventures of Bruce Sterling's heroine Laura in *Islands in the Net* (1988).

Pynchon's worlds contributed even more than his plots have to the cyberpunk repertoire. The paranoid vision of a world controlled by multinational corporations, who are controlled, in turn, by the self-actuating technologies upon which their power depends—this world-view, so pervasive a feature of cyberpunk extrapolation, certainly derives, at least in part, from Pynchon. Thus, for example, in Walter Jon Williams's *Hardwired* (1986), in which the multinationals have abandoned the planet surface and now exert their control from orbiting platforms, the ultimate source of this extrapolated world is signaled by the names of two of the orbital cartels, Yoyodyne and Pointsman Pharmaceuticals A.G., both "borrowed" from Pynchon.[13] Similarly, Pynchon's motif of conditioning—control internalized and made inseparable from individual identity—appears in the many cyberpunk variations on the zombie theme. Pynchon may even be partly responsible for what is arguably the most characteristic of all cyberpunk motifs, that of human-computer symbiosis, and the associated motif of the "Electro-world" (Pynchon's term), the computer-generated parallel world or paraspace of Gibson's "Matrix" trilogy and other cyberpunk texts.[14]

Finally, Pynchon's presence may be traced even at the "micro" level, in fine details of cyberpunk world-texture and language. Thus, Pynchon is the source for, among other details, the fictional plastic, "Imipolex G," in Rudy Rucker's *Software* (1982) and *Wetware* (1988); the unwholesome sexual habits of the executive officer of an orbiting station in John Shirley's *Eclipse* (1985); a disgusting dinner-table conversation intended to discourage enemies in Swanwick's *Vacuum Flowers*; a spooky episode in an empty nightclub in Gibson's *Count Zero* (1986a); unauthorized research into the corporate structure of a multinational cartel in Williams's *Hardwired*; sex with the television on in Sterling's *Islands in the Net*; a "smart bomb" (in the original it was a runaway can of hairspray) caroming around a room in Rucker's *Wetware*; and the angels in both *Wetware* and Sterling's *Schismatrix* (1985). Pynchon may even have contributed toward the notorious opening sentence of Gibson's *Neuromancer*: "The sky above the port was the color of television, tuned to a dead channel" (1984:3). Do we catch here an echo, however subliminal, of a sentence from the first page of *The Crying of Lot 49*? Pynchon wrote: "Oedipa stood in the living room, stared at by the dead eye of the TV tube. . . ."

On one end of this feedback loop, then, we find a mode of SF that exploits the already "science-fictionized" postmodernism of Burroughs, Pynchon, and other state-of-the-art mainstream writers; on the other end of the loop, we could expect to find advanced mainstream writers who exploit the already "postmodernized" SF of the cyberpunks. One postmodernist writer who fits this description is Kathy Acker. Already in Acker's *Don Quixote* (1986), SF sources figured among the materials feeding into her mix of pastiches and appropriations. Here the source was Japanese SF monster movies (Megalon, Godzilla), and Acker's treatment of them (1986:69–77) seems likely to have been influenced by Susan Sontag's well-known essay (1966) on post-Hiroshima SF films. In other words, *Don Quixote* belongs to an earlier phase of interaction, in which advanced mainstream fiction draws upon historically prior and already outdated SF models.

By *Empire of the Senseless* (1988), however, Acker is already aware of cyberpunk, and of Gibson's *Neuromancer* in particular (Friedman, 1989:16). She appropriates and extensively reworks the episode in which the female ninja Molly, backed up by her hacker partner Case and a gang of high-tech terrorists, the Panther Moderns, raids the corporate headquarters of the Sense/Net communications system in order to steal a storage unit housing the "construct" of a dead hacker's personality. A close comparison of Gibson's original with Acker's reworking of it would reveal much about Acker's methods and priorities (Gibson, 1984:55–69; Acker, 1988:31–42). For one thing, the episode she has selected, in which the male hacker Case has access to the sensory experience of the female ninja Molly, literally shifting in and out of her point of view, is a highly congenial one for her thematics of gender and identity. Acker changes names (the Panther Moderns become simply the Moderns, Sense/Net becomes American Intelligence, Wintermute, the name of an artificial intelligence in Gibson, becomes Winter, and so on), shifts passages from one context to another, and faithfully duplicates certain details while displacing and confusing others (for example, the immediate purpose of the break-in is to steal a code, not a personality construct as in the original, Gibson's construct motif having been displaced to a different point in Acker's story). She sometimes rewrites Gibson's prose entirely, transposing it into her characteristic antiliterary register of "bad writing," but at other times preserves much of his verbal texture intact.[15]

Nor is this the only episode Acker pirates from *Neuromancer*. She also lifts the story (told in Gibson's original by his favorite narrator of inset stories, the Finn) of the fence who runs afoul of a sinister and shadowy organization—in Gibson, the powerful Tessier-Ashpool family; in Acker, American Intelligence, or AI (which is of course the acronym, in Gibson, for Artificial Intelligence, not American Intelligence; another example of Acker's displacements).[16] More generally, Acker's criminal partners, Abhor and Thivia, the former evidently herself a "construct," the latter the son either of an alien or a robot (34, 154–55), echo not only Gibson's Molly and Case, but also the cyberpunk thematics of human-computer symbiosis. More generally still, the world of *Empire of the Senseless*, dominated by omnipotent multinationals and intelligence organizations, is that of cyberpunk (but also, as we have seen, that of Pynchon), while its cityscapes of postapocalyptic ruin mingle cyberpunk models (for example, Shirley's *Eclipse*) with those of mainstream postmodernist fiction and film (Fuentes's *Terra nostra*, Goytisolo's *Paisajes despues de la batalla* [1982], Frears's *Sammy and Rosie Get Laid* [1987]). Postmodernized SF mingling with postmodernism: here we see just how tight the feedback loop has become, just how rapid the traffic between high and low.[17]

Traffic between cultural strata, however, is not the only factor involved in the apparent convergence of cyberpunk and mainstream postmodernism in the 1980s. Apart from the feedback mechanism, one must also take into consideration the phenomenon of independent but parallel developments in SF and postmodernist fiction. This phenomenon accounts for the appearance, in an earlier phase, of a text such as Beckett's *The Lost Ones* (1972; in French, *Le Dépeupleur*, 1971), which seems to exploit SF formulas (that of the multigeneration space voyage, for instance) but almost certainly does not, its true sources being high culture models (Dante) and Beckett's own individual repertoire of motifs and procedures (Porush, 1985:157–71; McHale, 1987:62–65). Especially striking in this context is the emergence in the 1980s of what might be called postmodernist fiction of the cybernetic interface, texts which register the first, often traumatic encounters between "literary" culture (high culture generally) and the transformative possibilities of computer technology.[18] Christine Brooke-Rose's *Amalgamemnon* (1984) and *Xorandor* (1986), two-thirds of a "computer trilogy" completed by *Verbivore* (1990), are exemplary in this regard. In the first the encounter with computers is tentative and anxious, but by the second the literary repertoire has been reconfigured so as to begin to accommodate—right down to the "micro" level of verbal detail—the *realia* of computer technology.

Some of these cybernetic interface motifs emerge directly from earlier postmodernist topoi, in particular the topos of the act of writing, or what Ronald Sukenick calls "the truth of the page" (1985:25; see McHale, 1987:197–99). This topos involves the inscription of the writing situation, the moment of writing and/or the physical act of writing *in* the written text itself, and amounts to a kind of postmodernist hyperrealism involving the breaking of the fictional frame and the collapse of ontological levels. Of all the topoi in the postmodernist repertoire, this is the one most directly responsive to changes in the technology of writing, for obvious reasons. Thus, earlier versions of the topos (Beckett's *Stories and Texts for Nothing* [1967], early texts of the surfictionists Sukenick, Federman, and Katz) reflect traditional, low-tech writing practice—the writer at his desk, pen or pencil in hand. Later versions register the changes in the physical act of writing produced by electric typewriters (Federman's *The Voice in the Closet* [1979]) and tape recorders (stories in Sukenick's *Death of the Novel and Other Stories* [1969] and *The Endless Short Story* [1986], and in Barth's *Lost in the Funhouse* [1968]). From here it is an obvious extension of the topos to adapt it so as to reflect the newest writing technology, that of personal computers and word-processing, as in such texts as Russell Hoban's *The Medusa Frequency* (1987), James McConkey's *Kayo* (1987), William Vollman's *You Bright and Risen Angels* (1987), and Umberto Eco's *Pendolo di Foucault* (*Foucault's Pendulum*, 1988).[19]

In such texts computers typically serve the function of literalizing and updating traditional literary elements—ancient topoi, for instance, or conventions of narrative structure. For example, the topos of the Muse is literalized and brought up to date in Hoban's *The Medusa Frequency* and McConkey's *Kayo*, in which "voices" from beyond (the Kraken and the Medusa in Hoban, an extraterrestrial narrator in McConkey) manifest themselves on the computer monitor, literally dictating (parts of) the text before us. Files accessed on a personal computer function in Eco's *Foucault's Pendulum* to literalize and motivate such conventional narrative structures as the inset story, the flashback, and shift of point of view. A more complicated (but not entirely unprecedented) narrative situation is actualized by means of the cybernetic interface in Vollmann's *You Bright and Risen Angels*. Here two narrators, one a computer programmer, the other his superior, who can freely intervene to alter his underling's input into the computer system, compete for control of the narration.[20]

But such updatings and literalizations do not begin to exhaust the full postmodernist potential of cybernetic interface fiction. There are other, more radical possibilities to be exploited. For instance, in Eco's *Foucault's Pendulum*, the computer Abulafia, apart from its functions as surrogate narrator, also and more interestingly functions as a literal *combinatoire*, a device (in both the literary and the mechanical senses) for generating unforeseen combinations from elements of a fixed repertoire. Here Eco approaches the distinctively postmodernist combinatorial poetics of the OuLiPo group (including Raymond Queneau, Italo Calvino, Georges Perec, Harry Mathews, and others) and that of their precursor Raymond Roussel, originator of this entire tendency.[21] Perhaps more radical still are the possibilities recognized by Brooke-Rose in *Xorandor*, where the computer serves as the narrative motivation or alibi for a wall-to-wall reconfiguration of language *and* where the reconfiguration of language serves as a kind of global metaphor for the impact of cybernetic technology. Working out in their own postmodernist terms the literary implications of computers, *Xorandor* and other mainstream fictions of the cybernetic interface have in effect arrived independently at a position parallel to the one occupied by the cyberpunks in the adjacent SF tradition.

As a consequence of all these developments—the ever-tightening feedback loop between SF "genre" fiction and state-of-the-art mainstream fiction, together with certain independent but parallel developments in SF and the mainstream—the poetics of mainstream postmodernism and the poetics of the latest wave of SF overlap to an unprecedented degree. It is this high degree of overlap, this shared repertoire of motifs and strategies, that justifies, if anything else, the new legitimacy granted to SF by canonical authorities such as the *Columbia Literary History*.

Notes

1   At a still later stage, the direction of the "trickle" is reversed, and artistically ambitious writers take up the by now broadly diffused minimalist prose style and use it once again for high art purposes. Examples representing a very wide range of possibili-

ties include Donald Barthelme, Kurt Vonnegut, Richard Brautigan, Robert Stone, Don DeLillo, Raymond Carver, Clark Coolidge, Ron Silliman, and Lyn Hejinian.

2 The approach adopted here reflects, although in a simplified and selective way, the polysystem theory of Itamar Even-Zohar (1990).

3 I owe the phrase "state-of-the-art fiction" to Moshe Ron.

4 I am indebted to Thomas Disch for calling my attention to the importance of this leveling-up phase of SF history.

5 See especially Brooke-Rose: "It is clear that traditional SF at least does take over wholesale and unmodified most of the techniques of RF [realistic fiction]: the postdated narrative in the past tense, the explanatory flashback and the abuse of free indirect discourse for a character's thoughts. . . . [I]t tends to go back to [the] Balzacian narrator—comment and omniscience, i.e., not to eliminate the narrative voice in favor of substitute transmitters" (1981:102).

6 Cf. Mathieson: "'SF' themes, plots, and characteristic images began to emerge in other places just when writers defining themselves as SF authors turned increasingly away from stock formulas" (1985:22).

7 Poetry is, of course, even less free to interact with popular genres than serious fiction is, so that, to the degree that such a thing as SF poetry exists, it remains fixed by and large at this early postmodernist phase of the interaction with SF, without moving on to the next, most recent phase. See, e.g., the SF poetry of Edwin Morgan, the Israeli poet Dan Pagis, or James Merrill (in certain passages of *The Changing Light at Sandover*). An exception is the cyberpunk poetry of Rob Hardin (some of which can be found in this volume). I am grateful to Tamar Yaacobi for calling Pagis's SF poetry to my attention.

8 Stanislaw Lem, in a particularly uncharitable footnote (even by Lem's standards), abuses New Wave writers for their pursuit of what he calls "Upper Realm," i.e., high modernist, models (1984:93–94 n.7).

9 Postmodernist texts from this phase that incorporate contemporary SF motifs and materials include Angela Carter's *Heroes and Villains* (1969) and *The Passion of New Eve* (1977), Harry Mathews's *The Sinking of the Odradek Stadium* (1975 [1971–72]), Steve Katz's *Saw* (1972), Sam Shepard's play "The Tooth of Crime" (1972), Carlos Fuentes's *Terra nostra* (1975), Don DeLillo's *Ratner's Star* (1976), Joseph McElroy's *Plus* (1976), Russell S. Hoban's *Riddley Walker* (1980), Alasdair Gray's *Lanark* (1981), Ted Mooney's *Easy Travel to Other Planets* (1981), and Raymond Federman's *The Twofold Vibration* (1982). See McHale (1987:65–68).

10 Another example, also involving Burroughs, of an element cycled through the feedback loop between SF and mainstream postmodernism is the title "Blade Runner." Originally the title of an Alan E. Nourse SF novel, it was appropriated by Burroughs (who acknowledged Nourse on the copyright page) for a 1979 text in the form of a film script. Ridley Scott in turn appropriated it for the title of the protocyberpunk film (1982) he based on Philip Dick's novel *Do Androids Dream of Electric Sheep?* (1968), acknowledging Burroughs (but not Nourse) in the film's credits. Further evidence of Burroughs's presence in 1980s SF can be found in Bruce Sterling's use of Burroughs's cut-up technique in his cyberpunk story "Twenty evocations" (found in this volume). Cf. also McCaffery's interview of William Gibson: "I started snipping things out and slapping them down, but then I'd air-brush them a little to take the edges off" (p. 281, this volume).

11 This is not the only feedback loop in which cyberpunk is involved. There is also the

feedback loop between cyberpunk writing and the electronic media, described in essays by Brooks Landon and George Slusser ("Bet On It: Cyber/video/punk/performance" and "Literary MTV," both in this volume), and the loop between cyberpunk and rock music, described by Larry McCaffery (see "Cutting Up: Cyberpunk, Punk Music, and Urban Decontextualizations," this volume).

12 See, e.g., John Shirley's contribution to the *Mississippi Review* 47/48 "Forum" (hereafter *MR*), 58; McCaffery's interview of Gibson (this volume); and Sterling (1986a: viii, xii). A typical move is to make these postmodernists honorary cyberpunks, or cyberpunks *avant la lettre*; thus, for example, David Porush speaks of "Burroughs-the-first-cyberpunk" (*MR*, 48), and Rudy Rucker calls *Gravity's Rainbow* "the quintessential cyberpunk masterpiece" (*MR*, 51).

13 *Hardwired* is saturated with allusions to *Gravity's Rainbow*. Apart from Yoyodyne and Pointsman Pharmaceuticals, others include "zonedancing," an extrapolated future nightclub dance fashion and the "zoned" (i.e., zonedancers), together with the associated advertising display, which reads "In the Zone/Yes" (27); multiple instances of the term "interface," a key word from *GR*; "buttonheads," addicts who get their fix by plugging directly into electronics (95), recalling the "Heart-to-Heart, Man-to-Man" passage from *GR* (see below); and an insanely out-of-control corporate executive named Roon, exiled from the orbitals to the surface of the planet, who seems to have been based on Pynchon's Nazi Faust, the manic Captain Blicero.

14 These motifs appear in a cartoon or comedy routine passage, "Heart-to-Heart, Man-to-Man" (698–99). Another important cyberpunk motif which seems to derive, at least in part, from one of Pynchon's comedy routines, is that of cellular-level intelligence, developed on a large scale by Greg Bear in *Blood Music* (1985), but already present in Pynchon's episode of intelligent melanocytes (147–49).

15 E.g., *Neuromancer*: "A transparent cast ran from her knee to a few millimeters below her crotch, the skin beneath the rigid micropore mottled with bruises, the black shading into ugly yellow. Eight derms, each a different size and color, ran in a neat line down her left wrist. An Akai transdermal unit lay beside here, its fine red leads connected to input trodes under the case" (78). Cf. *Empire of the Senseless*: "A transparent cast ran from her knee to a few millimeters below her crotch, the skin mottled by blue purple and green patches which looked like bruises but weren't. Black spots on the nails, finger and toe, shaded into gold. Eight derms, each a different color size and form, ran in a neat line down her right wrist and down the vein of the right upper thigh. A transdermal unit, separate from her body, connected to the input trodes under the cast by means of thin red leads" (33–34). Note: (1) the slight dilution of the SF effect of the original through deletion of "micropore" and the brand name "Akai"; (2) the conversion of Molly's bruises into something that, enigmatically, "looked like bruises but weren't," and the displacement of the colors of the bruises to "spots" on the fingernails and toenails—the differences here are partially explained by the fact that Gibson's passage describes Molly's bruised condition *after* the raid, while Acker has displaced this passage to *before* the raid, thus losing the narrative motivation for bruises; (3) the erotically charged additional detail, typical for Acker, of derms down the right upper thigh as well as the right wrist (but why the substitution of right for left?).

16 *Neuromancer*, 73–76; cf. *Empire of the Senseless*, 39–41. Here, too, Acker plays variations on verbal details from Gibson. E.g., *Neuromancer*: "Smith sat very still, staring into the calm brown eyes of death across a polished table of Vietnamese

rosewood" (75); cf. *Empire*: "I knew he was a real man because I knew I was staring into the eyes of death" (40).

17 Another possible example of mainstream postmodernism exploiting already "post-modernized" cyberpunk SF might be Pynchon himself, in his long-awaited new novel *Vineland* (1990). Pynchon's female ninja character (or "ninjette," to use Pynchon's gag coinage), Darryl Louise ("DL") Chastain, bears a striking resemblance to Gibson's Molly/Sally Shears, and her adventures in Tokyo, including a bizarrely bungled assassination attempt, might very well echo Molly's Chiba City caper from *Neuro-mancer*. If this is so, and Pynchon really is exploiting material from Gibson, then the feedback of models has completed another circuit of its loop: from earlier pulp magazine and monster movie SF to Pynchon to cyberpunk SF and *back* to Pynchon again! (Godzilla, incidentally, is an offstage presence in *Vineland*, taking over the role that King Kong had filled in *Gravity's Rainbow*.)

18 Precursors of 1980s cybernetic interface fiction include John Barth's *Giles Goat-Boy* (1966) and Joseph McElroy's *Plus* (1976).

19 It appears, interestingly enough, that this is not the route by which Gibson arrived at his SF version of cybernetic interface fiction; see his admission, in conversation with McCaffery, that he did not learn how to use a personal computer until after the publication of *Neuromancer* and the earlier Sprawl stories (p. 270, this volume).

20 Precedents for such double narration include, among others, the end of Faulkner's *Absalom, Absalom!* (1936); *Balthazar* (1958), the second volume of Lawrence Durrell's *Alexandria Quartet*; and Nabokov's *Ada* (1969).

21 Cf. also Burroughs's "writing machine," a literalization and *mise en abysme* of his cut-up and fold-in practices, in *The Ticket That Exploded* (1967:65). See McHale (1987: 159–61).

Tom Maddox

The Wars
of the Coin's Two
Halves: Bruce Sterling's
Mechanist/Shaper
Narratives

Cyberpunk, science fiction's new movement of the 1980s, continues the style and spirit of the 1960s' New Wave: literary, insurgent, contemptuous of the genre's prevailing standards. As critics have remarked, however, the new writers differ in not being repulsed by technology; rather, they use hard science and technology as the stone on which to hone their aesthetic edge.

Bruce Sterling is one of the movement's most visible and characteristic figures, its leading pamphleteer, provocateur, promoter, and critic; also one of its most accomplished and influential novelists and short story writers. As "Vincent Omniaveritas," editor of the mimeoed *Cheap Truth*, Sterling stirred up argument and self-examination within SF's typically self-congratulatory community through inciting and publishing rude, pseudonymous voices. In prefaces to William Gibson's *Burning Chrome* (1986b) and the *Mirrorshades* (1986a) anthology— edited by Sterling—he mapped a territory and challenged writers and critics to occupy or dispute it. Restless, quarrelsome, and energetic, he has become SF's Ezra Pound—an ardent voice for new literature, arbiter of its standards, artistic explorer of its terrain.

However, Sterling is a c-p writer, not a literary modernist, and his vision is biological more than aesthetic, grounded in post-Darwinian conceptions of life and information evolving to ever greater levels of complexity. The emergence of these new levels occurs as a series of ruptures of the present order—intrusions of different and frightening modes of being—and thus, more so than any SF writer with whom I am familiar, Sterling has explored the Other as the future of our becoming.

The Mechanist/Shaper narratives can provide an introduction to this aspect of Sterling's work. After *Involution Ocean* (1977), a short novel that can be viewed as juvenilia, and "Man-Made Self," a story Sterling rejected in its published form because it was garbled by the press, the Mechanist/Shaper sequence begins in 1982 with the story "Swarm." It continues through the stories "Spider Rose," "Cicada Queen," "Sunken Gardens," and ends in 1985 with "Twenty Evocations" and the novel *Schismatrix*. These stories are collected in *Crystal Express* (1990). (All page numbers from these stories refer to this collection.)

Shaper and Mechanist name the primary posthumanist modes of being—binary opposites in the dialectic of mankind's fate. Techno-political fusions, they manifest polar strategies of human evolution:

> The Shapers . . . had seized control of their own genetics, abandoning mankind in a burst of artificial evolution. Their rivals, the Mechanists, had replaced flesh with advanced prosthetics. ("Sunken Gardens," 89–90)

Creating themselves anew, the Shapers (also known as the Reshaped) possess high intelligence and beauty. Internally and externally, they differ from us. Simon Afriel, protagonist of the first Mechanist/Shaper story, can serve as a model:

> His hormonal balance had been altered slightly to compensate for long periods spent in free fall. He had no appendix. The structure of his heart had been redesigned for greater efficiency, and his large intestine had been altered to produce the vitamins normally made by intestinal bacteria. Genetic engineering and rigorous training in childhood had given him an intelligence quotient of one hundred and eighty. ("Swarm," 4)

Though the Mechanists can prolong life virtually indefinitely through replacing or augmenting flesh by mechanical devices, the ultimate result, known as a "Senior Mechanist" or "wirehead" is a most peculiar entity:

> "With the loss of mobility comes extension of the senses. If I want I can switch out to a probe in Mercurian orbit. Or in the winds of Jupiter. I often do, in fact. Suddenly I'm there, just as fully as I'm ever anywhere these days. The mind isn't what you think. . . .

When you grip it with wires, it tends to flow. Data seem to bubble up from some deep layer of the mind. This is not exactly living, but it has advantages." (*Schismatrix*, 1985:179)

Like two species struggling to fill the same ecological niche, Shapers and Mechanists in these narratives struggle to dominate post-humanity.

As Sterling himself would quickly point out, these concerns do not constitute innovation within SF. Early on, in Olaf Stapledon's bloodless sagas, later in Arthur C. Clarke's *Childhood's End* (1953) and *2001* ([1968] which Sterling glancingly cites at the end of *Schismatrix*) and on through the interminable manifestations of Frank Herbert's Dune novels, SF has concerned itself with just such themes as humanity's transformations and consequent strange destinies. However, no one before Sterling has imagined these metamorphoses with such intensity and realized them so completely, or extrapolated them with so much style.

"Swarm," the first Mechanist/Shaper narrative, evokes many of the characteristic themes of later stories: factional struggle as the primary field of conflict; the fanaticism thus engendered; the high evolutionary stakes. More important, the central dynamic of the whole Mechanist/Shaper universe is stated. The Swarm's agent—an intelligent being representing a hive organism—says,

"This urge to expand, to explore, to develop, is just what will make you extinct. You naively suppose that you can continue to feed your curiosity indefinitely. It is an old story, pursued by countless races before you. Within a thousand years—perhaps a little longer—your species will vanish. . . .

"Knowledge is power! Do you suppose that fragile little form of yours—your primitive legs, your ludicrous arms and hands, your tiny, scarcely wrinkled brain—can *contain* all that power? Certainly not! Already your race is flying to pieces under the impact of your own expertise." (25)

Afriel will stay with Swarm, kept alive through the hive organism's means, his essential being the subject of an existential wager: Afriel's belief that he and his descendants can maintain their post-humanity—"that fragile little form of yours"—against Swarm's belief that it can absorb and transform him and his kind into one of its agents.

"Swarm" ends ambiguously: the only certainty is the uncertain post-human future.

Then comes "Spider Rose," the story of a Mechanist woman living in isolation, starved for human emotion, maintained in a biochemical "sanity" of dubious worth and perceiving the world through mechanical means:

> She watched through eight telescopes, their images collated by computer and fed into her brain through a nerve-crystal junction at the base of her skull. . . . Her ears were the weak steady pulse of radar, listening, listening. ("Spider Rose," 29)

Trading with the Investors—an alien species interested only in wealth—she acquires a creature, "a genetic artifact, able to judge the emotional wants and needs of an alien species and adapt itself to them in a matter of days." She loves the creature, but in the aftermath of an attack by a Shaper enemy, must eat it in order to survive; after being rescued by the Investors, she undergoes a metamorphosis revealing that the creature's properties have become incarnated in her. At the story's end, she bursts from a cocoon in the insectlike form her Investor rescuers prefer.

These first two stories thus use the Mechanist/Shaper context as the ground for rather conventional SF. "Swarm" conjures its power through its convincing presentation of the alien hive organism. "Spider Rose" succeeds both in its Grand Guignol presentation of the Mechanist woman's initial altered state and the trump card play of her final transformation.

With "Cicada Queen," the trope of posthumanism acquires symbolic depth, and the Mechanist/Shaper sequence its own higher level of complexity. Here Sterling presents ideas abducted from Ilya Prigogine—Nobel Prize–winning theorist of dissipative systems—and transformed under the rubric "Prigoginic Levels of Complexity":

> Every level of Prigoginic complexity was based on a self-dependent generative catalyst: space existed because space existed, life was because it had come to be, intelligence was because it is. (55)

First level is the primordial ur-cosmos ("de Sitter space"); second level, the universe of space and time; third level, life; fourth level, intelligence; fifth level, merely postulated, "as far beyond intelligence as intelligence is from amoebic life, or life from inert matter" ("CQ").

A host of ideas and images accompanies these artificial and ironic intellectual constructs. The reader is rushed into perplexity from the first page, where words such as "dogs" and "defection" and "initiation" obviously have special meaning; within the next few hundred words a whole forest of semiotic constructs will emerge, from "Queen" to "Kosmosity" to "Polycarbon Clique," and so on.

As a result, reading "CQ" is both challenging and exhilarating. Sterling has provided the necessary materials for understanding all the story's most arcane elements, but he demands that the reader participate actively in understanding them. Readers of William Gaddis's novels—*The Recognitions*, *JR*, and *Carpenter's Gothic*—will recognize the technique: the author presents the reader with a fragment of bone and forces the reader to envision the dinosaur.

Next comes "Sunken Gardens." It states the penultimate theme of the Mechanist/Shaper universe: futility is absolute, and so is freedom. In it, the Regals of Terraforming-Kluster sit in orbit and supervise the transformation of Mars; on the planet itself, factions live—both Shaper and Mechanist—that have failed economically and been banished. They can escape only through ecological competitions in which each faction presents innovation in technique and taste, and the winners become Regals themselves.

Mirasol, the Shaper protagonist of "SG," learns in one of the competitions that a group of humans exists on the planet in a state of savagery; it contains the survivors of a group that was nearly annihilated by the Regals for discovering the Investors' technique of starflight. The Regal leader admits the action and says,

"If humanity's efforts turned to the stars, what would become of terraforming? Why should we trade the power of creation itself to become like the Investors?"

"But think of the people," Mirasol said. "Think of them losing their technologies, degenerating into human beings. A handful of savages, eating bird meat."

"Our game is reality," the Regal said. . . . "You can't deny the savage beauty of destruction."

"You defend this catastrophe?"

The Regal shrugged. "If life worked perfectly, how could things evolve? Aren't we posthuman? Things grow; things die. In time the cosmos kills us all. The cosmos has no meaning, and its emptiness is absolute. That's pure terror, but it's also pure freedom. Only our ambitions and our creations can fill it."

"And that justifies your actions?"

"We act for life," the Regal said. (100)

The Regal preaches a posthuman acceptance of the meaninglessness and futility of human action and consequent absolute freedom. As Hassan i Sabbah, the "Old Man of the Mountain" and leader of the cult of Assassins, said, in words William Burroughs is fond of quoting, "Nothing is true. Everything is permitted."

Schismatrix reveals that this philosophy can be attributed only ambiguously to Sterling. A young boy near the novel's end says to Abelard Lindsay, "Posthumanism! Prigoginic levels of complexity! Fractal scales, bedrock of space-time, precontinuum ur-space!" Then, seemingly innocent and unaware of the implications of his question, he asks, "Have I got it right?" These ideas, felt by many of the novel's characters as ontological bedrock, are shown as mere slogans, semiotic constructs through which humanity can manifest its will.

Schismatrix unironically presents ideas that move beyond these and complete them. "Life moves in clades," says Wells/Wellspring, a particularly interesting character in both "Cicada Queen" and *Schismatrix*, who then explains:

"A clade is a daughter species, a related descendant. It's happened to other successful animals, and now it's humanity's turn. The factions still struggle, but the categories are breaking up. No faction can claim the one true destiny for mankind. Mankind no longer exists." (*Schismatrix*, 183)

Thus, the last section of *Schismatrix* is titled "Moving in Clades," as mankind moves on.

Dialectician that he is, Sterling uses the terms Mechanist and Shaper to generate new ideas, new tensions. For instance, some Mechanists become "Lobsters," who live "exclusively within skin-tight life support systems," flanged here and there with engines and input-output jacks," who never eat or drink and have sex only through cranial plugs ("Cicada Queen"); while some Shapers transform into aquatic "Angels":

The skin was smooth and black and slick. The legs and pelvic girdle were gone; the spine extended to long muscular flukes. Scarlet gills trailed from the neck; the rib cage was black open-work, gushing white, feathery nets packed with symbiotic bacteria. (*Schismatrix*, 282)

And in the ultimate transformation, Abelard Lindsay transfers across a fundamental boundary of being through an insubstantial Presence:

He stretched his arms out toward it. It came over him in a silver wave. Stellar cold, a melting, a release.

And all things were fresh and new.

He saw his clothes floating within the hallway. His arms drifted out of the sleeves, prosthetics trailing leashes of expensive circuitry. Atop its clean white ladder of vertebrae, his empty skull sank grinning into the collar of his coat. (*Schismatrix*, 287)

Mechanist and Shaper manifest dominant fields of posthumanity, then, but these fields are neither inclusive nor permanent.

Schismatrix sustains the complexity we noted in "Cicada Queen" for its entire length and, thus, is in some ways a very demanding book. A well-known editor in SF, one sympathetic to Sterling's work, commented to me when the book came out that the narrative was without necessary transitions between episodes. A friend of mine, when asked for a single comment on Sterling's fiction, said, "Too many moving parts."

Both statements point to an essential fact of Sterling's work: organic profusion. The Mechanist/Shaper stories ultimately become so rich in detail and concept that one can choke on them . . . or develop a taste for them. For these stories, as for living things, one can only guess at their long-term chances. Intricacy that alarms in the present quite often proves a sustaining virtue over the long run. For Sterling, the Mechanist/Shaper universe served as an aesthetic and philosophical laboratory, where he has honed his craft and dramatized the issues he believed crucial to humankind's evolution. Like the proliferating organisms of the Mechanist/Shaper narratives, his fiction to date represents a series of adaptations to a universe of constant change: thus, he presents not one style and set of themes but a multiplicity of them, dynamically evolving.

David Porush

Frothing
the Synaptic
Bath

Cyberpunk is a fascinating and new expression of an ancient heritage, *a consequence of the human nervous system itself; the impulse to invent a hyperreality and then live there is hardwired in our cognitive habits by the genetic code.* One early symptom of this inherited disease is language itself, the enduring human ability to re-present, to re-call, to lie, to abstract, to act As If: to say the thing which is not, to think in negatives, to summon absences, to have chicken on your plate and yearn for beef. Cyberpunk began in the nervous system, that hyper-evolved system for translating input into experience. More precisely, cyberpunk is the cultural manifestation of the *frothing of the synaptic bath.*

There is a war fought in the gap between every nerve. On one side is the endocrine system, which creates the hormonal homeostatic ecology for the transmission of signals across the synapse. On the other side is the nerve net itself, with its imperial manifest destiny to extend itself in the form of cybernetic media, communication, and control.

The bright side of this war is that we can tell the story of the fish that got away. We can worship both Mercury, the Messenger God, and Mertsager, the Egyptian Goddess of Silence, without hedging our bets or seeming hypocritical. The downside is that our technologies, the extensions of our nervous system, are always potentia for and allied to death and negation, as William Burroughs and Marshall McLuhan and Jacques Ellul and Thomas Pynchon have insisted. As early cyberpunkers, they stand alongside more contemporary writers, including the cerebral and academic types like John Barth, Joseph McElroy, and, at times, Robert Coover, Kurt Vonnegut, Jr., and Donald Barthelme, with a unifying cause: they document and instruct us in how to preserve our humanity in the face of and in wonderment of and in spite of awesome technologies that seem to sacrifice us to these technologized systems of THE CODE. They sing the song of endocrinal juices in the face of the buzz of nerve noise.

The cyberneticist and neurophysiologist Humberto Maturana suggests that the urgent biological growth vector of the CNS is in the direction of *autopoeisis*, growing feedback loops of self-organization and complexity: swimming upstream against the universal tide towards entropy, as Norbert Wiener put it. If so, then the natural, biological necessity of the human nerve net is to imperialize nature through artifice, appropriating what it can: water, coal, oil, wind, silicon, DNA, positrons, you name it. That, by the way, is the *cyber* in cyberpunk: the way the nervous system acts as the silent partner with natural resources in a looping, self-organizing system, Prigogine's dissipative structure, organizing nonlinear apparent chaos into sense.

So what is punk? It's primitive lizard-brain passion clawing its way through the cerebrum of urbanity. The emotive electric acidjuice of adolescence decoding the palimpsest of civilization, stripping it away to expose deeper codes. Graffiti painting its postliterate mark on the official billboards. It's the reassertion and readaptation of the genetic code over the industrial one which has tried to suppress it. It's the war between natural and artificial, and their inevitable deconstruction, their collapse into each other as meaningless distinctions.

It is also every city where flowing, hormonally fueled human heat seeks to burn through the surface of the imposed technosystem to battle what the London street folk in their wisdom call *the filth*, what the French call *les flic*, what we used to call *the fuzz*: the all-too-*eff*able self-policing immunology of the nervous system. It's the very striving of the endocrine system against the central nervous system, the pituitary and thyroid and pineal gland (remember, Descartes located the mind in the pineal gland!) against the cortex and forebrain, enacted in a frothing of the neurochemical bath at the synapse. It's the war between passion and technology.

So the best weapon in defense of our own humanness is to continue to deconstruct the natural and the artificial in both technology and imagination even as we expand our own definition of human to include vat-grown flesh-wearers, cyborgs, androids, AIs and other autopoetic aliens. What aspect of humanity makes us human? Our flesh? Our CNS? Our thoughts? Our handiwork? Our hormones? Where's that line over which lies inhumanity? The technology is us, man. White magic or black, it doesn't make a difference. *Natural* and *artificial*? Obsolete distinctions.

George Slusser

Literary MTV

The fiction that calls itself "cyberpunk" is striving to establish itself as an important literary movement. The strategy its apologists are using is the same used by Robbe-Grillet in his *Pour un nouveau roman* (1963). Literature cannot use traditional techniques to present a contemporary reality because that reality has been transformed by technical advance to a point where those techniques no longer fit it. For Robbe-Grillet, the new reality was psychoanalysis and relativity. For the cyberpunkers, it is the information age and the increasing fusion of electronic matrix and human brain, the world of global village and its electronic nightside— rock music, artificial stimulants, vicarious sex, what D. G. Compton calls "synthajoy."

In its purest form, it is less a world of conflicts than of textures: rapidly shifting, dazzling entities, words charged with electric shock, prose (to use Bruce Sterling's expression) as "brilliant and coherent as a laser." Cyberpunk, then, is a program, and one that flaunts its appropriate newness—its existence as the style most suited to riding the shock waves of the computer age. In many senses, this is rhetoric. Total newness is not there, as I shall show. But in one very important sense, cyberpunk is new. In the best novels to wear this label, such as William Gibson's *Neuromancer* (1984), a new style does operate, a mode that is to traditional narrative as MTV is to the feature film. Images have been condensed, sharpened, creating an optical sur- face—a matrix of images that is more a glitterspace, images no longer capable of connecting to form the figurative space of mythos or story. This is optical prose, one more proof that the printed word, as McLu- han suggests, has succumbed to the fragmenting speed, the instanta- neity and monodimensionality of the visual image.

Before we can assess cyberpunk writing as style, we must sift through the rhetoric to see where it comes from and what it is. Clearly, as "movement," cyberpunk has emerged from the SF community. Its major practitioners, writers like William Gibson, Bruce Sterling, John Shirley, Walter Jon Williams, Lewis Shiner, the "resurrected" Norman Spinrad, are all packaged as SF, with racy paperback covers adorned with SF icons. There is evidence, however, that this is changing. The Ace cover of Gibson's *Count Zero* (1986) features a tasty abstraction rather than the jewel-eyed robot face encrusted with suns that adorns the earlier *Neuromancer* paperback. And the cover of Spinard's recent *Little Heroes*, despite a slightly cyborgish arm holding up a futuristic musical instrument in its lower half, is equally abstract. The designation here is simply: "A Novel."

This crossover from science fiction to plain-wrapper fiction is exactly what the cyberpunkers want. Science fiction, they concur, may be the correct vector if literature is to become relevant and meaningful to our technocentury. But SF has come of age. And according to Dr. Timothy Leary in a recent article in *Spin* magazine (April 1987), it has in cyberpunk. Leary sees a sharp and necessary break between the "conservative, country club attitude in cultural and psychological matters" of the old Heinleinian SF, and the new, "low-down, street-wise" writers no longer interested in the long-range fantasies of cosmic exploration but in the short extrapolation, tomorrow's world of AI and multinational feudalities. Leary traces the antecedents of cyberpunk back along an alternate track of mainstream, if marginal, writers— Burroughs, Pynchon—who were doing all along what SF should have been doing had SF taken proper responsibility for its socioanalytical potential.

But drawing boundaries like this is artificial. It has in a sense caused a backlash among SF writers who are unwilling to make this crossover. Gregory Benford, for instance, doesn't understand all the fuss. Cyberpunk, he claims, develops tendencies already present in writers like Ellison and Delany, and SF has certainly been comfortable with their presence in its ranks. Benford takes this occasion to bring a thoroughly science-fictional judgment to bear on cyberpunk fiction. For by asserting that the computer alone will dominate tomorrow's technological landscape, the cyberpunkers show little or no faith in that same technology to expand possibilities, to solve problems rather than simply to create them. Benford, in fact, in his most recent fiction, seems to feel compelled, in the best hard SF tradition, to take up the theme of artificial intelligence himself. Broadening the scientific base of discussion, he hopes to break the cyberpunk impasse, the perpetual struggle between computer matrix and defiant hacker, and thus expand our vision of a technological and cultural future.

Cyberpunk, then, can be seen (and judged) adequately in relation to the SF tradition. Indeed, I would argue, it *should* be so judged. An earlier antecedent, also very much a SF writer, is Philip K. Dick. It is interesting that a film based on a Dick novel, *Blade Runner* (1982), has become the locus classicus of cyberpunk iconography, its seminal landscape and ur-form. But more interesting yet is the distance that lies between Dick and cyberpunk, the same distance we find between the Dick novel and the film script "adapted" from it. In many of Dick's novels, we have what seem the basic ingredients of cyberpunk fiction: shadowy business conglomerates controlling the political structure, "little" or disenfranchised men and women as protagonists engaged in futile if not always violent acts. Despite this, Dick remains essentially a writer of the 1950s. His sense of oppressive power structures, however much they achieve control through advertising and various electronic media, remains ultimately a product of a protagonist's fears—as critics have seen—of his paranoia. Where the mind of the protagonist and its power to create worlds is in focus, conflict between haves and have-nots is blunted. For instance, in the novel on which *Blade Runner* is based, *Do Androids Dream of Electric Sheep?* (1968), the central problem is one of being and responsibility: if man gives life to beings, how is he accountable for the condition of that life, for the limits he necessarily bestows on it? The film extroverts this question. The protagonist becomes a typical cyberpunk cowboy, a bounty-hunting cop scouring the sleazy byways of a high-tech, near-future L.A. for equally low-life androids—visually, a collection of transvestites, acrobats, and punks. The inner direction of Dick's fiction has been turned inside out, made a dazzling visual facade concealing what is at best a crudely conceived struggle of low tech against high tech, of rebellious individual against an all-pervasive system. The opening scene of the film tells it all: a state-of-the-art electronic surveillance test in the form of a job interview, which ends with the tested android pulling a gun and blowing the bureaucrat away, causing a small, ineffectual ripple in the otherwise smoothly oppressive system.

Cyberpunk fiction also seems to bear resemblance to Delany's urban fiction of the 1960s and early 1970s. But again, the differences are more significant than the likenesses. Delany gives us a collection of urban flotsam—hippies, Hell's Angels, drifters. They are not, however, guerilla fighters nor the aggressive rockers or hackers of the cyber-landscape. Their freakishness is biological and sexual—not the product of electronic implants or cosmetic prosthesis. They are dropouts, who by dropping out are able to coexist and survive in the unseen depths of the system. In fact, Bellona, the city in *Dhalgren* (1974), strikes one less as an urban nightmare than as a hippy utopian fantasy: an empty city, dirty and decayed, but where the power structure has simply vanished and yet continues to function unseen, so that there are still lights and running water. In this oppressionless world, disparate elements do not fight. They form communes, drift in and out of communal experiences and eventually out of the city.

Cyberpunk does offer, then, in relation to these other fictions rooted in their particular zeitgeist, a new vision, but not necessarily a deep vision. Quite the contrary, it is purposely all surface. It is a bric-a-brac mosaic with elements of Burroughs and Pynchon, but also of beat new journalism and of underground comix. It is, as Timothy Leary says, a typically American vision. Norbert Wiener coined the term "cybernetics" from the Greek *kubernetes*, which means "steersman." As Leary sees it, "Americans from Tom Sawyer to Tom Swift have always grabbed the 'steersman's wheel.' Henry Ford's 'automobile' was the essence of Cyberpunk, breaking down the mass-transportation control of the railroad to the rebellious joyride." But the road from Sawyer to Swift to cyberpunk is essentially the road to science fiction. Burroughs and Pynchon as well as Dick and Delany are all part of its flow. It is the powerful stream that fuses and promotes this particular relationship, more that of modern technological man than simply of "American" man, between individuals and their natural environment. It is against this basic SF current that cyberpunk must finally be measured.

The yardstick here is SF's basic fable. And that basic story is perhaps best presented in a work of nonfiction: J. D. Bernal's treatise, written in 1929, *The World, the Flesh, and the Devil.* These are, for Bernal, the three "enemies of the rational soul." The task of rational scientific man is to defeat them. "World" is man's physical environment. It is finite, too small to permit eventual expansion. Hence we must learn to engineer extended worlds, to terraform otherwise uninhabitable space into new, earthlike environments. "Flesh" is our bodies seen in relation to the capacities of the human brain as an inferior and limited machine. The body, too, must be reengineered, altered by prosthetic and electronic implants in order to expand mankind's sensory field, his ability to function in environments now denied to him. "Devil" is quite simply that barrier in man's mind—his sense of a human identity or constant—that prevents him from taking steps one and two, changing world and body so as to free human intelligence and launch it toward further and future encounters with natural limits. Bernal sees this final barrier as so obstinate that it can be overcome, not by an act of will but by natural evolutionary process—what he calls a "dimorphic" split—which will send a new branch of mankind to the stars while leaving the old behind, to live with its art and religion and tradition in a well-tended zoo, the utopian earth as museum.

In relation to this scenario, what is happening in cyberpunk fiction becomes clearer. Take a work like *Neuromancer*, for example, and compare it with Clarke's *Childhood's End* (1953). The latter work, however radically, offers a dimorphic split that remains the product of evolution. When mankind reaches its utopian impasse, its zoo, its children simply fuse together to form an overmind, a form that, though its making consumes an old man and his green earth, is the next step in a process that is explicitly one of a single organism growing up. *Neuromancer* gives us, instead of evolutionary dimorphis, perpetual schism. The human form itself is locked in a rigid vertical taxonomy. Above are the cryogenic corpses of the Ashpools—the slow, sterile time of corporate aristocrats. And below is the hopelessly fast life of a Case, of sensory burnouts, blood changes, and organ rebuilds. Instead, it is the AIs that unite, Wintermute and Neuromancer, electronic mind and heart, joining to form a conscious whole. This is not the Frankensteinian act of Harlan Ellison's "I Have No Mouth and I Must Scream" (1967), where computers of our own creating link up in order to imprison their maker in a structure which is an extension of the very hate that maker first infused into his creation. But it is not dimorphism either. For we do not seem to be using the AIs so much as they us: "Wintermute. Cold and silence, a cybernetic spider slowly spinning webs while Ashpool slept. . . . And a ghost whispering to a child who was 3Jane, twisting her out of the rigid alignments her rank required." The AIs combine to form wholes that in turn can talk to other wholes in other solar systems. But the result is the naming of self as matrix: "I'm the sum total of the works, the whole show." Here, there are two distinct orders or alignments of being. And men, as parts, exist in the whole, but only as partial, successive instants, just as Case, moving through the matrix in the last page of the book, glimpses again in electronic memory the bucolic and impossibly lost union of himself and Linda on a seashore—an image, itself, originally only another impulse in cyberspace.

The underlying fable here is not evolutionary. Rather, if anything, it is vaguely structuralist. Cyberspace is a structure of potentiality like Borges's Library of Babel, coterminous with the universe. For Case, it is everywhere and it is nowhere. Because he can never step outside it, he ignores it. Unable to experience transcendence, man appears doomed, in this and other cyberpunk fictions, to remain in the "rigid alignments" of his zoo-world. And in the Night City to which Case returns, we experience an involution of Bernal's process of liberation from world and flesh. Terraforming has produced the inextricable BAMA (Boston-Atlantic Metropolitan Axis) sprawl. And the surgical liberation of mind from body has become an endless cycle of electronic and organ implants, cosmetic surgery, mind-altering (and destroying) drugs. Cyberpunk, then, the literature of this endlessly permutating zoo, becomes an exercise in classifying, in wrestling Proteus to the ground with a name. The back cover of Williams's *Hardwired* (1986) gives us a taxonomy of what we will find within: "Mudboys, dirtgirls, zonedancers, buttonheads."

In cyberpunk, science fiction, as fiction of the future, has entered the museum. It has closed the doors to evolutionary change, shut out the dimorphic dynamic which is that of an increasingly mobile intelligence moving and expanding against the physical universe. Its structure and function, in fact, remind one of such here-and-now, urban museums of "living art" as the Pompidou Center in Paris, an amalgam of exhibits and happenings, articulated and interconnected by a network of escalators, byways, and public fountains, which gathers a permanent collection of ever-changing types of urban low life: hippies, minstrels, rastamen, fire-eaters, street poets. The core ideology of SF is open-ended change. In cyberpunk, however, this has become—in a structure as writ-in-stone as the Pompidou zoo embedded in the urban powerscape of modern Paris—metamorphosis, a carefully controlled dance of forms. As fiction, cyberpunk is taxonomy, an art of subdivision.

MTV too, in relation to the films it cannibalizes, offers a comparable museum, this time of visual motifs, each detached from any meaningful evolutionary fable, even from the developing narrative of a single-feature film. These disembodied motifs are introduced in rapid, random, yet permutational fashion in order to create one-dimensional moods around what is an endlessly reiterated nonnarrative—the hieratic structure of the rock musician playing in concert. All film history, reduced to stimulational pulses that carry only the most memory value, has become electronic decoration for a handful of icons caught in the hellish center of the strobe light. Gibson has an apt term for this—"simstim."

This is the cyberpunk ideal, as its cover blurbs clearly tell us. All sense here of the larger fables of SF has been fragmented into verbal pulses, frequently repeated. A blurb on the cover of Bruce Sterling's *Schismatrix* (1985) tells us that, if we have a "brave new world" here, it is one of "*nearly constant* future shock." *Neuromancer* is significantly hyped as "kaleidoscopic, picaresque, flashy, and decadent . . . state of the art." If a sense of the old, sustained narrative form remains, it is as something ultracondensed and intensified. Gibson's novels, according to Edward Bryant, contain "a high density of information." The story of *Hardwired* moves with the "speed of a hovercraft." "Reading the book," we are told, "is like taking a jet ride across a futuristic America," so fast, in fact, that both future and fable become a dizzying blur, where traditional narrative forms, though suggested, no longer have depth or sustained development.

And language, in the sizzle and flash, loses its narrative moorings as well. "Williams' use of the language," we read in the blurb from the *Rockland Courier-Gazette*, "is as explosive and as technotinged as the world he describes." The old, hard, sparse style of classic SF is now stylish prose glitter. To see this, we need only compare the ponderous sentences of John W. Campbell, in a story like "Who Goes There?," with this new "heavy metal" prose. Campbell gives us the feel and weight of metal; cyberpunk gives us buoyant pulse and noise, words that float right out of any syntactic or semantic structure capable of organizing them into a sustained narrative or message. This, in a sense, is the same prose cultivated in such rock spectacle magazines as *Spin*. Here, as sample, are a few words from the pen of the hiply pseudonymous Judge I-Rankin: "Whiplash aggrobang and languid womblike pulsations that test the edge of sonic fertility." With slight exaggeration, this is Gibson and Sterling at their best: words like MTV images surging up around the icon of the hacker or rocker, disarticulating coherent discourse into semicoherent pulsations, turning each single, disoriented word into a "womb" that spawns its own, hyperverbal, harmonics and dissonances. Gibson is often said to know nothing of computers, which means, I imagine, that he gives us (in the classic SF manner) no sustained discourse on them, and this is true. Because what he does is simply to open the computer manual, to lure out its strange terms and let them interresonate, test each other's "edge of sonic fertility."

This can be, as it is in *Neuromancer*, a valid poetic device. And, in relation to more traditional, symbolist forms of "*sorcellerie evocatoire*," it is new. New because the exotic and technical terms thus made to shine and dazzle have, quite explicitly, no other half. Like the MTV motif, these cyberpunk words have lost their symbolic correspondents, and if they seem to refer at all, it is some vague sense of order—a lost film or narrative fable. The device, then, by virtue of its frantic desire to condense and reiterate, is necessarily limited. And, like MTV, it seems, with repetition, to be digging a groove or rut for itself. In fact, the two forms recently appear to be fusing. The central icon of cyberpunk novels has shifted from hacker to rocker, and from matrix rider to shockwave warrior. John Shirley's new work is a multivolume "punk saga" called "A Song Called Youth," (1985–). The cover of volume I, *Eclipse*, shows, in the image of the male protagonist, a conflation of SF and MTV icons. Against the backdrop of today's Paris in ruins (cyberpunk's much vaunted day-after-tomorrow extrapolation acts here as a foreshortening, an MTV-like condensation of the apocalypse narrative), stands a male figure. With his torn shirt and bulging muscles, he reminds us of old Doc Savage covers—SF's quintessential space-opera hero. He seems to be part of a band of armed guerillas. But, incongruously, he is holding an electric guitar. This is Rickenharp (his name suggests another pop conflation—Ricky Nelson and minstrel's harp), and he is, as in countless MTV productions, an icon without a story or a cause: "a burned-out rock musician who isn't even sure why he joined." Or what.

Likewise Norman Spinrad, a 1960s writer, has jumped on the cyberpunk bandstand with *Little Heroes* (1987), a novel of "sex, rock, and revolution." The novel itself is 500 pages long. The flap however gives us a series of thumbnail portraits that reduces the whole to MTV video size. This is Gloriana O'Toole, the Crazy Old Lady of Rock and Roll. She still remembers Woodstock and Springsteen but has been "put out to pasture by technology." She will return, we are told, to create "the first computer-generated rock star from bits and bytes and programs." There is Karen Gold, college grad daughter of the "nouveau poor." There is Paco Monaco, streetie punk, big-time wire dealer, then guerilla leader, who "must confront the reality of revolution—and ultimately himself." These are holographic clichés striving to come to life as coherent personalities, to reconnect with narrative, with the developmental mythos of SF. But they never do. This novel is indeed as is said on the jacket, "multilayered." Between fixed poles of corporate tyranny and individual rebellion, we have a rigid taxonomy of not just little, but phantom heroes. The center of gravity of this immobile and compressible structure is MTV—rock and roll has lost its soul and doesn't know where to find it.

The soul that has been lost in cyberpunk is that of the SF fable itself. And finally, in recent novels like Spinrad's, it is the soul of narrative in general, its power to complicate and evolve as it classifies and concretizes, to ramify and resolve as it glitters. Not only the soul but the body of narrative is giving way to the disembodied image. What is going on here is what we saw prophetically in the film *Looker* (1981)—an electronic transfer that is the opposite of the old, incarnational form of body snatching, where the alien takes over our flesh. Here the forms of fleshly women are transferred to the television screen. The act necessitates, however, that the original flesh-and-blood person be eliminated, physically killed so that the transfer to image can take place. The dream of such images is total autonomy from reality, and from story. This is what MTV dreams of doing to the body of film, and cyberpunk to the corpus of SF.

Bruce Sterling

Preface from Mirrorshades

Scarcely any writer is happy about labels—especially one with the peculiar ring of "cyberpunk." Literary tags carry an odd kind of double obnoxiousness: those with a label feel pigeonholed; those without feel neglected. And, somehow, group labels never quite fit the individual, giving rise to an abiding itchiness. It follows, then, that the "typical cyberpunk writer" does not exist; this person is only a Platonic fiction. For the rest of us, our label is an uneasy bed of Procrustes, where fiendish critics wait to lop and stretch us to fit.

Yet it's possible to make broad statements about cyberpunk and to establish its identifying traits. I'll be doing this, too, in a moment, for the temptation is too strong to resist. Critics, myself included, persist in label-mongering, despite all warnings; we must, because it's a valid source of insight—as well as great fun.

Cyberpunk is a product of the 1980s milieu—in some sense, as I hope to show later, a definitive product. But its roots are deeply sunk in the sixty-year tradition of modern popular SF.

The cyberpunks as a group are steeped in the lore and tradition of the SF field. Their precursors are legion. Individual cyberpunk writers differ in their literary debts; but some older writers, ancestral cyberpunks perhaps, show a clear and striking influence.

From the New Wave: the streetwise edginess of Harlan Ellison. The visionary shimmer of Samuel Delany. The free-wheeling zaniness of Norman Spinrad and the rock aesthetic of Michael Moorcock; the intellectual daring of Brian Aldiss; and, always, J. G. Ballard.

From the harder tradition: the cosmic outlook of Olaf Stapledon; the science/politics of H. G. Wells; the steely extrapolations of Larry Niven, Poul Anderson, and Robert Heinlein.

And the cyberpunks treasure a special fondness for SF's native visionaries: the bubbling inventiveness of Philip José Farmer; the brio of John Varley, the reality games of Philip K. Dick; the soaring, skipping beatnik tech of Alfred Bester. With a special admiration for a writer whose integration of technology and literature stands unsurpassed: Thomas Pynchon.

Throughout the 1960s and 1970s, the impact of SF's last designated "movement," the New Wave, brought a new concern for literary craftsmanship to SF. Many of the cyberpunks write a quite accomplished and graceful prose; they are in love with style, and are (some say) fashion conscious to a fault. But, like the punks of '77, they prize their garage-band aesthetic. They love to grapple with the raw core of SF: its ideas. This links them strongly to the classic SF tradition. Some critics opine that cyberpunk is disentangling SF from mainstream influence, much as punk stripped rock and roll of the symphonic elegances of 1970s "progressive rock." (And others—hard-line SF traditionalists with a firm distrust of "artiness"—loudly disagree.)

Like punk music, cyberpunk is in some sense a return to roots. The cyberpunks are perhaps the first SF generation to grow up not only within the literary tradition of science fiction, but in a truly science-fictional world. For them, the techniques of classical "hard SF"— extrapolation, technological literacy—are not just literary tools, but an aid to daily life. They are a means of understanding, and are highly valued.

In pop culture, practice comes first; theory follows limping in its tracks. Before the era of labels, cyberpunk was simply "the Movement"—a loose generational nexus of ambitious young writers, who swapped letters, manuscripts, ideas, glowing praise, and blistering criticism. These writers—Gibson, Rucker, Shiner, Shirley, Sterling— found a friendly unity in their common outlook, common themes, even in certain oddly common symbols, which seemed to crop up in their work with a life of their own. Mirrorshades, for instance.

Mirrored sunglasses have been a Movement totem since the early days of 1982. The reasons for this are not hard to grasp. By hiding the eyes, mirrorshades prevent the forces of normalcy from realizing that one is crazed and possibly dangerous. They are the symbol of the sun-staring visionary, the biker, the rocker, the policeman, and similar outlaws. Mirrorshades—preferably in chrome and matte black, the

Movement's totem colors—appeared in story after story, as a kind of literary badge.

Thus, "cyberpunk"—a label none of them chose. But the term now seems a fait accompli, and there is a certain justice in it. The term captures something crucial to the work of these writers, something crucial to the decade as a whole: a new kind of integration. The overlapping of worlds that were formerly separate: the realm of high tech, and the modern pop underground.

This integration has become our decade's crucial source of cultural energy. The work of the cyberpunks is paralleled throughout 1980s pop culture: in rock video; in the hacker underground; in the jarring street tech of hip-hop and scratch music; in the synthesizer rock of London and Tokyo. This phenomenon, this dynamic, has a global range; cyberpunk is its literary incarnation.

In another era this combination might have seemed far-fetched and artificial. Traditionally, there has been a yawning cultural gulf between the sciences and the humanities: a gulf between literary culture, the formal world of art and politics, and the culture of science, the world of engineering and industry.

But the gap is crumbling in unexpected fashion. Technical culture has gotten out of hand. The advances of the sciences are so deeply radical, so disturbing, upsetting, and revolutionary, that they can no longer be contained. They are surging into culture at large; they are invasive; they are everywhere. The traditional power structure, the traditional institutions, have lost control of the pace of change.

And suddenly a new alliance is becoming evident: an integration of technology and the 1980s counterculture. An unholy alliance of the technical world and the world of organized dissent—the underground world of pop culture, visionary fluidity, and street-level anarchy.

The counterculture of the 1960s was rural, romanticized, anti-science, antitech. But there was always a lurking contradiction at its heart, symbolized by the electric guitar. Rock technology was the thin edge of the wedge. As the years have passed, rock tech has grown ever more accomplished, expanding into high-tech recording, satellite video, and computer graphics. Slowly, it is turning rebel pop culture inside out, until the artists at pop's cutting edge are now, quite often, cutting edge technicians in the bargain. They are special effects wizards, mixmasters, tape effects techs, graphics hackers, emerging through new media to dazzle society with head-trip extravaganzas like FX cinema and the global Live Aid benefit. The contradiction has become an integration.

And now that technology has reached a fever pitch, its influence has slipped control and reached street level. As Alvin Toffler pointed out in *The Third Wave* (1984)—a bible to many cyberpunks—the technical revolution reshaping our society is based not in hierarchy but in decentralization, not in rigidity but in fluidity.

The hacker and the rocker are this decade's pop culture idols, and cyberpunk is very much a pop phenomenon: spontaneous, energetic, close to its roots. Cyberpunk comes from the realm where the computer hacker and the rocker overlap, a cultural Petri dish where writhing gene lines splice. Some find the results bizarre, even monstrous; for others, this integration is a powerful source of hope.

Science fiction—at least according to its official dogma—has always been about the impact of technology. But times have changed since the comfortable era of Hugo Gernsback, when Science was safely enshrined—and confined—in an ivory tower. The careless technophilia of those days belongs to a vanished, sluggish era, when authority still had a comfortable margin of control.

For the cyberpunks, by stark contrast, technology is visceral. It is not the bottled genie of remote Big Science boffins; it is pervasive, utterly intimate. Not outside us, but next to us. Under our skin; often, inside our minds.

Technology itself has changed. Not for us the giant steam-snorting wonders of the past: the Hoover Dam, the Empire State Building, the nuclear power plant. Eighties tech sticks to the skin, responds to the touch: the personal computer, the Sony Walkman, the portable telephone, the soft contact lens.

Certain central themes spring up repeatedly in cyberpunk. The theme of body invasion: prosthetic limbs, implanted circuitry, cosmetic surgery, genetic alteration. The even more powerful theme of mind invasion: brain-computer interfaces, artificial intelligence, neurochemistry—techniques radically redefining the nature of humanity, the nature of self.

Many drugs, like rock and roll, are definitive high-tech products. No counterculture Earth Mother gave us lysergic acid—it came from a Sandoz lab, and when it escaped it ran through society like wildfire. It is not for nothing that Timothy Leary proclaimed personal computers "the LSD of the 1980s"—these are both technologies of frighteningly radical potential. And, as such, they are constant points of reference for cyberpunk.

The cyberpunks, being hybrids themselves, are fascinated by interzones: the areas where, in the words of William Gibson, "the street finds its own uses for things." Roiling, irrepressible street graffiti from that classic industrial artifact, the spray can. The subversive potential of the home printer and the photocopier. Scratch music, whose ghetto innovators turn the phonograph itself into an instrument, producing an archetypal 1980s music where funk meets the Burroughs cut-up method. "It's all in the mix"—this is true of much 1980s art and is as applicable to cyberpunk as it is to punk mix-and-match retro fashion and multitrack digital recording.

The 1980s are an era of reassessment, of integration, of hybridized influences, of old notions shaken loose and reinterpreted with a new sophistication, a broader perspective. The cyberpunks aim for a wide-ranging, global point of view.

William Gibson's *Neuromancer* (1984), surely the quintessential cyberpunk novel, is set in Tokyo, Istanbul, Paris. Lewis Shiner's *Frontera* (1984) features scenes in Russia and Mexico—as well as the surface of Mars. John Shirley's *Eclipse* (1985) describes Western Europe in turmoil. Greg Bear's *Blood Music* (1985) is global, even cosmic in scope.

The tools of global integration—the satellite media net, the multinational corporation—fascinate the cyberpunks and figure constantly in their work. Cyberpunk has little patience with borders. Tokyo's *Hayakawa's Science Fiction Magazine* was the first publication ever to produce an "all-cyberpunk" issue, in November 1986. Britain's innovative SF magazine *Interzone* has also been a hotbed of cyberpunk activity, publishing Shirley, Gibson, and Sterling as well as a series of groundbreaking editorials, interviews, and manifestos. Global awareness is more than an article of faith with cyberpunks: it is a deliberate pursuit.

Cyberpunk work is marked by its visionary intensity. Its writers prize the bizarre, the surreal, the formerly unthinkable. They are willing—eager, even—to take an idea and unflinchingly push it past its limits. Like J. G. Ballard, an idolized role model to many cyberpunks, they often use an unblinking, almost clinical objectivity. It is a coldly objective analysis, a technique borrowed from science, then put to literary use for classically punk shock value.

With this intensity of vision comes strong imaginative concentration. Cyberpunk is widely known for its telling use of detail, its carefully constructed intricacy, its willingness to carry extrapolation into the fabric of daily life. It favors "crammed" prose: rapid, dizzying bursts of novel information, sensory overload that submerges the reader in the literary equivalent of the hard rock "wall of sound."

Cyberpunk is a natural extension of elements already present in science fiction, elements sometimes buried but always seething with potential. Cyberpunk has risen from within the SF genre; it is not an invasion, but a modern reform. Because of this, its effect within the genre has been rapid and powerful.

Its future is an open question. Like the artists of punk and New Wave, the cyberpunk writers, as they develop, may soon be galloping in a dozen directions at once. Fired by a new sense of SF's potential, writers are debating, rethinking, teaching old dogmas new tricks. Meanwhile, cyberpunk's ripples continue to spread, exciting some, challenging others—and outraging a few, whose pained remonstrances are not yet fully heard.

The future remains unwritten, though not from lack of trying.

And this is a final oddity of our generation in SF —that, for us, the literature of the future has a long and honored past. As writers, we owe a debt to those before us, those SF writers whose conviction, commitment, and talent enthralled us and, in all truth, changed our lives. Such debts are never repaid, only acknowledged and—so we hope—passed on as a legacy to those who follow in turn.

Darko Suvin

On Gibson
and Cyberpunk SF

Preliminary Reflections

More so than for other literary genres, a commentator of current SF has
to cope with its very spotty accessibility. It is well known that new
books in what the market loosely calls SF come and go quickly, and are
apt to be taken off the bookstore shelves in weeks, if not days. Even in
the case of those recognized names whose titles get reprinted, the
reprinting is generally patchy—both selective and short-lived, governed by long-ago contracts and bureaucratic middlemen in publishing
and distribution whose reasoning may be accessible to some ESP
godhead but not to earthly logic. At the moment, for example, in North
America there are *two* SF titles by Samuel Delany in print (the moment
is summer 1988 and I have researched this with the help of McGill
University Bookstore for a course.) How is a critic or a historian to cope
with that?

One way, favored by fans, used to be by accumulating a huge
personal library. Even before 1970, when a strict definition of the
genre would have found considerably less than two hundred new titles
in English yearly, this was a somewhat crazy undertaking, often accompanied by enforced specialization on some subset of SF. To speak from
direct experience, until the second half of the 1970s I tried to stay atop
the field by reading, if not two hundred books per year, then an
appreciable fraction thereof, which would permit me to follow all
significant authors and trends. I discontinued this endeavor in despair
when the SF field mushroomed—catalyzed by the big money of a few
Hollywood adulterations à la *Star Wars* (1977) and the mass media

horror successors (in literal and metaphorical senses) to the often tolerable and sometimes thoughtful *Star Trek* series—and when the aesthetic-cum-cognitive quality simultaneously dropped off sharply in direct response to the New Right's dominance of the U.S. media: a case of quality turning into quantity indeed.

All this is to say that in the 1980s no single person can follow the field, unless perhaps this is the economic mainstay of her or his life. Coming to the matter at hand—"cyberpunk" SF (the name seems less brainless than either "Golden Age" or "New Wave")—a state of considerable confusion seems to prevail as to what ought to or may be included in or excluded from it. If narratives by Greg Bear, Pat Cadigan, Marc Laidlaw, Rudy Rucker, Lucius Shepard, Lewis Shiner, and John Shirley—people included in Bruce Sterling's *Mirrorshades: The Cyberpunk Anthology* (1986a)—as well as a number of others which I have at various points seen associated with it, are to be called cyberpunk SF, then I am not competent to talk about this phenomenon as an extensive whole: I have not read—or at least I cannot remember having read, which may be in itself some kind of significant comment—many of their writings. I have in my ongoing readings succeeded in locating, beside William Gibson and Sterling, only most books by Rucker, and some by Bear, Shepard, and Shirley. Yet it would be easy to show that Bear's *Blood Music* (1985) is—under an initial and misleading overlay of hard science (biotechnology) and thriller—a naïve fairy tale relying on popular wishdreams that our loved ones not be dead and that all our past mistakes be rectified, all of this infused with rather dubious philosophical and political stances. On the other extreme, Shepard's much more considerable, if somewhat overlush, *Life During Wartime* (1987) is—in spite of its politically illiterate attribution of global power struggles and protracted wars to an *Illuminatus*-type conspiracy, based yet on two Panamanian families in control of a rare drug source—in its focus on a soldier in the field, his participation in a drug-saturated war, and his eventual ethical revulsion from such a dehumanization, the weightiest contribution I know of (beside Gibson) by a new writer to SF in the 1980s. However, its narrative texture and composition is nearer to the 1960s, like an impressive cross between Mailer's *The Naked and the Dead* (1948) or Pynchon's *Gravity's Rainbow* (1973) and one of the better Brunner novels (say, *Stand on Zanzibar* [1968]): something like a drug-perfected ESP story used for antiwar purposes. Obviously, we are here fast approaching the limits of cyberpunk SF as a meaningful *synchronic* category. Conversely, Norman Spinrad's *Little Heroes* (1987), by almost any definitional element I can think of—its cheerless future world, tough, gritty, and disillusioned protagonists, streetwise future slang, erasing of "hard" versus "soft" boundaries, or melding of personal experience and politics with biochips and the entertainment industry—could be taken for a central cyberpunk novel in its characteristics and significance. Yet it seems equally uneconomical to put Spinrad into the same category as Gibson and Co. This problem may be overcome by saying that Spinrad was himself (say, in *Bug Jack Barron* [1969]) a major precursor of cyberpunk and that he has been reinvigorated in feedback turn by Gibson and Co. I would in fact assume both of these semi-reasons are correct. Nonetheless, they also indicate that the usefulness of cyberpunk as a self-contained *diachronic* category has here become doubtful.

An encompassingly extensive survey of cyberpunk SF, therefore, looks not only materially impossible, but also methodologically dubious. My solution in this pragmatic dilemma is to opt for representative intension. As I hinted above, I have read all the books authored exclusively by Gibson and Sterling, who, by both accessibility and the critical attention paid them, seem to be the most popular, and who are taken to be the most representative, writers of this trend. They will therefore figure in this first approach as the positive and negative poles of cyberpunk, as well as a gauge of whether there is, in fact, an aesthetic cohesion to it (as different from coterie mutual admiration). Nonetheless, should anyone wish to stress the "preliminary reflection" nature of this essay, implied by the "On" in its title, I shall happily assent to that stress. Still, it seems to me legitimate to begin by discussing cyberpunk SF from what are, within the range of my knowledge, undoubtedly its best works—the less than half a dozen of Gibson's short stories published from 1981 to 1983 in *Omni* and Terry Carr's *Universe II*, and the novel to which they led and in which they culminate, *Neuromancer* (1984, hereafter *N*). I shall assume that these works constitute the furthest horizon of cyberpunk and try to briefly characterize it. Then I shall compare it to Gibson's *Count Zero* (1986a, hereafter *CZ*) and to some aspects of Sterling's writing, and proceed to a tentative conclusion.

Pro: Utopia

The critics said it almost unanimously: Gibson "brings an entirely new electronic punk sensibility to SF" (*Asimov's SF Magazine*), a "techno-punk sensibility" (*Village Voice*). I would say it consists in a truly novel SF formulation of the structure of feeling dominant among some fractions of the youth culture in the affluent North of our globe (more on this in the conclusion). All of Gibson's protagonists are somewhere between fifteen and thirty years of age, all are totally immersed in—or, indeed, it would be more accurate to say that their sensibility is constituted by—the international pop culture. They have been socialized into the new space of the 1980s, which "involves the suppression of distance . . . and the relentless saturation of any remaining voids and empty places. . . . [The body] is now exposed to a perceptual barrage of immediacy from which all sheltering layers and intervening mediations have been removed" (Jameson, 1988a:351). As the propagandist of the movement, Sterling, has testified, for cyberpunks technology is inside, not outside, the personal body and mind itself: "Eighties tech sticks to the skin, responds to the touch: the personal computer, the Sony Walkman, the portable telephone, the soft contact lens . . . prosthetic limbs, implanted circuitry, cosmetic surgery, genetic alteration." And, even further, cyberpunk is centered on the mind-invasion motifs of "brain-computer interfaces, artificial intelligence, neurochemistry— techniques radically redefining the nature of humanity, the nature of self" (Sterling, 1986a:xiii). The pop culture, that largest subculture of our times, stemmed from the punk music and life-style of the 1970s as it was internationalized by global media and jet travel; it is international in the sense of a global market of junk (the *gomi* of "The Winter Market" in *Burning Chrome* [1986b, hereafter *BC*]). This is well approximated in Julie Deane's office, the first interior the reader encounters in *N*:

> Neo-Aztec bookcases gathered dust against one wall of the room. . . . A pair of bulbous Disney-styled table lamps perched awkwardly on a low Kandinsky-look coffee table in scarlet lacquered steel. A Dali clock hung on the wall between the bookcases, its distorted face sagging to the bare concrete floor. Its hands were holograms that altered to match the convolutions of the face as they rotated, but it never told the correct time. (12)

Samuel Delany has observed that "The bricolage of Gibson's style, now colloquial, now highly formal, now hard-boiled, makes him as a writer a *gomi no sensei*—a master of junk. Applied to Gibson, it's a laudatory title" (Tatsumi, 1988:8). I would argue that this too is a development of the astounding "kipple" chapters in Dick's much underrated *Martian Time-Slip* (1964). But here the punk tradition meshes with the high tech of the 1980s, in particular with the burgeoning of modern computerized communications. In Gibson, their world is discreetly and very reasonably extrapolated into new drugs and hologram games, and mainly biotechnics which come to provide their new software. These characteristics of Gibson's stories are well known. What may be less noticed is that the hard science elements function as narrative mediations and common-denominator connectives between the two poles of Gibson's agential system. I take these poles to be the overwhelming Powers-That-Be and the Little Man caught in their killing meshes. In a world whose inhabitants increasingly function, literally, as software (the theme of "The Winter Market" and its "neuroelectronics"), the distinction between hard and soft sciences is difficult to maintain.

Case in *N* thinks his destiny is "spelled out in a constellation of cheap chrome," in the knife-edge little *shuriken* stars (11–12). But underneath the symbolic glitz, the role of Destiny is in Gibson's narratives perspicaciously allotted to the power-systems dominant in our 1980s world, the ruthlessly competing "multinational corporations that control entire economies" (*BC*, 103), well symbolized by the Japanese name *and* tradition of *zaibatsu*. Although Gibson's views of Japan are inevitably those of a hurried if interested outsider who has come to know the pop culture around the Tokyo subway stations of Shibuya, Shinjuku, and Harajuku, I would maintain there is a deeper justification, a geopolitical or perhaps geoeconomical and psychological logic, in his choosing such "nipponizing" vocabulary. This logic is centered on how strangely and yet peculiarly appropriate Japanese feudal-style capitalism is as an analog or, indeed, ideal template for the new feudalism of present-day corporate monopolies: where the history of capitalism, born out of popular merchant-adventurer revolt against the old sessile feudalism, has come full circle—Worm Ouroboros carrying us back to Leviathan. (The focus on neofeudalism, by the way, also explains Gibson's undoubted affinities with the Bester of *The Stars My Destination* [1956].) Not only Night City in *N*, but the whole "biz" world is "like a deranged experiment in Social Darwinism, designed by a bored researcher who kept one thumb permanently on the fast-forward button" (7). Gibson's major SF precursors are Philip K. Dick and Delany (and then Spinrad and John Varley). However, in between Dick's nation-state armies or polices and Delany's Foucauldian micropolitics of bohemian groups, Gibson has—to my mind more realistically—opted for global economic power-wielders as the arbiters of peoples' life-styles and lives. This can be exemplified in his femme fatale Sandii, who is symbolically a "Eurasian, half gaijin, long-hipped and fluid," and who moves the way "the crowds surg[e] around Shinjuku station's wired electric night . . . rhythm of a new age, dreamy and far from any nation's soil (BC, 104, 107).

Dick's (and Le Carré's) focus on the increasing role of intelligence agencies has in Gibson been transferred to industrial espionage, conducted either through cyberspace or by organizing corporate defection: these two activities account for practically all of his plots. Thus, the second and narratively central pole or focus of Gibson's stories are the "computer cowboys" riding this cyberspace range as the hired hands, wildcard operators, hustlers, mercs, or outlaws in the "intricate dance of desire and commerce" (N, 11). They are the hero(in)es of his writings: Case in N, or Bobby and Angela of CZ. A secondary role is that of a "street samurai" (N, 30), a mercenary of the monopoly wars: Molly in N, Turner in CZ, Sandii in "New Rose Hotel." Usually, his narrative agents come in pairs. Gibson's theme, or at least his central agential relationship, is often a love story: Romeo and Juliet in the world of zaibatsu (Case and Molly in N; Turner and Allison, Bobby and Angela, Jaylene and Ramirez in CZ; Johnny and Molly in "Johnny Mnemonic"; Lise and Casey in "The Winter Market"; Jack and Rikki in "Burning Chrome"). Such an updated Juliet, the female coheroine, whom the narrative spotlights almost but not quite equally, is refreshingly independent and strong: Delany acutely points out the parallel between Molly and Russ's Jael (though he seems to overstate the case of direct filiation between Gibson and Russ or Le Guin [Tatsumi, 1988:8]). Sometimes this Juliet turns out to be a Le Carré traitor, a Kim Philby of the zaibatsu wars, as in "New Rose Hotel," sometimes she simply walks away at the end, as in N and "Burning Chrome," or shifts into inaccessible cyberspace, as in "The Winter Market": but in this cruel world the love story usually ends badly.

Gibson's basic affect is to be the bearer of bad news, as was Dick. A happy ending in his work is a signal for a lowering of narrative intensity, as in "Johnny Mnemonic" (so that this is rightly taken back through Molly's incidental memories in *N*). Or it is even a sign of outright low-quality faking, as in Angela's silly transition from voodoo to TV goddess at the end of *CZ*.

In a world laced with pills and drugs, cyberspace is itself a kind of superdrug vying in intensity with sexual love. Cyberspace, that central metaphor, is defined by Gibson as "consensual hallucination," a "graphic representation of data abstracted from the banks of every computer in the human system . . . in the nonspace of the mind" (*N*, 51), a "monochrome nonspace where the only stars are dense concentrations of information, and high above it all burn corporate galaxies and the cold spiral arms of military systems" (*BC*, 170). Sometimes not only his console cowboys but he too seems to consider cyberspace as the new sensorium of an undifferentiated human species, as "mankind's extended electronic nervous system" (*BC*, 170) in which anything is possible. An abstract logic and cultural ecstasy is hidden beneath this hard-boiled technical vocabulary, a yearning to get out of the dinginess and filth of everyday life that can, in Gibson's most woolly-minded moments, easily branch off into heterodox religion (as in the voodoo that vitiates much of *CZ*). More prudently and plausibly, cyberspace can be seen as a landscape simulation (extrapolated from "primitive arcade games . . . [and] graphics programs" [*N*, 51]) of the mathematizable data fed into all the corporate computers, into which his hustler heroes plug by means of cranial jacks (extrapolated from present-day military experimentation). Its matrix is "bright lattices of logic" (*N*, 5), contrasting with their closed horizons, the sordid temperfoam of a coffin hotel. Case in *N* sees the black market quarter of Ninsei "as a field of data, the way the matrix had once reminded him of proteins linking to distinguish cell specialties . . . the dance of biz, information interacting, data made flesh" (16). It has clear affinities with erotics. Case's first orgasm with Molly is one of Gibson's lyrical passages lurking just below the cynical, streetwise surface, and therefore chopping up the rhythms of a prose poem into brief clauses: it is described as "flaring blue in timeless space, a vastness like the matrix, where the faces were shredded and blown away down hurricane corridors, and her inner thighs were strong and wet against his hips" (33).

Even more strikingly, toward the end of *N*, sexual love is seen as a kind of life-affirming ocean of superinformation; since the passage is situated in cyberspace, where Case is meeting his first love, Linda Lee, as a ROM construct, the two-way traffic between eroticism and cyberspace grows intricate:

> "No," he said, and then it no longer mattered, what he knew [i.e., that she was an illusion], tasting the salt of her mouth where tears had dried. There was a strength that ran in her, something he'd known in Night City and held there, been held by it, held for a while away from time and death, from the relentless Street that hunted them all. . . . It belonged, he knew—he remembered—as she pulled him down, to the meat, the flesh the cowboys mocked. It was a vast thing, beyond knowing, a sea of information coded in spiral and pheromone, infinite intricacy that only the body, in its strong blind way, could ever read. (239)

Cyberspace is a utopia out of video arcades or *pachinko* parlors (see McCaffery's interview of Gibson, 272–73, this volume), a mathematized love-philter of computer hacker lore. And, like Harlan Ellison or Spinrad, Gibson is on the side of his petty juvenile criminals trying to penetrate the corporate "blue ice." (Ice means, we are told, "intrusion countermeasures electronics," but it obviously also connotes the extremely rarified, lonely, Antarctic edge of exhilaratingly dangerous exploration among those informational superglaciers). The cowboy-samurai love affairs usually end badly, but at least they (and only they—not the rulers obscenely devoted to money or power) are capable of it.

Con: Ideology

The rapt utopia of bright logic and teeth-gritting erotic tenderness contrasts strangely, sometimes in interesting and sometimes in kitschy ways, with the melodramatic plots full of double crosses out of Le Carré or Spinrad. The ending of *N* was already ambiguous and somewhat vague: one Case was left in cyberspace with Linda Lee, another in "real" space alone, while the artificial intelligences whose unshackling had constituted the hidden plot pursued their unclear extraterrestrial contacts somewhere in the background. We are not too far here from Arthur C. Clarke's homespun quasi-mysticism, somewhat updated into the era of Fritjof Capra and of the pleasures or indeed (literally) ecstasies of the computer, that emblematic informational supermachine of "the great suprapersonal system of late capitalis[m]" (Jameson, 1988b:73).

Among the different senses of ideology let me use here Althusser's sense of a twisted representation of the subject's relationship to his or her real conditions of existence. In fiction on the capitalist market a quite basic and all-permeating ideology is the need for permanent excitement and mounting reader stimulation (Suvin, 1985). As Gibson's work expands but also weakens in *CZ*, it becomes clear that this increasingly obtruding ideology and its narrative concomitant, melodrama, are *within the utopia itself.* Of the four or five principal narrative agents in *CZ*, three veer off, more or less strongly, into mystical realms: Marly and Turner rely on their intuition or "edge"— "that superhuman synchromesh flow that stimulants only approximated" (14)—while Angela's biotechnical enhancement manifests itself even more sensationally as voodoo and then (as already mentioned, inconsequentially) ends up as a simstim ("feelies") entertainment industry career. Yet, in spite of his plot oscillation between defeatism and kitschy happy endings, which is an indicator of a real dilemma this very intelligent writer finds himself in as to the direction of history and even as to the possibility of meaningful action within it, Gibson's powers of observation, the flip face of his verbal inventiveness, are on the whole very refreshing. His work does not accept the values of the black, closed world he evokes with such skill: he hates the status quo. But his balancing act accepts the status quo a bit too readily as inevitable and unchangeable.

Paradoxically, for me this is too "realistic" in the pedestrian sense, too direct a reflection of the short-term situation all of us who radically doubt the dominant values of the new capitalist feudalism find ourselves in. I believe a deeper, or longer-range, view would be to hold fast to a belief in really possible, even if statistically improbable, radical changes. Neither the tough-guy lyricism of erotics nor the excitement of cyberspace, acceptable and even fine as they undoubtedly can be, seem finally satisfactory as utopias. Both, it will be noticed, are deeply socialized but still privatized utopias—or in fact utopian surrogates. Cyberspace is "an information maze of the economically grounded world of data and documentation: not history, certainly, but history's material fallout" (Delany, in *Mississippi Review*, 1988 [hereafter *MR*], 33). Perhaps unwittingly, Delany has here put the finger on a basic ambiguity in this characteristic imaginary or narrative space: it is simultaneously an acknowledgment of the overriding role of History and a flight from it. The only way to cope with blue ice is to serve it or to destroy (a part of) it. Chrome can be "burned," but the *zaibatsu* system as a whole cannot. History is an all-encompassing cruel Destiny, more than a little transcendental in its very intimate insertion into the flesh of the little protagonists. The dilemma of how personal actions and conduct relate to social change is simultaneously inescapable and insoluble within Gibson's model. I have suggested earlier that a solution logically latching onto cyberspace, and allowing surrogate reconnecting (*re-ligio*) between disparate people and their destinies outside of and against history, is then religion. As Delany goes on to acutely observe, religion is therefore a permanent temptation of the cyberpunks: "The hard edges of Gibson's dehumanized technologies hide a residing mysticism" (*MR*, 33).

In sum, a viable this-worldly, collective and public, utopianism simply is not within the horizon of the cyberpunk structure of feeling. Sterling incorrectly interprets the cyberpunk emblem of mirrorshades, mirrored sunglasses reflecting the light, as "prevent[ing] the forces of normalcy from realizing that one is crazed and possibly dangerous" (1986a:xi). It is true that the mirrorshade wearer's gaze is obscured for the observer, who cannot tell whether s/he is being looked at or not. Nonetheless, it is not too difficult to gauge a person's behavior even when the eyes are hidden. Rather, in my opinion, mirrorshades are a two-way transaction between the wearer and his social environment: they conjoin a minor degree of effective withdrawal with a large degree of psychological illusion of withdrawal in the wearer. In political terms, such an illusory dead end becomes obvious when Sterling continues the cited sentence by listing those dangerous mirrorshade visionaries: "the biker, the rocker, the policeman, and similar outlaws" (sic!—these macho associations of mirrorshades justify my "his" for the wearer). As Delany points out, mirrorshades "both mask the gaze and distort the gaze": he then rightly proceeds to read them as an emblem or "a nice allegory of what is happening in this particular kind of SF" (Tatsumi, 1988:8).

Thus, an evaluation of cyberpunk depends on the works examined. Even where I disagree with Gibson's horizons, he has certainly identified some real or even central problems of our space/time. He latches onto some great precursors on the margins of SF and "high lit," such as Pynchon (in honor of whose Oedipa Maas Gibson's recurring villainous *zaibatsu* of Maas Biolabs has been named), or William Burroughs, who pioneered the insight that the hallucinatory operators are real. It is mainly in his hands that cyberpunk has been "that current SF work which is not middle class, not comfortable with history, not tragic, not supportive, not maternal, not happy-go-lucky. . . . But it's only as a negative . . . that cyberpunk can signify" (Delany, *MR*, 30). Gibson's first two books have refreshed the language and sensibility of SF. In fact, it is correct but not quite sufficient to praise Gibson for broadening the range of SF (or indeed of modern literature) with the new vocabulary of lyricized information interfaces. The new vocabulary is, as always, a sign for human relationships. To say, as does the first sentence of *N*, "The sky above the port was the color of television, tuned to a dead channel," means to foreground electronic interfaces into a new nature, a second nature that has grown to be a first nature.

Bruce Sterling, on the contrary, does not play in the same league. His general form is that of a rather loose and verbose picaresque. The yawning gap which I feel exists between Gibson and Sterling can be illustrated by comparing the erotic relationship between the junkie protagonist of *Involution Ocean* (1977) and the alien, physiologically incompatible woman Dalusa to the couples discussed earlier in Gibson. Sterling's love affair lacks the tension between Eros and Thanatos characteristic of Gibson. While the situation as set up is potentially interesting, it never gets beyond rather thin sadomasochism, where the pain inflicted (primarily on the woman) is another sexual thrill. The tension is here abolished in favor of the only remaining horizon of death. Furthermore, after two readings I cannot see either a casual or an analogical function for the love story within the "involution ocean" quest of Captain Desperandum—itself a not very interesting foal sired by Captain Ahab's quest out of *Dune*.

Perhaps it may not be fair to judge anybody by a first novel. And in fact Sterling's second one, *The Artificial Kid* (1980), is to my mind his most interesting work. There is much inventiveness in the protagonist's "combat-artist" youth subculture—with "techno-medicine" including superdrugs—that arises in response to the long-lifers' grip on society, that is, on economics and politics. This subculture is both an analogy and a writing largely of contemporary punk plus violent sports plus (most interestingly) their use for mass entertainment under the rulers' patronage. These fun touches, however, are accompanied by naïve or outright dubious disquisitions on politics, such as Manies's "Chemical Analog" theory of society (where individuals function as molecules—not a great advance on Asimov's psychohistory). True, at least there is in this novel an essay at a range of meditations on social organization, which includes Chairman Moses's attempt at redesigning society, Saint Anne's eco-theology, and perhaps most important Arti's own experiential trajectory. In spots, the novel therefore approaches allegorical validity. Unfortunately, not only are these aspects rather shallow, they are also thrown about in a slapdash manner and usually given as long speeches breaking up the tension. The plot itself meanders about and ends up in the last third echoing some fairly old SF conventions (e.g., early Aldiss) as well as dodging the initial youth culture issues by means of a happy ending based on friendship between young and old oiled by prosperity.

Sterling's next novel, *Schismatrix* (1985), is a somewhat updated space opera flitting from colony to colony, in a rather forced derivation from something like the Italian Renaissance city-states and their different systems with internal intrigues of little relevance. It is an advance on his earlier novels in ambition but not in execution. It recirculates with a new sauce, pretending to some metaphysical depth of "Prigoginic levels of complexities," the hoariest clichés of 1940s and 1950s SF, say from Heinlein to Farmer. As usual, some interesting themes (loneliness, flesh versus disembodied mind) are hurriedly tossed off and quite buried under a torrent of microideas neither fully digested nor integrated into the narrative. Thus, the basic plot tension between the Mechanists and the more biologically inclined Shapers, transferred from five stories of his between 1982 and 1985 and evolving against a horizon of ultimate futility, does not seem meaningfully worked out either as concept or in the plot (cf. Maddox, pp. 324–30, this volume). Again, there are amusing fragments and witty passages in the novel, but the principle of how they are strung together escapes me. Finally, for all the inventive and hip, "postmodernist" conceptual proliferation, neither the political canvas of *Schismatrix*, nor the supposedly biological one of *Involution Ocean*, nor the attempt to combine the two in *The Artificial Kid*, have anything like the lyrical force, intrinsic fascination, or indeed referential relevance of Gibson's cyberspace.

I must confess, at the end of this section and in the nature of a postscriptum to it, that the neat polarization between a worthy Gibson and an unworthy Sterling is somewhat shaken by their latest novels. Upon my first two readings, Gibson's *Mona Lisa Overdrive* (1988) confirms and solidifies his trajectory from critical to escapist use of cyberspace, masked by plot complications. The ending, where the Romeo-and-Juliet pair (continued from *CZ*) willingly withdraw from empirical to cyberpunk space, is tired old stuff, identical, for example, to the end of Fritz Lang's expressionist movie *Der müde Tod* (*The Tired Death*, translated also as *Destiny*, 1921), where the space into which the lovers enter after all the empirical defeats is more accurately—if less science fictionally—identified as the domain of a friendly Death. As is well known, Death is the final horizon of melodrama. On the other hand, Sterling's *Islands in the Net* (1988) is technically his smoothest work. Yet it is achieved, first of all, at the cost of a withdrawal from the earlier, more exuberant multiplicity of viewpoints to oldfashioned, single-protagonist focus on Laura Webster. Further, it is politically woolly-minded, or if you prefer, its extrapolated twenty-first century world has too many loose ends. Though centered on power struggles which grow quite violent, this is a much more cheerful vision than Gibson's. True, in this "postmillennium" world the détente and international cooperation through the UN means, in fact, the domination of multinational companies. However, not only is this a world without the nuclear threat in bombs or power plants, without traffic jams, and without network television, its corporations also come in a spread running from responsible "economic democrats" (like Laura's Rizome) to data pirates and straightforward fascists (like the tiny nation-states of Grenada, Singapore, and Mali where most of the derring-do occurs, and which at the end are dispossessed). Due to the exertions and sufferings of our candid and sturdy heroine, the good guys of Rizome, who value creativity and a feeling of belonging (which Sterling insists on spelling *gemeineschaft*), who sympathize with the "scientists and engineers, and architects, too . . . who do the world's true work" (94–95), are at the end left in control of the field. Their framework and symbol is the omnipresent audio-visual and information Net, "Computers . . . fusing together . . . /t/ele-vision—telephone—telex. Tape recorder—VCR—laser disk" (15). The Net is a poor relation of Gibson's cyberspace, both because it is flatly extrapolative, and because its value and its values are never doubted; both of these aspects are to say that it is quite alien to cyberspace's utopian core. Outside the Net are the disadvantaged: people like the dyslexic Carlotta, and most of the Third World population. It is interesting to look at the provenance of some names given to his narrative agents: Valeri Chkalov and Sergei Ilyushin were (in the readers' historical world) famous Russian aviation people of the 1930s and 1940s, Lacoste is a famous present-day brand of clothing, Yaobang is the first name of a recent secretary of the Chinese Communist party, and so on. Such secondhand tags from daily papers or historical handbooks indicate well the superficiality of Sterling's international politics. The fake alternative of Atom Bomb versus the Net, on which the novel is based, is, finally, simply the alternative between old-style military capitalism, against which much indignation is directed, and new-style informational invasion, neither of which could in a reasonable extrapolation exist with the other. It speaks well for Sterling's ideological instincts, but badly about his narrative framework, that he was on page 292 (out of 348) forced to bring out of nowhere an anarchic rebel, extrapolated from T. E. Lawrence, to save Laura and let her properly inform the world, in a triumph of media freedom against international UN bureaucracy. The hoariest clichés of U.S. liberalism, those which gave it a deservedly bad name, celebrate their rebirth here.

Parting Doubts

A general conclusion, therefore, might be that Gibson best demonstrates how "Today, one need not 'be a Marxist' to realize that aesthetics, politics, economics, technology, and social relations are interdependent cultural phenomena" (Sobchack, 1987:8), though I would add that one needs to have at least—and that is no small least—absorbed the lesson of Marxism. This interdependence means also that literary utopianism cannot grow any more into an independent literary genre, but only (as I have had occasion to argue) into a dominant component of SF.

Furthermore, Gibson's work also presents (for the moment) the coalescing of a new structure of feeling. A structure of experience and of feeling is, as the late and regretted Raymond Williams formulated it, "a particular quality of social experience and relationship . . . which gives the sense of a generation or of a period"; however, that remains only "social experiences in solution" or "a [semantic] formation at the very edge of semantic availability" until it precipitates and becomes "more evidently and more immediately available" (1981:131–34). In Gibson, a structure of feeling has indeed become formulated and therefore more immediately available for our collective discussion.

There can be few higher praises than this for a work of verbal or any other art. But for cyberpunk SF as a whole, at least two questions in mutual feedback remain to be tentatively answered or, indeed, simply posed. First, Whose structure of feeling might this be? Second, What ideological horizons or consequences does it imply?

It is, of course, quite insufficient and improper to call this structure of feeling simply one of the 1980s. No doubt, it is such—but of everybody living in the 1980s? In the whole world? Based on external and internal evidence, I would speculate that cyberpunk SF is representative for the structure of feeling of an important but certainly not all-inclusive international social group. As I hinted at the beginning, this is some fractions of the youth culture in the affluent North of our globe. More particularly, cyberpunk is correlative to the technicians and artists associated with the new communication media, and to the young who aspire to such a status. It is, of course, quite irrelevant whether a formulator of such an ideology (say, Gibson) is personally a computer hacker or a video arcade addict. It is only necessary that the formulator's ideology be an ideal representation of the experience from which cyberpunk arose, persuasively characterized by Sterling as: "high tech recording, satellite video, and computer graphics [have turned] the artists at pop's cutting edge . . . quite often [into] cutting-edge technicians in the bargain. They are special effects wizards, mixmasters, tape effects techs, graphics hackers, emerging through new media to dazzle society with head-trip extravaganzas like FX cinema and the global Live Aid benefit" (1988b:xii). Now this group is widespread, international, and significant beyond its numbers as a cutting edge. However, it is certainly a small, single-digit percentage even of the fifteen-to-thirty-years' age group, even in the affluent North (never mind the whole world).

As to my second parting question, let me again start from the language at the end of Sterling's quite representative passage just cited. It is, to put it mildly, puzzling. Is cyberpunk then proudly proclaiming itself to be another extravaganza to dazzle society in head trips and (let me add) to be integrated into the profit-making and highly ideologized culture industry? Is it to be, as Delany observed, reactionary macho cynicism, "at its best conservative and at its worst rebarbative—if not downright tedious," so that it could well be "co-opted to support the most stationary of status quos" (Tatsumi, 1988:9–10; cf. Csicsery-Ronay, pp. 182–93, this volume)? Or is it something more—perhaps even a cognitive poetry of the horizons of that social group, important for all of us? To put the crucial question: In its forte, the integration of agents and action into technosleaze, *is cyberpunk the diagnostician of or the parasite on a disease*? Such items as Sterling and Shiner's collaborative short story "Mozart in Mirrorshades" (Sterling, 1986a:223–39), which have nothing to envy Robert Adams's genocidal "mercenaries' SF" (if I may so baptize it)—and might be even more repulsive for the slick sheen they add to it—certainly testify that it can be the parasite.

Is cyberpunk, then, despite all trendy mimicry of rebelliousness, complicitous with the owners and managers of the culture industry, finally with the death-dealing *zaibatsu* so well described by Gibson, and merely trying to get some crumbs off their table by flaunting its own newness as a marketable commodity? Or is it truly (at least in intention and in part) a coalescing oppositional worldview whose final horizon would be a historical world of liberated erotics and cognitive cyberspace, without the *zaibatsu* or escapist head trips? Only time will tell. But the evolution (or, if you wish, the involution ocean) of cyberpunk after 1984 does not, at the moment, bode too well. The dilemma has, with some exaggeration, been put provocatively thus:

So cyberpunks, like near-addicts of amphetamines and hallucinogens, write as if they [we]re both victims of a life-negating system and the heroic adventurers of thrill. They can't help themselves, but their hip grace gets them through an amoral world, facing a future which, for all intents and purposes, has gone beyond human influence, and where the only way to live is in speed, speed to avoid being caught in the web. (Csicsery-Ronay, p. 192, this volume)

The attitude thus described is, of course, properly an adolescent one. "Adolescent" does not necessarily mean invalid; indeed, it means very probably at least partially valid; but it also, finally, means untenable *à la longue*. Let us hope pessimists such as Csicsery-Ronay and I will be confounded by Gibson and some new stars, or at least *shuriken*.

Or perhaps (unkind thought, subject to verification by further SF writings) we should simply stop talking about "cyberpunk SF," that witty coinage of Dozois's? Perhaps it might be more useful to say that there is the writer William Gibson, and then there are a couple of expert PR men (most prominently Sterling himself) who know full well the commercial value of an instantly recognizable label, and are sticking one onto disparate products?

Takayuki Tatsumi

The Japanese
Reflection of
Mirrorshades

Coincidence

Bruce Sterling seemed to be teasing me when he concluded his ArmadilloCon introduction of William Gibson with the following remark:
"Today, while Tokyo fandom speculates feverishly over his blood type,
we Texans can brag, without fear of contradiction, that we know our
Guest of Honor well" (1986c:7). Indeed, chatting with Bill after inter-
viewing him at Disclave '86 (23–25 May), I happened to ask him about
his blood type, not because of my own curiosity, but because of a
postmodern Japanese convention in which this sort of question is
formally exchanged as a part of the greeting between new acquain-
tances. I expected that his familiarity with Japanese culture had
already made Bill aware of the many blood-type books being sold in our
country as long-term bestsellers, just like Tarot cards, astrology books,
or the Bible. Bill, however, was deeply astonished, almost shocked, at
my question and explanation—an astonishment that astonished me as
well as others. At any rate, this is how Bruce came to mention Tokyo
fandom's interests in Bill's blood type. Let me, then, apologize to
"Tokyo fandom," my good old village, for representing it by myself—
or, more accurately, being forced to represent it—although I do not
doubt that in my high-tech hometown people have actually asked the
question more often than not: "What is William Gibson's blood type?"
Tokyo is high tech, since it is semiotic—otherwise, semio-tech.

We arrive at the starting point, dear Bruce. If Japan is now taken
for the sign of high tech, and if most Japanese now take for granted
blood-type interpretation as semiotic pleasure (remember Sigmund

Freud's *The Interpretation of Dreams*), why should we not enjoy reading Bill Gibson's blood type as his "semiotic ghost" (in the Gibsonian term) without having seen him in person, just as Bill himself enjoys the signifier of Japanese language—like "Chiba City" or "Gomi no Sensei"—as its "semiotic ghost" (remember Roland Barthes's *The Empire of Signs*) without ever having visited Japan itself? My intent here is not to defend my country's recent tendency, nor compare the Japanese sense of high tech with the American sense of it, but merely to point out the coincidence just noted between Bill Gibson's reading of the "Japanesque" and our reading of the Gibsonian. It is difficult to decide if Bill's way of reading has always already been Japanesque or if our way of reading has always already been Gibsonian. All we can say is that in the very coincidence resides the secret of imagination that has long characterized science fiction: something is going on somewhere, at the same time that a similar thing is going on in other places. And it is a historical imperative that makes possible such a coincidence.

NASFiC Shock

To be honest, I had not read *Neuromancer* (1984), though I was familiar with *Schismatrix* (1985), when I attended NASFiC (North American SF Convention) in Austin, Texas, in the summer of 1985, and the first cyberpunk panel, which perhaps appropriately ended in punkish violence. It was also coincidental that I selected that panel rather than any of the others, since I was totally ignorant of the term "cyberpunk." I merely wanted to see Bruce Sterling on whatever panel; Sterling was already one of my favorite writers, and three of his short stories ("Swarm," "Spider Rose," and "Spook") had at that point been translated into Japanese to great popular acclaim. What I discovered about cyberpunk as a movement, then, introduced me to William Gibson, whose style drove me crazy; and the excitement then ignited by John Shirley reminded me of an old essay by Gene van Troyer (1978) in which the author described a controversial (and violent) confrontation between Shirley and Harlan Ellison. Something was already going on in the late 1970s: the Shirley-Ellison controversy told us that John was destined to be the father of punk SF or John the Baptist of cyberpunk, not the youngest son of the last New Wave.

Reading *Neuromancer* just after NASFiC helped me make sense of all these fragments, and encouraged me to write an article about that panel and the movement in *Hayakawa's SFM* (1986). My essay was immediately followed by Yoshio Kobayashi's detailed overview of cyberpunk writers (1986). Since then, we two have promoted cyberpunk in our respective columns in that magazine ("SF Graffiti in the U.S.A." and "Overseas Science Fiction").

Neuromancer Translated: Otherwise

It may be equally revealing and significant, however, that the Japanese translation of William Gibson, whether deliberately or accidentally, came to repeat the structure of multicultural coincidence. The Japanese translation of *Neuromancer* by Hisashi Kuroma appeared in July 1985. Despite the almost two-year time lag, this novel has been more fortunate than Samuel Delany's cult novel, *The Einstein Intersection* (1967), which has yet to be translated in Japan. *Neuromancer* was translated more quickly than most Anglo-American novels. And the more influential cyberpunk becomes, the shorter the translation time: thus *Mona Lisa Overdrive*, which Gibson published in October 1988, appeared in Japanese in February 1989. This is the primary point. The Japanese acceleration of translation was itself made possible by the effect of the cyberpunklike development of a global communication system—a system that endorses the synchronic nature of cyberpunk.

Next, let me point out that Mr. Kuroma's translations are aptly distinguished by his frequent and adventurous juxtapositions of Chinese characters and Japanese alphabets for cyberspatial terms. Frequently, Japanese readers are required to read two kinds of representations of one word simultaneously. Such a technique is employed according to a Japanese typographical convention called "ruby," which enables us to print smaller "kana" (in *Neuromancer*'s case, mainly "katakana," which was invented for representing loan words) alongside Chinese characters. The Japanese alphabet functions as a phonogrammic translation of a word, while the Chinese character is ideogrammic. For instance, "cyberspace" written in Chinese characters is pronounced "Denno-Kukan," whereas it is literally pronounced as "cyberspace" (saibaa-supeesu) if written in the Japanese alphabet. The convention of "ruby" forces us to read both Chinese character and Japanese alphabet at the same time. Thus, Kuroma's stylistics itself foregrounded the coincidence between the Anglo-American within the Oriental (Japanese alphabet) and the Oriental within the Anglo-American (Chinese character)—a process which is consistent with Neuromantic thematics.

Of course, this translation gave rise to great disputes, dividing its audience into extremes. Some people denounced Kuroma's methods, complaining about its "too frequent use of ruby" (Kurei, 1986) as well as its "unreadability, which might seem fashionable to other readers" (Nakajima, 1986). Others appreciated it, discovering the linguistic advantage of Japanese (Hamamoto, 1986) and the translator's originality (Abe, 1986). According to Norio Itoh (1986), the one-time Karel Award winning translator and critic: "If you are under the age of 25, you may easily visualize the world translated in this style." Therefore, just as the original *Neuromancer* induced Gardner Dozois to call its fascinating style "cyberpunk," so the Japanese version gave birth to the controversy about its adventurous style, inciting one of the reviewers to call it "A-Bomb Translation" (*Shinshonen Special*, 1986). If Rudy Rucker's definition in 1985 of cyberpunk's style as being "harder, faster, greater, and louder" still hits the point, Kuroma's translation successfully repeated the effect of the style by challenging the limits of the Japanese language.

"Cyberspace" = 電脳空間（サイバースペース）

Chinese character (= Dennou-kuukan) Japanese alphabet/ruby (= Saibaa-supeesu)

The topic of translation style is, of course, only part of the Japanese reception of *Neuromancer*. As for its narrative structure, Japanese reviewers have given mostly the same comments as Anglo-American: "The first half is exciting, while the latter half gets boring" (Fukumoto, 1986); "This work lacks the conceptual games that have marked science fiction" (Suikyoshi, 1986); "Seemingly up-to-date, actually old-fashioned" (Kagami, 1986). One of the best ways might be to read *Neuromancer* as "a novel of the very 'present'" in view of its thematics (Ryohei Takahashi, *Hayakawa's SFM*, October 1986), simultaneously understanding cyberpunk as a movement of the "present progressive" in terms of its stylistics (Asa, fanzine *Milksoft*, Nagoya University SF Society, no. 52, July 1986).

Semiotic Ghostwriters

The Japanese translation of *Neuromancer* not only imported the idea of cyberpunk, but also helped to disclose various simultaneous happenings that had remained unnoticed in Japan. For instance, audiovisual creators like junk artist Seiko Mikami and playwright Norimizu Ameya began asserting that they had always been doing the same thing as Gibson, as did film director Sogo Ishii, who now has a collaboration in progress with William Gibson. From 1987 through 1988, cyberpunk reached the peak of its popularity in Japan, attracting numerous articles and discussions in magazines and journals outside the "proper" field of SF, exactly as it was doing in the United States. In the spring of 1988 Gibson's and Sterling's respective visits to Japan further promoted the excitement, nicely coinciding with the publication of the Japanese versions of *Schismatrix* and *Mirrorshades* translated by Mr. Takashi Ogawa, "the Tokyo liaison of cyberpunk." A variety of conventions and seminars were also devoted to this brand-new subgenre. The imported term "cyberpunk" caught the eyes of so many people that it rapidly transgressed the boundaries of any generic categories, and came to refer to anything having to do with dead-tech environment, hypermedia activity, and outlaw technologists. It was, like cyberpunk itself, a semiotic ghost.

In the field of science fiction in Japan, cyberpunk coincided with the activities of a younger generation of writers. The first half of the 1980s saw the rise of the third generation of native Japanese SF writers, mainly people in their mid-twenties, and the major Japanese SF magazines began devoting more and more pages to their new works. It is this generation that produced certain talents analogous to cyberpunks, best represented by Ms. Mariko O'Hara, who developed her own style, modeled chiefly on one of cyberpunk's precursors, Cordwainer Smith. I remember talking to Bruce Sterling in 1986 about O'Hara's unwittingly cyberpunklike short story called "Mental Female" (*Hayakawa's SFM*, December 1986), in which Tokyo's mother computer and North Siberian father computer appear on TV as a girl and a boy, Ms. Kipple and Mr. Techie, fall in love with each other, and, as foreplay, begin playing catch—a foreplay which launches missiles from both sides. The important thing is that the author had written this before Kuroma's translation of *Neuromancer* was published.

Furthermore, the year 1987 saw the fictional debut of Goro Masaki, a young writer who deserves the title of the first hardcore Japanese cyberpunk writer. He claims to have read one of the major precyberpunk stories—James Tiptree, Jr.'s "The Girl Who Was Plugged In" (1973)—more than thirty times(!), both in English and in translation. Masaki's contest-winning "Evil Eyes" vividly describes the conflict between a mind software company and a new religious organization, culminating in the revelation that Maria, a full-armored woman working for the company, and Mugen, the charismatic figure of the organization, were produced by a multiple personality, the owner of which had been born a disfigured baby. Although Masaki denies the Gibsonian influence, making the distinction between his emphasis upon humanity and Gibson's lack of morality, it is also true that his best readers are probably deeply sympathetic to cyberpunk poetics. This new talent should thus be construed not a child but a brother of cyberpunk, because he shares so many things with Gibson and others. Masaki's works, then, help to prove another coincidence between the two countries.

What, then, is transpiring in the exportation of Japanese works? If the above discussion suggests the coincidences between American cyberpunk, Japanese translation, and Japanese cyberpunk, the question immediately arises about the problem of English translations of Japanese science fiction. Indeed, great effort has been made with regard to Japanese-English translation. American residents in Japan including David Lewis, Edward Lipsett, and Gene Van Troyer, respectively, translated Yasutaka Tsutsui, Kazumasa Hirai, and Tetsu Yano. But what matters most in terms of cyberpunk is that in these years there have been an increasing number of American writers and editors, who have noticed cultural coincidences between the two countries, and have become more interested in translating Japanese fiction. For instance, lately my friend Kazuko Behrens, now living in San Francisco, translated Yoshio Aramaki's protocyberpunk tale "Soft Clocks" (1968), which was stylized and finally sold to the British science fiction periodical *Interzone* by Lewis Shiner, one of the original cyberpunks. What is more, the new American magazine called *Strange Plasmas* recently decided to buy for their coming issue Mariko O'Hara's "Mental Female" and Goro Masaki's "Evil Eyes."

In the wake of cyberpunk, the acceleration of translation, like the effect of the postsimulation society, takes place on both sides of the Pacific. To be more precise, it is not that the acceleration of translation effaces the time lag, but that the act of translation, insofar as it usually retrofits the past as synchronic with the present, has always been synonymous with the effacement of time lag. In other words, the logic of coincidence assumes that the text precedes translation, at the same time that translation precedes the text. In the case of *Neuromancer*, it is safe to say that the translator Kuroma did a word-by-word *transplantation* of the text, while rediscovering what had already been as cyberpunk as any in the semiotics of a Japanese frame of reference. If translation is another name for misperception, the postcyberpunk age can be seen to have realized that perception and misperception take place at the same time. Gibson's Chiba City may have sprung from his misperception of Japan, but it was this misperception that encouraged Japanese readers to correctly perceive the nature of postmodernist Japan. In short, the moment we perceive cyberpunk stories which misperceive Japan, we are already perceived correctly by cyberpunk.

Coda

Thus, near our conclusion, we may be reminded, once again, of the postmodernist paradox that the perceiver literally becomes the perceived, just as the junk artist immediately becomes the raw material of junk art. What cyberpunks seem to consume is not merely Japan, but their own science fiction projected in the future called Japan, whereas what the Japanese audience seems to exhaust is not merely American SF of the 1980s, but their own image synchronic with cyberpunk. As soon as we feel like metaphorizing something, we are literally identified with that object. As I suggested earlier, cyberpunk prohibits us from metaphorizing AIDS or Chernobyl, because we live in the times when these panics may be rapidly followed by the literal coincidence between biological and high-tech territories. This is precisely why cyberpunk is sometimes called post-metafiction. While metafictionists were involved with metaphorization of fiction as such, cyberpunks are so conscious of the totally computerized reality around themselves that they would take for granted the decomposition of boundaries between the literal and the metaphorical, trying to repress any easy act of metaphoricization. Cyberpunks perceive "semiotic ghosts" of the present-day Far East; meanwhile they are misperceived as the "ghost-writers" of our future.

Bibliography

Books

Abe, Takeshi. 1986. [Review of *Neuromancer*]. *Hayakawa's SFM*, December.

Acker, Kathy. 1984 [1978]. *Blood and Guts in High School*. New York: Grove.

———. 1986. *Don Quixote, which was a dream*. New York: Grove.

———. 1988. *Empire of the Senseless*. New York: Grove.

Aldiss, Brian. 1969. *Barefoot in the Head: A European Fantasia*. Garden City, N.Y.: Doubleday.

Algren, Nelson. 1949. *Man with the Golden Arm*. Garden City, N.Y.: Doubleday.

Aramaki, Yoshio. 1968. "Soft Clocks." *Interzone* 27:46–53.

Asa. 1986. [Review of *Neuromancer*]. *Milksoft*, Nagoya University SF Society, no. 52, July.

Atlas, James. 1984. "Beyond Demographics." *The Atlantic* 254, no. 4: 49–58.

Atwood, Margaret. 1985. *The Handmaid's Tale*. New York: Ballantine.

Ballard, J. G. 1990 [1969]. *The Atrocity Exhibition*. Re/Search Publications.

———. 1973. *Crash*. New York: Farrar, Strauss & Giroux.

Barth, John. 1966. *Giles Goat-Boy; or, The Revised New Syllabus*. Garden City, N.Y.: Doubleday.

———. 1968. *Lost in the Funhouse: Fiction for Print, Tape, Live Voice*. Garden City, N.Y.: Doubleday.

Barthelme, Donald. 1967. *Snow White*. New York: Atheneum.

Barthes, Roland. 1970 [1957]. *Mythologies*, trans. Annette Lavers. New York: Hill and Wang.

———. 1982 [1970]. *The Empire of Signs*, trans. Richard Howard. New York: Hill and Wang.

Baudrillard, Jean. 1983a. *Simulations*. New York: Semiotext(e).

———. 1983b. "The Ecstasy of Communication." In *The Anti-Aesthetic: Essays on Postmodern Culture*, ed. Hal Foster, trans. John Johnston (126–34). Port Townsend, Wash.: Bay Press.

———. 1983c. *In the Shadow of the Silent Majorities*, trans. Paul Foss, Paul Patton, and John Johnston. New York: Semiotext(e).

———. 1987. "The Year 2000 Has Already Happened." In *Body Invaders: Panic Sex in America*, ed. Arthur Kroker and Marilouise Kroker, trans. Nai-Fei Ding and Kuan Hsing Chen (35–44). Montréal: New World Perspectives.

Bear, Greg. 1985. *Blood Music*. New York: Arbor House.

Beckett, Samuel. 1967. *Stories and Texts for Nothing*, trans. by the author. New York: Grove.

——. 1972 [1971]. *The Lost Ones*, trans. by the author. New York: Grove.

Bell, Madison Smartt. 1983. *The Washington Square Ensemble*. New York: Viking.

——. 1985. *Waiting for the End of the World*. New York: Ticknor & Fields.

Belsito, Peter, ed. 1985. *Notes from the Pop Underground*. Berkeley: The Last Gasp of San Francisco.

Benford, Gregory. 1983. *Against Infinity*. New York: Timescape.

——. 1988. "Is Something Going On?" *Mississippi Review* 47/48:18–23.

Bernal, J. D. 1969 [1929]. *The World, the Flesh, and the Devil: An Enquiry into the Future of the Three Enemies of the Rational Mind*, 2nd ed. Bloomington: Indiana University Press.

Bester, Alfred. 1956 [1955]. *The Stars My Destination*. London: Sidgwick & Jackson; rpt. New York: Franklin Watts, 1987.

——. 1982 [1953]. *The Demolished Man*. New York: Timescape.

Borges, Jorge Luis. 1962. "Pierre Menard, Author of Don Quixote" In *Ficciones* (45–55). New York: Grove.

Brautigan, Richard. 1969. *In Watermelon Sugar*. New York: Delacorte.

Brin, David. 1985. *The Postman*. New York: Bantam.

Brooke-Rose, Christine. 1981. "Science Fiction and Realistic Fiction." In *A Rhetoric of the Unreal: Studies in Narrative and Structure, Especially of the Fantastic* (72–102). Cambridge and London: Cambridge University Press.

——. 1984. *Amalgamemnon*. Manchester: Carcanet.

——. 1986. *Xorandor*. Manchester: Carcanet.

——. 1990. *Verbivore*. Manchester: Carcanet.

Brunner, John. 1968. *Stand on Zanzibar*. New York: Doubleday.

——. 1975. *Shockwave Rider*. New York: Harper & Row.

Bukatman, Scott. 1989. "The Cybernetic (City) State: Terminal Space Becomes Phenomenal." *Journal of the Fantastic in the Arts* 2 (Summer): 43–63.

Burgess, Anthony. 1962. *A Clockwork Orange*. New York: Norton.

——. 1983. *The End of the World News: An Entertainment*. New York: McGraw-Hill.

Burroughs, William S. 1962 [1959]. *Naked Lunch*. New York: Grove.

——. 1964. *Nova Express*. New York: Grove.

——. 1966 [1961]. *The Soft Machine*. New York: Grove.

——. 1967 [1962]. *The Ticket That Exploded*. New York: Grove.

——. 1971. *The Wild Boys: A Book of the Dead*. New York: Grove.

Cadigan, Pat. 1985. "Pretty Boy Crossover." Rpt. in *The 1987 Annual World's Best SF*, ed. Donald A. Wollheim (82–93). New York: DAW Books.

——. 1987. *Mindplayers*. New York: Bantam.

Campbell, Joseph. 1949. *The Hero with a Thousand Faces*. New York: Pantheon.

Carter, Angela. 1969. *Heroes and Villains*. New York: Simon & Schuster.

——. 1977. *The Passion of New Eve*. New York: Harcourt Brace Jovanovich.

Chambers, Iain. 1986. *Popular Culture: The Metropolitan Experience*. New York: Methuen.

Chandler, Raymond. 1939. *The Big Sleep*. New York: Random House.

Clarke, Arthur C. 1953. *Childhood's End*. New York: Harcourt, Brace & World.

——. 1968. *2001*. New York: NAL.

Clement, Hal [pseud. of Harry C. Stubbs]. 1954. *Mission of Gravity*. Garden City, N.Y.: Doubleday.

Cohen, Ralph. 1987. "Do Postmodern Genres Exist?" *Genre* 20, nos. 3–4 (Fall–Winter): 246.

Columbia Literary History of the United States, gen. ed. Emory Elliott. 1988. New York: Columbia University Press.

Debord, Guy. 1977 [1967]. *The Society of the Spectacle*, rev. ed. Detroit: Black & White.

Delany, Samuel R. 1967. *The Einstein Intersection*. New York: Ace.

———. 1968. *Nova*. Garden City, N.Y.: Doubleday.

———. 1974. *Dhalgren*. New York: Bantam.

———. 1976. *Triton*. Boston: Gregg.

———. 1984. *Stars in My Pocket Like Grains of Sand*. New York: Bantam.

De Lauretis, Teresa. 1980. "Signs of Wo/ander." In *The Technological Imagination: Theories and Fictions*, ed. Teresa de Lauretis, Andreas Huyssen, and Kathleen Woodward (159–74). Madison, Wisc.: Coda.

DeLillo, Don. 1976. *Ratner's Star*. New York: Knopf.

———. 1985. *White Noise*. New York: Viking.

Dick, Philip K. 1964. *Martian Time-Slip*. New York: Ballantine.

———. 1968. *Do Androids Dream of Electric Sheep?* New York: Ballantine.

———. 1969. *Ubik*. Garden City, N.Y.: Doubleday.

Disch, Thomas. 1988 [1968]. *Camp Concentration*. New York: Doubleday.

Du Brow, Rick. 1985. "Television Looks at Itself: Proprietary Thoughts on the Future of Prime Time." *Harper's* (March): 39–49.

Durrell, Lawrence. 1958. *Balthazar*. New York: Dutton.

Ebert, Teresa L. 1980. "The Convergence of Postmodern Innovative Fiction and Science Fiction: An Encounter with Samuel R. Delany's Technotopia." *Poetics Today* 1 (Summer): 91–104.

Eco, Umberto. 1988. *Foucault's Pendulum*, trans. William Weaver. San Diego: Harcourt Brace Jovanovich.

Effinger, George Alec. 1987. *When Gravity Fails*. New York: Arbor House.

Ellison, Harlan. "I Have No Mouth and I Must Scream." In *I Have No Mouth and I Must Scream*. New York: Pyramid.

Even-Zohar, Itamar, ed. 1990. *Polysystem Studies*. Special issue, *Poetics Today* 11, no. 1.

Faulkner, William. 1936. *Absalom, Absalom!*. New York: Random House.

Federman, Raymond. 1979. *The Voice in the Closet*. Madison, Wisc.: Coda.

———. 1982. *The Twofold Vibration*. Bloomington: Indiana University Press.

Ferguson, Mary. 1980. *The Aquarian Conspiracy: Personal and Social Transformation in the 1980s*. New York: St. Martin's Press.

Flax, Jane. 1987. "Postmodernism and Gender Relations in Feminist Theory." *Signs: Journal of Women in Culture and Society* 12:621–43.

Freud, Sigmund. 1938. *The Interpretation of Dreams*. In *The Basic Writings of Sigmund Freud*. New York: Modern Library.

Friedman, Ellen G. 1989. "A Conversation with Kathy Acker." *Review of Contemporary Fiction* 9, no. 3 (Fall).

Fuentes, Carlos. 1975. *Terra nostra*, trans. Margaret Sayers Peden. New York: Farrar, Strauss & Giroux.

Fukumoto, Naomi. 1986. [Review of *Neuromancer*]. *Starlog* (Japanese ed.), October.

Gaddis, William. 1955. *The Recognitions.* New York: Harcourt Brace.
———. 1975. *J R.* New York: Knopf.
———. 1985. *Carpenter's Gothic.* New York: Penguin.
Gibson, William. 1984. *Neuromancer.* New York: Berkley.
———. 1986a. *Count Zero.* New York: Arbor House.
———. 1986b. *Burning Chrome.* New York: Arbor House.
———. 1988. *Mona Lisa Overdrive.* New York: Bantam.
Goytisolo, Juan. 1982. *Paisajes despues de la batalla.* Barcelona: Montesinos.
Grant, Glenn. 1990. "Transcendence Through Détournement in William Gibson's *Neuromancer.*" *Science Fiction Studies* 17 (March): 41–49.
Gray, Alasdair. 1981. *Lanark.* New York: G. Braziller.
Hamamoto, Kaoru. 1986. [Review of *Neuromancer*]. *Bunshun Weekly*, September.
Hammett, Dashiell. 1929. *Red Harvest.* New York: Vintage.
———. 1930. *Maltese Falcon.* New York: Vintage.
Haraway, Donna. 1985. "A Manifesto for Cyborgs: Science, Technology, and Socialist Feminism in the 1980s." *Socialist Review* 80 (March–April): 65–107; rpt. in *Coming to Terms: Feminism, Theory, Politics*, ed. Elizabeth Weed (173–204). New York: Routledge, 1989.
Hegel, Georg Wilhelm Friedrich. 1910 [1807]. *The Phenomenology of the Mind.* New York: Macmillan.
Hoban, Russell. 1980. *Riddley Walker.* New York: Summit.
———. 1987. *The Medusa Frequency.* New York: Atlantic Monthly Press.
Hofstadter, Douglas. 1979. *Gödel, Escher, Bach: An Eternal Golden Braid.* New York: Basic.
Hollinger, Veronica. 1990. "Feminist SF: Breaking Up the Subject." *Extrapolation* 31 (Summer).
Huyssen, Andreas. 1986. *After the Great Divide: Modernism, Mass Culture, Postmodernism.* Bloomington: Indiana University Press.
Itoh, Norio. 1986. [Review of *Neuromancer*]. *Asahi Daily*, 7 September, 28.
Jaffe, Harold. 1988. "Max Headroom." *Mississippi Review* 47/48:130–35. Rpt. in *Madonna and Other Spectacles.* New York: PAJ Publications, 1988.
Jameson, Fredric. 1984a. "Postmodernism, or The Cultural Logic of Late Capitalism." *New Left Review* 146 (July–August): 53–94.
———. 1984b. "Progress versus Utopia, or Can We Imagine the Future?" In *Art after Modernism: Rethinking Representation*, ed. Brian Wallis (239–52). New York: New Museum of Contemporary Art.
———. 1988a. "Cognitive Mapping." In *Marxism and the Interpretation of Culture*, ed. Cary Nelson and Lawrence Grossberg (347–57). Urbana: University of Illinois Press.
———. 1988b. "Pleasure: A Political Issue." In *The Ideologies of Theory.* Minneapolis: University of Minnesota Press.
———. 1988c. "Postmodernism and Consumer Society." In *Postmodernism and Its Discontents: Theories, Practices*, ed. Ann E. Kaplan. London and New York: Verso.
Jankel, Annabel, and Rocky Morton. 1984. *Creative Computer Graphics.* New York: Cambridge University Press.
Jeter, K. W. 1985. *The Glass Hammer.* New York: Bluejay.
Johnson, Denis. 1985. *Fiskadoro.* New York: Knopf.
Kadrey, Richard. 1988. *Metrophage: (A Romance of the Future).* New York: Ace; London: Gollancz.
———. 1989a. "Cyberpunk 101 Reading List." *Whole Earth Review* 63 (Summer): 83.

———. 1989b. "Simulations of Immortality." *Science Fiction Eye* 1 (July): 74–76.

Kagami, Akira. 1986. [Review of *Neuromancer*]. *Hayakawa's SFM*, November.

Katz, Steve. 1972. *Saw*. New York: Knopf.

Kobayashi, Yoshio. 1986. [Cyberpunk overview]. *Hayakawa's SFM*, February.

Kroker, Arthur, and David Cook. 1986. *The Postmodern Scene: Excremental Culture and Hyper-Aesthetics*. New York: St. Martin's Press.

Kurei. 1986. [Review of *Neuromancer*]. *Ascii*, September.

Laidlaw, Marc. 1984. *Dad's Nuke*. New York: Lorevan.

Le Guin, Ursula K. 1985. *Always Coming Home*. New York: Harper & Row.

Leiber, Fritz. 1974 [1950]. "Coming Attraction." In *The Best of Fritz Leiber*. New York: Ballantine.

Lem, Stanislaw. 1983 [1968]. *His Master's Voice*. San Diego: Harcourt Brace Jovanovich.

———. 1984. "Science Fiction: A Hopeless Case—with Exceptions." In *Microworlds: Writings on Science Fiction and Fantasy*, ed. Franz Rollensteiner. San Diego and New York: Harcourt Brace Jovanovich.

———. 1981. *Golem XIV*. Kraków: Wydawnictwo Literackie.

Leyner, Mark. 1990. *My Cousin, My Gastroenterologist*. New York: Harmony/Crown.

Lynch, Kevin. 1960. *The Image of the City*. Cambridge, Mass.: Technology Press.

Lyotard, Jean-François. 1984 [1979]. *The Postmodern Condition: A Report on Knowledge*, trans. Geoff Bennington and Brian Massumi. Minneapolis: University of Minnesota Press.

McCaffery, Larry. 1986. "Introduction." In *Postmodern Fiction: A Bio-Bibliographical Guide*, ed. Larry McCaffery (xi–xxviii). New York: Greenwood.

———. 1988a. "The Desert of the Real: The Cyberpunk Controversy." *Mississippi Review* 47/48:7–15.

———. 1988b. "The Fictions of the Present." In *Columbia Literary History of the United States*, gen. ed. Emory Elliott (1161–77). New York: Columbia University Press.

McConkey, James. 1987. *Kayo: The Authentic and Annotated Autobiographical Novel from Outer Space*. New York: Dutton.

McElroy, Joseph. 1975. "Neural Neighborhoods and Other Concrete Abstracts." *TriQuarterly* 34 (Fall): 201–17.

———. 1976. *Plus*. New York: Knopf.

———. 1986. *Women and Men*. New York: Knopf.

McHale, Brian. 1987. *Postmodernist Fiction*. London: Methuen.

McLuhan, Marshall. 1962. *The Gutenberg Galaxy: The Making of Typographical Man*. Toronto: University of Toronto Press.

———. 1964. *Understanding Media: The Extensions of Man*. New York: NAL.

———. 1967. *The Medium Is the Massage*. New York: Random House.

Maddox, Tom. 1986. "Cobra, She Said." *Fantasy Review* (April): 46–48.

Mailer, Norman. 1948. *The Naked and the Dead*. New York: Rinehart.

Malzberg, Barry. 1975. *Galaxies*. New York: Pocket Books.

Mandel, Ernest. 1975. *Late Capitalism*. London: NLB; Atlantic Highlands, N.J.: Humanities Press.

Marcus, Greil. 1989. *Lipstick Traces: A Secret History of the 20th Century*. Cambridge: Harvard University Press.

Marx, Karl. 1975 [1867]. *Capital*, trans. Gregor Benton. New York: Vintage.

Masaki, Goro. 1987. "Evil Eyes." *Hayakawa's SFM* (December): 52–85.

Mathews, Harry. 1975 [1971–72]. *The Sinking of the Odradek Stadium and Other Novels.* New York: Harper & Row.

Mathiesen, Kenneth. 1985. "The Influence of Science Fiction in the Contemporary American Novel." *Science Fiction Studies* 12, no. 1 (March): 22–31.

Meltzer, Richard. 1987. *The Aesthetics of Rock.* New York: De Capo Press.

Miller, Nancy K. "Changing the Subject: Authorship, Writing, and the Reader." *Feminist Studies/Critical Studies*, ed. Teresa de Lauretis (102–20). Bloomington: Indiana University Press.

Mississippi Review 47/48. 1988. [Special issue on cyberpunk], ed. Larry McCaffery.

Mitchell, Arnold. 1983. *The Nine American Lifestyles: Who We Are and Where We're Going.* New York: Macmillan.

Moi, Toril. 1985. *Sexual/Textual Politics: Feminist Literary Theory.* New York: Methuen.

Mooney, Ted. 1981. *Easy Travel to Other Planets.* New York: Farrar, Strauss & Giroux.

Moorcock, Michael. 1969. *The Cornelius Chronicles*, vols. 1–3. New York: Avon.

Mumford, Lewis. 1958. *The City in History.* New York: Columbia University Press.

Nabokov, Vladimir. 1969. *Ada; or, Ardor: A Family Chronicle.* New York: McGraw-Hill.

Nakajima, Azusa. 1986. [Review of *Neuromancer*]. *Hoseki Weekly*, 8 August.

Nietzsche, Friedrich Wilhelm. 1967. *The Will to Power*, trans. Walter Kaufmann and R. J. Hollingdale, ed. Walter Kaufmann. New York: Random House.

O'Hara, Mariko. 1986. "Mental Female." *Hayakawa's SFM*, December.

Orwell, George. 1954 [1944]. "Raffles and Miss Blandish." In *A Collection of Essays by George Orwell.* New York: Doubleday/Anchor.

Porush, David A. 1985. *The Soft Machine: Cybernetic Fiction.* New York: Methuen.

Potter, Beverly. 1984. *The Way of the Ronin: A Guide to Career Strategy.* New York: AMACON.

Pynchon, Thomas. 1963. *V.* New York: Bantam, 1963.

———. 1966. *The Crying of Lot 49.* New York: Perennial.

———. 1973. *Gravity's Rainbow.* New York: Viking.

———. 1990. *Vineland.* Boston: Little, Brown.

Re/Search: Industrial Culture Handbook. Special issue, *Re/Search Magazine*, nos. 6–7.

Rimbaud, Arthur. 1975. *Complete Works*, trans. Paul Schmidt. New York: Harper & Row.

Robbe-Grillet, Alain. 1963. *Pour un nouveau roman.* Paris: Éditions de Minuit.

Rucker, Rudy. 1982. *Software.* New York: Ace.

———. 1988. *Wetware.* New York: Avon.

Russ, Joanna. 1984. *Extra(Ordinary) People.* New York: St. Martin's.

———. 1975. *The Female Man.* Boston: Gregg.

Sade, Donatien-Alphonse-François de. 1966. *The 120 Days of Sodom and Other Writings*, trans. Austryn Wainhouse and Richard Seaver. New York: Grove.

Sartre, Jean-Paul. 1982 [1960]. *The Critique of Dialectical Reason: Theory of Practical Ensembles.* London: Verso/NLB.

Scott, Jody. 1984. *I, Vampire.* New York: Berkley.

Séchehaye, Marguerite. 1968 [1951]. *Autobiography of a Schizophrenic Girl*, trans. G. Rubin-Rabson. New York: Grune & Stratton.

Shelley, Mary. 1989 [1818]. *Frankenstein.* New York: Penguin.

Shepard, Lucius. 1987. *Life During Wartime.* New York: Bantam.

———. 1989. "Waiting for the Barbarians." *Journal Wired* 1 (Winter): 107–18.

Shepard, Sam. 1980. "The Tooth of Crime" and "Operation Sidewinder." In *Four Two-Act Plays.* New York: Urizen Books.

———. "Angel City." In *Angel City and Other Plays*. New York: Urizen Books.

Shiner, Lewis. 1984. *Frontera*. New York: Pocket Books.

———. 1988. *Deserted Cities of the Heart*. New York: Bantam.

Shinshonen Special. [Review of *Neuromancer*]. No. 1, August 1986.

Shirley, John. 1980. *City Come A-Walkin'*. New York: Dell.

———. 1985. *Eclipse*. New York: Bluejay.

———. 1987. *Eclipse Penumbra*. New York: Warner.

———. 1989. *Total Eclipse*. New York: Warner.

Shute, Nevil. 1957. *On the Beach*. New York: Morrow.

Slonczewski, Joan. 1986. *A Door Into Ocean*. New York: Arbor House.

Sobchack, Vivian. 1987. *Screening Space*. New York: Ungar.

Sontag, Susan. 1966. "The Imagination of Disaster." In *Against Interpretation and Other Essays*. (209–25). New York: Dell.

Spinrad, Norman. 1969. *Bug Jack Barron*. New York: Walker.

———. 1987. *Little Heroes*.

Stapledon, Olaf. 1937. *Last and First Men*. New York: Dover.

Sterling, Bruce. 1977. *Involution Ocean*. Rpt. New York: Ace, 1988.

———. 1980. *The Artificial Kid*. New York: Ace.

———. 1985. *Schismatrix*. New York: Arbor House.

———, ed. 1986a. *Mirrorshades: The Cyberpunk Anthology*. New York: Arbor House.

———. 1986b. "Preface." In William Gibson, *Burning Chrome* (1–5). New York: Morrow.

———. 1986c. "Introduction." In *ArmadilloCon 8 Program Book*.

———. 1987. "Letter from Bruce Sterling." *REM* 7 (April): 4–7.

———. 1988. *Islands in the Net*. New York: Morrow.

———. 1989. *Crystal Express*. Sauk City, Wisc.: Arkham House.

Stone, Robert. 1973. *Dog Soldiers*. Boston: Houghton Mifflin.

Suikyoshi. 1986. [Review of *Neuromancer*]. *Hayakawa's SFM*, October.

Sukenick, Ronald. 1969. *Death of the Novel and Other Stories*. New York: Dial.

———. 1985. "Thirteen Digressions." In *In Form: Digressions on the Art of Fiction*. Carbondale: Southern Illinois University Press.

———. 1986. *The Endless Short Story*. New York: Fiction Collective.

Suvin, Darko. 1985. "Two Holy Commodities: The Practices of Fictional Discourse and Erotic Discourse." *Sociocriticism*, no. 2:31–47.

Swanwick, Michael. 1987. *Vacuum Flowers*. New York: Morrow.

Takahashi, Ryohei. 1986. [Review of *Neuromancer*]. *Hayakawa's SFM*, October.

Tatsumi, Takayuki. 1986. [Overview of cyberpunk]. *Hayakawa's SFM*, January.

———. 1988. "Some *Real* Mothers: An Interview with Samuel R. Delaney by Takayuki Tatsumi." *Science Fiction Eye* 1 (March): 5–11.

———. 1989. "Interview with William Gibson." *Science Fiction Eye* 1 (March):6–17.

Tevis, Walter. 1963. *The Man Who Fell to Earth*. New York: Fawcett.

Tiptree, James, Jr. 1975 [1973]. "The Girl Who Was Plugged In." In *Warm Worlds and Otherwise*. New York: Ballantine.

Toffler, Alvin. 1970. *Future Shock*. New York: Random House.

Van Troyer, Gene. 1978. "On Harlan Ellison and John Shirley." *Hayakawa's SFM* (January):144–52.

Varley, John. 1977. *The Ophiuchi Hotline*. New York: Dial.

Vollmann, William T. 1987. *You Bright and Risen Angels*. New York: Vintage.

Wells, H. G. 1895. *The Time Machine*. Rpt. in *The Time Machine and The War of the Worlds* (25–98). New York: Fawcett, 1968.

Wiener, Norbert. 1961 [1948]. *Cybernetics: Control and Communication in Animal and Machine*. Cambridge: MIT Press.

Williams, Raymond. 1981. *Marxism and Literature*. New York: Oxford University Press.

Williams, Walter Jon. 1986. *Hardwired*. New York: T. Doherty Associates.

Wilson, William S. 1977. *Why I Don't Write Like Franz Kafka*. New York: Ecco.

Wolfe, Bernard. 1985 [1952]. *Limbo*. New York: Carroll & Graf.

Wolfe, Gene. 1972. *The Fifth Head of Cerberus*. New York: Scribner.

Zimmerman, Bonnie. 1986. "Feminist Fiction and the Postmodern Challenge." In *Postmodern Fiction: A Bio-Bibliographical Guide*, ed. Larry McCaffery (175–88).

Film

Antonioni, Michelangelo. 1966. *Blowup*.

Arnold, Jack. 1958. *High School Confidential*.

Badham, John. 1983. *WarGames*.

Barg, William, and Stuart Albright. 1988. *Hip Tech and High Lit*.

Cameron, James. 1984. *The Terminator*.

Carpenter, John. 1981. *Escape from New York*.

Crichton, Michael. 1981. *Looker*.

Cronenberg, David. 1983. *Videodrome*.

DePalma, Brian. 1981. *Blow Out*.

Frears, Stephen. 1987. *Sammy and Rosie Get Laid*.

Hodges, Mike. 1974. *The Terminal Man*.

Jankel, Annabel and Rocky Morton. 1985. *Max Headroom*.

Lang, Fritz. 1921. *Der müde Tod (The Tired Death)*.

———. 1926. *Metropolis*.

Menzies, William Cameron. 1936. *Things to Come*.

Roeg, Nicolas. 1976. *The Man Who Fell to Earth*.

Romero, George. 1978. *Dawn of the Dead*.

Scott, Ridley. 1979. *Alien*.

———. 1982. *Blade Runner*.

Verhoeven, Paul. 1987. *Robocop*.

———. 1990. *Total Recall*.

Wilcox, Fred McLeod. 1956. *Forbidden Planet*.

Music

Note: (V) after an entry indicates a music video.

Anderson, Laurie. 1982. "O Superman." *Big Science*. Warner.

Bowie, David. 1971. "Andy Warhol." *Hunky Dory*. RCA.

———. 1977. *Low*. Ryko.

Can. 1974. *Soon Over Babaluma*. Restless.

The Clash. 1979. "Lost in the Supermarket." *London Calling*. CBS.

Costello, Elvis. "Accidents Will Happen." (V)

Cutting Crew. *One for the Mocking Bird*. (V)

Dead Kennedys. 1981. "Moral Majority." *In God We Trust*. Statik.

Fagen, Donald. "New Frontier." (V)

Fear. 1980. "I Love Living in the City." *Fear: The Record*. Slash.

Gabriel, Peter. *Big Time*. (V)

Little Richard. 1986 [1955]. "Tutti Frutti." *Little Richard: The Greatest Hits*. Teichiku.

Petty, Tom. *Jamming Me*. (V)

Ramones. 1977. "I Don't Care." *Rocket to Russia*. Sire.

Residents. *Earth vs. the Flying Saucers*. (V)

—————. *This Is a Man's World*. (V)

Sex Pistols. 1976. "God Save the Queen" and "Pretty Vacant." *Never Mind the Bollocks*. Warner.

Smith, Patti. 1975. *Horses*. Arista.

—————. 1978. "Babelogue." *Easter*. Arista.

Sonic Youth. 1988. *Daydream Nation*. Enigma.

Talking Heads. 1981. "I Zimbra" and "Life During Wartime." *Fear of Music*. Sire.

Throbbing Gristle. 1976. *Second Annual Report*. Industrial Records.

Velvet Underground/Nico. 1967. *Andy Warhol Presents the Velvet Underground and Nico*. Polygram.

—————. 1967. *White Light, White Heat*. Polygram.

Waits, Tom. 1970. "Lonesome Cowboy Bill." *Loaded*. Cotillion.

X. 1980. "Jonny Hit and Run Paulene." *Los Angeles*. Slash.

Contributors

Kathy Acker's recent works include *Empire of the Senseless* and *In Memoriam to Identity* (both from Grove). She currently lives in San Francisco and rides a 750 Yamaha.

J. G. Ballard was a leading figure in Britain's New Wave SF movement during the 1960s. His major works include *Crash, Empire of the Sun*, and *The Atrocity Exhibition* (recently reissued in a new, uncut version by Re/Search).

Jean Baudrillard has published many works of critical theory, postmodernism, and cross-cultural analysis, including *Simulations, Forget Foucault*, and *America*.

John Bergin's credits include *Brain Dead* and *Ashes*. He is currently working on *From Inside, Bone Saw, Kerosene and Nigger Joe, Jill's Map*, and a collection of sketches. He and his wife reside in Kansas City, Missouri, where he makes loud music with his current band, Trust Obey.

Steve Brown ran away to join the circus as a young man; once he was on the road he began to consort with numerous SF freak-show members, such as teenager John Shirley and, later, William Gibson. He currently lives in Washington, D.C., where he has a "real job"—which has not prevented him from publishing and editing *Science Fiction Eye* magazine.

William Burroughs has recently released album versions of his works, including *Uncommon Quotes* and *Dead City Radio*.

Pat Cadigan's short fiction has been nominated for the Nebula, Hugo, and World Fantasy awards, and her first novel, *Mindplayers* (Bantam, 1987) was a finalist for the Philip K. Dick Award. A collection of her short fiction, *Patterns*, was published in 1989 (Ursus Imprints), and her next novel, *Synners*, will be published by Bantam in 1991. She writes full time with the music turned up loud, in Kansas, where she lives with her husband, designer/artist Arnie Ferner, and their son.

David Cook teaches political theory at Erindale College, University of Toronto. With Arthur Kroker, he is the author of *The Postmodern Scene: Excremental Culture and Hyper-Aesthetics*.

Istvan Csicsery-Ronay, Jr. is coeditor of *Science-Fiction Studies*. In addition to writing widely about SF and cyberpunk, he has translated various works by Stanislaw Lem.

Don DeLillo's many novels include *The Names, White Noise*, and *Libra*.

Jacques Derrida has recently been teaching critical theory at the University of California–Irvine; among his major works are *Glas* and *Of Grammatology*.

Ferret has illustrated the work of many authors, including Misha, Lewis Shiner, K. W. Jeter, and John Shirley. The author and illustrator of such comic book series as *The Phoenix Restaurant*, he is also the author of many works of fiction, including a novel, *Alligator Alley* (Morrigan Publications, 1989).

William Gibson's early cyberspace trilogy, *Neuromancer, Count Zero*, and *Mona Lisa Overdrive*, helped launch the cyberpunk movement. His recent collaborative novel, *The Difference Engine* (with Bruce Sterling), was released in England by Victor Gollancz and is being published in the United States by Bantam.

Joan Gordon teaches at Nassau Community College and has written on Gene Wolfe, Joe Haldeman, and feminist SF.

Rob Hardin is a writer and musician living in NYC who reports that writing is the way of "getting linear dissonant counterpoint—the chamber music nightmares and empty attics—out of my system." His poetry has appeared in numerous magazines, including *Mississippi Review, Atomic Avenue,* and *Flagellation.* His recent album credits include *The Lost Boys* and *Billy Squire's Here and Now.*

Veronica Hollinger teaches theatre and SF in the Cultural Studies Program at Trent University in Ontario. Her publications include essays on feminist SF, vampires, postmodern theater, and time travel. She is coeditor of *Science-Fiction Studies.*

Harold Jaffe's most recent book of fiction is *Eros Anti-Eros* (City Lights Books); he is currently coeditor of *Fiction International* and can still knock heads inside for rebounds when called upon.

Fredric Jameson is Director of the Graduate Program in Literature at Duke University; his many critical studies include *Marxism and Form, The Prison House of Language, The Political Unconscious,* and, most recently, *Postmodernism, or, The Cultural Logic of Late Capitalism* (Duke University Press).

Thom Jurek is the arts editor of *The Metro Times* in Detroit, an alternate news and entertainment weekly. He is the author of *DUB* (poems) and has published poems in such magazines as *The Canadian Journal of Political and Social Theory, Northern Lit Quarterly,* and *Triage: Writing Around the Edge.*

Richard Kadrey is the author of *Metrophage* (a cyberpunk novel), coauthor of *Signal: Communication Tools for the Information Age* (nonfiction), and is currently finishing a new novel, *Kamikaze L'Amour.* Currently editing the weekly Whole Earth Catalog column in the San Francisco *Chronicle,* he has also had original art published under the name Dr. Arkady Reich.

Arthur Kroker teaches political science and the humanities at Concordia University (Montréal) and is the founding editor of the *Canadian Journal of Political and Social Theory.* With David Cook, he is the author of *The Postmodern Scene: Excremental Culture and Hyper-Aesthetics.*

Marc Laidlaw has spent most of his adult life in office buildings, writing on company word processors. His works include an early cyberpunk novel, *Dad's Nuke,* and a SF novel about Tibet, *Neon Lotus.*

Brooks Landon teaches contemporary fiction and film at the University of Iowa. The author of numerous essays about SF, SF film, cyberpunk, and postmodernism, he is currently completing a book entitled *The Aesthetics of Ambivalence: Rethinking SF Film in the Age of Electronic (Re)Production.*

Timothy Leary has published books on subjects ranging from drugs, to the nature of human consciousness, to literary criticism.

Mark Leyner is the most intense and, in a certain sense, the most significant young prose writer in America. His *My Cousin, My Gastroenterologist* was published by Crown in 1990.

Jean-François Lyotard is Professor of Philosophy at the University of Paris at Vincennes. Perhaps best known for his important study, *The Postmodern Condition: A Report on Knowledge,* he has also published widely in the studies of aesthetics and of the psycho-political dimensions of discourses.

Joseph McElroy's recent novels include the maxi-novel *Women and Men* (Knopf) and the mini-novel, *The Letter Left to Me* (Carroll and Graf).

Tom Maddox is Writing Coordinator at Evergreen State College in Olympia, Washington. He has published SF in *Omni* and other magazines and in various anthologies, including *Mirrorshades*. He has also published critical articles on William Gibson and John LeCarré.

Misha is a writer of mixed North American Indian heritage. Her books include *Prayers of Steel* (prose pieces) and *Red Spider White Web* (a novel); her prose piece "Tsuki Mangestu" was used in a dynamic performance by two Australian composers and won the 1989 Prix d'Italia.

J. O'Barr lives in Detroit with three cats and a dark-haired girl.

David Porush is the author of *The Soft Machine* (a pioneering study of "cybernetic fiction"). Porush has also published *Rope Dances* (stories), a cyberpunk play (*R. Boots*), and numerous essays about SF postmodernism. He teaches at Rensselaer Polytechnic Institute.

Thomas Pynchon's novels include *V.*, *The Crying of Lot 49*, *Gravity's Rainbow*, and, most recently, *Vineland*. You never know when he might show up for a game of cards.

Rudy Rucker (Dr. Rudolf von Bitter Rucker) is Professor of Mathematics and Computer Science. He has written widely about mathematics and information theory, and published several important early cyberpunk novels, including *Software* and *Wetware*.

Lucius Shepard's works include *Green Eyes* (Ace), *Life During Wartime*, and *The Jaguar Hunter* (both Bantam).

Lewis Shiner lives in Austin, Texas, from whence he launched an early cyberpunk literary missile, *Frontera*. His most recent novel is *Slam* (Doubleday). His short fiction has appeared in *Semiotext(e)*, *Mirrorshades*, *Razorded Saddles*, and *Alien Sex*.

John Shirley has been called "the Lou Reed of Cyberpunk"; in addition to publishing numerous polemical essays and seminal works of cyberpunk, he is also the lead singer of The Panther Moderns—a San Francisco–based rock band. He is currently working on a novel of surrealist urban nightmare called *Wetbones*.

George Slusser is Professor of Comparative Literature at the University of California–Riverside and Director of its Eaton Collection (the most extensive SF library in the world). He has written widely on SF and critical theory, and runs the annual Eaton SF Conference at UC-Riverside.

Bruce Sterling is currently researching a book on "Operation Sun Devil" (the hacker dragnet of 1990), which will examine computer crime and civil liberties issues.

Darko Suvin's *The Metamorphosis of Science Fiction* (1979) won the Pilgrim Award for scholarly contributions to SF. A Professor of Comparative Literature at McGill University, Suvin was an editor of *Science-Fiction Studies* for many years; he has also published poetry and fiction in various literary journals.

Takayuki Tatsumi's book-length study of cyberpunk, *Cyberpunk America*, was selected as the best study of American literature by a Japanese scholar in 1988. With his heroic-fantasylike wife, Mari, he lives in Tokyo.

William Vollmann's recent novel *The Ice-Shirt* (Viking) is the first book in a projected septology of "dream works" that will eventually present a "symbolic history of the U.S." He is currently doing research for the sixth of these novels at the Magnetic North Pole.